The Black Swan Event
A Dr. Mike Murphy Novel

By Matthew J. Messina, DDS

Keep Smiling!

The Black Swan Event

ISBN 978-0-9852208-1-5

Published by:
Matthew J. Messina, D.D.S.
20390 Lorain Road
Fairview Park, OH 44126

First Printing 2013

Adore God. Love your neighbor as yourself,
and your country more than yourself.
Be just. Be true. Murmur not at the ways of Providence.

Thomas Jefferson

Ad Majorem Dei Gloriam

Prologue

His eyes snapped open, instantly alert. The quiet of the room was violated in just the slightest way, the sterile peace disturbed by the sound. Even though they had heavily soundproofed the room, he was aware of any noises that seemed out of place, no matter how faint.

Scrunch. There it was again—the muffled sound of a shoe on gravel. *Count to 30*, he thought. *There it is again!* Pacing from one side of the wall to another, he imagined, the perimeter guard on his regular rounds, turning, grinding his boot on loose stones and retracing his steps. Though he had never been out of the room, his military training let him place the sounds and envision the world outside his apartment. *Who am I kidding? It's my prison!*

After waking up months ago to find himself in this confinement, talking to himself had become a habit. For a prison, it was well appointed...a one-bedroom condo with a comfortable bed, sitting area, and a small kitchen featuring granite countertops and stainless appliances. Like a luxury hotel room, with everything stocked for him—sunny yellow walls with a cream colored plush carpet—gold framed prints of pastoral scenes—gray fabric couch and two leather armchairs. All the comforts of home! Except completely sterile. The TV channels seemed to be there, but over time he had figured out that they all broadcast outdated news events.

He climbed out of bed and stretched to his full height of six feet. Walking over to the window, he touched the glass. The blinds between the panes were completely closed and he had no way of opening them. The bright yellow glare of sunlight seeped around the edges and the glass was hot to the touch. The clock on his bedside table said 7:00 am, but he had determined by carefully watching the daylight around the windows that it really was nearly midday. He had tried to change the clock, but they kept changing it back when he was out for his daily exercise period, running in the hallway. It had become something of a contest of wills. He was not about to give in and let them win. He set his jaw firmly and bent down, resetting the alarm clock to noon.

It troubled him that he had been unable to figure out who *they* were. He had been shot down on a mission in Afghanistan and had woken up here in captivity. His efforts to comprehend the nature of his situation had allowed him to determine very little. He was in a warm climate, based upon the heat on the windows. Much warmer than where he had been in Afghanistan. Of that he was certain. Though the apartment was filled with cameras, he had identified a few areas out of the reach of surveillance. In one of these blind spots, he had been digging at the sheetrock, discovering a limestone wall beneath the thin layer of drywall. In fact, the base stone seemed to be ancient, cold stone bricks set without mortar, anchored firmly to the earth. However, the corridor where they let him run was freshly poured cement, dimly lit by open bulbs hanging from the low ceiling, hastily strung to provide meager light to the passageway.

His guards were always hooded. Heads covered so that only their eyes were showing. They were heavily armed and appeared to be highly trained military—Special Forces types by the look of them. They never spoke, just prodded him with their rifles. He had no problem getting the message. The more he thought about it, he realized that he had far more questions than answers.

Another day in paradise! He began his usual routine of exercise. His efforts to stay fit kept him sane. He wasn't about to give in, no matter how much they were messing with his mind. He thought of his children, two beautiful daughters. How old would they be now? Five and three, if his calculations of his time here in confinement were correct. He said a quick prayer for their safekeeping. He sat down on the floor and began his sit-ups.

His head snapped around at the sharp click of the lock on the door. As it opened, he saw a smile on the face of the only captor he had ever met.

Though the time of her arrival was never the same, she was constant in being the only variation in his boring existence. He had tried to place her looks and accent to latch onto any clue about the nature of his captors. But her identity was as obscured as the rest of his condo. Clad in blue jeans and a gray t-shirt today, she was Caucasian, but slightly darker skinned. Strikingly beautiful, with jet-black hair cropped short. Close set eyes over a long nose. Her smile was warm and inviting, but somehow hollow, almost rehearsed. *Maybe she was a model?* She had appeared daily during the early stage of his captivity, seemingly wanting to chat. He expected some sort of interrogation, but none had ever occurred. She simply spent a half-hour or so talking. It always felt like an uncomfortable blind date, just making small talk, since he had no intention to let any relationship develop. He was at a loss to make anything of what was going on here. W*hy are they holding me?*

Her visits had become less frequent as his time here had extended, so that now he was increasingly surprised when she arrived. With a look of frustration on his face, he rose and walked over to the couch, sitting down heavily. He motioned her to the high-backed wing chair where she always sat anyway. "Have a seat!"

Her smile hardened as she sat down, perched expectantly on the edge of the chair, folding her hands in her lap. Her voice was cheerful, yet cold as ice. "So Colonel, what shall we talk about today?"

6

Chapter 1

It was a bright, sunny morning as the black Mercedes sedan wound its way through the streets of Washington DC. Traffic was light for a Saturday and the driver found it easy going to weave through the maze of one-way streets until he reached the Potomac River. The car had diplomatic plates, but that didn't help when they met the congestion just past the Lincoln Memorial. Independence Drive SW was slow passing the Korean War Veterans Memorial, but as they turned onto West Basin Drive, traffic stopped. To the right of the new Martin Luther King Jr. Memorial, a tour bus had become entangled with a taxi. Nothing was moving in the general commotion.

With a sigh, the lone occupant of the back seat tapped the window divider and motioned to his driver that he would get out and walk. Nodding in reply, the driver eased off to the side and unlocked the doors.

Stepping out of the car into the sunlight, the man gently closed the door and stood, taking a moment to straighten the crease in his pants. Taking his bearings, he began to walk at a brisk pace into Rock Creek Park.

It was getting warm. As the day wore on, the oppressive heat and humidity would get the better of sane people and drive them indoors for the air conditioning. For now, eager to get out and enjoy the morning, the residents of Washington had come out in force to bask in the sunshine. The locals were running, biking, and even laying out in swimsuits on blankets, soaking up the warmth. It was a casual Saturday on the National Mall, which made the appearance of the tall man with the purposeful stride all the more jarringly out of place walking down the sidewalk.

His silver hair shined in the sun, tightly cropped against his head. Rimless glasses sat low upon his nose, accentuating the high cheekbones and angular line of his face. He was just under six feet tall, thin, but full of energy. In a word: wiry. His complexion was the color of parchment and even the warm glow of the sun could not change the sense that he needed to be outdoors more. He could have been any older gentleman in his sixties out for a walk, easily ignored by the younger crowd inhabiting Rock Creek Park this morning, but he was impossible to miss, clad all in black. His suit was tailored, black coat and slacks, black shirt, with impeccably shined black leather shoes and belt. The round white collar, cinched snugly against his neck, marking him as a Roman Catholic priest.

He stopped at a fork in the sidewalk, considering which path to take. Lifting his nose a bit in the air, he cocked his head and listened. The sharp chirp of a whistle to his left caught his attention. With a quick nod, he stepped briskly on, following the sound under the canopy of trees just coming into full bloom. A group of bikers braked suddenly, squealing to a stop and staring, not wanting to run him over as he strode across the bike path. He fixed them with his gaze and nodded a 'thank you,' slowing slightly.

The lead biker, wearing a Georgetown t-shirt, stammered "Good morning, Father!"

The man stopped and turned back. "Bless you, my son. Have a wonderful day." His voice was crisp and clear, precise and formal, with a note of command.

The biker managed a stumbling "You too, Father." They watched him proceed on, wondering what purpose would bring him out this morning. The biker looked to his fellows, "That's no ordinary parish priest!"

"What makes you say that?" His girlfriend was skeptical, regarding him dubiously as she reached for her water bottle.

"Did you catch the gold pin on his lapel?"

"Yea, I saw it, shining in the sun. So what?"

"I've spent enough years in Catholic school to know that emblem! It was the tri-Regnum over crossed keys. That's the symbol of the Vatican. His accent was clearly American, but he works for the Pope. That's an odd combination. I just wonder what he's doing here?"

She clipped her water bottle back on her bike and shifted her weight. "Well either go ask him, or lets get going!" The other couple riding with them voiced their approval.

"OK, Cindy. You win! I guess we'll just have to wonder what's up."

"He probably needs the exercise and forgot to pack his sweats. You never know. Keep your eyes on the news! Maybe you'll see him again." She pushed off and took the lead, setting a brisk pace, riding out of the park toward the Jefferson Memorial, yelling back at her friends to keep up.

Chapter 2

Father Lawrence Albers, Director of the Vatican Library, was indeed on a matter of great importance in Washington DC. His sources had informed him that he could find the people he sought in Rock Creek Park, at least until noon on Saturday. As he rounded the corner of the path and exited the tree line into the wide-open space that had once been the polo grounds, he stopped to find that the park had been converted to sand volleyball courts. There were at least a dozen nets up, each court filled with pairs of players. The fans were reclining on blankets around the courts.

The large crowds brought energy to the field, cheering on the teams. A banner over the registration tent proclaimed that this was the Cherry Blossom Classic, the premier summer tournament for sand volleyball in Washington. It was a gorgeous morning for a sand tournament and it appeared that the players and spectators were making the most of it.

Squinting into the sun, Fr. Albers worried he would have a tough time finding his quarry, so he stepped back into the shade of a cherry tree to survey the situation. By far the largest crowd surrounded the center court, closest to the registration tent. The match there was intense, with fans loudly cheering each point, hooting and waving red, white, and blue towels.

The referee whistled for the serve and play began. The match was between teams of two. The pair on the near court was a tall redhead and a slightly shorter guy in red board shorts, his brown hair now darkening with sweat. After serving, red shorts played defense. The opposing team passed the ball and attempted a spike back over the net. The redhead partially blocked the shot and red shorts dove into the sand, smoothly passing the ball back up. His partner gently set the ball. Red shorts had rolled over, bounced up and jumped, powerfully hitting the ball into the open corner of his opponents' court. Landing lightly on his feet, red shorts arched his back, puffed out his chest and howled, "Woooo!" He smacked hands with his partner in a hi-five and trotted back to serve again, brushing the sand out of his hair and pushing the front up out of his eyes.

Fr. Albers smiled. *Some things never change.* He knew those mannerisms well. Michael Patrick Murphy, his student at Saint Ignatius High School in Cleveland Ohio so many years ago, had been playing Junior Olympic volleyball since the age of eleven. "Murph" had been a captain of the Ignatius Wildcats, leading them into the state tournament and earning himself all-state honors his senior year. Though his career path had moved on to greater things in the last ten years, Murph always returned to volleyball as a release and a chance to feed his competitive nature. Fr. Albers had need of the talents of his former pupil, so he set off across the green, heading straight for the show court.

As he approached, Fr. Albers could see the match was close. Even though he had no real interest in sports, he could recognize Murph's opponents as a team he had seen on TV in the last Olympics. Asking another spectator when he came up to the crowd, Fr. Albers was told that this was a celebrity match between the Olympic team of Garth and Rodriguez and local DC dentist Murphy and his partner Owen McAndrews, some old friend of Murph who had just been on the Olympic US Men's indoor volleyball team. The match was close, with the crowd pulling for the local DC guy, just thrilled to see a very competitive game.

Having located one of his targets, Fr. Albers knew the other couldn't be far away. He scanned the crowd carefully, finally spotting her reclining on a blanket, cheering every point. He moved through the crowd, people making a path for the black-clad priest, their eyebrows rising at the sight. He approached her from behind, so as not to disturb her as she chatted with her friend sitting next to her. She had been easy to find as well, he thought. Though she never tried to call attention to herself, Caroline Chamoun was difficult to miss. Petite, at barely five foot tall, she sat on the blanket, leaning back on her arms with her legs extended. She had the lithe build of a distance runner, which she had earned through years of competition in track and cross-country. Carli was of Egyptian-American heritage and her bronze skin glistened in the sun, set off by the white short shorts and orange halter-top. Her auburn hair was pulled back into a ponytail and her sunglasses were pushed up onto her head. Carli had a casual elegance that combined with her energetic personality to make her simply beautiful.

Murph's girlfriend since college, Carli had been in Cairo on an archeological dig when her radical discovery had caused the Egyptian authorities to try to silence her. Murph had traveled to the Middle East to rescue her and their escape had started a chain of events that had changed the historical understanding of the pharaohs, and nearly killed the two of them in the process.

Standing behind her, Fr. Albers interrupted loudly enough for Carli and her friend to hear, casually commenting, "I'm glad to see that Michael's shoulder is better. That is quite a nasty scar!" He pointed at a three inch wound over the left shoulder blade that was just fading into Murph's tan. The scar remained stubbornly pink, but he was moving well enough to play volleyball again, diving all over the court with his usual reckless abandon.

11

Carli answered without looking up. "It's not as strong as he would like yet, and I'm not thrilled he's playing so soon. He'll be sore tomorrow, but I can't stop him. He can be stubborn at times."

She began to turn around. "Thanks for asking...Yee!" She spotted Fr. Albers and jumped up, leaping at him and wrapping her arms around his neck with a hug, nearly knocking him over. "Father! It's so great to see you!"

He gently placed her back on the ground and looked down at her bright green eyes, smiling. "It is I who am so delighted to see you, Caroline."

"Why didn't you tell us you were coming?" She chided gently, "We would have … baked a cake, or something..."

"This is not purely a social call," he cautioned. "I have a favor to ask of you, and Michael. But that can wait until later. Let's enjoy the end of the match." He gestured toward the court.

Carli cupped her hands around her mouth and shouted, "MURPH."

His head snapped around as he was preparing to serve again. Looking over at where Carli was, he smiled, and then stopped, his jaw hanging open, as he recognized the tall priest standing next to her. She grinned and indicated to Fr. Albers with both her hands like Vanna White turning a letter.

Murph waved weakly and started a question, mouthing "Why..." but Fr. Albers pointed back to the referee on the stand above the net, gesturing for Murph to serve. "Finish the match first," he suggested.

Nodding agreement, Murph returned to the task at hand, while Carli invited Fr. Albers to sit down with her. She introduced him to her friend. "This is Jane Mitchell, my roommate. She is an MBA student at Georgetown. She's from Cleveland too."

"Pleased to meet you, Jane. I taught at St. Ignatius for many years before going to the Vatican."

"Yes, Father." Jane nodded, her blond ponytail wagging, "My brothers had you for AP European history."

"How are Grant and Peter doing?"

Jane was stunned. "I can't believe you remember!" His memory for names was legendary, but even Jane and Carli were shocked. "Grant is in New York and Peter is a Navy lieutenant. He is a helicopter pilot in the Mediterranean now."

Carli filled in the details. "Jane and I met running. We share an apartment in Georgetown while I finish my Ph.D. in Archeology. I have been taken on as a doctoral student at Georgetown so I can finish the exhibit at the Smithsonian."

"Ah!" Father Albers pushed his glasses up on his nose. "I want to hear all about the Mummy and the Pharaoh Queen. But that is better done over dinner, I think. And I suspect we had better pay closer attention to the volleyball game. I sense the match is at its climax."

Fr. Albers was indeed right. McAndrews had just powerfully blocked a ball, leading to another loud pair of "Wooooo's" and a chest bump in celebration. Murph went back to serve with the score 20-17 in favor of the Olympians. With 21 points needed to win, it would be a tall order for Murph and Owen. Murph took the ball and threw it up in the air for a running jump-serve. The ball streaked over the net and landed in the back corner, barely an inch inside the line. An Ace! 20-18. He took the ball again and went back to serve.

Murph tossed the ball up and jumped, but instead, this time hit the ball open handed. The ball floated over the net, fluttering without spin like a knuckle ball. Difficult to return, especially for the tall hitter Garth, he shanked the pass out of bounds. 20-19! Murph clenched his right fist, swinging it up in front of his face. "COME ON!" he shouted, seemingly into the inside of his wrist.

Owen took the ball from the ref and handed it to Murph. "One more!" He clapped his hands and turned to face the net, a determined look in his eye.

Murph considered his serve options. Looking across the net, he could see that they had taken a step forward, going closer to the net to get the softer float serve. Murph tossed the ball high and hit a hard jump serve, aimed right between his opponents. Rodriguez and Garth were professionals though, and Rodriguez turned and dove, getting one arm on the ball and passing it up toward Garth at the middle of the net. McAndrews moved forward to block and Murph slid into the open side of the court to the right. Instead of setting the ball for Rodriguez, Garth tapped the ball over with the back of his hand. It sailed over McAndrews, heading for the open sand on the left side of the court. Murph saw the tip, but could only dive helplessly as the ball landed softly, just out of his reach. Face down in the sand, he could hear the crowd moan. 21-19! He pounded the ground with his arm, but then pushed himself up and managed a smile.

McAndrews reached down and pulled Murph to his feet. He and the big redhead ducked under the net and congratulated the Olympians, earning a hug from each. The crowd applauded the valiant effort, happy to have seen such an exciting match.

Carli ran over and jumped into Murph's arms. He lifted her easily into the air and swung her around. At 6' 2", he towered more than a foot over her when he set her back down. "Not bad for an old man?" He looked happy, receiving the congratulations from the fans around them, but she could see he was drained from the effort.

"Considering what you have been through, there's no shame in losing to professionals!" She touched his shoulder and he winced a bit, in spite of himself. "Let's get you home for a good hot shower. No one wants your autograph anyway," she laughed, then wrinkled her nose. "Besides, you stink!"

Murph realized she was right. While Rodriguez and Garth signed programs and posed for pictures, Murph thanked Owen and walked over to help Carli pick up their blanket and picnic cooler. He came over to his old teacher, smiling broadly.

Murph shook hands with Fr. Albers, but resisted the temptation to embrace him, since he was sweaty and covered with sand. "Welcome to DC, Father. I'm so glad to see you. We have so much to tell you!"

"Yes. And there is so much that I want to know. But you, to be frank, are a sight." He shook his head and laughed. "Carli and I have planned everything. She tells me you have become something of a gourmet during your time in Washington, and she has promised me an excellent dinner at your condo later tonight. I will have my driver deliver me at seven and I will bring the wine."

"That sounds fantastic. But we have a lot of work to do, it seems!"

"Indeed you do." Fr. Albers turned to Carli and bowed slightly, "until later!" He walked away from the crowd and toward the road, his black diplomatic car idling in the shade of the cherry trees.

Murph inclined his head toward Carli and let out a low whistle. "What could he be doing here? He never does anything spontaneously. Everything has a plan and a purpose." He pulled on a faded Ohio State volleyball t-shirt and flip-flops.

"He said he needed a favor from us, but didn't say any more. I guess we'll find out tonight!" She took his hand as he picked up the cooler. "In the meantime, you have some cooking to do!"

"It seems you have promised something special from me. Now I have to figure out what I want to cook...to impress a man who lives in Rome." Murph furrowed his brow, thinking as they walked. "I *will* need the help of my favorite sous chef!" He leaned down to kiss her on the cheek.

"Of course," she smiled happily, "I can't think of anywhere I'd rather be!"

Chapter 3

Carli and Jane had biked back to the house they had rented near the Georgetown University campus. It took Murph about 30 minutes to walk to his condo on 6th Street NW. As the Clinical Director of the Washington Center for Esthetic and Reconstructive Excellence, Murph was the lead dentist in a large, multiple-specialty practice located just one block off the National Mall. He had chosen the penthouse condo since it was straight north of the Center and he could easily run the 15 blocks down 6th Street each morning. Given the traffic in Washington DC, the less driving he had to do, the better!

Murph intended to shower quickly, but the warm water reminded him of how sore he really was after the volleyball match. It had been the longest he had played since his injury and now that the adrenalin from the competition had worn off, he was beginning to realize just how uncomfortable his shoulder was going to be as the day wore on. He lingered in the shower a bit longer, then dried off and dressed quickly. He kept his hair short for just such an emergency, toweling it dry and running his fingers quickly through it to fluff it a bit. Clad in a cream polo shirt and blue linen slacks, he was dressed for dinner, just in case time became tight while preparing the meal.

Whistling softly, he dashed out the door and pulled his car out of the garage. As he eased the Mustang into traffic, he slipped on his sunglasses and enjoyed the bright sunshine of summer. On days like this, he wished he had gotten the convertible, but, in reality, he wouldn't trade his dark Highland green Ford Mustang for anything. It was the type of car Steve McQueen drove in the movie "Bullitt" and for a movie buff like Murph: it was the ideal ride.

He shifted gears absentmindedly while alternately planning his menu for dinner and trying to figure out what had brought Father Albers all the way from Rome. Murph had been a student at Saint Ignatius High School in Cleveland, Ohio when he had become friends with Fr. Albers. The Jesuit educator had been summoned from teaching Advanced Placement European History at St. Ignatius all the way to Rome in order to become the Director of the Vatican Library. With his installation as Francis I, the new Pope expressed a desire to bring new blood to the staid leadership of the Vatican.

Fr. Albers was one of many new faces in powerful positions in Vatican City.

It was less than a year ago that Murph had led Carli, while on the run from Cairo and Arab gunmen, into the safety of the Vatican. With the help of Father Albers, they had begun the process of solving the mystery that led to their being chased across Europe, before returning to Washington and confronting their adversaries. Murph's shoulder felt a twinge just thinking about it!

An angry HONK of a horn brought Murph back from his daydreaming. He waved at the impatient Toyota behind him and turned right onto S Street. It was becoming humid already, especially here in the low land that was Georgetown. He pulled up in front of the two-story white row house that Carli shared with Jane. In spite of himself, Murph grinned from ear to ear as she bounced down the walk from the door. Carli had changed into a pale green floral sundress, sandals, and carried a raspberry sweater in her hand, for later when it got cooler. Her auburn hair was pushed back from her face by the sunglasses resting on her head. That was Carli in a nutshell—fashionable, stylish but never overdone—well planned and ready for anything—simple and fun, yet somehow graceful and elegant all at the same time.

Murph jumped out of the car, ran around and opened the door for her. She looked up at him and winked, "Goin' my way?"

He leaned down and kissed her lightly on the forehead. "Anywhere you want to go, just say the word!"

"Well," she pursed her lips in mock thought, "I would like Paris, but for now, how about the Farmer's Market."

"An excellent idea!"

He got back in the car and slid away from the curb. Murph looked over, noticing that in spite of her bronze complexion, she had gotten a bit too much sun and the tip of her nose was turning pink. "You missed a spot with the sunscreen."

She wrinkled her nose, her eyes crossing as she tried to focus on the tip. "I know! It's a bit tender already. At least the opening of the exhibit was two weeks ago, so if it peels, it's OK. You should talk! They say only mad dogs and Irishmen go out in the sun, and I think you're both!"

Murph laughed. "No comment." He could feel the prickliness of the sunburn on his back and shoulders already, but he didn't want to admit it to Carli. She had told him to put on sunscreen before the match, but he had refused, saying he didn't want the sand to stick to his skin. Since he had started playing volleyball at ten years old, he was always diving on the floor to never let a ball drop if he could get to it. Today had been no different and he had the sand abrasions to go with the sunburn to prove it.

Quickly changing the subject, Murph asked Carli if she had any thoughts about what to serve for dinner.

"I'll make the salad, and I have a new recipe I want to try for coconut cake for dessert...but don't think that I don't know you went without sunscreen. I can see the Irish in you reddening through that Italian skin tone. You'll be tan next week, but you'll be sorry tomorrow!"

Murph couldn't help smiling. "Yes, Dear," he deadpanned. She was right, as usual. Murph was half Irish. His mother was Italian and he had inherited her chestnut hair, brown eyes, and ability to be out in the sun. He had to go through a tender Irish period to build his base, but tanned well enough in the end.

Carli was of Egyptian-American descent. The sun loved her and she had a healthy bronze glow throughout the year, no matter how deep the snow outside. As Murph went pale in the winter, Carli just seemed to manufacture her own sunlight and stayed ever beautiful. He took his hand off the gearshift and squeezed her hand playfully.

She inclined her head and looked at him, batting her eyes. He began to get lost in those green eyes. They were easily her most striking feature. Gorgeous, emerald green eyes, slightly too large for her face, yet somehow perfect—expressive and playful. When she smiled, the corners of her eyes crinkled, implying that she knew a secret. Something you didn't know! From when they first met, Murph had been captivated by her eyes and had been lost ever since.

"Stop that!" He blinked, chiding her without really being able to sound stern, and looked back at the road ahead. "We have work to do! You *know* you distract me that way!"

"Have it your way," she giggled, wrinkling her tiny little nose. "Ow! That hurts." She touched the tender tip of her upturned nose. "It's more burned than I thought." She rolled her lower lip into a pouty face.

"Enough of the boo-boo lip. I know you're tougher than that. I've seen you in action." It was his turn to laugh now. "Well, we're here. Let's see what's for dinner!"

Chapter 4

Murph and Carli enjoyed the farmer's market and had been there often enough to be known to many of the vendors. Given Murph's exposure on TV in the reality show "The Dental Apprentice," he was easily recognized. Even though he hadn't won, as the runner up he had been the fan favorite. He always was the friendly one, looking out for the little guy, and the viewers had been rooting for the nice guy to finish first. It hadn't happened, but in the end, Murph had gained a bigger prize.

Carli's sunny disposition and beauty made her remarkable. No one knew who she was, but everyone wanted to be the guy with her. Put together, the two made a striking couple. Murph, tall and more serious, and Carli, a petite smiling bundle of energy.

They breezed through the market, selecting the freshest ingredients recommended by their vendor friends. If he had the time, Murph would come to the market every day and choose what to cook based upon what looked good, just like the little old ladies with their pull carts. It had an old-world feel that reminded Murph of the historic West Side Market in Cleveland, where he grew up going with his parents on weekends. He had developed a love of cooking because it made him feel like home with family and friends.

Packing their groceries in the back seat, the Mustang smelled of fresh vegetables and coconut as they drove back to the condo. Murph's home in Washington was a 1600-square-foot penthouse on the third floor of a walkup in the Shaw area of Washington DC. Typical of Murph, it was not impressive from the outside, yet comfortably appointed on the interior. With two bedrooms and two baths, it was ideal for his occasional visits from his family and friends. He considered serving dinner on the rooftop deck, since the views of Washington were stunning, but Carli worried that it was too hot and sticky now and would become cool and damp later. Since it was July, Murph agreed she was right.

They settled in to prepare the meal, working easily on the ample granite counter space in the kitchen. Having selected fresh tilapia, Murph cleaned the filets, seasoned them and set them aside. He turned on some jazz, and the haunting strains of Stan Kenton's Malaguena began to play. Murph took Carli's hand and twirled her around. She pirouetted with practiced grace and he kissed her lightly on the forehead.

Her eyes widened, "What was that for?" She stood there smiling with a knife in one hand and the strawberry she had been cutting in the other.

"Nothing. I just love having you here." He bit the strawberry out of her fingers and turned her back around. "But you better keep chopping. The salad comes first, you know."

She sighed and picked up another strawberry. "If you would stop eating it as fast as I make it, it'll get done." She wagged the paring knife at his face and shooed him off.

Murph opened a bottle of Pino Grigio for Carli, pouring a glass of the crisp white wine and then chose a bottle of Plumpjack Merlot for himself.

Carli accepted the glass and tasted the wine. "Excellent choice! It'll be perfect with your tilapia. Why the red?"

"This Merlot is my favorite. I know, white with fish, but life is short..."

"That works for me!" She took another sip and returned to tossing her strawberries in with the goat cheese and candied walnuts on the salad.

Murph rolled the deep purple liquid around the glass and savored its aroma. He drank and smiled. "Ahhh!"

He looked at his watch and frowned. "I better get going, or we'll be calling out for pizza!"

"That would be ok with me, but I promised Fr. Albers something special. You better get your gourmet on and get moving. Chop! Chop!"

"Yes Ma'am!" Murph picked up a knife and returned to cutting chives for the sauce.

In the end, dinner was expertly prepared with time to spare, featuring field greens with goat cheese, walnuts, and strawberry vinaigrette; broiled tilapia with a mustard chive sauce, grilled asparagus and pine nuts; and an incredibly light 13-layer coconut cake for dessert. No finer meal could be had in Washington and they had thoroughly enjoyed preparing it.

Knowing Fr. Albers as they did, they were not surprised when the doorbell chimed precisely at 7 pm. Murph's eyes widened with expectation.

He touched his wine glass to Carli's, the ding reverberating in the kitchen. "Time to get some answers!"

"Indeed!" She took his hand and squeezed. Then they walked expectantly to the door together.

Chapter 5

Murph opened the door to see the sun-shadowed outline of his teacher and friend, but also found an unanticipated surprise. Father Albers stood quietly, impeccably dressed as before in black suit, shirt and white priest's collar. Beside him was a young priest, barely over five-foot tall, who appeared to be making his best effort at mimicking his leader. A shock of red hair refused to lie down and blew across his face in the breeze. He pushed it back and re-positioned a pair of round, heavy rimmed glasses with the thickest lenses that Murph could ever remember seeing. His pale skin was dotted with freckles across his cheeks and nose. Where Fr. Albers was serious, the little priest couldn't stop grinning and fidgeting, shifting his weight from one foot to the other.

Carli, looking around Murph, took in a sudden, involuntary breath, and Murph quickly covered for her, "Good evening, Fr. Albers!"

"Hello, Michael. May we come in?" His tone, as always, was deep and evenly modulated, not unfriendly, but very formal.

Carli recovered from her shock rapidly, and with her usual grace. "Please..."

Father Albers entered the room with long, even strides. The little priest burst past the doorway like a small terrier and circled Fr. Albers, waiting to speak.

"I am sorry to bring another guest without calling in advance but, as you can see, he so wanted to come. May I introduce my research assistant, Father Bernardo Foa?" Fr. Albers precise diction gave the last name two syllables and pronounced it *fo-Wah*.

Fr. Foa burst forward, as if unleashed, and pumped Murph's hand with a vigorous handshake. "Call-a me Bernie!" He then took Carli's hand and kissed the back, near the wrist. "I am-a so glad to meet you! Murph and *Caro-leen-a*! I hav-a heard so much about-a you from Father Albers."

Murph looked a bit taken aback at all this attention. Carli noticed that Fr. Albers smiled slyly at his discomfort and suspected that this was no accidental meeting. Murph poured wine for his guests and settled everyone in the living room to talk. He quickly added another place setting at the table, very thankful that he had prepared an extra piece of fish – he had been planning to eat it for his own dinner later in the week. *No leftovers,* he thought to himself, *but at least I don't have to pull a loaves and fishes thing for dinner tonight.*

He returned to find that Bernie was beginning to settle down since introductions had been made. His initial canine analogy was still appropriate.

Father Albers had been describing how he had been dispatched to the US on Vatican business and had been assigned Fr. Foa as a research assistant. Bernie was fresh out of the seminary, with a boundless supply of energy. He also was fluent in English, if accented, and eager for an adventure away from his home in Italy.

Murph refilled his Merlot and settled in on the couch next to Carli. "So then, what brings you to Washington, Father?"

"All in good time, My Son. First, I am interested in the details of your adventures. When last I left the two of you, you were running down an alley in Zurich with an order of extradition to Egypt—for murder—hanging over your heads."

Carli turned pale as she remembered. The emotions came back to her in a flood, as if it were yesterday. Seeing that she was struggling, Murph held her hand and began the tale.

"We made contact with my dentist colleague in Zurich, Klaus Jantzen. With his help, we traveled to Munich and collected another piece of the puzzle. The G20 conference happened to be ending there and we caught a plane ride back to DC courtesy of Senator Brooks Borlon, whom I'm sure you remember."

"Ah, yes," Father Albers clarified for Bernie Foa, "Brooks was another one of my students at Saint Ignatius High School when I was a teacher."

"Once we returned to DC, things exploded rapidly." Murph didn't know how much to say. "I'm not sure what you have heard?"

Fr. Albers was sitting upright in the chair, carefully considering the story as it unfolded. "The reports we received in Rome were that there was a terrorist attack in Washington aimed at the Egyptian, Dr. Manesh Farouk. Though Dr. Farouk was killed, you foiled the bigger plot and stopped the leaders of the terrorist cell. Farouk was your employer at the Center for Esthetic and Restorative Excellence, was he not?"

"Yes. He was a fine man, and I'm sad he is gone. There's so much more I wish I could ask him." Murph was finding this particularly difficult.

"What you heard is the official story," Carli continued, picking up the pieces. "We figured out what Hamid al-Said and the Egyptians were looking for and collected the remainder of the Pharaoh's gold before they could. At the end, it's so crazy that even I don't believe it when I say it. There are really only a handful of people who know exactly what happened." She took a deep breath. "The short form is that Murph solved the mystery and lifted the Curse of Sekhem Ka."

Bernie's eyes widened and Fr. Albers nodded for her to continue.

Murph set down his wine and finished the narrative. "The mummy was returned to Cairo, along with that thug from the Brotherhood, Omar Bengdara, who, I expect, will recover from his wounds. He's too mean to die. The story we released to the media indicated that tracking down the 'terrorist cell' uncovered some exciting Egyptian history and artifacts. Carli was tasked with deciphering the scroll and hieroglyphics. Her exhibit on the Pharaoh Queen, Banthaira, opened two weeks ago in the Museum of Natural History at the Smithsonian. It is an impressive presentation. She did a fantastic job and will be receiving her PhD from Georgetown University after the fall semester."

Father Albers concurred. "I visited the exhibit today. It is truly exquisite. I was unaware of the sophistication of dentistry and medicine in ancient Egypt and the elaborate rites for sending the dead into the afterlife. Simply fascinating!"

Carli blushed at the praise.

"The ceremonial dagger on display with the jewelry and mummy of the Pharaoh Queen was especially interesting." The priest slowly probed for more answers. "The width of the blade seems remarkably similar to the scar on Michael's back, don't you think?" he asked, raising his eyebrows.

Murph involuntarily moved his left shoulder and Carli reached over to massage it protectively. He sighed. "You are most perceptive, as usual. It has taken a lot of physical therapy to get the strength and range of motion back. If Banthaira hadn't hit my shoulder blade straight on, I wouldn't be here talking to you now." He felt a chill and shuddered. "It was a close thing."

Carli put her arm around Murph's neck, pulled him close, and kissed him on the cheek. "He's the toughest guy I know. He saved me, and a lot of other people as well. It was hard to see him wounded, but he has worked hard and he's stronger now than before, lifting weights and learning yoga for flexibility."

"I'm not the only one with scars from that adventure." Murph lifted Carli's chin, and Bernie gasped. Though she did a good job concealing it, if you looked closely, a thin pink line ran across her neck from under her left ear to the middle of her throat. "That's from the same blade. She tries to minimize her involvement, but Carli's no innocent bystander. She had as much a part in stopping them as I did."

A tear formed in the corner of her eye and began to trace the line of her cheek. Murph gently wiped it away before it could roll far.

"I suspected as much. There is strength in the both of you and the Lord has need of that power to do His work. I will not ask more, for it is not appropriate for a guest to come into a house and cause distress to his hosts."

"It's no problem, Father. You are one of a very few people with whom we can ever share that story." Murph rose and extended a hand to Carli. "Let's have some dinner! I've had enough adventure to last a lifetime!"

Carli smiled as she stood up, the color returning to her face. "Amen to that.

Chapter 6

Since the hour was getting late, they decided to serve the salad and the main course together. Murph ladled the mustard chive sauce onto the broiled tilapia, arranged the asparagus, and brought out the steaming plates. Carli distributed the salad and garnished it with the vinaigrette as Murph refilled the wine glasses. With everything in place, they settled in for dinner.

"It's a-beautiful. Thank-a you so much!" Bernie was truly impressed.

"Michael, will you say the blessing?"

"But Father, I thought with you being the priest and all..."

"Michael!" The Jesuit's tone was gentle, yet insistent.

Murph took a deep breath:

"Bless us, Oh Lord and these, thy gifts, which we are about to receive…"

Father Albers arched an eyebrow. Bernie just giggled.

Carli kicked him under the table, squeezing his hand for emphasis. "How old are you? Five?"

Murph smiled from ear to ear. "Just kidding!" He cleared his throat, closing his eyes. Deepening his voice a bit, he began slowly, savoring each word:

Lord, teach me to be generous.
Teach me to serve you as you deserve;
To give and not to count the cost,
To fight and not to heed the wounds,
To toil and not to seek for rest,
To labor and not to ask for reward,
Save that of knowing that I do your will.

They all intoned "Amen" and looked up. Bernie was grinning and Fr. Albers nodded, looking pleased.

Carli was confused. "Is there some Jesuit inside joke I'm missing here?"

Father Albers thought for a moment and shared, "The Prayer for Generosity of Saint Ignatius of Loyola is never out of place, even as a blessing for dinner."

Murph laughed. "When in doubt, go with tradition. We said that prayer nearly every day of high school."

"I'm-a impressed that you-a remember that ten years a-later—after graduation."

"Jesuit education does leave a mark!" Murph raised a fork. "Now let's eat before the fish gets cold."

* * * * * *

Murph had cleared away the plates after dessert, while Carli was enjoying the praise of her superb coconut cake. He refilled the coffee cups and sat down. Fixing Father Albers with his gaze, Murph tried to finally get at the heart of the matter. "Alright Father, this is clearly not just a social call. What brings you to Washington?"

The Jesuit priest leaned forward, placing his elbows on the table and touched his long, bony fingers together like a tent. He seemed to be considering his thumbs for a time, then took in a breath and began:

"Since I was called to Rome by the Holy Father, he has periodically sent me on tasks to obtain information for the Vatican. Many of these errands are of a highly sensitive nature. This is one of those times. It is well known that I am here in Washington, but the 'official story' as you say, is that I am here to see the two of you and that it is purely social. Nothing could be further from the truth."

He paused a moment, waiting. Sensing that he had their complete attention, he continued, "The Holy Father is seeking to either prove or dispel the accusations levied against the Church by her many critics. Of special interest to me is the fact that the Pope is committed to evaluating allegations that, during World War II, Pope Pius XII did not do all he could to help the protect Jews of Europe from the Nazis. Before being elected Pope, Pius had been the Papal Nuncio to Germany and as the Vatican representative had worked closely with many men who rose to power in the Nazi regime. My early research leads me to believe that Pope Pius did not want to be seen as openly hostile to the Germans, since Vatican City remained free while initially trapped inside fascist Italy and then in an Italy occupied by the Nazis. He did, however, work behind the scenes to allow local priests to help protect the vulnerable. Speaking out from inside a police state like Germany would have gotten people arrested and killed. Pope Pius XII made an agreement with the Nazis that allowed the church to continue to operate in Germany in exchange for the Pope not condemning Hitler's regime. Instead, the Pope privately issued orders that eventually began an organized campaign to protect and rescue as many Jews as possible, providing false birth certificates, religious disguises, and safe keeping in cloistered monasteries and convents. After the war, the Israeli government acknowledged that the Catholic Church had saved thousands of Jewish lives."

"I hadn't ever heard that." Murph was impressed. "It's an interesting project, but what can you do here? And how do you need our help?"

"All in good time, my son." He held up his hand, palm outward. "I have uncovered evidence of a pathway that led Jews out of occupied Europe, passing them from one parish priest to another, through the mountains of Italy, and eventually to Rome. The trail leads to America—and there is a recently discovered cache of documents that may help us."

Carli took a sip of ice water and thought aloud, "It sounds like some sort of Underground Railroad, like they had during the Civil War to get escaped slaves out of the South."

"Quite so. It appears to be an ancient road, actually. The path follows the Via Francigena, a pilgrim route in use since the 11th century, leading from Canterbury through the Alps eventually to Rome. Each group of pilgrims would plot their course, traveling from town to town, visiting monasteries, abbeys, castles, and churches along the way. From France, the road led through the Susa Valley, the "Valley of the Abbeys" to Turin. Another member of my staff is now investigating the cities of Avigliana and Susa for evidence of the existence of such a Jewish underground railroad."

Bernie couldn't contain himself any longer. "What-a we do here is check out Post Office Box 1142, of-a course!"

"What?" Both Murph and Carli were completely confused.

Father Albers looked sternly at Bernie. Thoroughly chastised, he looked down and intently studied his coffee.

The Jesuit continued. "There is an old Army facility outside Alexandria Virginia called Fort Hunt. It was known during World War II as Post Office Box 1142, the address where mail was sent to reach the men and women stationed there. It had a clearance so top secret that most people in the U.S. had no idea of its existence. Only recently, have the activities at Fort Hunt gained any exposure and an amazing tale is coming to light. Pour me another cup of coffee and I will tell you a bedtime story the likes of which you have never heard before."

Chapter 7

Murph lit the gas logs in the fireplace and they all settled back down in the living room, Carli cuddling against Murph on the couch and Bernie in a leather armchair, his smile returning with the change of scenery. Father Albers stood beside the fire, as if to lecture, looking completely at ease. He was an engaging storyteller anyway and this story proved to be captivating.

"Located on the Potomac River, just over eleven miles south of Washington DC, Fort Hunt had originally been part of George Washington's estate at Mount Vernon. It had been in use as a coastal defense installation dating back to the Spanish American War. In 2006, the National Park Service completed the renovation of Fort Hunt Park as a picnic spot. During the dedication, a park ranger was detailing the history of the park, including its use as a hospital during World War I.

A visitor attending the ceremony raised his hand and said. 'I used to work here during World War II.' Taken aback, the ranger asked what the man meant, and the following story unfolded.

In 1942, a highly classified military intelligence unit was created at Fort Hunt, known only as PO Box 1142, as Fr. Foa indicated, for the mailing address of its over 1000 personnel. The unit was responsible for interrogating Nazi Germany's top military officers, government officials and scientists as they were taken prisoner during the war. In a way, Fort Hunt was the Guantanamo Bay of its day. The mere existence of this camp and its intent violated the Geneva conventions on POW protocol, as the Red Cross and German government were not notified of the presence of captives until long after they had been transferred out of Fort Hunt to traditional POW camps. The extraction of information by the staff at PO Box 1142 was done without torture, interrogation, or cruelty but it did involve a level of deceit.

Nearly 4,000 POWs spent some time in the camp's 100 barracks, ringed by barbed wire and watchtowers. The barracks and grounds were bugged, allowing conversations to be surreptitiously monitored and recorded. Through the unit's efforts, the Allies learned about German research in such areas as rocketry, jet engines, U-boats, microwaves, infrared technology, and the atomic bomb.

Often the personnel monitoring the POWs had little or no understanding of the information they were recording. They passed the details along for interpretation by their superiors.

Remember the V1 and V2 rockets that rained mass destruction on England? They were the world's first long-range missiles and were truly terror weapons used on the civilian population. The staff at Fort Hunt overheard two German naval officers talking in their room, 'Don't worry, once the work at Peenemunde prevails, Germany will be victorious.' It only took the Allies about a month to target the exact location where the rockets were being made and then the British successfully bombed the Peenemunde site.

Another key program based at Fort Hunt was the Military Intelligence Research Section, which studied documents in order to give the interrogators information to extract confessions from POWs. They provided details to make the Americans seem to know far more than they actually did. For example, when Army researchers spotted a newspaper photo of German General Erwin Rommel surrounded by other generals at his daughter's wedding, they used it for leverage against another general who was captured and brought to 1142. An interrogator would say, 'We already know most of the information we need, and by the way, how was the wedding? We know you were standing next to general so and so, and when he was captured, he gave us plenty of information, so you might as well talk.'

The Army gathered a large group of German-speaking personnel and many of the men stationed at Fort Hunt were refugees from Germany. They were often Jews who had been young boys when Hitler came to power and their families fled. They had language proficiency, cultural background and a personal knowledge of many of the cities and villages where captives had lived.

The tales of Fort Hunt are emerging as one of the best-kept secrets of the war. After their service, the personnel at the fort were sworn to never reveal what they had done there. Unlike modern Washington, where secrets cannot be kept for a day, the men who served at 1142 never broke their silence. The details of Fort Hunt were declassified in 1977, but no one ever contacted the veterans and released them from their confidentiality agreements. Sadly, most of the history of the camp is dying with the veterans at an alarming rate.

Realizing their mistake, the National Park Service is racing to contact the surviving personnel from Fort Hunt and collect their stories. They have created a library of the declassified documents from PO Box 1142 and are including the narratives from the former workers. The records are now available for public viewing on site at Fort Hunt—and that is where you come in!"

Bernie had drifted off during the lecture, since he had heard it all before. His chin rested comfortably on his chest and he was breathing deeply. Murph and Carli had enjoyed the history lesson, but were still confused about their part in the search. Murph shrugged his shoulders. "Other than just two more pair of eyes, why us?"

"The primary reason is that I enjoy your company. However, what I neglected to tell you is that during Fr. Foa's initial search of the documents, he narrowed the field to a manageable group. Within the pile of records of specific interest to me, there are several notebooks that could benefit from examination by people of your specific talents."

"Which are?" Carli, ever the researcher, was intrigued.

"Caroline, you speak French fluently and there is a file of transcripts from Vichy French officers and officials. Fr. Bernardo and I are both fluent in German, so that is under control. I need help with a collection of private confession notes written by a trio of Roman Catholic priests. In order to shield the privacy of the confessional, yet keep their agreement with the military to record everything, they kept journals and vowed never to release the information to the authorities."

"I get that file because I'm Catholic?"

"No, Michael. You have been assigned those files because they are written in Latin!" Father Albers smiled broadly like the Cheshire cat.

"Oh, great! Just what I always wanted. Can't we find an Honors Latin IV class looking for a project?" Murph whined, but Carli elbowed him in the ribs.

"No, Michael. I'm afraid this is a private matter and you are the man for the job. I know your skill in the ancient language and have complete faith in your ability!"

The sparkle in Carli's eyes signaled her excitement. As an archeologist, she enjoyed the search, digging through piles of history. Murph preferred more action, but knew when he was out-voted. His fate was sealed. "How do we do this?"

Father Albers had done his homework. "I know your day off is Wednesday. Father Foa will have everything prepared for us before then. I would appreciate it if you could give me a full day. I believe we can complete the review of the documents on Wednesday if we work diligently."

Carli reviewed the calendar on her iPhone, tapping with a manicured finger. "I can move my meeting and free up the day. This is great."

Murph seemed more concerned. "I have a lot to do this week. We have been invited to the Inaugural Dinner at the White House."

"But that's not until Saturday!" Carli looked sternly at Murph. "We owe Fr. Albers. You can make the time!"

"OK. You win. I'll clear my calendar for Wednesday." Murph smiled a tired smile. Fr. Albers nodded his approval. "I'll request one of the Ford Explorers from the Center. That will be big enough for me to drive us all down comfortably."

Father Albers seemed curious. "The dinner at the White House is for Senator Borlon, is it not?"

"Yes. When President Biden went into a coma after his heart attack, it was only five weeks after his inauguration. Vice President Buchanan then became acting President. President Biden's death last month created a vacancy and Brooks Borlon was recently confirmed as the new Vice President. The country is coming out of a period of mourning, so they are having a State Dinner at the White House as a low-key inaugural party. The Vice President was kind enough to invite us." Murph had been genuinely surprised when the invitation bearing the Presidential Seal had arrived. "I toured the White House with my 8th Grade class from St. Angela's, but Carli has never been inside."

"I'm so excited!" She giggled like a kid on Christmas Eve. "It's a once in a lifetime chance.

"I was also invited to represent the Vatican. I am pleased to know that I will have friends to meet when I am there."

Murph thought to himself, *I should have expected that. It's another reason why he's here in D.C.* "We'll get the research done this week and celebrate at the White House on Saturday. Sounds like a very full week!"

"Indeed. I suppose that I should wake Fr. Foa and depart." The Jesuit looked at his watch. "My driver will have been waiting for a few minutes now, and you will need to hustle to get Caroline home before midnight." He arched one eyebrow.

"Indeed," Murph mimicked, rising from the couch and pulling Carli up.

"I am staying at the guest house in the Jesuit residence at Georgetown. My cell number remains the same as before."

"Excellent, Father." Murph calculated the driving time. "I will pick up Carli and then get you at 7:30 on Wednesday morning."

"Thank you for a fabulous dinner and even more stimulating conversation." He shook Murph's hand warmly. In spite of his formal demeanor, Carli gave Father Albers a hug and he cracked a rare smile.

Bernie awoke with a start and stammered his thank you, clearly embarrassed at having fallen asleep. Murph got their suit jackets and saw them out.

As he closed the door behind them, Carli nestled into the crook of his arm, resting her head on his chest. He held her close with his arm around her shoulders. "Well, that wasn't what I expected. It's a simple research project." She sounded almost disappointed.

"I know. I'm glad its not a big deal—but it seems like a long way to come to get us to help him read a couple of old diaries, even if they are in Latin!"

"I guess we'll know more on Wednesday." She turned and glanced down at her watch. "You better hurry. I hear that I turn into a pumpkin at midnight!" She started for the kitchen and looked over her shoulder, winking at him.

Murph reached out for her, but Carli ducked under his arm and started running. "Last one there washes the broiler pan!"

Chapter 8

The week passed quickly and Wednesday arrived with a rush. Murph was already tired from running around even though it was just past dawn when he parked the Mustang at the Center. Where the weekend had been sunny and warm, the middle of the week had been marked by grey skies and rain. Though it was currently dry, the heavy, leaden storm clouds foretold of wet weather to come.

The Washington Center for Esthetic and Restorative Excellence was an imposing granite and brick edifice just adjacent to John Marshall Place Park on C Street. Sitting just a block off the National Mall, it was in the middle of everything and Murph's home away from home. At 6:30 am, the parking lot was nearly deserted as he ran in the back door and up to his office. Efficient as always, Margaret had a note on his desk, detailing his schedule for the rest of the week and the keys he needed today. Murph scanned the schedule and shook his head. *No time to breathe,* he thought to himself. *How am I ever going to get this all done?* A full schedule of patients tomorrow and Friday, then teaching a study club at the Center on Saturday—the enormity of it all scared him. *No point in stressing. It'll work out. It always does.* He sighed and pocketed the keys to the Ford Explorer.

He locked up and dashed out the back, fearing that he would be late. He made it through the Dunkin' Donuts drive thru quickly enough and managed not to spill the coffees while negotiating the narrow streets in Georgetown, pulling up in front of Carli's house at the arranged time of 7:15.

Murph popped the lift gate as she came down the walk. Where he looked drab in black slacks and a grey golf pullover to shed the rain, Carli was radiant in a lavender sweater set and khaki slacks. She carried a basket of fruit and muffins as well as chicken salad and croissants for lunch. She had even made chocolate chip cookies! Murph took her load and placed it in the back of the SUV next to the cooler of water bottles and Diet Coke he had packed. He helped her in the car and absentmindedly pecked her on the cheek. He climbed into the car and reached for the gearshift.

Carli grabbed his hand and looked him sternly in the eyes. "OK Murphy! What's going on?"

"Why?" He sounded evasive, in spite of his efforts to be casual.

"Since you dropped me off on Sunday, you haven't called. You've barely texted me! I know you have that TMJ course on Saturday but you've taught that one before. Something's up. I can feel it."

"It's no big deal. Work's been real busy and I have a lot of things to do this week. I really couldn't spare today, but I need to make time for Fr. Albers. I owe him that."

"Alright...but I'm not sure. I know you and there's something you're not telling me." She pursed her lips and shook her head.

Murph reached over and pushed her hair back over her ear. He leaned over and kissed her. "After I get through this week, it will all be a lot easier. You'll see!" His smile was warm and inviting.

"Well, OK." She relaxed a bit. "I'll take your word for it."

"Good thing. We have to get going. Father Albers will be waiting!"

* * * * * *

"They are here." Bernie called back to Fr. Albers. He couldn't mistake the white Ford Explorer with the logo of the Washington Center for Esthetic and Restorative Excellence on the door. As Murph parked and opened the doors for the two priests, Bernie couldn't resist asking, "Why-a the white car with the big symbol of the Washington Monument on the door?"

Murph chuckled. "Can you think of a better color for a dentist than white? We use these SUV's to pick up patients and run other errands for the practice. They are very effective mobile billboards for the Center, so they have to be a bit showy. I borrowed this one today for the drive. It's only 35

36

minutes to Fort Hunt Park but it will be much more comfortable than the Mustang for the four of us."

Bernie looked sad. "I was-a hoping for a ride in the Mustang."

Murph smiled. "Don't worry. I'll let you drive it while you're here. You can do your best Steve McQueen imitation."

Bernie beamed. "I can't –a wait." He rubbed his hands together "Does it have a stick-a shift?"

Carli just shook her head. "You guys are all the same."

Still talking cars, Murph took a sip of his coffee and pushed his way into the growing traffic. He and Carli narrated the tour of Washington DC as they crossed the gray ribbon of the Potomac River into Virginia near Theodore Roosevelt Island. They wound through the narrow streets of Arlington, eventually passing around the Marine Corps Memorial, much to the appreciation of Bernie Foa. It was a favorite of Murph's as well, so he slowed down while driving past. He always marveled at the power of the image of the Marines raising the flag on Iwo Jima. The commitment and sacrifice displayed by the Marines was legendary. "Semper Fidelis," he whispered.

It must have been a bit louder than he intended. "Amen," added Fr. Albers quietly.

They left the memorial and eased onto George Washington Parkway.

The bustling traffic swept them along past Reagan National Airport and downstream paralleling the Potomac through Alexandria. They enjoyed the view as the city opened into more green spaces, with the slowly moving waters of the Potomac on their left and the rolling pastures of George Washington's historic estate, Mount Vernon, spreading out on their right. Murph drove swiftly to the park that had once been Fort Hunt. The entrance led them to an open parking lot. The impending rain had scared off any other visitors. It appeared that the little party would have the place to themselves, which would suit their purpose perfectly.

Murph parked in front of the newly constructed visitors center and they got out. Bernie went in ahead to greet the ranger in charge, while Murph gathered up the picnic basket and cooler. Father Albers led Carli to the door with Murph in tow. The low brick building was unremarkable but sufficient. The flagpole was protected by a granite marker recognizing the contributions of the men and women who had served at PO Box 1142.

Murph stopped beside the plaque and looked around. He surveyed the flat grass fields and tried to imagine the barracks, watch towers and barbed wire of the prison camp that had been here 60 years ago. A light rain was beginning to fall as he turned and entered the building.

The main hall contained displays of the history of the camp. Murph's mental picture turned out to be fairly accurate as he examined pictures of the facility when it was home for 1000 prisoners and their captors. The artifacts in glass cases showed the way the barracks and grounds had been bugged.

Murph pointed at one of the listening devices, "It's tough to call this a bug—it's nearly two feet long!"

Carli was trying out a station where the park service had set up headphones. You touched the button and heard tapes of the prisoners talking, the same way the staff at the camp listened and made notes. The recordings were in German, but even if you couldn't understand the language, the urgency and concern in the words came through just fine. Fear needed no translation.

Father Albers motioned them to a separate room in the back where Bernie and the park ranger had spread out boxes and files for them. "You each have your records to examine. Please let me know when you find something interesting."

Murph and Carli considered their stations. A pile of musty old hand-written notes in manila files, and next to them, several yellow legal pads and pencils.

Murph couldn't help himself. "This looks like fun," he observed dryly, setting down his coffee.

"That's enough out of you!" Carli scolded him, but she had been thinking the same thing. "We better get started."

Chapter 9

Carli made herself right at home, putting her ear buds in and starting her iPod to keep out any distractions. She spread out the files and a note pad. With a look of calm concentration on her face, she took to the task with enthusiasm.

Murph, on the other hand, looked distracted. It was tough for him to focus, as he kept checking his iPhone for texts and emails. He kept it in his hand in his lap, since Carli had frowned each time it had buzzed, shaking the table. He spread out the files and quickly made a survey of what was in front of him.

Three priests had made records of their confessions. One, Father Larkin, had only been at Fort Hunt for two months. His file was very small and Murph reviewed it quickly. His notes were simple. It looked like the files of a man who was simply doing what he was ordered to do and nothing more. Murph could empathize. There was so little here that Murph put the file aside as unlikely to produce anything interesting.

The second group of records that Murph examined was much more detailed. Father John MacLaughlin didn't hear confessions as much as he had conversations with his charges—long, involved, deep conversations. His file read like a collection of short stories. Murph started to enjoy this, in spite of his predisposition against being here. It was actually fun to read MacLaughlin's conversational Latin, if you could call a dead language conversational. Fr. John seemed to be a nice guy, his notes were casual and Murph was really beginning to like him.

Three hours passed surprisingly quickly. Father Albers called a halt to the search. Carli served the chicken salad croissants that she had prepared. They hoped to go outside and stretch, but a steady, drenching rain was falling. They ate quietly, each one alone with their thoughts.

Murph could sense that Carli was troubled, her brows deeply furrowed as she chewed. "What's wrong?"

"There were very few prisoners here who spoke French as a primary language, so I don't have much."

Father Albers agreed. "Yes, most were German and there were a few Italians. Any Frenchman would have been either a collaborator in occupied France or a Vichy officer. Why? Have you found something?"

"Nothing to do with Jews or the Holocaust, but there are transcripts from a Frenchman who sounds like a raving madman. It's just creepy!"

"Captivity will affect the sanity of a man sometimes. What is he talking about? "

"His name is Marcel Bloch. He was a physician and I think he was part of the crew of a German submarine that was captured and brought here to Fort Hunt. He keeps babbling about *the fire* and how he needs to confess. He thinks he's going to burn and the fear is consuming him. He's driving the rest of his barracks crazy. Either they get some psychiatric help for him or his bunkmates are going to kill him. One way or the other, I don't think this is going to end well." She shuddered at the thought.

Murph thought for a minute. "If he was a French Nazi, he would probably have been Catholic. Let me see if he went to confession. It sounds like he needed it. What was his name again?"

"Bloch. Marcel Bloch."

Carli came over as Murph started paging quickly through the notes. He hoped that Bloch had Father John as his confessor, since the notes could be much more enlightening. Finding an English word like a name among Fr. John's tightly written Latin proved to be much easier than Murph had thought. It only took a few minutes to find the confession notes of one Marcel Bloch. Murph was not surprised to discover that this confession had its own section. As he began to read, his eyes grew wide.

Father Albers and Bernie Foa carried over chairs and sat closely. Carli leaned against Murph's back, peering over his shoulder. The story that unfolded wasn't just creepy, it quickly progressed into a nightmare.

"I've got it right here. Father John MacLaughlin's notes are very thorough even when he heard a mundane confession. This narrative is huge and contains so much more detail. He met with Marcel Bloch on several occasions. Bloch was the ship's doctor for the submarine U-513, which was captured in 1944. Bloch's confessions were a mess, with the man rambling—feeling this compelling need to confess.

Bloch keeps referring to *the fire*. Fr. John wonders if there was a real fire that nearly took Bloch's life. The Frenchman also lives in mortal fear of judgment before God and being consumed by eternal fire in Hell. Father John is troubled, because he can't grant absolution to Bloch. He can't decide what penance is appropriate, because...oh, my God!" Murph gasped and pushed back from the table.

Carli jumped. "What is it?"

Murph leaned back to the document and traced the words with his finger, unable to believe what he was reading.

"Bloch admitted to more than 200 murders! He tells the story of his medical practice in Paris in 1944. Bloch let it be known on the street that he could get Jews safely out of France and keep them from being shipped out to concentration camps. Jewish families would come to his office and he took their money and valuables in trade for their safety.

Bloch told them that since he was a physician, he could vaccinate them before sending them on the difficult journey from Paris out of German occupied territory to neutral Spain. Instead of vaccines, he injected them with morphine...and then killed them! Bloch was a serial killer!"

Carli was horrified, thinking of the scene. She turned a sickly gray. Murph got her a chair before she collapsed and opened a bottle of water for her.

As terrible as the tale was, Murph felt compelled to keep translating. "Fr. John details Bloch's confession that he dismembered the bodies by cutting them up so that he could dispose of them more easily. Bloch did not seem upset at the carnage he was creating, but he hated *the boy*. Fr. John writes that Bloch was sedating a family when a ten-year-old boy broke free. The boy grabbed medicine bottles off Bloch's desk and threw them at the doctor. They missed him, but crashed into the fireplace. One of the bottles contained ether, which exploded and caught the drapes on fire. The blaze spread rapidly, engulfing the building. The boy escaped and continues to haunt Bloch in his dreams. As the firemen arrived, Bloch knew he couldn't hide the evidence of his crimes, so he fled Paris. He made his way to the French coast and signed on with the submarine to get out of the country."

Father Albers had been sitting in his usual pose, hands folded in a peak with the fingers supporting the angle of his jaw. He cleared his throat. "I have heard rumors of murderers like this operating under the Nazis. In a police state like the Third Reich, no one asks questions or looks too closely at their neighbors. If a family went missing, no alarm would be raised, especially if the family were Jewish. People went missing all the time and it was not healthy to make inquiries."

Carli still looked like she was going to be sick. Murph held her hand and tried to offer a bit of hope. "Fr. John says that Bloch was ranting that *the boy* probably got help from *that meddling priest Father Gaspard.* Maybe the boy got away."

Father Albers urged him to push on. "Michael, is there any more?"

"Yes. Father John had seen the face of evil within the madness. He was troubled that he had learned something in the confessional that he couldn't absolve and not report. He violated his oath and contacted one of the Fort Hunt interrogators about what Bloch had told him. Father John is really at a loss to know what to do. He laments that this will haunt him for the rest of his life. He offers no penance to Bloch and urges him to tell everything he knows to his captors as a way to make amends. He urges Bloch to pray to God for absolution because there is no earthly power that can help him."

"Who was the officer whom Father MacLaughlin told?"

Murph looked at the manuscript carefully. "Captain Frederic Arnold."

Father Albers looked to Bernie. "See what you can find."

* * * * *

Murph held Carli close as they stood, staring out the window at the rain. There was nothing to say while Bernie and Father Albers were searching the interrogation records with the help of the park ranger. Murph had tried to talk to her, but she was too disturbed to speak and just wanted to feel the safety of his arms around her.

"Here it is." Father Albers pushed his glasses further up on his nose and looked up. "Marcel Bloch was brought in with the crew of U-513. Bloch had escaped Paris in April 1944 and made his way to the French port of Brest. He met the commander of U-513, Kapitainleutnant Heinz Klemper, just as the submarine was ready to begin another patrol in the Atlantic. The submarine needed a ship's doctor and Bloch needed a way out of France. Neither man asked many questions. The confined spaces on the U-boat drove Bloch mad. The crew of U-513 reported being happy to have been captured and getting away from the lunatic."

"I can-a imagine that!" Bernie nodded in agreement.

"Captain Klemper would not agree. U-513 had sunk the British steamer S.S. Dover early in the patrol. Klemper had been accused by the British and Americans of shooting survivors of the Dover when they took to their lifeboats. He believed that the British would try him as a war criminal and agreed to talk if he could avoid being turned over to the British.

Captain Arnold questions both Klemper and Bloch about the submarine's mission. Klemper is then passed along to the British for trial anyway. Bloch confirms what he had confessed to Father MacLaughlin."

Murph sighed. "Well, that's it then."

"Not exactly." Father Albers turned the page. "The day after Bloch is confronted by Fred Arnold, the prisoner walked toward the fence surrounding the interrogation center and

43

began to climb over. The doctor continued to climb after guards had ordered him to stop. Marcel Bloch was fatally shot while attempting to escape from Fort Hunt."

"Sounds more like suicide," Murph observed rather casually.

"Coward!" Carli spat out the words.

"I believe that Dr. Bloch has met his judgment...without absolution." Father Albers tone was icy. "The tale does not end there. Arnold and MacLaughlin meet again and agree to keep following the story. MacLaughlin is obsessed with finding out what happened to the boy."

"I agree with him." Carli gazed out at the rain, determined. "He's the only happy ending that could possibly come from this."

"Arnold writes that Fr. John intends to travel to the Vatican as soon as possible to try to find out what happened to the boy and track down this Father Gaspard. Arnold plans to interview the commander of the ship that captured the U-513 when they came back in port. The initial interrogation occurred on the ship and he thinks there might be something else that Bloch may have said.

The U-513 was forced to the surface by bombs and depth charges from the USS Nassau. Sixteen of the crew of the U-513 were killed, but 40 survived and were brought to the Nassau. The Captain of the Nassau was apparently an extremely smart officer. He knew that Captain Klemper of U-513 was a wanted war criminal and idly threatened to turn him over to the British navy. That got Klemper scared and he began talking, and the rest of his crew talked as well."

Bernie had been cross referencing the story and read from his computer, "I'm-a not completely sure, but the Cap-i-tan of the Nassau was a Commander Donald..."

"Williams." The certainty of Murph's voice cut through the gloom. "Captain Don Williams, United States Navy, retired. He's 104 years old, but sharp as a tack and living in Arlington. Would you like to meet him?"

Chapter 10

Carli grinned, her smile warming the room. "You never cease to amaze me!"

"Why?" Murph shrugged his shoulders. "Don was one of my first patients when I started working at the Center. He's the nicest guy in the world. After he left the Navy, he was a very successful businessman. He even was the International President of Kiwanis. He's the oldest patient I have, but if there is anything else to know about Bloch, he'll remember."

Father Albers passed the file in front of him over to Bernie. "Father Foa, please make copies of the pages we have discussed while Michael contacts Captain Williams. This seems to be a promising lead that we should examine."

Bernie Foa spread out the records and began meticulously snapping images into his iPad.

Murph pulled out his iPhone and Carli shook her head slightly. "You remember his number?"

"No, silly. But I can access the Center's computer patient records." Murph paused while he punched in his username and password. "This is one of the benefits of computer based patient records. If I get a call after hours for an emergency, I can call up a patient's records to make sure I know if they have any drug allergies or medical concerns before I call in a prescription. I also can see tomorrow's schedule to offer them a time to come in and have me take a look at whatever the problem is." Murph grabbed a pencil and quickly made notes. "Here it is."

He logged off the office computer and dialed the number, putting the phone on speaker so everyone could hear.

"Hello?" The voice was raspy, but then he coughed and it became stronger. "Can I help you?"

"Hi Mr. Williams. It's Doctor Murphy!" Murph was talking slowly, to be clear.

"Oh, hi Mike! What's up? My teeth are fine!"

Murph laughed. "That's good. I wouldn't have expected any less since I saw you just last month." Not knowing how to bring up the subject, Murph opted for the direct approach. "I was talking with a friend about the war...the Battle of the Atlantic. I remember we talked about your ship capturing U boats..."

"That's right," he said with a laugh. "Tough business, that."

"My friend is working on a research project and he was interested in one specific case. The U-513…"

Before Murph could continue, Don cut him off. "I wondered when someone would look into that. It's taken over 70 years, but...I've seen lots of things in my years in the Navy, but that was the darnedest!"

"Why do you say that?"

There was a slight pause. "I've never seen the crew of a ship so happy to be captured. The sailors couldn't get off the boat fast enough to get away from that crazy Frenchman...the doctor!"

"Doctor Bloch?"

"Mike, are you working with the Army on this?"

"No. Why?"

"I can't hear you really well, you're breaking up." He paused but the line sounded fine to Murph, "Can you come by in person?"

"Sure! It's on my way. Besides, I'll bring Carli with me."

"That's great. You talk about her so much. She sounds so perfect, I want to see if she's real."

Carli blushed.

Murph shouted to be sure Don could hear, "We'll be over in less than an hour."

"Sounds good. I'll put on a fresh pot of coffee!" and the line went dead.

Carli was impressed. "He seems like such a nice guy."

"But there's something he doesn't want to say on the phone." Murph was puzzled. "This is a 70-year-old story but there's a cloud over it. It stressed us all to read it. We hear about serial killers far too often these days, but this feels different."

Father Albers was in agreement. "Any time I deal with the Holocaust, it makes me ill. Dr. Bloch is an extension of that. Such evil has a power that transcends time."

Carli shivered again. "Let's pack up and go see what Captain Williams has to say."

Murph didn't have to be asked twice. He helped Bernie rearrange the folders and return them to the ranger, while Carli tidied up and closed the picnic basket.

When they were ready, Murph tossed his Styrofoam coffee cup to be recycled. "I could use another cup of coffee and Don's a widower, so I'm sure he would love some of your chocolate chip cookies—and that pretty smile."

Chapter 11

Once again, the drive back up the George Washington Parkway was uneventful, since they were travelling the opposite direction to the prevailing afternoon traffic rushing out of Washington. Murph had no problem locating the address. Don Williams was living in Arlington Village, a bright, cheerful new retirement home just outside of downtown Arlington. Though he was 104 years old, Don had his own apartment in the assisted living side of the facility. He had told the front desk that he was expecting Dr. Murphy and friends, so they entered without delay. As the little party walked down the corridor, Murph could smell the coffee brewing. Don was true to his word and the coffee was ready, done the Navy way, black and strong, to keep you awake on the midnight watch.

The door was ajar, so Murph knocked and pushed it open, stepping through the threshold. The apartment was spare, but comfortable. Along the back wall of the room, a twin bed and nightstand sat underneath the window. The middle of the room had a pair of high backed leather armchairs facing a TV mounted on the wall where it could also be seen from the bed. The door led into a short hall that passed the bathroom. As he stepped in further and said, "Hello?" he was greeted from the left.

"Hi, Mike! C'mon in!"

The front of the apartment was a small kitchen area, really just a sink, mini fridge and microwave, but it gave the appearance of home. Don was pouring coffee into two large mugs, with the logo of the USS Nassau proudly on the side.

Murph went over and shook hands warmly with Don Williams. Though he had never been a tall man, Don had been markedly shrinking in recent years. His legs were still long, but the compression of his spine had left his upper body out of proportion with his overall height. His hair was closely cropped, white snow around the back of his head with a few wisps on the top. He placed his mug on the tray of his walker, waving off Murph's help and moved to a chair. Even though it was July, he had khaki slacks on and a navy blue cardigan sweater over a pressed white collared shirt. The room was meticulous, everything in its place. Murph had expected no less, knowing Don as he did, but Carli was impressed.

Murph introduced Carli, Father Albers, and Bernie. Don motioned for Carli to sit next to him in the "comfy chair" while Murph retrieved the folding chairs Don had asked him to get from the closet. By the time Murph had everyone settled and was savoring his coffee, Carli had already shared her cookies. Don was enjoying one and praising Carli. "Just like my wife used to make!"

Don was a charmer and loved to have visitors, but he was well aware that there was a purpose to their coming. He patted Carli's hand, "Much as I love the company, I know there is something you want to know. How can I help you?"

Murph explained Father Albers's role in the Vatican and the fact that he was researching the Holocaust. Their search had led them to Marcel Bloch, who had led them here.

Don put down his mug and took them back to 1944. "It was summer of 1944, soon after the D-Day invasion. The

German soldiers and sailors could see the handwriting on the wall, but the fanatical Nazis in command still felt they could win the war. I was in command of Task Force 22.4, with the escort carrier USS Nassau and the destroyer escorts USS Pope, Pillsbury, Chatelain, and Flaherty. We had been warned of a wolf pack of U-boats working the convoy lanes out of Norfolk. We discovered the U-513 recharging her batteries on the surface. When she dove, we were able to force her back to the surface and she surrendered. It was the strangest thing..."

"Why is that?" They had decided that Murph would lead the interview while the others just listened and Bernie made some notes.

"The crew couldn't get off the ship fast enough. The Captain and the Frenchman kept arguing and my executive officer had to take them off the U-boat at gunpoint. Once they were on the Nassau, we separated the officers and crew, as was the standard procedure. I then had to put the doctor and other officers in different rooms as well. The stress of living in such a small, confined space as a submarine had worn them to a raw nerve."

"What about Dr. Bloch?"

"Mad as a hatter, that one! Kept ranting about *the fire* and some *boy*. I really didn't talk to him that much. Remember, there was a war on and we needed to find out what the U-boats were doing. I concentrated on Captain Klemper. I convinced him that I could help him avoid being hanged as a war criminal by the British if he talked. It wasn't a lie, mind you, but I did stretch the truth a bit. In the end, he sang like a canary. And once he started, so did the rest of his crew."

Don was getting dry, so he took a sip of coffee. "Ahh. We reached port and transferred the whole lot of them together with my interrogation reports to some Army unit called PO Box 1142. I didn't think about crazy old Dr. Bloch again for some time. We were transferred to the Pacific and took a Kamikaze hit off Okinawa. It damaged a few of the officer's cabins, including the one where we had stashed Dr. Bloch. The repair crew found a logbook, some sort of diary written in

French that had been stuffed in the bulkhead. The crazy SOB must have worked his fingers raw to open a panel and hide the book there. I can't read French so I just kept it until we got back to port."

Murph and Carli exchanged glances. "That's interesting!"

"That's nothing! When we got back to Norfolk, this Army Captain came to see me."

"Captain Arnold?" Murph wanted to be sure.

"That's the fellow, a really squirrely guy—clearly military intelligence, although I'm not so sure about the intelligence part, if you know what I mean." He laughed to himself, "That's an oxymoron, you know, military intelligence!"

Murph chuckled along with Don. It was an old joke. "What did Arnold want?"

"I thought he would want to know about Klemper, but he had nothing but questions about Bloch. He seemed to know more than I did, so I wasn't able to help him much. He said that Bloch had tried to escape and gotten himself shot. Sounds like a suicide, if you ask me."

Murph nodded. "That was our impression too. What did Arnold say about the logbook?"

Don frowned and was quiet. "That's the part that I'm not proud of." The Navy man looked suddenly old and tired. "Mike, will you help me?" Don extended his hand and Murph pulled him up. Don stood as tall as he could and pulled down his sweater, straightening it.

Murph held his arm as he walked, unsteadily, over to a card table at the foot of his bed and pulled back the tablecloth. Carli's eyes opened wider in surprise. Partially hidden in shadow was the unmistakable shape of a bank safe. Don knelt down with some difficulty, but twirled the combination with prac-ticed skill. The lock opened with a satisfying *click*. He pulled back the door and reached inside. From buried in the back, he produced a thin, leather bound folio and showed it to Murph. Don leaned on Murph and stood back up, walking triumphantly back to his chair.

Handing the book to Carli with a sad smile, he said, "I just didn't like Arnold. His manner left me thinking that there was more he wasn't telling me. I didn't trust him, so I didn't tell him about the logbook. I know it wasn't right, but I have always rationalized it by telling myself that since Bloch was already dead, it didn't matter."

Carli patted him on the hand. "I know you did the right thing. I think the diary will be more valuable now than it would have been back in 1944."

"Thanks, dear. You know how to make an old man feel better." Don's smile was worn. He was tired—relieved to be rid of the burden. "Just what's in that folder anyway?"

Murph had his suspicions, but it was time to be sure. "Marcel Bloch was not a ship's doctor. He was really a serial killer. He had been luring Jewish families to his office in Paris by letting them believe that he could get them out of occupied France before they were shipped to concentration camps. Once he had them, he drugged and killed them. He was a monster!"

"Oh my God!" Don sobbed.

"The only thing that stopped Bloch was a young boy who accidentally started a fire and burned down the building." Murph had been watching Carli. She looked up from the diary with tears in her eyes.

He walked over and squatted down next to her, holding her hand. Murph spoke quietly, encouraging her. "It's OK. Tell them what's in here."

"It's a log, with the names of all the Jews he killed, arranged by family and the date of their death." Her voice broke. "He even cataloged their possessions and the money they paid for safe passage. There are more than 300 names here."

They all sat in stunned silence. Carli turned to the last page. "The last entry is a family of five. The youngest was a boy of 10. His name has been circled so many times that the pen has nearly worn through the page." She traced the name with her finger, her voice falling to a whisper. "His name was Simon Cohen."

Chapter 12

With tears in his eyes, he felt ashamed that his fear of needles had made him sick. He wiped the traces of vomit from his mouth with his handkerchief as he walked into the room. He had come out of the bathroom suddenly and watched as his father slumped to the floor after the doctor had finished the injection. Though he was only 10, he knew something was terribly wrong. The doctor had told them he had to give them vaccinations before they could travel. He saw the bodies of his sisters crumpled in a pile, like coats thrown on the bed. He reached out to them and touched a handful of dark brown hair, soft and smooth. His mother...

Simon screamed and Dr. Bloch looked up suddenly, realizing that there was still one left. The doctor smiled, his lips a thin line. He reached down to his exam table and picked up another syringe, pointing it menacingly at the boy. Simon dashed to move to safety, ducking behind the doctor's desk to put a barrier between himself and the physician. Dr. Bloch just shook his head and began to walk toward the boy.

Simon's eyes scanned the room. The door to the waiting room was on the far wall, past Bloch, and the doctor was already approaching...slowly...deliberately. Both of them knew he had all the time in the world. Simon was trapped.

On the edge of the desk in front of him, Simon noticed several glass bottles, the largest of which held about a half gallon of a clear liquid. He grabbed it and threw it at Dr. Bloch. To Simon's surprise, the doctor didn't try to get out of the way. He tried to catch it. Simon's throw, made in haste, had been aimed at the doctor's head, but was so poor that it sailed over the outstretched arms of the doctor and crashed at the base of the wood stove that heated the room.

The decanter shattered and the ether it contained exploded in a fireball. In seconds, the brocade curtains were aflame. Simon had been thrown back by the force of the explosion but bounced off the wall and ran forward. The room filled with smoke, burning his eyes. He looked for the doctor, but he had been knocked to the ground in the blast and Simon couldn't see him.

Simon ran, not knowing where to go, unable to see in the smoke but panic driving his legs. A hand grabbed his ankle and he fell. Kicking out, he realized that the hand belonged to his father, his body sprawled on the floor, reaching out in death to save his son's life. Now below the smoke, Simon could clearly see the door and crawled toward it. He opened the door and the wind rushed in, adding oxygen to the fire. The flames brightened to a blinding yellow. Simon turned back to see the bed engulfed in flames. He smelled the burning hair and screamed, running from the building in panic.

Simon Cohen sat upright in bed, sweat on his bald head, rolling down his cheeks and tracing the wrinkles on his neck. His breath came in gasps, causing a wracking cough. The smoke of the fire still choked him. The smell of burning hair was as revolting today as it had been 73 years ago. He guessed it would be with him forever.

"Johnson!" His voice cracked, but quickly strengthened. "JOHNSON!"

The butler entered the bedroom carefully, the half-light of moon filtering around the edges of the heavy curtains. Johnson was hurrying, as much as he dared while straightening his jacket and vest, running his fingers through his black hair to flatten it. *English butlers do not run*, he told himself. He crossed the long expanse of the room to reach the bed at the far wall. The massive bed dwarfed his employer whose wispy white hair was disheveled and whose silk pajamas were stained with sweat.

"Sir?" Johnson raised an eyebrow. He knew that Cohen had been reliving the nightmare again. Would it be the pills or the cognac he wanted this time?

"Dammit, Man, where have you been?"

"So sorry, Sir" Johnson soothed. "But it is 3:30 in the morning. What can I get for you?"

"Wake Diedre and have her begin making the arrangements. We leave for Washington as soon as possible. There is too much at stake!" The fire still burned in Simon's eyes.

"But, Sir?" Johnson always expected the seemingly irrational from his employer, but this was odd, even for him. "We arrived only a few days ago and opened the estate..."

"Are you deaf, man? I said today!" Cohen was still out of breath, "I feel like someone has stepped on my grave!"

Chapter 13

They stood in a tight group, huddled under the portico of the Jesuit residence in Georgetown. It had been an exhausting day. Living in the mind of a madman had drained them all.

Don Williams had settled in for the evening, thrilled to be free of his burden at last. He slept soundly, knowing that Murph would get the diary to the proper authorities. Murph had told him that the Germans had created a center where the Nazi archives of the Holocaust were to be kept and open to the public for review. The diary would be taken there and it would provide closure for the families of the hundreds of names it contained.

Father Albers would return to the Vatican to search for the trail of Father Gaspard and to see if Father John MacLaughlin had ever reached Rome. With names to go on, the threads of a trail might be found, and the Vatican maintained the records to make such research possible.

Bernie Foa would stay in America to finish the review of the documents of Fort Hunt and to see if he could find any more about Bloch's interrogator Captain Fred Arnold. Bernie mentioned Murph's promise of driving the Mustang and Murph agreed that he wouldn't forget. That left Bernie smiling from ear to ear at the prospect.

Murph drove quietly through the rain to drop Carli off. She snuggled against his arm as darkness settled in and fell asleep. He kept on going until he was back at his place and carried her inside. She opened her eyes and drowsily said, "Thanks. I really didn't want to be alone tonight."

He kissed her lightly on the forehead. "I know. It's been a tough day, but it's all over now. We can relax and get ready." He smiled. "In a couple of days, I'll take you to dinner at a big White House here in town."

Chapter 14

Saturday came in a hurried rush. Murph had hardly talked to Carli, and that contact had been by text. The seminar on TMJ ended late so Murph was forced to shower and dress at the Center. Luckily, he had anticipated the problem and brought his tuxedo in the morning.

To be more correct, Margaret had foreseen the time crunch and had reminded Murph to bring everything to get ready at the Center. The widow of the founder of the Washington Center for Esthetic and Restorative Excellence, Margaret Farouk had taken over as its CEO with Manny Farouk's untimely death. Murph had been become the clinical director and chief dentist. Though Murph was the popular public face of the Center, Margaret's steady hand and excellent business instincts had seen to the continued growth of the practice.

Murph could only guess at Margaret's age, but he suspected that she was older than the late 30's she appeared to be. Always there to keep him organized, she mothered Murph like the son she never had. Her black hair pulled back in a tight ponytail, she came into Murph's office as he struggled with his bow tie. She looked down her nose over her half glasses, smiling at his difficulty.

"Can I help with that?"

"Please. I never could do one of these! Can't I use one of the pre-tied ones?"

"Certainly not!" She chided. "This isn't prom. You're going to the White House. It's a big night!"

Margaret reached around him and finished the knot. "You almost had it anyway."

"I know." Murph pecked her on the cheek sweetly. "I just wanted you to know I still need you."

Margaret blushed. "Enough of that. You get in enough trouble for the bunch of us here." She picked up his jacket where he had tossed it over a chair and helped him put it on. She smoothed the shoulders. The tailor had allowed enough room for his broad shoulders to move easily, yet the jacket tapered quickly to Murph's narrow waist. She patted him on the back in approval.

Murph twirled around and tugged at his shirtsleeve, adjusting his cuff link and watch. He looked down at her and flashed his best movie-star smile. "Bond. James Bond!"

"You better believe it!" She took off her glasses and brushed a tear from her eye. "I'm so proud of you!"

Murph hugged her tight. "Oh, Margaret. Thanks for getting me ready."

She pushed him away. "I'll just get tears on your jacket!" She wiped her eyes and put her glasses back on, quickly trying to quash the emotion by getting back to business. She walked quickly to his desk and picked up the manila envelope she had laid there earlier in the afternoon. "Here's you invitation. The limo driver was chosen because he is familiar with the routine for White House dinners, so you don't have to worry about getting there. He'll drop you off and you can go in through the portico. He knows where to pick you up afterwards as well. His cell number is on his card, here..." she handed Murph the business card and he dutifully put it in his pocket, not telling her that he had already entered the number into his phone.

"Yes, Mom!" He chuckled.

"Really!" She shook her head in mock anger and then continued. "There is no such thing as *fashionably late* at the

White House. It is rude to the President and First Lady. Your timing is set to arrive 15 minutes early so you can move swiftly through security. Get up to the main floor quickly to be in position to greet the President and Vice President when they arrive."

Though Murph had heard this lecture before, he knew it was good to make sure he didn't miss anything. This opportunity wouldn't come around every day.

"Make sure you talk with equal enthusiasm to the people on your left and right. The person sitting next to you will likely be one of the most prominent people in the country. Remember, don't lobby. That's considered very bad form. If you can't remember which fork to use, just imitate the First Lady. You'll never go wrong that way."

Carli had been concerned about etiquette and Murph appreciated that Margaret had taken her to lunch this week at the Willard Intercontinental Hotel to practice. "Thanks again for easing Carli's fears. She'll make sure I drink from the water glass on my right and use the bread plate on my left."

Margaret stopped and sighed, smiling. "So you have learned something from me."

"I'll be fine. My parents started me on the right track and you've finished the teaching. I'm ready to go."

"Murph, you certainly look the part. I trust your ability to talk with anyone. You have always been the master of the social ju-jitsu that you do. It never ceases to amaze me how you can make friends instantly, anywhere you go."

"It's an Irish gift." Murph shrugged, embarrassed at the compliment.

"It's your greatest talent. Tonight is a once in a lifetime opportunity, so use it!"

Murph glanced at his watch. "Thanks for the pep talk, but it's time to go." He took a deep breath and, for the first time his carefully crafted façade of calm control cracked.

Margaret reached out and grasped his arm. "Do you have it?"

Murph held out his left hand and turned over his arm, slowly opening his clenched fist, extending his palm upward. The sunlight filtering from the window caught the diamond and it sparkled like fire. The thin platinum band had been so small that Margaret had not noticed it on his pinky.

Margaret reached out and cradled his hand in both of hers. The diamond solitaire was just over 1.5 carats, perched high over a pair of smaller triangular diamonds that framed the center stone. Margaret knew that it had been Murph's choice that the center stone was not huge, but of exceptional quality. She could see by the dazzling array of colors sparkling before her that he had succeeded in finding a nearly flawless diamond with an exceptional cut.

"It's beautiful!" Margaret closed Murph's hand around the ring. "Does Carli suspect anything?"

"I don't think so. She's suspicious of something. I've been a bit preoccupied this week—rather distant—but I've told her I had a lot to do at work this week. I think she's buying it, but I'll be glad to get it over with tonight. I hate trying to do things behind her back."

"You're not a very good liar—which is a good thing, I guess."

" I know. She reads me so well. That's why I've tried to stay away from her this week."

"The Vice President is OK with this?"

"It was Brooks's idea in the first place. He said, 'What better place to get engaged than at the White House? Just be sure she's going to say YES!' He's enjoying the sneaking around more than I am. He nearly spilled the beans two weeks ago when he was in the office having his teeth cleaned."

The intercom chirped and a cheerful voice interrupted them. "Limo's here!"

"Thanks, Laurie!" Murph looked at Margaret in desperation. "Time to go, I guess."

"Do you love her?" Margaret looked into his eyes.

"More than anything in the world."

She smiled. Just saying it out loud gave him the peace he had needed. "Then relax and enjoy the night. Make sure you send me the pictures!"

She led him to the door and out the hallway. Not to be outdone, the entire staff was waiting in the lobby to see him off. They had set up the music, so when Robin touched the iPod, Murph walked out to ZZ Top's *Sharp Dressed Man* blaring from the speakers.

Murph hugged them all and dashed out the door to the waiting limo, energized for the most important night of his life.

Chapter 15

Running out the entrance of the Center, Murph squinted against the bright sunshine as he went down the steps two at a time. He trotted to the waiting black town car and was pleased to see his old friend Murray step out from behind the steering wheel. Leave it to Margaret to see to it that everything was in place to make the night as easy as possible for Murph.

During Murph's time on *The Dental Apprentice*, Murray Eisenberg had been a frequent driver. While most of the cast treated the staff as furniture, Murph preferred their company to the other contestants. Embracing him like along-lost brother, Murph lifted the teddy bear that was the little driver. Not much more than five feet tall, Murray was a round ball with short arms and legs, twinkling eyes, and a keen sense of human nature. Time spent riding with Murray was a lesson in getting people to talk. He was the master!

"Murray! So glad to see you!"

"Aw, Doc. I wouldn't miss your trip to the White House for anything. I'm so proud of you."

"You taught me everything I know about putting people at ease and then interrogating, err interviewing, them."

"You're a natural. I just showed you the finer points."

"Well, if the dentistry thing doesn't work out," Murph offered, "I'll make a great bartender."

"You got that right!" Murray winked. "We better step on it to get that little filly of yours!"

Murray reached for the car door, but Murph waved him away. "I got it."

Murray looked sternly at him. "You can let yourself in now, but if you reach for that door yourself when we are at the White House, I'll break your arm. That's my job!"

Murray ran around the car, as Murph began get in. Murph looked back up at the Center, waved and gave a thumbs-up. He mouthed *Thank you!* to the window of the CEO's office, where he assumed Margaret would be watching. And of course, she was.

Murph settled into the plush leather back seat of the Lincoln and gladly took the ice-cold bottle of water that Murray offered. He sat back and relaxed as Murray expertly moved through the DC traffic. In his late sixties, Murray was the owner of the car service, which meant he picked his own clients and only drove the most important people in Washington—or the people he really liked. And Mike Murphy was one of those special ones.

Being the driver to the most powerful people in town, and a keen listener, made Murray exceptionally well informed. During the 20-minute drive to Georgetown, Murray gave Murph the inside scoop on the political landscape in the district. Murph felt that he had the equivalent of a full CIA briefing for the dinner tonight. He was as ready as he ever would be when they pulled up in front of Carli's row house.

Having been warned, Murph dutifully waited for Murray to come around and open the door for him.

"Much better, Boss!" Murray did his job with flair.

Murph patted him on the cheek as he got out. "Thanks, Old Man!"

Murray smiled and looked him up and down to make sure he was perfect. "OK, James Bond. Go get her!"

Murph nearly flew up the walk and rang the bell. The door opened and he tried to hold his excitement in check. "Hello, Princess…"

His voice caught in his throat. Caroline Chamoun was indeed breathtaking. Her auburn hair was pulled over in a low, side ponytail and draped down her left shoulder. She wore a black, short-sleeved illusion neckline dress with a scalloped lace bodice leading down to a full tulle knee length skirt. She sported a lime green grosgrain ribbon bow at the waist to accent her slim figure. To meet Murph's height, and add length to her legs, she wore nude LK Bennett patent leather pumps. She carried a sparkling Kate Spade green pineapple clutch. Completely tasteful, it was understated, yet sexy in its simplicity. She twirled, fluffing the skirt. Stopping like a ballerina, she struck a pose, placing one hand into a side seam pocket, looking at him intently.

Like the first time he met her, Murph reached out and took her hand...and couldn't say anything. Carli batted her lashes and he looked deeply into her emerald green eyes. Time stopped and he was lost. He could stay here forever!

"Dr. Bond, I presume?" She broke the spell, smiling sweetly. "I think we should be going." She pulled the door closed behind her and slipped her arm into Murph's. "Have I told you how dashing you are in a tux?"

"Not recently." Murph was struggling to find his tongue, picking it up off the ground. "But I like it."

They reached the car and Murph noticed that Murray had a wide-eyed open-mouthed expression that Murph was afraid he shared.

Carli leaned down and kissed Murray lightly on the cheek. "Hi, Murray! I'm glad to see you tonight. I feel so much safer knowing you're driving. My date seems a bit distracted, shall we say?"

Murph shook his head to clear it and settled into the back seat beside Carli. It was going to be tough to focus this evening.

Chapter 16

Their timing was perfect. As Murray approached the security checkpoint, Murph could see a line of limos and town cars beginning to stretch behind them. No sooner had the secret service guard motioned Murray to stop, when another black-clad attendant opened the car door. Murph stepped out, deliberately straightened his jacket, and reached in for Carli's hand.

Her shapely, tanned leg ended in the nude pumps, four-inch heels settling lightly to the ground. Every head turned to see which A-list actress would appear, since a leg that fabulous had to be connected to someone beautiful. Murph helped her rise and she fluffed her dress, tossing her hair and sweeping it back to one side as she blew Murray a kiss. She blushed slightly, realizing that every eye was on her.

Murph took her arm and led her between the lines of the Marine Honor Guard, all in their dress blues, white gloves, and swords. They passed through security easily. Murph had been concerned that the ring box would have been discovered in the x-ray body scan. Rather than risk spoiling the surprise, he had devised his plan to wear the ring himself on his left hand. It was working so far. Once past security, he slipped the ring off and settled it deep in his pants pocket.

The couple moved into the Yellow Oval Room of the White House for the informal reception as the guests arrived. Murph got Carli her glass of Chardonnay and he selected a Cabernet. He lightly tapped his glass to hers. The gentle ding was lost in the general noise of talking. "You look marvelous! I might as well be invisible, since all eyes are on you."

Carli blushed. "I didn't want to make a big impression. But Margaret suggested this dress."

"It's perfect. You *are* stunning—all the more beautiful since you aren't trying." Murph pulled her close and nuzzled her neck, whispering in her ear, "Just remember, they all want you, but you're going home with me!"

"Wouldn't have it any other way!"

"Murph!" The voice cut through the room and Murph looked up, over Carli's head, to see a blonde Navy officer striding over. Murph disengaged his arm from around Carli and set his wine glass down on a nearby table.

"Patrick!" Murph met the Lieutenant in a bear hug, as they slapped each other on the back. "How have you been?"

"Excellent! I'm at the Navy Yard for a while after being at sea for a year. That's how I get to do these ceremonial gigs."

Murph guided his friend by the shoulders and turned to Carli.

She regarded them both with a sly smile. "Is there anywhere we can go that you don't know someone?"

Murph looked at Patrick and shrugged. "Nope," they said in unison.

"I would like to introduce Carli Chamoun...the best thing that ever happened to me!"

Patrick shook her hand. "Believe me, you are, without a doubt, the best thing..."

Murph cut him off. "Carli, this is Lieutenant Patrick Whitmore, a classmate of mine at Saint Ignatius. He was one of my best friends in high school."

Carli stood beside Murph as the two old friends began to catch up. It didn't last long, as Patrick noticed all the uniformed officers beginning to move toward the end of the room. All of the branches of the military were represented, looking sharp in their dress uniforms.

Patrick excused himself. "Sorry, got to go back to work."

The officers formed an honor guard at the base of the stairs and snapped to attention. The United States Marine Band, "The President's Own," had been providing background music and now played four *ruffles and flourishes*. The attention of everyone in attendance turned to the head of the Grand Staircase.

Murph and Carli recognized the familiar face of the newly confirmed Vice President, Brooks Borlon, with his wife Emma on his arm. Then they were joined by the man of the hour, broad smile warming his face, the power of a nation in his eyes. He waved to the crowd and nodded. The Marine Band began the unmistakable strains of "Hail to the Chief" as he descended the marble stairs. There could be no doubt; the President of the United States had arrived.

Chapter 17

The President and First Lady, followed by the guests of honor, Brooks and Emma Borlon, were escorted down the length of the Cross Hall. They took up positions outside the entrance to the State Dining Room and a receiving line formed immediately. Murph and Carli allowed the rush of eager guests to pass before joining the queue at a more leisurely pace. They had ample time to observe their friends.

Brooks Borlon had the easygoing look of a career politician. With sandy blond hair that showed not a hint of gray, it was only the crinkles in the corners of his eyes when he smiled that gave away his age. He greeted each guest warmly, shaking hands with him or her. His enthusiasm was infectious. He clearly loved the stage and drew energy from the crowd.

Emma stood by his side, bravely smiling and making small talk. Carli nudged Murph and whispered, "Emma would rather be anywhere than here! Her smile looks painted on."

"I know," Murph allowed. "She's trying too hard and her smile is too big. It's forced."

"I feel so sorry for her." Carli frowned. "Please, no politics for you!"

"Not a chance! This is too much work." He was stopped by a polite voice behind him.

"Excuse me, young man." The gray-haired woman in a glittering black sequined dress adjusted her shawl and patted Murph on the arm. "The President looks so young. How did he get elected?" Murph couldn't place her accent. Her English was formal and her voice steady and firm, despite her apparent age.

Murph took a deep breath, but before he could speak, Carli interrupted him.

"His story is so sad, but it ends happy, " began Carli as she edged closer to the Grande Dame. "Franklin Buchanan was a congressman from South Carolina. He had a young daughter and his wife was pregnant with their second child. As the pregnancy neared its end, the doctors discovered that she had an extremely aggressive form of breast cancer. Another daughter was born healthy, but Gayle Buchanan passed away from the cancer."

"Oh my!" She covered her mouth with her hand. "I had no idea."

Carli nodded in sympathy. "Congressman Buchanan was distraught. His wife's parents took over care of their grandchildren while he tried to deal with his grief. He was an Air Force Academy graduate and pilot, so when his reserve unit was activated and sent to Afghanistan, he had a decision to make. Though he could have taken a deferment as a sitting congressman, he chose to go.

During his deployment, he was shot down while protecting some Marines. He parachuted safely and was picked up by the Marine patrol. The soldiers came under fire and many were wounded. As they were being evacuated by helicopter, Colonel Buchanan picked up a rifle and helped the Marines hold off the Taliban fighters. Buchanan and the Marine lieutenant in command were the last two to get in the helicopter. The Marine was wounded and Buchanan lifted him and threw him into the helicopter. Just then, an explosion, "

"A mortar shell hit just behind them..." Murph couldn't help himself, but Carli's scowl shut him up. It was her story, after all. "Sorry."

"As I was saying, an explosion right behind him knocked him out. Colonel Buchanan was lifted into the helicopter and taken eventually to the military hospital in Germany. He was in a coma for a while. When he came out of the coma, he needed therapy. His nurse stayed by his side during all that time. They fell in love, and there she is, still by his side."

"Jane Buchanan was his nurse? What a wonderful story!"

"Yes, it is. Congressman Buchanan was awarded the Medal of Honor for his actions and he was a perfect choice to run as the Vice President with President Biden. He was so popular that he helped the Democratic ticket win the election easily."

"Ah, yes. That part I know." She nodded her head and her blue-gray curls bobbed. "I am Marie Eberle, the new Ambassador from Lichtenstein. Thank you for making my time in this line pass so swiftly."

"It was our pleasure," Carli confirmed. They were almost at the head of the line.

Marie had one more question, and it was direct. "Who are you that you were invited to the Inaugural Ball?"

Murph looked sheepishly down at his shoes. "May I introduce Miss Caroline Chamoun, PhD candidate in Archeology at Georgetown University? I'm Mike Murphy, a dentist here in Washington and..."

"An old friend of mine!" Vice President Brooks Borlon's voice cut through the buzz in the foyer, giving Murph a big hug as he turned around, then kissed Carli on the cheek.

Emma Borlon embraced Carli, hanging onto her like a life preserver. "Thank God you're here! Someone normal to talk to," she whispered.

While Emma and Carli talked, Murph introduced Ambassador Eberle to Brooks and the VP made small talk with her before passing her on to the President.

Brooks shook Murph's hand again, "Ready for a fun night?"

"Yes, Sir! Thanks again for inviting us."

Brooks collected Murph and Carli, one on each arm. "There are so many politicians around, I need a few friends I can count on!"

Carli reached out and squeezed Emma's hand. "You know you can always rely on us!"

Brooks winked. Murph turned a bit as Brooks released them and suddenly heard, "Frank, may I introduce you to some old friends of mine...Dr. Mike Murphy and Caroline Chamoun."

Chapter 18

"Frank Buchanan! Glad to meet you!"

Murph's hand was enveloped in an iron grip. He squeezed back, their hands firm as their eyes locked. Murph appraised the most powerful man in the world. The President was a bit shorter than Murph's 6'2", but where the dentist was long and lean, the President was stocky and solid. A firm brow and the slightly crooked nose of a fighter marked his face, giving Frank Buchanan the rugged good looks that people admired in a politician. There was an aura of power in the man and he clearly was in complete command of the moment.

"The famous Murph and Carli! Brooks has told me about your past adventures. Not exactly a typical day at the office for a dentist, now is it?"

"No, Sir. It was not." Murph confirmed.

"I have to tell you, Doc, I really don't like dentists much."

"That's OK, Mr. President." Murph's hand was still bound in the handshake. "I really don't like politicians much either."

Jane Buchanan reached out and shook Carli's hand gently. The tension in the room was rising.

Frank Buchanan released Murph's hand and laughed heartily, breaking the spell. He clapped Murph on both arms at the shoulders. "Brooks, I can see why you like this guy! Not many people around here will stand up to me, but I've met you 30 seconds and you're willing to stare me down." He reached over to Carli, shook her hand and pecked her on the cheek. "Welcome to the White House. We're so glad you are here!"

"Thank you, Sir." Murph scooped up the stunned Carli in his arm and began to lead her past the First Lady, who flashed a sly smile at them.

President Buchanan stopped them in their tracks. "You know, Doc, I'm really glad that I have good teeth. I haven't had problems in years."

"That's very good, Sir. I'm always happy to give good news to people when they have a check-up."

"My wife isn't as lucky. She was missing two upper front teeth and she just had them replaced with implants. Why don't you show them off, Jane?"

The First Lady flashed an embarrassed smile.

"Beautiful," Murph observed. "Congenitally missing lateral incisors are genetic, so there is no shame there. The advances in implants have allowed dentists to resolve that issue with excellent results. I'm glad to see that you are happy."

The President wouldn't let it go. "Yep. I always tell her that she has the expensive mouth, compared to me."

"Be careful not to pick on her, Mr. President." Murph felt badly for the First Lady. "No one is bulletproof forever. Remember, gloaters never prosper!"

The tension began to rise again, but Frank Buchanan took it in stride. In fact, he seemed to like confrontation. "As I said, I like this guy!" He grabbed Murph by the back of the neck and shook him. "Go enjoy your dinner."

Murph and Carli quickly escaped and entered the State Dining Room, making their way toward the table assigned to them.

Carli came to her senses after a few steps and stopped, stepping in front of Murph and placing her palm on his chest. "What the hell was that all about?"

Murph shrugged. "After hearing the 'nothing personal Doc, but I hate dentists' line for the hundredth time, I've decided not to take it anymore."

"But, the freaking President of the United States??" She hissed, beside herself with concern.

"I don't know why, but he was pushing me. So I decided to push back. It seemed to work out OK."

"You never cease to amaze me, Murphy." She just shook her head, at a loss for more words.

They reached their table and were pleased to find that Father Albers had been assigned to the same place. Much to Carli's disappointment, he suggested they not sit next to each other in order to increase the number of new people they would meet. She knew he was right and they did their best to make conversation with all the guests around them.

On Murph's left was the Secretary of the Treasury, Malcom Scott, who proved to be as boring as Murph had feared upon finding out who he was. Seated to Carli's right were Shimon Perski, the Israeli Ambassador, and his wife Sarah. They were charming dinner companions and Carli's enthusiasm and tales of her findings in Egypt made captivating conversation. By dessert, Murph and Carli had earned a standing invitation to visit them in Israel.

Dinner concluded with a short speech from the President thanking everyone for coming. The guests were led from the State Dining Room into the East Room of the White House where round tables surrounded a small dance floor. A 20-piece orchestra sat ready on a raised stage.

As they crossed the dance floor in front of the stage, the bandleader crouched down in front of his grand piano and waved, "Murph!"

Murph left Carli and trotted over, shaking hands like an old friend with the pianist while Carli continued with Ambassador Perski, Sharon, and Fr. Albers to a table adjacent to the dance floor.

As he rejoined the party, Carli was curious, "You have friends everywhere. Was that another patient?"

Murph smiled. "Not mine. Dave Tabar is from Cleveland. He's a good friend of my Dad's. His group, *The Pulse*, is really popular back home. Brooks..." Murph looked up at the Israeli Ambassador and corrected himself. "I mean the Vice President didn't want to spend a lot of taxpayer money on his

Inaugural Ball so he arranged for old friends to come play. I hear they are even going to use some celebrity impersonators instead of the A-listers. This should be a treat. I've heard *The Pulse* before and they're really good!"

Murph and Carli had politely taken the seats with their back to the dance floor so that the other guests would have the best view. The lights dimmed and a single spot found Brooks as he took to the stage with a few remarks, thanking everyone for their support in this time of change and promising to do his best as the Vice President.

The Pulse began to play as background, and the sounds of rock guitar filled the room. "For those of you not from Cleveland, that's Funk #49 by The James Gang." Brooks walked across the stage and hi-fived Dave Tabar at the piano. "Just remember, the Rock 'n' Roll Hall of Fame is in downtown Cleveland. Why, you ask? " Brooks jumped off the stage onto the dance floor. "Tell 'em, Drew!"

The spotlight left Brooks and centered on actor Drew Carey as he entered the stage as the band shifted to the song *Cleveland Rocks!* Brooks left the dance floor in the relative shadow, patting Murph on the back as he walked by. He rejoined Emma, the President, and First Lady at the head table.

The Pulse continued their survey of rock 'n' roll with another Clevelander, Chrissie Hynde and *The Pretenders*. Murph felt another hand on his shoulder. He turned to see the white glove of a Navy officer and followed the blue sleeve up to the face of Patrick Whitmore. He wasn't smiling now.

"Murph. There's been a medical emergency, and you're the closest doctor. Can you help?"

Without hesitation, Murph was out of his chair. He pressed Carli on the shoulder and kept her seated. "Just stay here. I'll be back soon...I hope."

Sticking to the shadows on the edge of the dance floor, Murph crouched down and followed Lt. Whitmore as they tried to avoid drawing too much attention. They disappeared from view around the stage and out the door into the hallway.

Chapter 19

Nearly 15 minutes had passed and Murph had not returned. Carli was beginning to become concerned. She scanned the room, but all the attention was on the stage. The President and First Lady were still there. *That's good,* she thought. *But where are Brooks and Emma?*

As if on cue, Emma Borlon sat down next to Carli and Brooks pulled up an open chair. "I'm glad to see you guys," Carli blurted out. "Murph was taken away to help with a medical emergency and then I couldn't find you. I was beginning to worry."

Brooks furrowed his brow in concern. "Medical emergency? No one told me about any emergency."

Emma patted Carli's hand. "It can't be anything serious then. I'm sure he'll be right back."

The band changed performers again and the crowd cheered.

Well, it's one for the money,
Two for the show,
Three to get ready,
Now go, cat, GO.

The white suit of the Elvis impersonator sparkled in the spotlight as he jumped down from the stage and shook his hips on the dance floor.

But don't you step on my blue suede shoes.
You can do anything but lay off of my blue suede shoes.

Elvis moved from table to table around the dance floor, working the crowd as he sang. Carli leaned in toward Emma and commented, "Its too bad Murph isn't here. He loves Elvis."

The music softened to a ballad and Elvis' deep voice crooned,

Wise men say, only fools rush in

A white silk scarf draped over Carli's shoulder and she was captured in the spotlight. Her face turned beet red and she began to panic.

But I can't help falling in love with you

She looked up and realized that everyone at the table was smiling from ear to ear. She turned around and saw Elvis standing over her, smiling, tall, and with a twinkle in his eyes.

Shall I stay
Would it be a sin
If I can't help falling in love with you

"Oh my God..." Carli covered her mouth with her hand, recognition beginning to dawn.

Elvis reached down and swept her in his arms, lifting her up and twirling her around, her silk skirt fanning out. Pat Whitmore stepped out of the shadows and placed a chair on the dance floor. Elvis gently set Carli down and went to one knee.

Like a river flows surely to the sea
Darling so it goes
Some things are meant to be

Elvis lifted his right hand to his forehead and pulled off the greased black wig and sideburns, tossing it to the ground. Murph reached into his pocket and took out the ring. He reached up and held Carli's hand, showing her the diamond between his fingers. It sparkled like fire in the spotlight. Without missing a beat, he kept singing,

Take my hand, take my whole life too
For I can't help falling in love with you

The band held the final chord as Murph quietly asked the question, "Caroline...will you marry me?"

The tears flowed down her cheeks. All she could do was nod. She finally managed a whisper. "Yes."

Murph put the ring on her finger and lifted her off the chair. He held her close and kissed her deeply. The crowd cheered. Murph looked up to Dave Tabar on the stage. The bandleader was smiling and clapping loudly. Murph gave him thumbs up and *The Pulse* moved on to the next set as a Michael Jackson impersonator came on stage. The spotlight left and Carli reveled in the sudden darkness, clinging to Murph. She looked down at the diamond sparkling on her finger, her vision blurred with happy tears.

Chapter 20

"You were all in on this?" Carli sounded irritated, but her smile took the sting out of the words.

Emma hugged her and took her hand to study the ring. "Yes. Murph has been planning this for a long time."

"Hey, it was my idea to do it at the White House!" The Vice President tried to appear indignant, but he just laughed and shook Murph's hand, pulling him into a bear hug.

Pat Whitmore stood off to the side smiling broadly, his white-gloved hands clasped behind his back. The rest of his Naval buddies were with him now, thrilled that their otherwise boring evening had become quite the show.

The White House photographer had taken pictures of the proposal and twitter was abuzz with the news already. Murph left Carli with Emma and Sarah Perski while he went back to the restroom to change out of his Elvis costume.

Sarah embraced Carli. "You are a lucky woman. Such elaborate planning shows devotion, and a flair for the dramatic."

"That's my Murph," she agreed. "Never a dull moment!"

Murph returned, looking once again like James Bond. He took Carli's hand and kissed it sweetly. "Hello, my Dear. Having a memorable night at the White House?"

She smiled and nestled her head on his chest. "Unforgettable!"

The concert appeared to be wrapping up. Murph looked around and realized that President Buchanan had left the East Room. The Vice President was also making the rounds and saying goodbye. He waved at Murph from across the room and Murph tossed him a salute.

"Time for us to call it a night." Protocol said that the audience waited for the President to leave, then danced one more dance. It was considered impolite to linger too much longer.

Murph and Carli accepted the congratulations again from their table and began to make their way out of the ballroom. As they neared the door, Murph felt a powerful hand grip his shoulder.

"Doctor Murphy?" The voice was deep, almost a growl.

"Yes." Murph turned around. It was unusual for him to have to look up, but the man who stopped him was at least four inches taller—African American, powerfully built—dark suit—earpiece in his left ear—clearly Secret Service.

"I'm Agent Collins. The President requests your presence."

"I suppose we can't say no to that!" Murph smiled and extended his hand. "Nice to meet you, Agent Collins."

Darnell gripped Murph firmly and smiled, broad white teeth lighting up his face. His mood softened, "I'll lead you up to the private residence. Please follow me." And he set off at a brisk pace, Carli working hard to keep up with his long strides in her heels.

The race ended in a small alcove where another Secret Service agent stood silently, holding open the door to an

74

elevator. Agent Collins allowed Carli to enter first, followed by Murph. Collins got in and pressed 2. The door closed quietly, leaving the three of them to examine the wood paneled interior. Looking up, Murph noticed the mirrored ceiling, his reflection looking small and insignificant in the large elevator.

Carli's eyes widened and she turned on Agent Collins. "Wait a minute. I know you! You're Darnell Collins, the power forward from Georgetown. You single handedly beat the Buckeyes in that NCAA tournament basketball game."

Murph looked closer at the Secret Service agent. "That's right. We were at that game where Georgetown went on to the Final Four. It was tough to watch you cut down the nets. You scored, what, 35 points to lead the Hoyas past Ohio State?"

Collins smiled sheepishly. "It was 33—probably my best game in college. Thanks for remembering!"

"You were a junior then. Did you play in the NBA?" Murph asked.

"I got drafted in the second round by the Atlanta Hawks but blew out my knee in a summer league game. They released me before training camp and I never played in an NBA game."

Carli frowned. "That's too bad."

Darnell shook his head, smiling. "No, not really. It was the best thing that ever happened to me. I had surgery and went back to Georgetown to rehab my knee. Coach and the staff were so great to me. They convinced me to finish my degree, and here I am."

"That's fantastic. How did you get assigned to the White House so quickly? You're pretty young for this job."

Collins shrugged. "When I finished training, Vice President Biden picked me for his protection detail, probably because I'm from Delaware. There aren't that many of us, so Mr. Biden wanted to look out for someone from home. When he was elected President, I moved up here with him. Now that he's gone," Collins swallowed hard, "I'll probably be moved to another assignment. President Buchanan has put several of his own agents on the detail but he hasn't gotten around to replacing me yet."

As the lift slowed, Collins held the door and beckoned them to exit with his open hand. "Welcome to the second floor of the White House. No one enters here without the specific invitation of the President. I'm sure that you'll quickly realize why you're here."

Murph raised an eyebrow, but Darnell just chuckled. Carli reached out and took Collins' hand. "We're glad to meet you. Best of luck in the future!"

Murph shook his hand warmly as well. Darnell relaxed a bit. "Thanks, Doc! I could use a good dentist. Would it be OK if I called your office for an appointment?"

"I'd be happy to add another friend to my practice!" Murph reached into his jacket pocket and gave the agent a business card. "Just give us a call."

Collins pocketed the card and led them down the corridor, their steps leaving footprints in the deep pile of the straw colored carpet. They stopped at a heavy wooden door and the agent reached down and held the knob. He hesitated for a moment, shifting back into character as the stern secret service agent. "The President is in the Treaty Room. He uses it as his study, or often the place where he will watch the game on TV. Thank you for coming."

Collins twice rapped his knuckles sharply on the door and pulled it open, shaking his head sadly. "Good luck."

A voice bellowed from beyond the doorway, "Where's that damn dentist? Get him up here, NOW!"

Chapter 21

The wheels touched down with a squeal and the roar of the jet engines died down to a low buzz. The Learjet taxied off the runway and over to the executive terminal at Reagan

National Airport. The moon was rising, making the dew on the tarmac glisten. It was a beautiful, calm night in Washington.

Diedre walked back from the cockpit, rubbing the back of her hand over her tired eyes. It had been an eight-hour flight, but she hadn't been able to rest at all. Though she was not yet 30, she clearly felt too old for this. She took a deep breath and braced herself for the storm to come. "Mr. Cohen? The pilot says that it will take more than an hour to clear customs at this time of night."

"Don't they know who I am?" He growled. "That's unacceptable.

"Yes, Sir." Her tone was soothing. "He told them, but it is a Saturday night and there aren't many customs agents available. It will be well after midnight when we are cleared."

"Damn it!" He spat it out. "Johnson?"

"Yes, Sir." The butler was always there, but Simon Cohen never took it for granted. "What can I get for you, Sir?"

"Have the car ready to pick us up as soon as we are free of this. We can't go into the district tonight. It will be too late to meet with them."

Diedre confirmed the plan. "I have arranged for your suite at the Ritz Carlton in Pentagon City. We have an appointment for first thing tomorrow morning."

"If that is the best you can do." The old man scowled but relented. "Get me a Scotch. I'm just jittery. It's only one night after all. I'll think more clearly in the morning."

Johnson went to the bar and poured a generous two fingers of the golden liquid and added a pair of ice cubes. He went to put the bottle back—thought better of it—and poured more into the glass. It was going to be a long night.

Chapter 22

Murph took a deep breath and stood tall. Taking Carli by the hand, he stepped quickly into the room, subconsciously shielding her with his body.

Darnell Collins called over Murph's shoulder, "Dr. Michael Murphy, as you requested, Mr. President!" The Secret Service Agent shut the wooden door with a heavy thud.

Murph scanned the room quickly. The Treaty Room was adjacent to the Yellow Oval Room, which was directly above the Oval Office. As such, both rooms shared the same superb southern view onto the Ellipse. The Washington Monument shone brightly, transfixed in the spotlights, dominating the view out the windows in front of the confused pair entering the room.

On their left was a massive Renaissance Revival style table that had been in the room since 1898, when President William McKinley used its surface for the signing of the peace treaty with Spain that ended the Spanish-American War. On the wall above the table was the painting by artist Theobald Chartran that commemorated the event. *This really is a Treaty Room!* Murph thought.

President Buchanan had converted this room to his private study, with plush leather armchairs and a couch facing an 84-inch Sony Ultra HD TV mounted on the wall. The Washington Nationals baseball game was on, but no one appeared to be watching.

The President's Chief of Staff, Paul Ramon, stood up from a chair and motioned for Murph to come in. As the gate-keeper to the President, Ramon was an extremely powerful figure who usually remained hidden from the public eye. His black hair was cut short on the sides, but his longer bangs drooped down his forehead. His heavy dark-framed glasses always seemed to be down on his nose and he absentmindedly pushed them back up while he walked over to greet Murph and Carli.

As Murph walked deeper into the room, he heard a faint "Psst!" from the side. Framed in the doorway to the Yellow Oval Room, Jane Buchanan put a finger to her lips indicating quiet and waved Carli over. Pleased to make her exit so easily, Carli squeezed Murph's hand and quickly darted for the door. The First Lady seemed to giggle and reached out for Carli's hand. They both admired her engagement ring and disappeared into the next room.

Ramon shook Murph's hand limply. "Thank you for coming!" It was impossible to guess the age of the Chief of Staff. Murph figured he was over 40 and less than 60, but that was as close as he could venture. "I think the President will be glad you are here as well." The voice was thin and reedy.

Murph considered his words carefully this time. "I'm glad to help in any way I can..."

"You damn well better be!" The President rolled over on the couch and sat up, growling, "This is all your fault, Murphy!"

"I'm not sure I understand, Mr. President." Murph took half a step back.

"You cursed me!" Buchanan held an ice pack against his lower jaw, but took it off and waved it at Murph. "*Gloaters never prosper,*" he mocked. "Now look at me!" The President tossed the ice pack down on the cherry coffee table in disgust. He picked up a half empty tumbler of Scotch and downed the rest in one gulp.

Murph stood with a bewildered look on his face, shrugging his shoulders at Paul Ramon.

"After leaving the dinner, the President came up here to watch the ballgame. He bit down and now is in a great deal of pain—with his tooth."

The President leaned over at Murph and pulled his lower lip back with his finger, showing his right molars. "*Shee!* It's right shere—*thish* one."

Even in the dim light, Murph could see that a molar was cracked in half and that the gums around the tooth were bleeding. A half eaten bowl of popcorn on the table was all the additional information Murph needed to complete the picture.

"Does anyone have a flashlight?" Murph guided the President to one of the leather chairs as Darnell Collins was summoned with the light. A quick glance at the tooth confirmed Murph's fears. The President's lower right first molar was fractured in half, with the un-popped popcorn hull wedged in the tooth. It had a massive old silver filling that had finally given way.

"Well, Mr. President, as I feared, your six-year molar is fractured through the middle. It's a two rooted tooth, but now it's broken in half."

"You're damn right it is. I was just sitting here watching the game, and now it's killing me. It's not like I was doing anything dangerous."

Murph considered mentioning the popcorn hull lodged in the tooth, but decided there was nothing to gain by pressing that point. "We really have no choice but to get that tooth out of there. I can make the pain go away as soon as I numb up the area, but it has to go. I can fix almost anything that goes wrong with a tooth, but a vertical fracture through the root is the end of the road."

Murph helped the President place the ice pack back on the area, which seemed to help a bit with the pain. Reaching into his jacket, Murph pulled his phone out and began to dial.

"What the hell are you doing?" The pain was making the President more irritable than ever.

"I can have my staff meet us at the office by the time we get there."

Paul Ramon reached over and tapped to end the call before it connected. "I'm sorry, Dr. Murphy. For security reasons, you'll have to do this one yourself. This is enough of a risk as it is."

"Can I at least call my limo driver and let him know that we won't be needing a ride home?"

80

"Yes, just don't give any indication of where you are going and with whom."

The President stood up and began to pace. "Just get this damn show on the road—and get me another Scotch!"

Chapter 23

Murph quickly called Murray and told him that they had been invited to stay for an after-party. Murray thanked him for letting him go so quickly, though he was sad not to be able to hear how the proposal had gone. Murph promised to give his driver all the details and got off the phone.

They collected Carli and the small traveling party set off from the White House for the short drive to The Center for Esthetic and Restorative Excellence. The black limo was without the usual trappings of the President, as they opted for stealth over the security of a police escort. It was a tight fit for the President, Murph, Carli, Paul Ramon, agent Collins and his partner Ron Kerner. Given the President's foul mood, no one spoke for the duration of the ride.

They pulled into the darkened parking lot behind the Center and stopped near the door. Agents Collins and Kerner studied the street while Murph scanned his ID card and entered his security code to open the building and shut off the alarm. He was turning on the lights as the President burst past him into the hallway, still holding the ice pack to his jaw. Murph led him into the main surgical treatment room and seated him in the dental chair.

This was the largest treatment room in the Center, designed for teaching purposes. Murph chose this suite as he expected that the President was not going to be left alone during treatment. Agent Collins took up a position behind the President where he could easily observe the entrances to the room. Agent Kerner looked uncomfortably at the medical instrumentation and mumbled an excuse about needing to check the perimeter. He quickly left the room as Murph passed out surgical masks for Collins and Paul Ramon. They were close enough to warrant the masks, but wouldn't need surgical gowns.

Carli was preparing to help Murph, so he gave her a lab coat to cover her dress and set out a box of gloves small enough for her petite hands. He bent down and whispered "Thanks" in her ear.

Reaching for a clipboard, Murph handed the President a medical history form and a pen. "While I get things turned on here, please take a minute and tell me about your medical history. Don't worry about the contact information. We know your address!"

Buchanan looked up from the paper with a scowl. "You're enjoying this way too much, Doc. You're too darn happy."

Smiling, Murph asked, "You would rather see a grumpy dentist?"

Buchanan shook his head and groaned, turning his attention to the medical history form.

Murph reached over onto the counter, picked up the TV remote, and handed it to Carli. "Why don't you see if you can get the Nationals game on the cable. It will help take his mind off things."

"Sure thing!" She busied herself with helping keep the President occupied and provided water bottles for the secret service agents.

Murph returned, having changed out of his tuxedo and into surgical scrubs. He scanned the medical history and was relieved to see that the President had no significant medical issues. "Now, let's get a better look at this tooth!"

Murph eased the President back in the dental chair and performed his exam. "I'll need an x-ray of this, but first, let's get you numb and make the pain go away."

"It's about time," the President grumbled.

Murph placed the topical anesthetic and then injected the local anesthetic slowly.

The President's eyes grew wider. "Wow, Doc. That didn't hurt a bit. I'm impressed!"

"We aim to please." Murph smiled. "Thanks for noticing!"

The President relaxed almost immediately as the anesthetic took away the pain. Murph led him to the panoramic x-ray machine. "This will give us a complete look at the tooth and all the surrounding area. It's digital now, so we'll see it on the monitor right away."

The dentist took the image and brought the President back to the treatment room. Murph put the image on the monitor. It didn't take a dental degree to find the tooth that was broken in half.

"Aha," Murph pointed anyway. "That tooth had a root canal in the past, as you can see by the white material in the roots. The tooth has a huge old filling and broke right down the middle. It never had a crown placed on it." Murph looked past the President to the rest of his audience and continued teaching. "When a tooth has had a root canal, the nerve is removed, as well as the blood vessels, and a gum rubber filling material is placed to seal the tooth. Without the blood supply, the tooth dries out internally and becomes brittle. A crown helps keep it from fracturing." Murph patted the President on the shoulder reassuringly. "The good news is that you have plenty of bone to put in an implant to replace this tooth—but that's a discussion for another day. Let's get this bad one out now."

With the pain gone, the President had nearly fallen asleep. Murph readied his instruments and swiftly extracted the fractured molar. As he lifted it out with the forceps, the President seemed surprised. "That's it?"

"I can put it back in and do it again slower if you like," Murph quipped.

Carli laughed, and, out of the corner of her eye, she caught sight of Darnell cracking the slightest hint of a smile as well. The President failed to see the humor of it all and began to frown again.

Murph packed the extraction site with cotton and had Buchanan bite down. Agent Kerner saw the bloody tooth on the surgical tray, turned green, and quickly excused himself from the treatment room again. Agent Collins crossed his arms and sighed.

Murph cleaned the extracted tooth and examined it to be certain that he had removed the entire tooth without leaving any fragments behind. He commented casually, "Mr. President, would you like to have the tooth to take home? You could put it under your pillow. Maybe you'll get some partial credit from my friend, the tooth fairy?"

"Very funny!" He mumbled through the cotton gauze.

"This is interesting." Murph held the cleaned molar up to the light for everyone to see. "This tooth has an unusual pink cast to the enamel. That's rather odd."

Paul Ramon stepped closer. "Why is that?"

"A pink tooth is very unusual. The only thing that causes a tooth to look like this is the use of a chemical called resorcinol when the root canal is done. The resorcinol in the filling material leaches out and stains the dentin, the inner part of the tooth, with this pink color." Murph blurted out without thinking, "What's odd is that resorcinol is banned in the US. It's only used by dentists in Russia."

Carli's eyes widened, but she bit her tongue. Murph observed a momentary glance from Ramon to the President. Collins was a statue in the back of the room.

The realization of what he had said hit Murph like a hammer. He had to find a way out—and quickly!

"Sometimes, pink tooth can also be caused by pulp polyps or internal resorption."

"I should hope so! This is just preposterous!" The President's anger was rising and his face was reddening.

"Wait a minute." Murph was dancing now. "You served in Europe in the Air Force, didn't you, Mr. President? I wonder if this root canal was done by a Russian trained dentist there?"

"Yes—well, that's true." The President blustered. "I can't remember when this tooth was done, but I remember having a toothache when I was stationed there."

"Well, it doesn't really matter. The tooth is gone now and we can move on to healing. You don't have to worry about it any more. I'll just make it disappear."

Murph took the extracted tooth and slipped it into a small sterilization pouch to throw into the medical waste. He removed his gloves, wadded them up with the tooth and tossed them into the medical waste container. He opened his clinic jacket, took it off and tossed it casually on his dental stool.

Murph reached into the cabinet and pulled out the written post-extraction instructions. He gave the paper to the President and reviewed the details. The air had come out of the room and everyone just wanted to be done. Buchanan rose quickly and shook hands with Murph.

"Thanks, Doc. I feel so much better. I still don't like dentists, but I'm glad you were here to help."

Murph smiled. "That's what friends are for!"

Paul Ramon turned to Carli. "Congratulations on your engagement. I'm sorry that we took away from your night."

Carli smiled. "It certainly has been a memorable evening!"

Murph shook hands with Ramon and Collins, then addressed Buchanan. "Mr. President, I'm happy to help you replace this tooth with an implant. Just have your staff call the office for an appointment and I'll do a full exam and discuss your options with you. Just let me know."

"I will." The President growled. "But for now, it's been a long night. Let's all go home."

Murph escorted the group out the back and waved as the limo drove away. He closed and locked the doors, then rested his head against the cool metal. The adrenalin was starting to wear off, and he suddenly felt very tired.

Chapter 24

Murph walked slowly back to the treatment suite. He passed Carli sitting at his desk, chatting excitedly on her cell phone. He heard her say, "But, Mom..." and he smiled. He took his time cleaning the surgical suite.

As he finished, Carli entered the doorway, standing with her arms crossed. Her hair had begun to fall, stray wisps down in front of her eyes.

Murph strolled over to her. "How are Mom and Dad?" he asked dryly.

"Mom's as excited as I am. But, somehow, Dad seemed like he already knew!"

"I asked his permission a few weeks ago—when they were in town for the opening of your exhibit at the Smithsonian."

She punched him lightly in the arm. "No wonder he's been so strange lately."

"He was pleased that I was getting around to proposing, but he wanted to know what had taken me so long."

"I've had the same question from time to time!" She looked down at her finger.

Murph took her hand and kissed it. "Was it worth the wait?"

"Absolutely! It's been a night I'll never forget."

"Good thing you're still wide awake—it looks like we're going to have to walk home." Murph turned off the overhead light. "I'll get changed and we can go."

Murph picked up his clinic jacket and reached into the pocket. He pulled the pouch with the pink tooth out and held it up with a flourish.

Carli whistled softly. "You're a sly one."

"I palmed it when I wadded up my gloves. I threw the gloves out and slipped it into the pocket. I don't know what, but something's very wrong here." He held the tooth up between his fingers. "It's true that there are a couple of things that cause pink tooth, but I've seen this before. This tooth has had a Russian root canal—I'd stake my life on it."

He walked into his office and worked on his computer for a minute and shut it down while he took off his scrubs. Murph slipped the tooth and a thumb drive into his pocket as he changed back into the tux, leaving the bow tie loose.

He turned off the light in his office and his iPhone rang. Murph looked down and was surprised to see Murray Eisenberg as the caller. He answered immediately, "Murray! Where are you?"

"I'm in your parking lot. It's getting late for you. Cinderella needs to get home!"

"We'll be right out."

Murph laughed as he walked out toward Carli. She looked puzzled to see him talking on the phone.

Murph pointed at the phone and took Carli's arm. "Come, my dear. Our chariot awaits!"

"Murphy. You do know how to show a girl a good time!"

"That's why you find me so irresistible!"

She nestled under his arm and laughed. Murph turned out the lights and set the alarm.

They walked out to the waiting town car, and Murray let them in.

Murph was curious. "How did you find us?"

"Aw, Doc. It was easy." Murray smiled as he put the car in gear. "You're such a bad liar. I just waited and when I saw a plain black, but very beefy limo pull out from the White House, I followed you here. I hid out in the parking lot of the Canadian Embassy over there and came over after they left."

"I'd love to tell you the story, but I can't betray patient confidentiality. That one we'll keep to ourselves."

"That's OK, Doc. I'm really more interested in hearing about earlier." Murray looked back quickly into the back seat. "That finger of yours is really sparkling in the streetlights, Miss Caroline! I've heard there's quite a story about that."

Murph sat back and smiled as Carli told the tale. Her excitement made all his hard work worthwhile. Everything had gone exactly as he had planned.

Murray dropped the happy couple off at Murph's condo, receiving a kiss from Carli and a handshake and hug from Murph. They waved as Murray's black sedan melded into the dark, then turned and went up the walk, arm in arm.

Chapter 25

Murph looked over at Carli, her hair all splayed out on the pillow, snuggled tightly in the down comforter. Her breathing was steady and even. She was sleeping soundly, so he slid out of the covers as quietly as he could and padded out to the kitchen. The clock on the stove said 4:30 am. By all accounts, he should have been exhausted, but he hadn't been able to sleep at all.

Rather than fight it, he had decided to just get up. He poured himself a glass of orange juice and walked into his office. He turned on the desk lamp to its dimmest setting and opened his laptop. With a sigh, he pulled the pouch containing the President's tooth out of the pocket of his tuxedo pants and retrieved the thumb drive as well. He inserted the memory stick into the computer and downloaded the image he had stored.

The ghostly black and white image of the panoramic radiograph he had taken filled the screen. He picked up the tooth and turned it around in his fingers, examining it in the half-light. He tried to tell himself this all had been a dream, but the pink tooth still stared back at him.

He thought a minute and decided not to wait any longer. He reached over and disconnected his iPhone from the charger. Paging through his contacts, he found the name he was seeking.

Murph considered that it was the middle of the night, but rationalized that if she wasn't awake, she wouldn't answer the call. He shrugged and tapped the phone number. It only took two rings until a bright, perky voice answered.

"Lieutenant Beerman!"

"Hey, Andrea! It's Mike Murphy!"

"Hi Murph! I was hoping to talk to you, but not this soon."

""You're awfully cheerful for 4:30 in the morning."

"Hey, it's the Department of Oral Surgery at Walter Reed Medical Center. We never sleep!"

Navy Lieutenant Andrea Beerman was a second year oral surgery resident who had studied with Murph during his time at The Pankey Institute. Murph had seen her several times since her posting to Bethesda, Maryland and had invited her to be part of his implant study club at the Center for Esthetic and Restorative Excellence.

"Andrea, I need a favor."

"Sure thing, anything for a friend. But if you're calling before 5:00 am, this must really be important."

"I was hoping you were on call, but having a quiet night. This one is a little odd, and I need your complete secrecy."

"Ahh. Secrets are my specialty. And you know I love this cloak and dagger stuff you are always into."

"Can you access the military patient database? I need to see the prior radiographs for a patient I'm seeing."

"Sure thing. Who's the patient?" Murph could hear her fingernails clicking on a keyboard, opening the database.

"Franklin Buchanan." Murph hated to say the name out loud, but he was committed now.

There was a low whistle on the other end of the line. Then silence.

"Andrea? Are you still there?" Murph gave her some time. "You don't need to do this..." The line sat quiet for a while, and then the clicking resumed.

"It's OK. I was worried that it would be locked, but I'm in. Why do you want to know?"

"I can't tell you much, due to patient confidentiality, but let's say that the patient had an incident and I had to remove a tooth. Now I need to do an implant and I want to compare radiographs with the one I took tonight before I plan the surgery."

"OK, I can buy that." The clicking continued. "There's not much here. Colonel Franklin Buchanan had a pano and some bitewings taken during his last flight physical, right before he deployed with his wing to Afghanistan. I'm sending them to your email address now."

Murph felt a hand on his shoulder and nearly jumped out of the chair. He looked up to see Carli, bundled up in a Georgetown sweatshirt to ward off the chill.

Murph put the phone down on the desktop and changed it to speakerphone. Carli leaned in a bit and announced her presence, "Hey, Andrea!"

"Hi, Carli." Andrea's excitement broke the tension of the moment. "Congratulations! Wow, that's such great news!"

"Uh, thanks?" Carli stammered, "How did you know?"

"Hey, it's been a boring night on call. Besides, if Murph decides to go all Elvis in the middle of the White House, don't be surprised that it blew up all over Twitter. Someone had a cell phone out and the video is going viral. You should check it out!"

Murph covered his face with his hands. Carli chuckled, "I should have known. There is no subtlety with this guy. Somehow everything ends up being a big deal!"

"You're so lucky. Just remember to invite me to the wedding!"

"Sure thing!" Carli could hear someone calling Andrea in the background.

"Hey, Murph, I've got to go. Trauma coming in."

"Thanks, Andrea." Murph heard the ding announcing the arriving email. "Did I ever tell you you're too nice to be an Oral Surgeon?"

"Yeah, like every time you see me," Andrea sighed. "One of these days I'm going to take you up on your offer to come work at the Center."

"The job is yours anytime you get tired of dealing with trauma in the middle of the night."

"Don't temp me." Then she was gone, leaving Murph and Carli staring at the phone.

Chapter 26

Carli slid around behind Murph and massaged his neck and shoulders. He leaned his head back against her and closed his eyes.

"I'm sorry to wake you up. I was hoping you would keep sleeping."

She kept working the knots out of his muscles. "It's OK. I couldn't rest with you gone." She leaned over him and tapped the computer screen. "Let's get this over with and look at what she sent you."

He looked up at her sternly, "I can just forget about tonight and delete that email. If I open the file, I may find out something I'd rather not know."

"If you delete that file, you're not the man I fell in love with."

"Then we're in this together." Murph pulled her down and kissed her. "Let's find out what's going on."

He opened the email and downloaded the images. He expanded the panoramic x-ray that Andrea had sent over and placed it next to the image he had taken earlier tonight.

Murph rubbed his eyes, shaking his head in disbelief. "It's worse than I thought!"

"What do you see?" Carli's voice was a whisper.

"I had no doubt that the President's pink tooth was the result of a Russian root canal. I was trying to figure out how he could have been treated by a Russian-trained dentist. But this..."

He pointed to the area behind the lower molars in the two films. "You can have your wisdom teeth extracted, but you can't grow them back!"

"What??"

"Colonel Franklin Buchanan had no wisdom teeth when he deployed to Afghanistan. The President has four badly impacted wisdom teeth in his jaws. The man I took a tooth out of tonight… is not Franklin Buchanan."

Chapter 27

Carli slid over to the leather armchair next to the desk and sat down heavily. She drew her legs up under her and hugged her knees. Murph pushed his chair back and looked his future bride in the face.

"We could just act like this never happened?"

She shook her head slowly, "But that wouldn't be our style. We're better than that."

He smiled. "That's my girl. I don't know where this leads, but we can't just let it lay there." He picked up the tooth again, marveling at its pink hue, taunting him as he turned it in the light. " The most powerful man in the world isn't who he appears to be. It could be dangerous to probe for the truth."

Carli smiled back, mocking, "I laugh in the face of danger!" But then she shuddered involuntarily. "As I learned in the study of archeology, *truth* is a matter of philosophy. We have to begin with the *facts*—and then see where they lead."

"OK, here's what we know. Colonel Franklin Buchanan had x-rays taken before he went to Afghanistan. He was shot down there and ended up in a military hospital in a coma. After a time in rehab, he emerges as a hero and successfully runs for office. He's elected Vice President and then assumes the office of the President with the death of Joe Biden."

"Right." Carli stood up and began to pad back and forth in her bare feet. "Somehow, the man we met tonight is not the same man who went to war. There was a switch made sometime."

"Why would someone want to substitute the President?"

"Slow down, Murph. We don't have nearly enough *what* to even begin to start thinking about *why*."

"That's true. In fact, we really don't know very much at all."

Carli sat down abruptly with a defeated sigh. "I know."

"Well, we have to start somewhere. I'll meet with Brooks Borlon and share what we have found out. Maybe he has a simple explanation for this. There are a lot of possible reasons why someone would want to replace the President—but none of them are things I want to even begin to think about."

Carli stood up again and walked over to Murph. She reached out and took the pouch with the tooth from him. "One thing I'm sure of—we need to make sure that this is kept safe. I'll take the tooth. I know just where to put it."

"Good idea." Murph turned to his computer and began to save the x-ray files. He reached into his backpack and pulled out several thumb drives. He saved the files of the two images onto a drive and gave it to Carli. "Let me see that tooth again for a minute."

He took the tooth and photographed it with his phone. He uploaded the image to his computer and gave the tooth back to Carli. Murph combined the images of the panoramic x-rays and the photo of the tooth into one file. He duplicated the file and saved it onto three of the thumb drives.

Carli realized what Murph was up to and went into the kitchen, returning with several sheets of paper towel and small zip-loc storage bags. Murph addressed two envelopes, pulled stamps out of his drawer and placed the proper postage on them. One portable drive was going to his father in Cleveland. The other was addressed to Lt. Andrea Beerman at Walter Reed. Carli wrapped the thumb drives in the paper towel and sealed them in the plastic bags. Murph closed the envelopes and looked up at Carli.

"Backups are ready." He chuckled. "It all feels so James Bond."

She agreed. "I know. Let's go for a run and figure out what's next. I always think better when I'm exercising."

They quickly changed and headed for the door. Murph stopped and went back to his desk. He picked up his backpack and put his computer and power cord into the bag, as well as the envelopes.

He shouldered the backpack and followed Carli out the front. "Let's go deliver the mail while we're out!"

Murph locked the door and they began to run, the first light of day turning the eastern sky pink. Murph marveled at the grey obelisk of the Washington Monument, visible in the distance as they ran south on 6th Street toward the National Mall.

The first rays of sunshine touched the tip of the Washington Monument, exactly as designed by the architect of the capital city. No building was taller than the monument, assuring that the first light of each day would illuminate the capstone of the monument. The eastern face of the capstone contained the Latin inscription *Laus Deo*—praise be to God.

Murph thought as he jogged beside Carli, *Praise be to God, indeed.*

Chapter 28

The limo carrying Simon Cohen swiftly cleared security and rolled to a stop under the awnings that shielded the portico from any prying eyes. The doorman opened the door and stepped back.

"Good morning, Mr. Cohen." He indicated to the door with a white-gloved hand. "They are expecting you."

Without a word, the billionaire stormed up the stairs and through the open doorway. His assistant Diedre and Johnson, the butler, hurried to keep up. Diedre smiled a tired look of thanks to the doorman as she flew past.

Cohen entered the hallway and stopped. He stood tall and straightened the jacket of his dark gray suit. *Men of my stature do not rush,* he told himself. He pulled out the white cuffs of his shirt and adjusted the cuff links. His black tie was adorned with a blue paisley design. He tightened the tie and buttoned the jacket. He started again, using long, slow strides to move deeper into the building.

His pace was matched by two Secret Service agents, who now accompanied him. He didn't need them to guide him. He knew exactly where he was going and moved with a clear purpose. He reached the elevator and they escorted him up to the second floor, where he passed straight to the Treaty Room.

Cohen burst through the door without knocking, finding President and Mrs. Buchanan eating breakfast at the mahogany table. In the painting above them, President McKinley was surveying the signing of the treaty ending the Spanish-American War, looking down upon the coffee and pastries spread where the treaty had once been.

The President glanced up from his coffee and waved, though Cohen was already approaching. "Good morning, Simon! Come in and join us!"

The Secret Service agents had retreated to the hallway. Johnson entered the room last and shut the door behind him. Diedre split the distance between the door and the table, looked around, and spotted Paul Ramon silhouetted in the window. She moved closer to Ramon as he moved nearer to the table.

The President had remained seated, so Simon Cohen stalked up to him and looked down his long nose. "I'm glad you are feeling better this morning," his tone was curt. "I understand you had an interesting evening."

"State dinners are always tedious. This one no more than most."

"NO!" Cohen slapped his palm onto the table. "I was referring to your unscheduled visit with the dentist!"

"That worked out really well, actually." The President waved his hand casually. "It was convenient that Dr. Murphy was here anyway. He's very talented. I didn't feel a thing when he took out the tooth and I feel fantastic today!"

Cohen turned around, shaking his head, and then transfixed the President with an icy stare. "You fail to see the danger here and that concerns me greatly. I have worked too long. This requires meticulous attention to detail!"

"It's no concern. No one will ever know I had a tooth pulled."

"It's not about the tooth!" Cohen exploded with fury. "He knows the tooth was pink and that will make him suspicious."

The President rose to meet the angry billionaire's gaze, using his six-inch height advantage over the old man. "It doesn't matter. I have already arranged for any evidence to be removed and if he becomes a problem, then he can be eliminated."

Cohen cooled a bit. "We cannot afford any hint of suspicion. And Dr. Murphy may not be as easy to eliminate as you think. He was the guest of the Vice President, was he not?"

The President nodded.

Diedre coughed quietly in the background. "Ah, hem."

Cohen turned on her, his eyes flashing. "You wish to add something?"

"Yes, Sir." She began meekly, pushing her blond hair over her ear and touching the iPad she held constantly. "I think you should all see this."

She set the iPad on the table as she explained. "Dr. Michael Murphy was a contestant on *The Dental Apprentice* TV show, which aired on NBC. He is very well known nationally as a result of his being the runner-up and the clear fan favorite among the contestants. This is from this morning's show."

Diedre touched the screen and the video from *The Today Show* began with host Erica Hill.

"Hey, Lester. Here's some happy news from Washington! At the White House last night, former *Dental Apprentice* star Mike Murphy used the occasion of a State Dinner to propose to his long-time girlfriend Carli Chamoun – and he did it in a big way! Here's some video of the event."

The video clip showed Murph, as Elvis, singing and proposing, to the cheers of the crowd.

Lester Holt narrated the clip, ending with, "And that's how you make a lasting impression. It will be a wedding we'll all be waiting for."

""With a start like that, I can't wait. Hopefully, we can get them on the show before the big day!" Erica laughed as they went to commercial break.

Diedre touched the screen again to stop the video.

Cohen glared past his assistant to the President. "What are your plans, Mr. President?"

"I have dispatched a team to destroy the computers at his dental clinic to eliminate the x-rays. He tossed the tooth into the medical waste container, so the team will recover that as well. Without any evidence, even if he suspects something, he'll keep quiet."

Cohen thought a minute and looked to Diedre. "They will have the computer data backed up, probably offsite."

She nodded in agreement. "That would be a standard procedure for the office. The backup may occur automatically overnight, so the images may have already left the office."

Cohen turned to the President and opened his arms wide, palms up, questioning, "So?"

The President just opened his mouth, but no words came out.

Paul Ramon came to his rescue. "We can have our people hack into the system and destroy the backup data. That should solve any problem."

"Good. Get it done! Let's be sure that there are no loose ends. We are too close to have any mistakes now." Cohen scanned the group. "I hope that you have acted quickly enough to contain this damage."

Buchanan found his voice again. "I am the President of the United States. No dentist is going to get in my way."

"That may be true..." Cohen reached into his suit pocket and withdrew his phone. "But I never take chances."

He scanned his contacts and selected one.

The phone rang only once and clicked. "Yes." The voice was clipped.

"Cyrille, I have a matter in Washington that may require your talents."

"Yes?"

"Come immediately!"

"Yes." And the phone went dead.

Chapter 29

Murph had left Carli at the Museum of Natural History. She intended to check on her exhibit and look at the comment cards that had been left by visitors. It was something she did routinely. The responses were nearly unanimously positive and reading them always made her feel good.

Murph continued jogging the short distance across Pennsylvania Avenue and through John Marshall Place Park to the Center for Esthetic and Restorative Excellence. Crossing "C" Street, he was nearly run down by a gray panel van speeding west that turned onto 6th Street NW and disappeared. The van driver wore dark sunglasses and a black ball cap and military style fatigues.

Murph had jumped back onto the sidewalk, shaking his fist at the receding van. He continued to the Center parking lot, stopping dead in his tracks. The rear door to the Center had been pulled off its hinges and lay on the ground.

Murph dashed to the doorway, noticing that the security keypad appeared fried, with a burn mark discoloring the brick around it. He entered the darkened hallway and waited a few seconds for his eyes to adjust from the sunlight. Moving more cautiously, he came to his private office. Looking in, he discovered his computer ripped out from under the desk. The connection cables dangled and the monitor lay face down on the floor, shards of broken glass littering the room.

Murph continued his quick tour, finding the surgical suite ransacked as he expected. The realization of the goal of the attack was dawning, as he discovered all of the computers in the office missing. The security cameras had also been smashed.

Murph entered the lobby at the front of the clinic and spotted the body out of the corner of his eye. Outside of the elevator, he found the crumpled form of Dr. Kevin Browne, bloodied and leaning against a wall. Murph knelt down and felt for a pulse. Thankful that Kevin was alive, Murph examined the cut above his left eye. Murph quickly collected some cotton gauze and stopped the bleeding with light pressure. A knot was already growing and the eye was turning black with the bruise.

Murph took out his phone and called 911. Kevin began to arouse and Murph held him still.

"Kevin, is anyone else in the building?"

"No. I'm the only one here." Kevin pushed himself into a sitting position and rubbed the back of his neck.

Murph sat back on his haunches and kept pressure on the laceration. "What happened?"

"I was working in the lab downstairs, getting ready for patients Monday when I heard a loud BANG up here. I came out of the elevator—only made it a half step when this big guy in a black jump suit whacked me with a club or something."

"Did he say anything?"

"He said, 'Doc, if I was you, I'd forget everything!' I told him I didn't remember anything worth forgetting. He hit me again and I blacked out."

Kevin was over 6 foot tall and in excellent shape. If he thought his assailant was big, then that was saying something. "How do you feel?"

"My head is killing me and my vision is blurry. I'm afraid I have a concussion. I played hockey in college and I've been hit hard over the years, but nothing like this!"

"I agree with the concussion. I've called 911, and they'll be here soon. Don't worry, Kevin. I'll take care of you."

"What's going on?"

"Someone broke in to the Center and stole all the computers. I think they thought you were me. You can't identify anyone, so you're in the clear. We'll get you to the hospital, and they can evaluate your head. You're going to end up with a nice scar there, but that will make a big impression with the ladies!"

"Well, that's good, at least."

The sirens could be heard in the distance, so Murph sat joking with Kevin until the paramedics arrived. They dressed and stabilized the wound then took him to the ER for evaluation.

Murph answered the police questions and described everything he knew of the attack, but not mentioning the late-night visit of the President. Margaret Farouk arrived soon after the police. The security company had alerted her to the break-in.

Margaret looked at Murph, raising an eyebrow knowingly.

"I'll explain later," he told her.

Margaret went into her office and pulled the inventory of the computers. She completed the police reports and began making calls to have the damage photographed and repaired.

Murph pulled aside the lead police officer and they surveyed the wreckage of the office. "Officer, I'm concerned that whoever did this may also have gone to my home. Can you have someone come with me and see if it's OK?"

The officer thought a moment, and then nodded. "Grady!" A young patrolman looked up from poking through the trash with a pencil, looking for clues. "Take the Doc to his condo and let me know what you find."

"Yes, Sir."

Officer Seth Grady had been on the DC police force for only six months and he was eager to help. Murph got in the passenger seat of the cruiser, and it took only minutes to cover the short distance up 6th Street to the condo.

They pulled into the driveway and could immediately see the front door smashed in. Officer Grady called in to his Lieutenant the address of the additional crime scene and drew his weapon. He motioned for Murph to stay but the dentist shook his head no.

"Then stay behind me until I'm sure they're gone."

They moved cautiously up the walk and entered the condo. The rooms were more thoroughly ransacked than at the Center and the perpetrators had gone. Grady holstered his gun and surveyed the scene with Murph.

"Well, Doc, someone sure was looking for something."

"Yeah, I just wish I knew what!" Then he muttered to himself, "There's a lot I wish I knew."

Chapter 30

Murph stepped outside his demolished condo and called Carli. To his relief, she was fine but shocked to hear about the attack. He told her to wait at work until he could come for her.

Murph then called Murray in case the driver had been spotted last night.

"No, Doc. All quiet here. But it sounds like someone is trying to tell you something!"

"Well, I got the message. Just you be careful. I don't want anything to happen to you."

"Doc. I can take care of myself. You don't need to worry about me."

"Well then, can you pick up Carli at work and bring her here?"

"Sure thing. I'm on my way."

Murph called Carli and told her to watch for Murray. The police had finished and just left when the black town car pulled up and let Carli out.

She ran to Murph and hugged him. Murray waved and was off.

Murph let her go, and she ran up into the condo. He followed her in. Instead of finding her crying, he was pleased to see her standing in the living room—hands on her hips—jaw set in fury.

He walked up to her and took her chin in his hand, lifting it up so he could look her in the eye. "The deeper we dig, the more dangerous it will get. They've removed the evidence and sent us a clear message."

"I know. But this also let's me know they're scared that we've found something."

"True enough. It confirms my suspicions that it's no simple mistake that the President's dental records don't match."

"Now we just have to figure out why!"

"We need to act like nothing's happened while we figure out a few things. This is just a burglary, and I've got to get the office back to normal."

Murph tried to set the door back in place and was able to get it so that, at least from the street, it looked closed. He drove Carli in the Mustang back down to the Center.

The ever-efficient Margaret already had a crew on site repairing the door. The staff was arriving to clean up the mess and make the office ready to see patients in the morning.

Murph and Carli called Margaret into his office and closed the door. Carli gave Margaret a big hug.

"Congratulations on your engagement," Margaret began, "but it appears that a fiancé wasn't all you picked up last night."

"It was a night we won't soon forget!" Murph proceeded to tell Margaret the events of the last day. Her eyes grew bigger with each sentence.

"That's amazing!" She leaned against the desk. "So what are you going to do?"

Murph explained, "We need time to understand what's going on. So we're just going to have to act like nothing has happened and that we're too scared to talk. I can't tell anyone anything since I don't have a clue what we really do know anyway."

Carli looked at him frowning, "If that's the best way you can put it, you *had* better keep quiet. That sounds just crazy!"

"At least they didn't get this," Murph patted the backpack with his computer. "And we mailed the copies of the files on thumb drives while we were running this morning." Suddenly Murph looked up in panic. "But what happened to the pink tooth?"

"The tooth is safe." Carli smiled. "I gave it to an old friend of mine to hold for us."

Chapter 31

It took a long evening of hard work for Murph and the staff but the Center was ready to see patients on Monday morning, as scheduled. Murph began the morning staff meeting with words of thanks for the efforts of his team. Their professionalism and dedication made everything possible. Margaret smiled in the background as Murph singled out Sue, Robin, Juliann, Laurie, and Sharri for high praise.

"It has been a tough weekend, but we have to make it seem that nothing happened. The patients can't know that anything is amiss." It made the speech easier to give knowing that they all agreed with him.

The office was cleaned and prepared. Temporary computers even were up and running with the office management software in place. Murph had a tough day ahead, since he had not only his own full schedule to see, but also some patients for Kevin Browne. Kevin had been released from the hospital but was home recovering from a concussion and unable to work.

Sue and Robin were seating the first patients when Margaret called Murph aside.

"There's one more issue."

"Why not!" Murph rolled his eyes.

"The backup data appears to be corrupted. It's not loading into the computers."

"That's odd. The company that handles our data storage is the best out there."

"I know. They have been able to give us an old copy that they archived in hard disc form on the first of the month. But we have lost the most current data."

"Margaret, I smell a rat." Murph went to his desk and pulled out his iPhone. He selected a contact and had the phone dial.

"Hey, Doc!" the voice drawled, stretching it out to "Daaawk."

"Hi Billy! I wanted to catch you before you went to court. I have a problem and need your help."

The law firm of McGinty and Gibbons had represented the Center for years. Its partners, Billy McGinty and Joe Gibbons, had taken a liking to the young Murph from the beginning. They were among the most connected attorneys in Washington, and Murph valued their advice.

"What's the problem, Doc?"

Murph quickly explained the burglary, including the theft of computers and the apparent damage to the office database. "I don't know why, but I suspect a cyber attack."

"Sounds like it," Billy agreed. "Let me get my people working on it. Do you have the numbers on the police reports?"

"Sure." Murph shuffled the papers on his desk and found the copies of the reports. "Here they are."

"OK, Doc, you just do teeth and I'll see what we can find out."

Chapter 32

All in all, it was a normal Monday—a mix of advanced dentistry and simple care. Murph was unusual, in that he derived the same pleasure out of redesigning an entire smile as repairing a denture, if the patient was happy. Monday was enjoyable because he had some of his favorite patients in for their visits.

Shirley needed an adjustment for her denture. Murph asked her to describe where it hurt. She admitted that she was very pleased and the teeth were extremely comfortable, but there was one minor problem.

"It only hurts when I laugh," she confided.

"Well, then. I need to tell you jokes until we figure out where to adjust."

They all laughed, found the sore spot, and successfully adjusted it.

Murph was still chuckling as Shirley prepared to leave. "I know I'll remember this adjustment forever."

"Me too!" Shirley laughed loudly. "And it feels great now!"

He gave her a hug and walked her out.

The next patient was an elderly lady. Always impeccably dressed in a skirt, blouse, jacket and low heels, Valerie David was nearly 90. Sitting upright in the dental chair, she took Murph's hand when he came in and sat down.

"I am oldt," she announced in her heavy accent. It was the way she began every visit.

"You are still young, " Murph countered as he always did, "but your teeth have quite a bit of mileage."

She smiled, "Doktor. You are so kind. But today, I do look oldt."

Murph had to admit that today she was right. She had broken off one of her upper front teeth near the gum line and her lip was sinking into the space, distorting her smile. She was very proud and the inability to smile was weighing heavily on her.

"This will take some work, but you're in the right place. I know we can fix that."

She patted him on the hand. "I know. I trust you."

After x-rays and an examination, Murph determined that he could save the tooth with a root canal and post, immediately giving back her smile

Valerie sat back happy and let Murph get to work. After anesthetic, the tooth was easily prepared and the nerve tissue removed. Completely comfortable, she drifted off to sleep. To complete the root canal, a gum rubber type sealer was placed. Removing the excess material required a heated instrument, so Murph struck a match to light the alcohol torch.

With the scratch of the match, Valerie's eyes snapped open and she inhaled the smoke, the sulfur smell permeating the small treatment room.

"Louisa. Not Louisa." Her voice was a whisper. "Don't take my sister."

Murph looked at Sue over his mask, his eyes widening. It was clear that Valerie was no longer with them. Smells are the most potent memory triggers, and Valerie was now on a journey far in her past. She gripped Murph's hand and explained, wanting him to see.

"The flames were all around. They ordered the convent burned as they left. The Nazis took Louisa. She was 14. I was only ten and hid in the basement with the other children. The priest kept us there so they would not find us. Through a tiny window, I saw them take poor Louisa to the young Nazi officer. He stood, silhouetted in the fire, barking orders as the convent blazed around him. He was SS. I could see the death's head emblem on his hat. They dragged her and dropped her on her knees in front of him. He looked down and lifted up her chin with his riding crop. He sneered, waved his hand, and they carried her to one of the trucks. They loaded everything from the storeroom onto the trucks and drove away into the mountains." She began to cry softly, tears rolling down her cheeks and onto the dental bib.

Murph held her hand. "Do you know what happened to Louisa?"

"No," she whispered. "I never saw her again. After night fell, the priest took us out of the cellar and into the woods. He led us to Rome, and I came to America."

The memory was 70 years old, but the emotions were as fresh as yesterday. Murph knew from previously talking with Valerie that she had been orphaned at a young age and lived in a convent in the Italian Alps. He had never heard this part of the story before.

"Mrs. David, do you remember the name of the priest who helped you?"

"Yes, Doktor. It was Father Henri. He was French, I think, but spoke excellent Italian. He was our shepherd, keeping us safe from the Nazi patrols while we were on the run."

"How many children were with you?"

"Twenty-two orphans—some were French, some Italian—Catholics. Many were Jews. At ten, I was the oldest—along with the Jewish boy." She began to sob.

"That's such an amazing story of sadness, and courage."

She wiped her eyes and looked at Murph intently. "It is a miracle that I am here and that I am oldt!"

"You are here because you have a task that still needs to be done. God has a purpose for you."

Murph was able to quickly finish the root canal and build up the tooth. He prepared it for a crown and placed a temporary. The esthetics of the resin crown were excellent, and Valerie's smile was restored.

"There's that beautiful smile again."

"Oh, Doktor." She admired the result in the mirror. "It is wonderful. Thank you!"

"I only ask that you smile and show off for people."

"You know that I always smile." She hugged him and left to make an appointment to finish treatment.

Murph realized that it was well past 5:00 pm. He suddenly felt extremely tired. He took off his mask and glasses, remarking to Sue, "Just when you think you have heard it all..."

"I know," she agreed, "that certainly was amazing. Everyone has their story, but that one sounds like a movie script."

"Indeed. I'm glad she felt comfortable sharing it with us. We know her so much better now."

Murph completed his notes in her chart and returned to his office, rubbing his tired eyes. He slumped in his chair and closed his eyes for a moment. His break lasted only seconds as his phone began to vibrate.

Chapter 33

Murph opened his eyes and tried to focus on his phone. Though blurry, he made out that the caller ID said William McGinty. He picked up the phone from his desk and keyed it to answer.

"Hello?"

"Doc! You've gone and done it now!"

"Hi, Billy. What do you know?"

"Well, Doc, if you judge a man by his enemies, you are the most powerful guy in Washington."

"Is it that bad?"

"In some circles, this would be a badge of honor!" Billy laughed, "but I'm not sure you will see it that way."

Murph sighed. "Give me the details."

"OK, first the break-in. My sources tell me it wasn't the FBI or CIA, and the Justice Department appears clear. The spooks at the CIA are fingering the National Security Agency. Well trained, military type operation. Tough people. Don't cross them, Murph."

"Believe me, I try not to."

"The cyber attack on your database is another thing—high level of capability with big-time computing power. The effort was to wipe out all records of the last few days—highly targeted and very effective. Any data you lost is never coming back. My forensic computer analysts..."

"Hackers?" Murph couldn't help needling Billy even in the face of mounting bad news.

"Fine, it sounds so cheap when you put it that way, but yes—my *hackers* traced this right up Pennsylvania Avenue to the top of the food chain." Billy paused for effect. "Then they were shut down in a big way."

"Thanks, Billy. That's what I was afraid of."

"Murph, all kidding aside now," Billy's tone changed and he was deadly serious, "you are involved with some powerful forces here in Washington. Anything that starts in the Oval Office will end very badly for you if you aren't careful. Is there anything you want to tell me?"

"Billy, I have more questions than answers right now, so I'll keep you in the dark—for your own good." He stopped for a moment, thinking. "Thanks for all your help! I'll let you know when I figure something out."

"Well, OK, but be very careful. This isn't like getting you out of a ticket for jaywalking."

Murph set down the phone and opened his laptop computer. He transferred another copy of the files to a flash drive, wrapped it, and placed it into an envelope. He quickly wrote down his suspicions on a note and tossed it in as well. He addressed the letter to Billy McGinty but included no return address. He placed the proper postage and sealed the envelope.

Murph packed up his computer and changed out of his scrubs. He gave the envelope to Robin and asked her to drop it in a mailbox near her home. She looked puzzled but agreed.

Having done all he could do for one day, Murph called Carli as he walked out to his car. She had made dinner and invited him over to her apartment, since his place was still a

109

mess. He was tired and thankful, so he settled in for the drive through DC traffic to Georgetown.

Chapter 34

After Murph's long day at the office, Carli had chosen well in preparing a light summer salad with seared salmon. They settled in to relax on the couch and Murph filled her in on his day. On the ride over, he had been debating about sharing Billy McGinty's ominous information, but, in the end, he decided that she needed to know what they were up against.

Carli pushed herself upright against the arm of the sofa and crossed her legs, sitting on them. She looked straight at Murph. "So any thoughts we had of this being some kind of a mistake are out the window?"

"That would be the way I see it. The President is an imposter and the White House had made a significant effort to cover up any evidence that we might have had. We just don't know who is responsible and why."

She nodded her head once. "That's so much more clear than yesterday!"

Murph cocked his head to one side. "Why does that matter?"

"Because it makes our next move easy!"

"How so?" Murph was curious now. Where he was often reflective, she had the talent of being decisive.

"We know something is wrong. A powerful force has pushed us." She smiled a sly smile. "It's time to push back!"

"Before we do that, we need more information—and we could use some protection." Carli's clarity had given Murph direction and a plan was forming.

"What should we do now?" Sitting still bothered her, so she was eager to start something—but she was completely unprepared for what he said next.

Murph looked at his watch. "I think we should go for a run!"

Chapter 35

Murph sprang up off the couch, leaving Carli sitting there dumbfounded as he trotted out to the Mustang and retrieved his gym bag from the back seat. He changed quickly into his workout clothes as she changed, as well. They left her apartment, and he led her at a brisk pace north on Wisconsin Avenue.

As they ran, Murph kept looking at his watch. Carli couldn't stand the suspense any longer, so she had to ask, "Where are we going? And why does it matter what time it is?"

Murph smiled like the Cheshire cat. "The Naval Observatory, of course!"

"Because that's where the Vice President lives!"

"Excellent, my Dear!" Murph quickened the pace. "And Brooks Borlon is a creature of habit. He always runs at 9:00 pm. I hope we can catch him running the circle with only a small protection detail."

Murph touched the screen on his iPhone and studied the map as they ran. It was a tough slog, uphill from Georgetown. The pulsating blue dot that represented their position crept closer to the arc that was Observatory Circle NW. The Naval Observatory sat atop one of the higher points of Washington DC. Observatory Circle was the street that circled the summit like the brim of a hat.

Murph was pleased to see the Holiday Inn Georgetown appear on their right, and he led her down the sidewalk, entering the grounds of the Naval Observatory. Running down the jogging path, the canopy of trees created a darkened tunnel. They left the park and reached the deserted pavement of Observatory Circle.

Murph slowed to a walk and scanned the area. "Now we need some luck." There was not a soul in sight.

Carli grabbed his hand and pulled him to the left, taking the lead. "Don't ask me why, but most people run on a circular track in a counterclockwise direction. If we go clockwise, we'll increase our chances of running into them."

"That's why I love you."

"I know—I'm full of useless information." She giggled. "I have to admit it, this feels really weird. When I ran track in high school, the races always went counterclockwise."

"It's that way for NASCAR and the Indy 500, too. I guess we're just going against the grain."

She looked over her shoulder back at him. "Or like salmon swimming upstream!"

Murph pointed ahead. "Well, aren't you just the smartest fish in the school!"

Carli turned, grinning. "I guess I win the prize."

Jogging straight toward them was Brooks Borlon, flanked by two secret service agents. Murph waved as they came closer. The agents put themselves between the Vice President and Murph until Brooks called out to them like old friends.

"Hey, Carli and Murph. If it isn't my favorite recently engaged couple!"

The agents relaxed visibly and allowed Murph and Carli to get close enough for Brooks to hug Carli and shake Murph's hand.

"Beautiful night for a run!" Murph wiped sweat from his forehead.

"Fantastic. I'm just getting started, so why don't you two run along with me. Just take it easy on an old man."

"You aren't old, and you are in excellent shape, Senator." Murph corrected himself, "Err, I mean Mr. Vice President."

"Thanks, Murph! And don't worry about titles. That whole Mr. Vice President thing is really clumsy. Just call me Brooks."

"That's going to be tough, Sir." Carli fell in step with Brooks as they started off. "I suppose I could try."

Murph offered, "I guess I'll just keep it to Mr. Borlon. It's shorter."

Brooks just laughed. The secret service agents had drifted back a bit. Close enough to provide security, but out of immediate earshot.

Brooks set the pace, glancing over at Murph. "I know the two of you love to run, but I'm also not naïve enough to think this was a chance meeting. Something's up if you wanted to see me outside of normal hours."

Murph looked straight ahead as he spoke, maintaining the pace. "You are very perceptive. We have had an exciting time since the dinner Saturday night."

Carli kept a subtle lookout to be sure that the agents stayed back far enough. Murph quickly described the extraction and the pink tooth. He explained the most common cause of that problem and their suspicions.

Brooks was quick to jump on a possibility. "It must be a mistake. He probably had that root canal done while he was in Europe or Afghanistan."

"That's what we were hoping, too, but then the Center and my condo were broken into, and the computers were destroyed. All to wipe out this image."

Murph held out his iPhone and showed Brooks the photo of the pink tooth and the x-rays of the President before and after his deployment to Afghanistan. Brooks let out a low whistle, immediately grasping the significance when Murph pointed out the sudden appearance of impacted wisdom teeth where they had not been before.

"Any hopes we had of being wrong were dashed when I found out today that the attacks were traced to the NSA."

Murph was going to continue, but Brooks held up a hand. They ran in silence for a few minutes, before the Vice President motioned for Murph and Carli to come closer.

"The first time we met, the two of you told me a highly improbable story about an ancient curse that turned out to be true. This tale has the potential to have much greater impact. This truly is a Black Swan event."

He paused for effect before continuing. "British ornithologists spent their lives cataloging and detailing the appearance and behavior of swans, secure in their unassailable belief that swans were white. In 1697, Dutch explorer Willem de Vlamingh discovered black swans in Australia, shattering the popular paradigm in zoology. It only took the sighting of one, single, and quite ugly bird to turn the scientific community on its head."

Murph frowned. "But it makes sense that swans could be in different colors. Why was that such a shock?"

"That's the nature of black swan events." He counted on his fingers as they jogged. "First, the event lies outside the realm of reasonable expectations, since nothing in the past can convincingly point to its possibility. Second, it carries an extreme impact. And finally, after the fact, thanks to human nature, we find a way to rationalize, concocting explanations that make its occurrence seem predictable."

"So the terrorists flying planes into the World Trade Center on 9-11 was a Black Swan event?" Carli's eyes widened with realization.

"Correct." Brooks agreed.

"But Pearl Harbor was not." Murph was beginning to understand. "Because the War Department had considered the possibility and developed plans in advance..."

Brooks finished the thought, "But no one listened to the analysts because the leadership didn't want to believe them."

The Vice President stopped suddenly and faced Murph, motioning for his protection detail to stay back. "This is precisely the problem we have. You have uncovered an inconceivable event that, if true, would be so shocking that the country wouldn't want to believe it."

Murph clenched his fists. "But we can't ignore it. I won't accept an imposter as the President of the United States! Who knows what damage he could do."

"Neither will I." Brooks reached out and put his hand on Murph's shoulder. "However, we need incontrovertible proof in order to confront the problem. You know who and what may have happened. If we show people the answers to when, how, and, most importantly, why this was done, we can change the trajectory of the country."

Carli stood tall, challenging, "We'll do our part to uncover the truth, but we need to know that you'll be there to back us up in the end."

"I'll be there for you." The Vice President smiled, but it was a politician's easy smile. "What can I do to help you?"

Murph thought for a minute. "Nothing, right now. We wanted someone to know what our suspicions were. We have placed copies of the x-rays in secure locations. You are too far on the inside to do anything."

"Sadly, you're right. Being Vice President sounds great, but there really is little power in this job."

"We're going to figure this out, no matter how far it goes." Carli was defiant.

"I don't like it, and I don't want to believe it." The Vice President thought for a minute. "It took a lot of guts to come talk to me, since there's a good chance that I'm involved." Brooks pointed at his security detail. "I could easily have my two armed friends there arrest you for threatening me." Murph saw the agents tense when Brooks motioned to them.

Carli winked. "But you haven't. And you're not going to, because this was all news to you." She sounded very sure of herself. "I could see it in your body language as Murph was telling you."

Brooks smiled and the Secret Service agents relaxed again. "I'm as puzzled and angry as you are. However, before challenging a popular sitting President, we must have more than just suspicions. And we have to figure out who stands to gain from controlling the Presidency."

The Vice President reached out and shook Murph's hand while he spoke. "We've been talking too long and I don't want my detail to get too suspicious. You've got me spooked and looking for the man behind the curtain." He hugged Carli. "I need the two of you to figure this out. Not for me, but for the good of the country. Let me give you my private number. It's a secure line."

115

Murph entered the number into his phone as the Vice President gave it to him. "Thanks. We'll keep you up to date on our progress."

Brooks Borlon gave a mock salute and jogged off, with his Secret Service detail in tow. They left Murph and Carli standing in the growing darkness, feeling truly alone.

Chapter 36

They ran in silence for a few minutes, lost in their own thoughts. It was an easier jog now, coming downhill from the Observatory.

Carli frowned. "All this discussion of Black Swan events in history is interesting enough, but I don't think it's really helping us at all."

"Oh, I don't know." Murph's mind was racing. "It strikes me that the common denominator here is that no one immediately accepts the event, because it challenges the prevailing beliefs. We can get ahead if we simply accept the fact that the President is an imposter and don't fight it."

Carli tried to see where he was going with this. "OK, so the President is bogus. So what?"

"Precisely!" Murph's eyes flashed. "Let's start with the rationalization."

Carli snorted, "Huh?"

"The terrorists wanted to create the maximum amount of chaos and fear, so..."

Carli snapped at the bait. "So they hijacked planes and flew them into buildings."

"Right." Murph found himself running faster now. "So they replaced the President with an imposter..."

"Because??" Carli leaned in with anticipation.

"Uhh... I've got nothing." Murph could sense a glimmer of something, but it remained elusive, in the shadows at the edges of his mind.

116

"That's what I was afraid of." Carli tried not to sound too harsh. "It's a step in the right direction, though."

"I think so, too. I just can't put my fingers on it." Murph kept running, the rhythmic crunch of his shoes on the pavement gave order to his thoughts. "Let's look at it this way—what powers does the President have that someone would want?"

"Just about anything! Proposing legislation, foreign policy, even launching a military strike!" Carli threw up her hands. "He's the most powerful man in the world."

"True. But Franklin Buchanan has only been President for a few months. Have there been any major changes in policy for his administration?"

Carli stopped in her tracks. Murph had to dodge to avoid running her over and tripped. He spun around and landed heavily on his butt, looking up at her.

"That's it!" she shouted, reaching down to pull him up. Murph just pulled her harder and she collapsed into his lap laughing. "You're a genius."

He held her tight, but she didn't say anything more. When he couldn't take the suspense any longer, he pushed her away and held her shoulders. "Are you going to tell me?"

"I don't have a clue what the President's doing—but we finally have a question that we can research! I don't know the answer but I know how we can find out!" She pulled him close. "And that's real progress."

"OK." Murph remained skeptical as they got to their feet. "So let's go home. We've got work to do."

Chapter 37

The President returned from his daily briefing from the CIA, NSA, FBI, and the State Department. The tension and instability in the world gave him a headache each morning, dealing with the doom and gloom inherent in current events.

He strode into the Oval Office and tossed his binder onto the desk with a thud. He rubbed his temples and sat down heavily in the leather chair. He leaned back and put up his feet on the desk, clasping his hands behind his head. His eyes had nearly closed when he spotted the dark form on the couch, sitting quietly, observing him.

"Unhhh." The President breathed in with a rush. "Why don't you wait outside like everyone else?"

"Because I am not like everyone else." Simon Cohen's tone was quiet—firm and even—pleasant, but commanding. He rose from the couch and approached the desk.

Franklin Buchanan tried to keep his relaxed pose, but as the billionaire came closer, he sat upright, resting his arms on the desktop. Cohen was not a tall man, so when he leaned his hands onto the Resolute Desk, his eyes met the President at nearly the same level. They locked eyes for a moment, then Buchanan glanced down at the briefing notes in front of him.

When the President looked up again, Cohen had turned to stare out the window at the South Lawn. "What business brings you to the White House so early?"

Cohen turned back. "You know full well—but there has been a complication."

"I have heard nothing."

Cohen picked up the binder and leafed through it. "You are well informed, but you do not see."

"Everything is going along according to the plan."

Cohen placed the binder in the crook of his arm. "Yes. My years of work are coming to fruition. Your part in the play is going well. It has been a virtuoso performance so far."

Buchanan smiled at the rare praise, but the corners of his mouth drooped as soon as it formed.

"The dentist has talked to the Vice President."

"But he knows nothing!" It was a hiss.

"Dr. Murphy has very little information, yet he sees with clarity. This I respect, and fear."

"He can't hurt us. We have come too far."

Cohen relaxed for a moment, and his shoulders drooped. "There is so much momentum that I know the plan cannot be stopped. It is because I can see no way that he can challenge us that I am concerned."

The President reached for the phone on his desk, "I'll call in the Vice President and we can dispatch him to the meeting of the Organization of American States in Buenos Aires. The Secretary of State was going to go, but I can send Borlon and get him out of Washington for two weeks. Then, we'll figure out something to keep him busy until it's over."

Cohen let out his breath heavily. "No, the Vice President is not the problem. He is too new to the job and too much of a politician to be an issue. Put down the phone."

Buchanan complied. "Then what?"

Simon Cohen reached into his pocket and extracted his phone. He touched the contact and the phone rang—once only.

"Yes." The voice was deep, slow and measured.

Cohen sighed. "Cyrille, Dr. Murphy has become a distraction. Please persuade our young dentist not to be a hero. Show him what is at stake."

"Yes."

Chapter 38

Simon Cohen left the White House and returned to his suite across the Potomac River in Pentagon City. It was only a 15-minute drive but it gave him the time he needed to think. He settled heavily into the plush chair in the sitting room, considered the time difference, and selected another contact on his phone.

After a few rings, a cheerful female voice answered, "Hello, Mr. Cohen! How are you this evening?"

"It is a fine morning here in Washington, Ariella. Thank you for asking. I have a task for you."

"Certainly, Sir. I'm happy take care of whatever you need."

"There has been an unexpected intrusion here. It is nothing, but I am a man of caution. I need you to ask about the dentist."

"Yes, Sir. It is important to leave no stone unturned at this point. Please text me your questions and I will let you know."

"Thank you, Ariella. Shalom!" He touched the phone and ended the call.

* * * * * * *

Murph completed another successful day with patients and completed his paperwork on the computer in his office. Each staff member leaned in through his door as they finished their tasks so he could say goodnight. As usual, he was the last to finish. He shut down the computer system and was pleased that it was beginning to run normally again. They had recovered all the patient data except the one group of files from Saturday. He knew that was gone forever, except for the copies that he had secreted around the city.

Murph changed into slacks and a golf shirt, locked up the office and walked to the parking lot. Tossing his backpack into the trunk of the Mustang, he slid behind the wheel and turned the key. He felt the pressure of the cold steel of the gun barrel against the back of his head and stiffened.

Looking into the rearview mirror, the face glaring at him was expressionless. Coal black eyes. Pale skin, almost pink. The head was completely shaved and, oddly, the man had no eyebrows. His nose was flattened at the tip, as if it had been broken in a fight at a young age. His lips were a thin line, drawn taut.

"Drive!" The voice was low and quiet, smooth and commanding.

"Where would you like to go?" Murph tried to sound light and friendly.

"To Georgetown. That is where you were going anyway, was it not?"

Murph thought the accent was vaguely European but his captor spoke excellent English. "Oh, I don't know. I was thinking of going to the ballpark. The Nationals are playing tonight."

"Tsk-tsk. But Miss Caroline will be so disappointed if you do not pick her up. She is expecting you soon." He pushed the gun slightly harder against Murph's head. "You had better start. The traffic to the University can be terrible during rush hour."

Murph put the car in reverse and looked over his shoulder to back out of the parking space. He glanced down at his assailant. The small rear seat of the Mustang was completely filled by the bulk of the man. His massive shoulders and upper arms were bursting from the tight t-shirt that was attempting to contain them. The pistol contacting his neck had gotten Murph's attention, but the raw power of the man stuffed behind Murph was palpable.

Murph pushed into traffic and began the drive across downtown Washington. He began to consider his options. He could probably dive out of the car before the gunman could dislodge himself from the back. Murph tried to assess the positioning of his captor out of the corner of his eyes as he made each turn.

Murph heard a menacing laugh from the back seat. "Do not work so hard at figuring if I can get out of this seat. Just concentrate on your driving. Even if you could get out, that would just keep Caroline waiting longer—although she will not be lonely. Several friends of mine are helping her pass the time on the bench in front of the Georgetown University library."

"How??" Murph shut his mouth before he gave anything else away. If they knew that Murph was to pick Carli up at the library, they had been reading her texts. Murph's mind raced, trying to remember what else he had been discussing on his phone today. He decided to take the direct approach. "So you have been reading my texts. Why don't you just ask me what you want to know?"

"Doctor Murphy, what you know is of no importance to us. What I am here to discuss concerns what you are going to forget."

Murph drove in silence for a few more minutes. "I know that the President of the United States is an imposter." Might as well play a trump card first.

"Yes. And for that I should pull the trigger right now." The barrel pinched against the bone, then eased away. "However, you are a well-known person in the city. Your popularity will save you—for now."

Murph swallowed hard. The Mustang turned off Prospect Street and onto the campus. On the order of his passenger, Murph pulled up short of the Lauinger Library and stopped. He looked over the seat at his assailant, "So where do we go from here?"

"You will let me out now. You know so very little that you need not concern yourself with attempting to learn any more. That would be a poor choice for you—and for Miss Caroline. She seems like such a nice girl. Please get out of the car and stand on the curb."

Murph did as he was told. His assailant opened the passenger door and unfolded himself from the back seat. His body was oddly shapen. His legs were long, yet he had a short torso and giant arms. His head was small, yet more menacing since it was shaved clean. He slipped his pistol into his belt and surveyed Murph.

"I should end it now. From evil comes a greater good." Their eyes locked. "You should give up any thoughts of being a hero. That only works in movies. It will not go well for you if we meet again."

"Just in case we do, what is your name? I hate being threatened by strangers."

"Bastien. Cryille Bastien." He turned and began to walk away. "It was nice to meet you, Doctor. Have a nice wedding!"

"Don't be disappointed if you don't get an invitation!" Murph shouted at his back.

Cyrille just waved and kept walking away.

Chapter 39

Murph took a deep breath and climbed back into the Mustang. Steadying his hands, he continued down the tree lined street. He spotted Carli sitting on a bench in front of the library. She glanced quickly from side to side, then sharply leaned her head to indicate the man on her left. Murph waved casually as he pulled up. He jumped out of the car and ran around, opening the passenger door.

Carli seemed less scared than irritated. Murph went up to her, but spoke to the middle-aged man in the gray jacket sitting on the other end of the bench.

He spoke quietly, through clenched teeth, while smiling for the benefit of anyone looking, "I already talked to Cyrille. You can put away the gun and leave us alone!"

The man nodded but continued to sit.

Murph took Carli's hand. It was cold as ice. "Come on, honey. Let's go get dinner!"

He seated her in the car and closed the door. As Murph got in and started to pull away, Cyrille's *associate* rose from the bench. Another younger man emerged from the shadows of the building, looking like a student, his hands in the pockets of his sweatshirt. Murph couldn't resist flipping them the bird as he drove away.

He accelerated down Prospect Street, to Canal Road then raced across the Key Bridge, crossing the Potomac River into Virginia. He swerved suddenly onto the George Washington Memorial Parkway and was relieved to see that no one appeared to be following them. He pulled off at the first parking area and shut off the car in the shade of a tree.

Murph reached over and pulled Carli close. The tension released and she sobbed, breaking down and crying on his chest. He held her tight and kissed her hair.

"The last part of the drive was so much more pleasant without the goon in the back seat holding a gun to my head!"

She looked up at him. "Who were they?"

"I don't know. They are connected to the President. They had intercepted our texts—so they could be NSA." Murph spoke slowly as he continued to think. "The goon, Cyrille, didn't sound American. He was pale skinned and shaved bald with big buggy eyes, but a small head. He had huge arms—kind of a troll."

"When I came out of the library to wait for you, the kid in the sweatshirt asked if I knew what time it was. As I looked down at my phone, the older guy came up beside me and grabbed my arm. I could feel the gun in his pocket as he led me to the bench. He told me to sit and wait, but that's all he said. Sweatshirt disappeared, but he obviously only hid near the building."

"They had it all figured out. We can't use our phones anymore."

"What did they want?"

"Well, Cyrille wanted to shoot me, but someone higher up seems to think that we're too popular to get rid of that easily. He told me to forget everything that I thought I knew." Murph took her hand and squeezed it. "He told me not to be a hero—that's for the movies."

She sighed. "What have we gotten ourselves into?"

"We could do what they say and just forget it."

"Why would we do that? I don't have many pet peeves, but..."

Murph smiled, "but you can't stand anyone telling you that you can't do something!"

She nodded, her eyes narrowing. "We will not be intimidated."

Murph studied her face—her jaw firmly set, nostrils flaring, fire in her eyes—and burst out laughing. "The President has no idea what he's done!"

"When I get scared, I get really angry." She crossed her arms.

"Take it easy, Tiger. We'll get them, but I'm not letting you out of my sight." Murph started the car again and headed out into traffic, working his way back toward home. "We need to get out of Washington for a few days. We also need information. And when you need information, who do you call?"

"Rocco Meroni."

"Precisely. Time to visit our favorite Mafia informant."

Murph battled his way across the Potomac and headed for his condo. He activated the hands-free phone in the car and dialed Derek Whitman.

"Molar Airlines. Where would you like your magic carpet to go today, Dr. Murphy?" The voice was dripping with sarcasm.

"Hey, Derek. Get your lazy ass up and preflight the plane."

"Your wish is my command."

Despite the banter, Derek and Murph had been close friends since his time on *The Dental Apprentice*. Derek was the lead corporate pilot for the Center for Esthetic and Restorative Excellence, so technically Murph was his boss, but they kidded each other like brothers.

"Where do you want to go, Murph?"

"Rome. We need to visit some old friends."

"So...the lovely Carli will be joining us on this trip. This is getting sooo much better!"

Carli cut in. "I can hear you."

"Oh, sorry Carli. Didn't realize—well, err—how've you been?"

"I'm great Derek. Can't wait to see you."

"Sorry to break up the reunion, but I think we'll have some time to catch up." Murph tapped his watch.

"Yeah, about eight hours in the air—if I remember right. When do you want to leave?"

"How soon can you be ready to go?"

"It'll take me a couple of hours to ready the flight plan, get us gassed up, and bring Kurt out here."

"That's fine. We'll get packed and meet you at the hangar at Reagan Airport. I'll bring the sandwiches for the flight, just tell me what you want."

"Sounds good. No matter what they say, you're a great boss!"

Carli laughed and wrote down the order for Derek and Kurt, the copilot.

Murph cut off the phone call. They had a lot to do in the next couple of hours, but they both were used to traveling light and packing quickly.

After stops at each apartment, Murph ended at the Center, where he left the Mustang parked in the secured lot and dropped his keys on his desk. Margaret met them at the Center, where Murph and Carli explained what had happened in the last two days and their plans for the near future. Margaret wished them good luck and gave them each a hug.

Murray picked the couple up in the town car and whisked them out of DC. Sunset was turning the Washington Monument golden as the eastern sky darkened to purple as Murph and Carli arrived at the executive terminal at Reagan International Airport. With a wave, they left Murray and boarded the Gulfstream G550. White with burgundy stripes, it was the height of executive transportation. Smooth and fast, it would deliver them to Rome in style.

Kurt Anson folded the stairs and closed the door as Murph helped Carli settle in. The whine of the engines began as Derek's voice drawled over the speaker.

"Thank you for flying Molar Airlines. Please sit back and enjoy your eight-hour flight to Rome. You will also be enjoying a six-hour time change, so we will be arriving around noon—tomorrow—assuming we don't fall asleep up here—since we're flying all night. Kurt, you brought the coffee, right? What, no coffee? Oh, boy, Houston, we have a problem."

Murph keyed his intercom, chucking, "Cut the comedy and just fly, OK?"

"Oh, fine. Everyone's a critic. Just remember, don't complain to us about the bumps!"

With that, they were off, heading east into the darkness.

Chapter 40

The door opened suddenly, catching him completely off guard. She had never come in the evening. *Something is happening,* he thought to himself. He was in the kitchen, pouring himself a glass of orange juice, so he poured another one for her as well and came out to greet her.

"Good evening! Can I interest you in a glass of juice?"

"Thank you, Colonel."

He walked to the kitchen table and placed her glass down. He pulled out a chair for her and she perched herself on the front edge. He sat down across from her and took a sip of the juice.

"It's late for you. Something special to talk about today?"

"Nothing important," she purred. Her raven hair was loose tonight, not pulled back in its usual ponytail. She also wore heavier makeup and had a necklace and earrings on. "I'm curious about how you know the dentist, Dr. Murphy."

That startled him. "I have no idea what you are talking about." He had been trying to anticipate her questions, figuring out where she as trying to go. This one came completely from left field.

"Dr. Michael Murphy. Do you know him?"

He searched his memory, trying to see any danger here. "No."

"He was on American TV. They call him Murph." She was becoming insistent.

"Maybe. My wife watched that *Dental Apprentice* reality show. I think he may have been on it?"

"Did Dr. Murphy ever do fillings on you in the service, or take out your wisdom teeth?"

"No. My wisdom teeth were taken out in high school. I haven't had a filling in years."

She stood up so abruptly that her chair fell over. She stormed out the door, leaving it lying on its back. He sat there dumbfounded, staring at the door as it slammed shut and the heavy locks clicked home.

Chapter 41

The phone rang quietly so Johnson, the butler, answered it quickly. "Yes, Sir." He nodded involuntarily. "Yes, I will get him."

Simon Cohen was in his usual spot for the early evening, sound asleep sitting upright in his desk chair. Johnson had only to touch him lightly on the shoulder and he was instantly awake.

Cohen turned and considered Johnson. The butler extended his hand, supporting the phone in his palm. "Mr. Bastien, Sir."

Cohen snatched up the phone. "Yes, Cyrille?"

"I spoke with Doctor Murphy earlier. He is not easily frightened."

"That is what concerns me."

"I should have eliminated him."

"No. He has done nothing directly to endanger our plans. I respect his abilities."

"He cares deeply for the girl. She gives us leverage."

Cohen thought a moment. "That is something to remember." He ended the call and set down the phone. The billionaire tapped his fingers together and stared into the distance. The TV was on in the background, CNN muted, the close captioning adding to the general chaos of information on the screen.

Without looking back, Cohen said, "Scotch."

As Johnson prepared the glass at the bar, the phone rang again.

Cohen reached down, smiling when he recognized the incoming call. He touched the screen to answer, but said nothing.

"Mr. Cohen?" The voice was melodious.

"Hello, Ariella. It is always so nice to hear your voice."

"Thank you, Sir." She paused slightly, but when he didn't respond, she continued. "I have spoken with the Colonel."

"Yes?"

"He knows nothing. He has excellent dental health. His wisdom teeth were removed before he attended the Air Force Academy."

"Thank you."

"I'm sorry that I couldn't get the information you wanted about the dentist."

"No, indeed. You have confirmed my fears. He is not a government agent. It is merely bad luck." He took a sip of the scotch. "The fates have conspired to add a random factor to challenge our plans." He took another drink. "Thank you for your service."

"It was my pleasure," Ariella said. "Will I be seeing you soon?"

"That is unclear. I will be there before the end, but for now, it remains to be seen what role Dr. Murphy has to play in our little show. I must stay here to direct." Cohen touched the phone to end the call. He took another sip of scotch and continued to stare into the distance, lost in his thoughts, long into the night.

Chapter 42

The Gulfstream jet cut smoothly through the European sky. They were still an hour away from arrival when Derek Whitman left the cockpit to rouse his passengers.

He found them sound asleep in the plush leather seats on opposite sides of the center aisle. Carli was curled up in a ball, buried in a blanket Murph had thrown over her. Murph was stretched out. His long legs extending as far as possible, his head was back with his mouth open. Derek suppressed a laugh.

He reached out his hand and touched Murph on the shoulder. Instantly awake, Murph touched his lips with his finger. "Shh."

Derek nodded. "About an hour. You can freshen up and be ready before landing." He headed back to the controls.

"Thanks."

Murph stretched his arms, hearing his neck and shoulder pop and crack. He ducked his head and went back to the galley. He started the coffee maker and poured orange juice from the fridge. He came back and kissed Carli on the forehead, the only exposed skin in the bundle of blankets. "Wake up, sleepy. Almost there."

She stretched like a cat, pushing the blankets off. She ran her fingers through her hair and collected it into a ponytail, securing it with an elastic cloth that she had kept on her wrist.

Carli accepted the steaming cup of coffee; cream and sugar, just the way she preferred. "Mmm. Excellent. Thanks."

"Derek says we have about an hour. We set the flight plan to arrive at Ciampino Airport, which is the small executive airport in Rome. We can take a taxi into the city."

"Probably a good idea not to use your phone to call any friends."

"Yeah. I thought so." Murph took a gulp of the coffee. "I'm sure they know we are going to Rome, since I told Derek that on the phone intentionally. But I don't want to advertise what we are going to do when we get there. Rome feels like home for me, and I want to use that advantage."

"Well, we had better get ready. I'm sure I look hell."

"Actually, I think you look fantastic." Murph reached over, laughing. "Especially with the blanket fuzz in your hair."

"Really!" She slapped his hand away playfully.

Carli went into the bathroom and freshened her makeup and brushed out her auburn hair. She looked ready for anything, in silver sandals, white slacks, denim shirt and a scarf.

Murph had prepared breakfast. They ate quickly then he shaved and dressed as well. It was the customary look for

Murph in Rome; black loafers and slacks, white oxford shirt and a grey sweater. Out of habit, he stocked the backpack with two water bottles and several granola bars. Carli looked at him. He shrugged. "You never know when we may get hungry."

The Gulfstream had begun its descent and the familiar landscape of verdant green hills bordered by the deep blue of the Mediterranean filled the window. Murph sat down and stared out as Carli came over and leaned on his back, placing her chin on his shoulder so she could see as well. Murph had spent a semester in Rome while in college at Ohio State, and he had visited several times since then. He spoke Italian well and loved the culture. For him, it was a city filled with friends.

It was a crystal clear day in the Eternal City. Their landing pattern carried them over the city itself, the monuments spread out across the Seven Hills of Rome. The cupola of Saint Peter's Basilica passed beside the jet, and Murph sighed. Carli squeezed her arms around him.

"It draws me here, like coming home."

"I know." She agreed. "You are at peace here. One of these days, we'll get to relax, and you'll show me around. Every time we come here, we're in a rush."

"Sadly, this time is no different." Murph nestled his head against her neck. "We need answers, and we need them fast."

The jet touched down smoothly and taxied to the Executive Terminal. Derek shut down the engines and opened the door. "How long will you be here?"

"I'm not really sure." Murph hated to be vague with his old friend, but he really didn't know. "You and Kurt can hang out for a while unless Margaret sends you somewhere else. I'll call you when I get a better idea."

"Sounds good to me. We need a day to rest anyway before we can go. I like Rome. Lots to see and the food's good." He shook Murph's hand and they embraced. "You two have fun—and don't go getting into any trouble this time."

"Yes, Dear." They all laughed.

Murph and Carli took their travel bags into the terminal and presented their passports to the Italian Customs agent waiting inside. The agent began asking about their plans while in Rome in a cool, efficient manner. When Murph answered in fluent Italian, the agent brightened considerably. They chatted easily about Rome, and Murph received suggestions on a new restaurant to try near the Spanish Steps.

The agent examined their bags and had nearly cleared them when his supervisor came over. Capitano Dalia Liriano was a stout, matronly woman who clearly took her duty to protect the borders of Italy seriously.

"Momento, Doctor Murphy." She held up her hand.

Murph introduced himself and Carli in Italian, but Liriano stepped closer.

"I will speak in English, so Miss Caroline can understand without translation."

"Thank you, Capitano." Carli appreciated the gesture.

"Is there a problem?" Murph wondered.

"No. You are always welcome in Rome. Especially a guest whose Italian is as exemplary as yours. How long did you study in Rome?"

"A semester in college, but I have also been here a number of times since then."

"It appears that you continue to practice."

"My mother is Italian, and my grandparents were born here. I do try to keep up."

Capitano Liriano smiled warmly. "I have no orders to stop you. I will give you a bit of information though." She reached out and held Murph's wrist. "We were instructed to inform the US Government upon your arrival. We have also been asked to tell them when you leave and where you are going."

"Is that unusual?" Carli tried to sound curious, fighting her growing sense of alarm.

"Unusual, but not remarkable in itself. We receive warnings about the arrival of travelers every day." She measured them both with her eyes. "What is odd is that the request did not come from your State Department. I was given a special contact number at the White House. It makes me wonder…"

Murph felt a chill up his spine as her grip tightened on his wrist.

"What would make the President take an interest in the travel plans of a simple dentist and his fiancé?"

"I have no idea, Capitano. We are here to visit old friends at the Vatican."

"Please be careful, Dr. Murphy. Rome is a beautiful city, but it can have a dark side. Try to stay in the light." She released his arm and waved them through.

Chapter 43

Murph led Carli quickly out of the terminal. He found a phone just outside the door and dialed the direct line for Father Albers. Murph's prayers were answered when the priest answered right away.

"Michael. It is so good to hear your voice."

"Thank you, Father. I appreciate hearing yours as well ... more than you know." Murph's heart was still pounding. "Carli and I just arrived in Rome. Much like the last time, we have arrived suddenly and in some distress."

"Michael, my son. Sanctuary is always given at the home of Saint Peter to those faithful who but ask for it. Present yourselves at the gate and the Swiss Guards will bring you straight to me. I will have rooms made ready for you to spend the night."

"Thank you, Father. As usual, we have a tale to tell."

"Then I will have dinner prepared. Your old friend Father Mahoney loves a good story as well as I do—and he thinks better on a full stomach." The priest laughed. "I will let him know you are here."

"Thank you. We will see you later this afternoon."

Murph hung up the phone and hailed a cab for them. He gave an address not far from the Vatican and the taxi sped off toward central Rome. They clattered over the cobblestone streets, across the Piazza dei Quinti, and onto Via Germanico, pulling up in front of a simple wooden door. Above the entrance, the sign proclaimed *The Clevelander*.

Murph paid the driver and pushed open the door, entering the dark interior. Their eyes fought to adjust to the dim light, but before the bar became visible, the booming voice of Rocco Meroni projected from behind the heavy wooden bar.

"I'd know that silhouette anywhere. Welcome home, Murph!"

Where Murph was long and lean, Rocco was stout, but built like a bull. He came around the bar and hugged Murph like a bear, lifting him off the ground like he was a child. He turned to Carli and enveloped her, the hug nearly knocking the wind out of her.

"Carli too. What a special occasion!" He stepped back and looked them over, remarking quietly, "Of course, this means that something evil is afoot."

Murph started to protest, "Well, it's not really that bad..."

Rocco ushered them to a booth in the back of the bar. The crowd was small now that it was after lunch. The TV's had the live feed of the Cleveland Indians on. The Tribe was at home playing the hated Yankees. The walls of the *Clevelander* were covered with pennants and jerseys of the Cleveland Indians, Browns and Cavaliers.

Rocco and Murph had been friends for years. They had graduated from rival high schools in Cleveland, Murph from St. Ignatius and Rocco from St. Edward, but had come to Rome together for a semester in college. While Murph loved Rome, Rocco had fallen in love in Rome. He had married an Italian girl and never left. *The Clevelander* was his little bit of home and had been a refuge for Murph and Carli in the past.

Rocco let them settle into the red leather bench and returned with a chilled glass of Pinot Grigio for Carli and a frosted mug of beer for Murph.

"No Guinness for you. It's too early in the day for a heavy beer."

"Thanks." Murph eyed the amber liquid and enjoyed a sip. "Excellent lager. What is this one?"

Rocco said, "Peroni Gran Riserva. I thought you would like it."

Carli sipped the wine and smiled. "Thanks, Rocco. You are always a marvelous host."

"It's easy to be gracious for a beautiful woman." He pulled a chair over to the end of the table and settled in to talk. "So, what brings you two back to Rome?"

Murph had been considering this during the flight. Rocco was far more than the humble bar owner that he seemed to be. Murph knew that he was connected to the Mafia and suspected that the ties led fairly high up, considering his lifestyle far exceeded that of a simple barkeep. If he wanted information, Murph needed to begin with the truth.

Lowering his voice so that it became hard to distinguish in the background hum of the bar, Murph quickly laid out the basics of what they knew and what they suspected. "In the end, we have the evidence of the President not being who he claims to be, but we don't know to what purpose."

Carli added, "I was looking to see if there had been any major change in legislation since President Buchanan took office, but the Executive Branch has not launched any new initiatives and is not lobbying for any current legislation in Congress. There have been no significant Executive Orders signed, and he has proposed no candidates for confirmation. It appears that nothing is going on domestically."

Rocco considered the story, rubbing the stubble on his chin with a massive hand. "Wow. That's quite a bedtime story. You should write a movie!"

"But we don't know the ending." Murph shook his head sadly. "What we want to find out is who is influencing the President? Is there someone who has his ear or would benefit from access to the White House?"

Carli leaned in, closer to Rocco. "I think there's a good chance that the secret has to do with foreign policy. That's why we're here."

Rocco flashed a broad grin. "Then you've come to the right place. I'll check with my sources and see if I can shed some light on this."

Murph reached out and grabbed Rocco's burly forearm. "Thanks, my friend."

Rocco laughed, rolling from deep in his barrel chest, "It's not for you. I mean, we're old friends and all—but this one," he patted Carli's hand, "I told you before, she's a keeper. Anything for her."

Murph reached across the table, took Carli's hand, and showed Rocco the engagement ring on her finger.

Rocco kept laughing, "Finally ... I mean congratulations. It took you long enough!"

"That seems to be the general opinion," Murph deadpanned. "But you're married! And Sofia is so lovely."

"True enough." Rocco agreed. "We're even then. We both have exactly what we want. And I'll get you the information you need."

"We're going to visit with Father Albers for dinner."

"Invitations to dine at the Vatican. You two are special!" Rocco went over behind the bar and reached into a cabinet. He selected a bottle of wine and returned. "Give this to Father Albers for you to enjoy with your meal."

Murph studied the label. "Giacomo Conterno Barolo Monfortino?"

"It's the longest aging Italian wine. Native Italian nebbiolo grapes, aged in casks for many years. A deep, mineral flavor with wildberry and spices. It's one of his favorites."

"Thank you. It sounds fantastic." Murph carefully placed the bottle in his backpack.

"You won't be disappointed." Rocco looked back as a group of customers came through the door. "Well, back to work for me. I'll call you when I know something."

Murph stood up and leaned closer to Rocco. "Don't call my phone. They're reading our texts and intercepting our calls. The NSA is under the control of the White House, so I can't use anything that would put us on the grid. I'll call you here in a couple days."

Rocco nodded. "Good luck!"

Chapter 44

Murph and Carli left the darkened interior of *The Clevelander* and were nearly blinded by the bright sunlight of late afternoon. Murph pulled her back into the shadow of the building and started to hail a cab.

Carli held his hand down. "Let's walk. It's only eight blocks, if I remember right."

"We do have more luggage with us than last time," he gestured at their roller bags.

"It's such a beautiful afternoon and I would love to enjoy the sights this time!"

"Your wish is my command." Murph took her by the hand and they set off up the narrow Via Germanico.

The last time they had been in Rome, they had run the distance to the Vatican, being pursued by Arab gunmen out to capture them. Murph led Carli on a leisurely stroll this afternoon and narrated his tour of the Via Terenzio. They approached the grey shadow of the walls of the Castel Sant' Angelo. The circular fortress, once the tomb of the Roman Emperor Hadrian, sat on the bank of the Tiber River and provided a scenic approach from the center of Rome to Vatican City.

Carli noticed the statue mounted at the highest point of the castle. "Who is that, looking down at us?"

Murph smiled. "The Archangel Michael, my namesake. Legend has it that Pope Gregory had a vision of the angel, standing atop Hadrian's Tomb, sheathing his bloody sword, which signaled the end of the plague in Rome. The Pope had the statue erected and changed the name to Castel Sant' Angelo, Castle of the Holy Angel."

"I do feel safe here," Carli mused.

They continued their journey and entered the Via della Conciliazione; four lanes wide and all traffic moving in one direction—toward Vatican City. The six-story tan and yellow buildings glowed cheerfully in the warm Italian sun. The sidewalks were filled with pedestrians, and tour busses moved about, while Vespa scooters dodged between them.

Murph tugged Carli's arm and led her along the sandstone columns of the streetlights, 30 feet above them. Palm trees swayed in the light breeze. Their pace slowed, walking almost mesmerized, drawn toward Saint Peter's Basilica. They moved into the square through the pass created by the cream and white buildings that bordered the gateway to the Holy City. Saint Peter's Square was really a circle at its entrance, with the spokes centering on the red granite Obelisco Vaticano placed in the middle of the piazza by Bernini in 1586. Stopping in the shadow of the obelisk, Carli slid under Murph's arm. He held her tight and they turned slowly around, marveling at the sights, statues of the saints, standing atop the walls, looking down, studying the faithful as they scurried across the sea of cobblestones.

Sighing, Carli leaned her head against his chest. "I could stay here all day."

"I know. I always feel that way when I'm here. But we have an appointment for dinner!"

Murph led her toward the Fontana Maderno, its waters cascading into the white granite basin, overheated tourists standing down wind to cool off in the spray. The boundaries of the square were colossal Tuscan colonnades, four columns deep. In the corner of the square, Murph aimed for the opening in the barrier between the last pillars of the Colonnato del Bernini, passing into the shadows of the Palazzo Apostolico.

Across the garden, up a short flight of stairs, stood a double door, flanked by two Swiss Guards in their renaissance uniforms of blue, red, orange, and yellow striped tunics, topped with a black beret. They stared down coldly at Murph and Carli, who looked for all the world like lost tourists, trailing luggage.

Much to the guard's surprise, Murph addressed them in flawless Italian, informing them of their appointment with Father Albers and asking to see the priest at the registration desk for admittance. The guards remained impassive, but one opened the door and held it for them.

Approaching the desk, Murph explained their appointment to the older priest manning the entrance. He rubbed his glasses and considered the request. Before he could dial the phone, a booming voice came down the hallway and everyone turned.

"Michael, me boy! And Caroline, as well." Short and round, with a ruddy complexion and a large nose, Father Brian Mahoney looked every bit the Irish country friar. His easygoing, jovial manner brought life to the dreariest event, and he was a prized guest for dinner, always having a joke or tall tale to tell.

Carli ran over and gave him a huge hug, much to the disapproval of the registrar. Murph greeted his old teacher with a firm handshake and embrace as well.

"Hi, Father. Thanks for meeting us!"

"Michael, I wouldn't miss it for the world." He arranged for their luggage to be taken to their rooms and led them deeper into the Vatican. "I can't wait to hear the rest of your story. I asked Albers, but the killjoy is so sparse with words that I barely get the facts out of him. He doesn't have the blarney in him!"

"Oh, I don't know." Carli offered. "He can tell a story when he wants to."

"Ha! You obviously haven't spent enough time with me!"

Murph agreed. "We're not in a rush this time, so we can enjoy your hospitality tonight. I want to hear what you've been up to here in Rome."

"Nothing compared to your mummy quest." Father Mahoney walked with them through the Vatican apartments and up to the private quarters of the senior Vatican clerics.

"And that Elvis thing! I did see the video." He clapped Murph on the back heartily. "Don't quit your day job, me boy. You'll starve." Both Carli and the priest laughed at his discomfort, and eventually Murph joined in.

Reaching the top of the stairs, they crossed a polished marble hallway and reached a heavy wooden door, banded with iron. The brass nameplate proclaimed:

Rev. Lawrence Albers
Director
Bibliotheca Apostolica Vaticana

"He has come a long way since being your teacher." Father Mahoney became serious.

Murph agreed. "Yes, my junior year in high school seems a long time ago."

"Books are the least of his duties these days. He has a team of investigators working for him. He is now in charge of special projects for the Pope."

Murph stepped to the door, raised his hand, and rapped crisply, twice, on the door.

"Enter!" came the muffled voice from beyond.

Murph reached down and opened the latch, pushing open the heavy weight of the door. They crossed the threshold into the inner sanctum of both an old friend and one of the most powerful men in Rome.

Chapter 45

Murph entered the room first, with Carli and Father Mahoney trailing behind. It was a large space, enough for a massive mahogany conference table surrounded by twelve high-backed green leather chairs. The far wall was cut by two sets of French doors that opened onto the balcony. The doors stood ajar, cream linen drapes hanging limp in the heavy summer air.

"I am glad that you can join me for dinner, but I must say that I'm surprised to see you in Rome so soon."

Father Albers rose from behind an imposing cherry desk, which bisected the end of the room opposite the table. He looked fatigued at the end of a long day, still in his black shirt and slacks, but his white priest's collar lay on his desk and his shirt collar was open.

"Hello, Father. Thank you for your invitation. I always appreciate your hospitality." Murph met him in the middle of the room and shook his hand.

Carli burst past Murph and gave the priest a warm embrace and a kiss on the cheek. He smiled and visibly relaxed.

"Let us enjoy our dinner—and talk of why you are here in such a rush."

Murph reached into his backpack and pulled out the wine. "Before I forget, I have a gift for you from Rocco Meroni. He said it was one of your favorites."

Father Albers studied the bottle and nodded. "Indeed it is. I enjoy the subtle flavors that come from its age. Time allows the notes of berry and spices to mature and blend. Like many things, time permits a richness to develop and we can discover the nuances if we have the patience to examine it well."

"Oh, I don't know." Father Mahoney shook his head, "I rather prefer a good beer, vintage this month. Wine's too much work."

They all laughed and settled in at the table.

"Father Albers," Murph indulged a question that had been nagging at him, "how do you know Rocco?"

"Like you, when you were here, I grow nostalgic occasionally and need to reconnect with Cleveland. I go to *The Clevelander* sometimes for a touch of home."

"I know that Rocco is easy to talk to," Carli followed Murph's lead. "That must make you feel comfortable."

"Rocco is a much better listener. It is his greatest talent." Albers looked at Carli and she averted her eyes downward. "Yes, your suspicions are right. Rocco is an excellent source of accurate information, which I find valuable as an outsider in a city historically known for intrigue."

"I'm sorry, Father." Murph interjected. "We don't mean to pry..."

"No offense, my son." He smiled sadly. "My days here seem to be filled with ferreting out information and managing secrets. I look forward to your visits. As old friends, we can be open with one another. We go back to another time, when life was simpler." He took off his glasses and rubbed them with his napkin. "But enough of my challenges, tell me what brings you to Rome!"

Murph took the wine from the priest and proceeded to open it and share it around. While the meal was served, Murph and Carli filled Father Mahoney in on the rest of the mummy's tale and the proposal. After a couple of glasses of wine, Murph even favored them with a short rendition of *Only Fools Rush In*.

As they sat back from the table filled with chicken marsala, potatoes and salad, Father Albers called for coffee and biscotti and then released his butler, Fernando, for the night.

As the door closed, Murph focused on the task at hand, detailing the discovery of the Presidential imposter, sharing the x-rays as evidence. Carli laid out their plan to research changes in policy within the administration.

"Very scary!" was Father Mahoney's assessment.

"Indeed." Father Albers had perked up with the discussion and the puzzle that now lay before them. "I believe that you are on the right path. If you find what there is to gain, then you can identify who is behind the plot."

"That's why we're here." Murph closed his computer with a click. "The Vatican is a state unto itself, so I'm sure there are people here who monitor foreign policy around the world. I have to believe that there has been some change in US

142

policy in the last few weeks—since the inauguration of President Buchanan—that would indicate who stands to benefit."

The librarian nodded. "I will make some discreet inquiries tomorrow." He pointed across the table, "However, it appears that we have lost Father Mahoney—Brian!"

The priest had been fast asleep, with his chin resting on his chest, hands folded in his lap. With the mention of his name, his eyes snapped open. "Why yes, I agree!"

Carli reached over and patted him on the shoulder. "That's OK, Father. I'm tired too."

"Well then, we can discuss our plan for tomorrow over breakfast…"

But before Father Albers could finish the sentence, there was a rapid knock on the door and it burst open. A middle-aged priest charged into the room and approached Father Albers.

"Excuse' please, Father."

He was shorter than Murph, medium build with black, curly hair and a narrow, tightly trimmed moustache under his nose and angled to the corner of his mouth, right over his upper lip. His coal black eyes were darting around the room.

"I have found him!"

Father Albers held up his hand and the priest stopped. "Manners—Allow me to introduce another of my assistants—Father Salvatore Falcone."

Falcone quickly shook hands with Murph and Carli, then looked expectantly at Father Albers.

"Now, Father Sal, what was it you were dying to tell us?"

The words burst out in a torrent, "I have found him! We were looking for any clues and found a thread. I traced it back and he's alive!" Sal clapped his hands together as if that settled everything. "And I know where he is!"

Murph looked at him, exasperated, "Who's alive?"

"Father Gaspard, of course!"

Carli gasped. "The priest who led all the children out of Nazi occupied France?"

143

"Si, signora!" He nodded vigorously.

Murph frowned, "but he would have to be a 100 years old!"

"Ninety-eight!" Sal grinned. "He is being cared for in the monastery Sacra di San Michele."

Father Albers walked back to his desk and touched his computer mouse, bringing the monitor to life. "Hmm. Saint Michael's Abbey is in the Susa valley, near Turin."

"Si." Father Sal moved closer to Albers. "I want to go question him quickly. They say his health is poor. But he only speaks French!" Sal looked defeated.

"But I speak fluent French," Carli offered.

"Ahh, Signore. Thank you!"

Murph contemplated the map on the computer. "That looks like quite a ways from here."

"Indeed. It is about six hours by car." Father Albers picked up the phone on his desk and dialed, "That means you will need to get an early start tomorrow." He arranged for a car to be ready by 7:00 a.m.

Murph stood there with his mouth open—then shut it with a snap. "I know when I've been had."

Carli laughed. "It will be a nice adventure. Father Albers needs a day to check on things for us here, and I've never seen the Alps."

"True enough. I've heard a lot about the Piedmont Region of Italy, but I've never been there either." He considered Father Sal. "I guess you have two companions for your trip."

"Bellisimo! I have much to prepare. Thank you, Father." He bowed slightly and was gone as quickly as he had come.

Father Albers left the desk and put his arms around Murph and Carli. "I appreciate your willingness to go with Father Falcone. He is a dogged researcher, but very head-strong and direct. He lacks your *people skills*, as it were. I feel much better knowing that you two will be with him."

Carli agreed with enthusiasm, "I'm glad to be going. I never thought I would be able to meet someone like Father Gaspard, and I can't wait to hear what he has to say. His

144

memories need to be chronicled to add to the oral history of the war."

"He's 98. He may not remember much."

"Oh, Murph. Think positively. Besides, it will be a beautiful drive."

"That's the part I'm looking forward to."

Then we must get you two some rest." Father Albers led them to the door. "Father Mahoney will show you to your rooms. Your luggage has been placed in each one for you. Sleep well and I will see you off in the morning."

"Thank you, Father, for an interesting evening."

Murph couldn't help wondering if Father Sal's sudden entrance had really been such an unexpected surprise. He had learned over the years to be skeptical of coincidences.

Chapter 46

Morning came quickly for Murph. The gray hint of dawn had begun to color his window when he rose from bed and prepared for the day. After a quick shower, he dressed for travel. Murph always tried to not to look like a tourist, so he began by thinking like an Italian.

The first thing Italians look at is your shoes and then the quality of the fabrics. Italians are very fashion conscious, but they also are highly respectful of traditions and customs. Since their journey would end at an abbey, Murph selected conservative clothing. Black leather loafers, black silk slacks, and a charcoal gray linen shirt—long sleeves and open collar. He decided to leave his computer and backpack here at the Vatican with Father Albers, but packed a small overnight bag.

Coming down into Father Albers's office, he found that Father Mahoney and Carli had already arrived. Carli looked every bit the Italian maiden in skinny designer jeans with peach camisole and gray linen jacket, so that her shoulders were covered when entering the church. Her sandals were stylish. She had avoided the American preference for flip-flops that so irritated the locals. Her makeup was minimal, looking natural, accentuating her golden complexion with a hint of eye color and lipgloss. With her hair pulled back into a ponytail, she was relaxed and ready.

Murph ran over and gave Carli a quick peck on the cheek. Father Albers had arranged a light breakfast, and Father Sal joined them for the meal. As they were finishing, Bernardo entered carrying a large manila packing envelope.

He handed the envelope to Father Albers and whispered something to him.

Father Albers gestured for Bernardo to give Murph the package. "Michael, this has just been delivered for you."

Murph took it and opened the seal. He reached in and removed two iPhones and an iPad mini, which was protected in a lime green case.

Murph handed the iPad to Carli, "By the color, I assume this is for you!"

He turned on the phones. The first one powered up with a beautiful screen photo of the Trevi Fountain. The other phone had a background picture of the green and yellow Eagle mascot of Cleveland St. Edward High School.

Carli laughed. "Well, I guess we know who these came from!"

"That Rocco is always such a funny guy! Remind me to send him something with the Ignatius Wildcat on it." Murph quickly activated the phone's camera. Carli tilted her head and flashed a movie-star smile. Murph snapped the picture and made it his background. "Much better!"

Father Albers sat there smiling, while Sal looked befuddled. The Jesuit priest leaned over to him and whispered, "Old high school rivalry."

Sal said, "Oh, I see." But it was clear that he didn't see.

Murph scanned the contact numbers in the phone. There were no names he recognized. On a hunch, he selected Bella, and Carli's phone rang.

"In case these phones are lost, the contact info appears unconnected to us. You were listed as Bella, or beautiful. I'm trying to find Rocco."

Carli consulted her phone. Her contacts included a Doctor and a Dentist. She touched Dentist and Murph's phone rang. "That wasn't very original."

They both scanned the contacts for a minute before Carli looked up. "There is a contact for *The Clevelander* with the right address and primary phone number. There's also one that says Ed Eagle."

Murph examined his screen. "I have the same contact. Let's try it." He touched the secondary phone number.

Immediately, the phone was answered by Rocco's voice. "Yeah, I know. You won the bet. Indians beat the Yankees 4 to 2, Salazar got the win, and Kipnis had a walk-off homer. You won all three parts. Just come in tomorrow, and I'll give you what I promised you."

Murph managed a quick, "Thanks," as the line went dead. He shrugged his shoulders.

"In case someone was listening, he sounds like a bookie," Carli offered. "We have to go in person tomorrow to 'get what he promised' I guess."

Father Albers rose from the table. "You now have phones and a tablet computer that are not connected in any way to you, so if you keep your communications guarded, you may stay off the grid and out of sight."

The priest went to his desk and took out an envelope. He withdrew 1000 euro in smaller bills and gave them to Murph. "Don't use your credit cards unless you have to. You should be back tomorrow. There is a guest hostel at the abbey where they will put you up for the night."

Both Murph and Carli thanked Father Albers profusely but he dismissed it. "You are going on an errand for me. Please find out what you can, take Father Gaspard's statement, and then come back."

He led them down into the courtyard of the priest's residence of the Vatican, where Father Sal had pulled up in a black Fiat 500. Murph and Carli stopped in their tracks.

Sal jumped out of the tiny, egg-shaped car and ran around to open the passenger door, leaning the front seat forward to allow Carli to enter the back.

Under his breath, Murph asked Carli, "Does he realize that I'm 6' 2"?"

"Hey, I'm only five feet tall and that back seat looks tight."

Father Albers patted them on the shoulder and gently shoved them toward the car.

Carli slid into the back behind the driver, turning her legs to the side to fit. Murph positioned the passenger seat as far back as he could and folded himself into the car as Sal closed the door. Father Albers patted the roof of the car and Sal engaged the clutch. They shot out of the courtyard, through the gate and into the early morning traffic of Rome.

Chapter 47

Sal proved to be an excellent driver, moving swiftly north, from Rome to Florence and then to the coast. They bordered the Mediterranean from Pisa to Genoa, then raced toward the mountains, climbing to Turin. They traveled west of Turin, stopping in the little village of Avigliana for lunch.

Sal stopped to fill the fuel tank. Murph unfolded himself from the car and reached in to help Carli out. He stretched to his full height and lifted his arms over his head, locking his hands together and pulling, feeling a satisfying pop from his shoulders and neck.

"Now I know what one of those origami birds feels like."

Carli lightly punched him in the shoulder. "Quit your whining. It's been a beautiful drive."

"True enough. Let's see if we can get something from the locals." Murph gestured to Sal that he would get their lunch and Sal nodded.

Murph and Carli walked into the town square and entered a few local shops. With Murph's command of Italian, it was quick work to buy what they needed. Fifteen minutes later, Murph was being treated like a long-lost son of the village.

They walked out to where Sal had parked the car and was sitting on the grass. Carli turned to Murph as they walked. "You never cease to amaze me."

Murph looked down at the bag in one arm and bottle in the other. "What? Cheese, bread, summer sausage, excellent local wine? Lunch like an Italian!"

Sal was impressed. "You eat like a local, not like an American tourist. You speak the language and are polite and respectful, especially of the elderly. It is no wonder they love you." He tore off a hunk of bread and produced glasses from the back of the Fiat as Murph opened the red wine. "It doesn't hurt your cause that Carli is gorgeous, you know!"

Carli blushed. "I know," Murph agreed, then continued in a mock hushed tone, "but don't let her find out, it will go to her head."

She reached out and whacked him. He feigned injury, but poured the wine anyway.

They enjoyed lunch in the summer sun in much the same way that travelers had for centuries. Avigliana sat along the road from Turin to France. The "new" town had been built in the 12th century on the ruins of the old town. For the modern population of around twelve thousand, little had changed. Pilgrims still traveled the road through the Susa valley from France to Turin.

"How close are we?" Murph hated to break the peaceful rest, but he knew they still had a job to do.

Sal thought a minute. "About 20 minutes. It should be 10 km."

149

Carli wondered, "That's six miles. Why so long?"

Sal pointed in the distance, "Because we are going up there!"

Across the valley, in the distance, they could make out a massive stone structure on the peak of the mountain. The leafy green of the trees on the mountainsides made a perfect back-drop to spot the yellow stone of the abbey. It appeared to be perched precariously on the edge of a cliff.

Sal pointed to the lake below the city where they sat in Avigliana. "We have to go around Lago Grande and then climb. The road bends around so we can make it up the side of the mountain, just like the horses did years ago."

"How high up is the abbey?" Murph was amazed. "I can't believe they built that structure up there starting in the 10th century!"

"It is a miracle. Sacra di San Michele is over 3,000 feet up from the valley floor. At the peak of Mount Pirchiriano, it has a commanding view of the entire Susa valley."

They reluctantly packed up their meal and climbed into the Fiat again. As Sal again attacked the narrow, twisting roads, he began the tale of Sacra di San Michele.

"The original church was a Benedictine monastery, founded in 983 C.E. Legend has it that Saint Michael, the Archangel, appeared to a hermit in a dream and told him to build a church on this spot. It really is one of the greatest

150

construction achievements of the Middle Ages. Thousands of tons of rock were hauled on the backs of donkeys from the valley below. It was one of the most important religious sites in Europe as it was crucial as a stop on the Christian pilgrimage route from England, France, and Spain through the Alps to Rome.

"The original monastery has crumbled over the years, but the main church sanctuary dates from the 13th century and is an excellent example of the transition from Romanesque to Gothic design."

As Sal concentrated on a particularly nasty hairpin turn, Carli added, "that's right. Churches were major construction projects that continued in stages for generations. Over time, the styles would change and the architecture adapted as they went on building."

Sal accelerated on a straightaway, talking as fast as he was driving. "One part of the old monastery that still exists is a staircase known as the *Scalone di Morti*, the stairway of the dead. It was called that because the niches and alcoves beside the stairs contained the skeletons of the earliest monks, entombed in the walls, buried so they were visible."

Carli shuddered. "Even to an archeologist, some customs are really creepy!"

Sal laughed. "The monks in the last couple hundred years agreed with you, so they covered them up."

Murph was thrown against the door as the tires squealed, barely making it around a corner. Looking down the sheer cliff, he blurted out, "Jesus, Mary, and Joseph!"

"Pray for us!" Sal chuckled.

"No offense," Murph asked, "but what was your profession before the priesthood? Taxi driver?"

"No. I am the son of a farmer." Sal answered innocently enough, "I grew up in this valley and went to school in Turin." He shifted to a lower gear, the engine straining as the road became even steeper. "At the top of the stairway of the dead of is an archway, the Zodiac Door. It is surrounded by frescoes, scenes from the Old Testament. The opening is etched with

151

signs of the Zodiac on the doorframe. It symbolizes the passage from earth to the heavens. Through the arch is an open terrace with the most wonderful view of the Alps in all Italy. You are so high that it is as if you can touch the sky."

Murph could see the vertical wall of the abbey extending up from the sheer rock face of the mountain. "They built it that way so as to be as near to God as possible. Shorter distance for their prayers!"

"It's breathtaking!" Carli's eyes were wide with excitement.

"That terrace is part of one of the most interesting legends of the abbey." Sal was telling bedtime stories now, as his mother had told him. "A young maiden, Alda the beautiful, had taken refuge at the abbey to avoid the amorous attentions of a local Lord. He sent his soldiers to Sacra di San Michele to bring her to him. She threw herself from the monastery tower to protect herself from capture, but angels saved her and returned her safely to the ground."

Murph laughed. "I love old stories like that."

"Wait—that's not how it ends. But when she boasted about her rescue and attempted to jump again, the angels refused to protect her and she plunged to her death."

"That certainly changes the moral of the story. Scripture says you should not test God."

"Exactly." Sal nodded, never taking his eyes off the road. "The monastery fell into decline and there were only three monks remaining in 1622 when it was abandoned. It was reopened in 1835 by the Rosminian Fathers. There has been extensive restoration since World War II. Pope John Paul II visited the abbey in 1991, the first Pope to go in hundreds of years. I had just graduated from the seminary then. It was a great honor for me to be there when he blessed the sanctuary."

The Fiat bounded over the last rise and skidded into the parking lot at the base of the abbey. Murph and Carli quickly eased out of the car and looked up at the imposing stone face of the Sacra di San Michele.

Chapter 48

Father Albers had not contacted the Abbot in advance of their visit. Surprise seemed to have some benefits, but Murph was a bit worried about gaining access without some authority. That concern proved to be completely unfounded, as Father Falcone was immediately recognized as a returning son of the parish. The homecoming would have gone on the rest of the day, but he was able to convince the staff of the urgency of his task.

Abbot Cosimo was an affable, rotund man of 70. "Life here at the abbey is simple—and rather boring. We love guests, even unexpected ones."

Murph and Sal apologized for their unannounced arrival and explained that they were interested in interviewing Father Gaspard to collect his memories of the war for an oral history the Vatican was compiling.

Cosimo was happy to comply and took the group down the hall, introducing them to the monk in charge of the health of the retired priests in residence at the abbey.

Brother Almaric was seated at his desk, but rose immediately when the Abbot entered. Where the abbot wore the long, black cassock of a parish priest, Almaric preferred the alb, a long, linen vestment with tapered sleeves. His was made of a brown, coarse cloth and was gathered at the waist with a rope cincture, the cord used as a belt to gird the alb.

Almaric was tall and dark, his olive skin appearing to have seen many days in the sun. His hair was trimmed in the traditional tonsure of a monk, scalp shaved bald at the top of his head and down to a band of black hair about an inch wide, starting at the temple, over the ears and around the back of the head. His neck was shaved below the ring of hair. He could have easily been one of the founding monks from a thousand years ago.

Cosimo introduced Father Falcone, Murph and Carli as emissaries for Father Albers in Rome and asked that Brother Almaric help them in talking to Father Gaspard. Almaric nodded, smiling, and the Abbot left.

Almaric turned, suddenly staring coldly at them, and scoffed, "You have made a long drive from Rome for nothing! Gaspard has not spoken in weeks. His time is near. You should have called first and I would have saved you the time."

Carli smiled sweetly, "Can we see him?"

Almaric snorted. "What would be the point?"

Murph stepped in front of her, closer to Almaric, and spoke quietly, firmly, "If he is near death, then what harm is there in seeing him? Then we can tell the Vatican that Father Gaspard is gone and his memories are gone with him."

Almaric turned on his heel, robes flying. "As you wish! Follow me!"

He swept out the door into the hallway, calling for a nurse to join them.

The group hurried to follow. Carli stamped her foot, "How rude!"

Murph, Carli, and Sal were shown to a dormitory wing of the monastery. The average age of the clergy worldwide was certainly increasing at a rapid rate and the retired residents of the Sacra di San Michele clearly demonstrated that. Father Gaspard had been given the first room on the hall, just off the courtyard. It was a Spartan cell, with just a small bed—really just a cot, and a washstand. A small dresser stood along the wall, and a chair sat under the window. A gnarled staff of wood, his walking stick, leaned against the dresser.

Father Gaspard lay in the bed, shriveled from his advanced age. The room smelled of death. His hair was ghostly white and long, splayed out on the pillow. He lay on his side in a slightly relaxed fetal position—mouth open, eyes closed. His eyes were sunken deep in their sockets and his cheeks were hollow. He had lost all of his teeth, which contributed to the skeletal appearance of his face. His breath-ing was shallow. A faint rattling told Murph that his lungs were filling with fluid. An IV dripped slowly next to the bed, the line connected to a blue vein easily visible through the ancient priest's nearly transparent white skin. As Brother Almaric had said, it was clear that Father Gaspard did not have long to live.

The nurse, Sister Elena—tiny and painfully young, went over to Father Gaspard and moved to wake him.

Almaric stopped her with a command and waved her to the corner of the room. She retreated like a dog that had been kicked.

The monk bent over the priest, shouting, "Father! You have guests!" Gaspard did not respond. Almaric patted him on the cheek and called again, "Father Henri?"

Almaric turned to Murph, spread his arms and opened his hands. "See, as I told you. Even if he were awake, his mind is gone. All he has done recently is babble."

Carli moved forward and sat down in the chair, taking the old man's hand gently in both of hers. Almaric moved to stop her, but Murph intervened, blocking the monk and placing his hand on his chest.

"We came a long way from Rome." Murph stared him down. "Do not begrudge us the chance to visit with Father Gaspard. We need only a few minutes this afternoon … and he seems to have all the time in the world."

"Suit yourself." Almaric snorted and left in a huff. Elena stayed cowering in the corner.

Carli began to speak quietly in French, patting his hand. "Father Henri? It's OK. We are here with you. Just relax and let go. Heaven awaits you." After a few minutes, he opened his eyes, blinking and trying to focus.

His voice was a croak, "Louisa? Is that you?"

Sister Elena gasped, but Murph put his finger to his lips to gently shush her.

Carli soothed. "No, I'm Caroline."

"Louisa, I have missed your visits. It has been so long."

"Father Henri, I am not Louisa. My name is Caroline. I'm from America."

"Oh. America." His eyes looked off, searching. "Valerie!" He struggled to sit up. "Valerie, you have come home!"

Elena shouted, "It's a miracle!" and made the sign of the cross. Father Sal did as well.

Murph bent down over Carli's shoulder and moved a pillow to support the old man. He whispered to Carli to play along. If Father Gaspard wanted to see Valerie, they should try to fulfill the wish of a dying man.

"Yes, Father. I have come home."

Tears streamed down his face. "Oh, Valerie. When I sent you to America during the war, I thought Louisa was lost. After the war, Louisa found me and we thought you were lost. Now you have returned—we must find Louisa." He moved to get up, filled with a renewed sense of purpose.

Brother Almaric burst through the door and ran to Father Gaspard, pushing him back onto the pillows. The old priest's eyes widened.

"What are you doing?" The monk challenged Carli. "He is a frail old man who should not get excited." He pulled a syringe from the pocket of his robe and injected it into the IV line.

Carli looked at Gaspard's face and was horrified to see his eyes begin to gloss over, the life fading from them. "Murph!" she screamed.

Almaric shoved Carli into Murph and they both toppled to the floor, falling over the chair. The monk turned and headed for the door. Sal moved to block his path.

Almaric pushed the smaller priest out of his way, but Sal stood his ground, "What did you put in his IV?"

"Nothing but THIS!" Almaric jabbed another syringe into Sal's chest, driving the plunger home. Leaving the syringe in place, he shoved the priest aside.

Elena caught Sal as he fell, cushioning the blow as they both crashed to the floor. Murph sprang to his feet and helped Carli back to Father Gaspard. She held his hand and patted his cheek, speaking to him again in French. The ancient priest reached up a bony hand and clutched the lapel of her jacket.

Murph bent down to check Father Sal. His breathing was shallow but he reached out his hand and held Murph's as he said, "Do not let him get away!" Elena was stroking his hair, tears beginning to fall.

Murph squeezed Sal's hand. "Hang on!"

Scanning the room, Murph grabbed the walking staff and dashed out the door, following the robed monk across the courtyard.

Chapter 49

Entering the courtyard, Murph was just in time to see the brown robes of Brother Almaric disappear into the doorway on the opposite side. He raced across the piazza and entered the darkened hallway.

BANG! The wooden doorframe above Murph's head exploded. He could feel the splinters in his cheek and scalp. BANG. Murph ducked back out into the courtyard as the bullet whizzed by.

Murph could see another door across the hall from his current position. He took a running start, sliding feet first, baseball style, low across the tile floor. BANG. The bullet zinged over his head as he slid safely into the room. He looked around the door, down the hall.

Running footsteps could only mean one thing, so Murph turned and followed them. Frescoes honoring the Blessed Virgin flashed by as Murph ran in pursuit. He noticed the statues in veneration of Saint Christopher, the patron saint of pilgrims, and quickly prayed that the saint would watch over him. The corridor ended at the church sanctuary. Diving through the door, he crouched down behind the last pew as another shot embedded in the solid wood of the door behind him.

That's four, he thought, *how many bullets does he have?* Murph peered over the pew and spotted Brother Almaric on the altar. BANG. The wooden pew to his left splintered. Murph had counted more than ten pews to the altar—too far to run at a man with a loaded gun.

"What is going on here?" Murph looked over the pew to see Abbot Cosimo and another priest burst into the sanctuary through an arch in the transept, to the right side of the altar. "Brother Almaric! What are you doing?"

To Murph's horror, Almaric aimed the gun at the abbot and fired. BANG. BANG. Murph vaulted over the pew and charged up the center aisle. He could see Cosimo spin around, falling to the floor.

Murph ran, holding the staff in both hands near the end, like a baseball bat. He waved it high over his head and yelled.

Almaric recognized the new threat and turned to face Murph. He extended his arm, pointing the gun straight at Murph's chest.

Murph was flying down the aisle but he realized that he wasn't going to make it. He cleared the last pew and had ten feet to go. Almaric was in front of the altar, three steps up from the floor of the sanctuary.

Almaric looked at Murph and smiled. To Murph, the barrel of the gun appeared massive, growing larger with each step. Murph closed his eyes, waiting for the sound.

CLICK! Almaric's eyes widened. CLICK. CLICK. He squeezed the trigger again and again.

Thank you, Lord. He only had a seven shot magazine.

Murph reached the base of the altar and swung down with the staff. The head of the walking stick struck Almaric on the left side of his neck. The staff shattered and the monk collapsed against the stone table, crumpling to the floor.

Murph kicked the pistol away from the prone body of the monk, sending it back down the aisle. He tossed the stump of the staff as well and ran to Cosimo. The Abbot was down on the floor, a bloodstain spreading on his cassock.

Murph started to unbutton the cassock, lamenting that a priest's cassock had 33 buttons, symbolic of the years of the life of Jesus. After undoing the first three, Murph grabbed the opening and pulled, tearing the cassock open at the neck. Cosimo appeared to have been hit by one bullet, in the shoulder.

Murph used the abbot's stole as a bandage to staunch the bleeding and sent the other priest for help. Cosimo's eyes opened. He groaned.

Murph supported his head and eased him onto his back. "You've been shot, Father—but only once—in the shoulder. You'll be OK. I've sent for help."

"What is going on?" he could only manage a whisper.

"I don't know. Almaric drugged Father Gaspard. I chased him here and he started shooting. He's down over by the altar." Murph turned to point at the body, only to see Almaric stagger out the archway behind the altar.

Cosimo also saw Almaric moving. "I am fine. Go get him, my son!"

Murph stood up and surveyed the sanctuary. He could hear the running footsteps coming from the hospital wing. He bent down and squeezed Cosimo's arm. "I hear the nurses coming."

Cosimo nodded and Murph stood up. He saw the gun on the floor in the center aisle. He ran behind the altar and peered carefully through the archway. Murph followed cautiously, moving slowly down the hallway until he reached a staircase. It extended up as far as he could see, hundreds of steps. He could see sunlight streaming through the archway at the top of the stairs. Beside the steps were dozens of dark alcoves and niches. *Scalone di Morti*, Murph thought, scratching his nose to keep from sneezing from the dust.

Brother Almaric leaped out of the shadow of a nearby alcove, throwing his rope belt over Murph's head, around his neck. The monk put his knee in Murph's back and pulled, intending to strangle his prey.

Luckily for Murph, his left hand had been up to his face. The rope pulled against his arm as well as his neck, reducing the choking force. Murph reached around and grabbed a handful of coarse robe with his right hand. With a surge of adrenalin, the dentist lunged forward, lifting the monk off his feet and flipping him over Murph's shoulder onto the steps. The shock of hitting the stone knocked his breath away and Almaric released the grip on the cincture. Murph fell to the ground gasping, fighting to untangle himself from the rope. Almaric got to his feet, turned and ran up the stairs, robe flying around his waist.

Murph sprang up and chased after the monk, taking the stone steps two at a time. The monk reached the terrace first, disappearing through the Zodiac Arch. Murph followed seconds later and found the Brother Almaric standing on the ledge, waiting for him, balancing a thousand feet above the valley floor.

Murph skidded to a stop in front of the monk. "Wait! Come down from there!"

Almaric shook his head slowly, "You do not know what you do not know—and your searching will come to nothing!" He spat at Murph's feet.

"You didn't have to kill him. Why?" Murph pleaded.

"From evil comes a greater good!" Almaric stared coldly at Murph, spread his arms wide and leaned backward, falling in slow motion. Murph could hear the screams from below.

Feeling suddenly very tired, Murph walked over to the railing of the terrace and looked out on the majesty of the Alps. He indeed felt close to God. He stared down and found the form of Brother Almaric, spread eagled on the tile roof of the newly constructed gift shop at the Abbey, just a few feet away from the thousand-foot drop into the valley.

With a heavy heart, Murph walked back down the stairway of the dead one step at a time.

Chapter 50

Murph re-entered the church sanctuary and found Abbot Cosimo sitting up, his left shoulder bound with a dressing. The chief nurse, a matronly woman in her sixties, looked sternly at Murph. When he inquired about Cosimo in Italian, she softened and informed him that the bullet had passed through his shoulder without striking any major organs.

The Abbot was pale and his expression was strained with pain. He met Murph's gaze and asked, "Brother Almaric?"

Murph shook his head no. "I need to check on Gaspard and Falcone."

The nurse grabbed his wrist and confirmed his fears.

161

Murph slowly retraced his steps. When he came to the shattered doorframe, he reached up and touched his head. He pulled several splinters out of his hairline. He walked across the courtyard and came to Father Gaspard's room.

Carli sat by the old man's side, holding his hand in hers. She had closed his eyes and mouth. His lips were blue. Father Henri was gone. Carli looked up at Murph, streaks of tears down her cheeks and she drew his eyes to Father Sal.

Sister Elena sat on the floor, sobbing. Sal lay on his back with his head in her lap. His hands were folded. He appeared to be sleeping peacefully, except his eyes were open.

Murph knelt down and closed Sal's eyes with his fingers. He made the sign of the cross over his friend and said a silent prayer. Murph could hear the sound of sirens, fading in and out as they weaved back and forth on the road to the abbey.

Murph went over to Carli, knelt down beside the bed and took the priest's hand out of hers. He positioned Gaspard's hands as if in prayer. He was at peace. Carli turned to Murph and collapsed onto his shoulder. He wiped the tears from her face and kissed her on the forehead.

She touched the dried blood on his face, tracing it back to the source on his scalp. Her eyes widened as she noticed the abrasions from the rope burn on his forearm and neck.

"I heard shooting..."

He nodded, touching her lips with his finger, but she continued, "What about Almaric?"

"Like Alda, he threw himself from the tower—but the angels were not inclined to protect him."

Murph gathered her in his arms and held her close in silence.

Minutes later, the relative peace was shattered by the arrival of police and medics. Murph and Carli gave their statements. The medics removed the splinters from Murph's head and cleaned the wounds. The coroner removed the bodies of Gaspard and Falcone, and the police took the body of Almaric off of the roof.

The Abbot proclaimed Murph a hero for tackling the murderer, but Murph and Carli felt the weight of suspicion from the rest of the Abbey. Life had been quiet there for hundreds of years, until the Americans had arrived, shattering the peace with gunshots and death.

Murph received approval from the local police chief to return to Rome. Sister Elena embraced them both. Murph had taken the car keys from the body of Father Falcone before the police had arrived. He and Carli had agreed that it would be best for them if they returned to the Vatican as soon as possible. With a heavy heart, Murph started the Fiat and wound their way down the mountain. The light of the setting sun turned Sacra di San Michele into a golden jewel against the verdant green of the mountain.

Chapter 51

Murph drove with purpose, turning his aggression into speed as the kilometers flew by on their way down the boot of Italy. In spite of the rapid pace, it was still well after midnight when they approached Vatican City. Murph was considering his options for when the Swiss Guards turned him away.

He was astounded when the Fiat was waved past the guard station and into the courtyard. Murph shut down the Fiat and they got out of the car, stretching their sore, tired limbs. Bernardo, Father Albers's butler, came running to greet them.

"Thank God you are safe." He ran over and embraced Carli. "We heard the terrible news!"

Murph accepted the hug from Bernardo as well. "Father Sal became a good friend. We will miss him dearly."

"I am sure that you are exhausted. Let me see you to your rooms and we can discuss the details tomorrow."

"Grazi… Thank you."

Murph took Carli's bag and then went to their rooms. Breakfast was set for 7:00 a.m. with Father Albers. As tired as he was, sleep wouldn't come for Murph. They had found a few more pieces of the puzzle, but the whole picture eluded him. He drifted off to a fitful slumber seeing the vision of the monk tumbling backward off the railing into the abyss.

Murph rose, showered, and completely packed. He had come to one conclusion overnight. They needed to return to Washington. He rapped on Carli's door and asked her to prepare to leave as well.

Father Mahoney appeared to guide them and once again they gathered in the office of the Vatican librarian. Much to their surprise, Rocco Meroni was there as well.

Rocco grabbed Murph's hand and pulled him into a hug, pounding his back. "You don't waste any time getting in trouble, do you?"

"Yesterday was terrible. We made a new friend and lost him in the same day."

Father Albers said a prayer for the souls of Father Gaspard and especially for Father Sal. "Father Falcone gave his life in the service of God. May he find everlasting peace."

They all made the sign of the cross. "Amen."

Father Albers took charge of the meeting. "So that these deaths may not have been in vain, let us consider what we have learned."

Carli began with Gaspard. "Father Henri was a priest who traveled from village to village, wandering the Alps for 70 years, preaching and searching. I'm not sure what he was looking for, but he thought I was Valerie—or her sister Louisa. He had apparently helped Valerie leave Europe during the war and Louisa had stayed in Italy."

"Believe it or not," Murph interjected, "I have heard a similar story from a patient in Washington. I think we should return to D.C. immediately and check it out."

"I agree." Carli took Murph's hand. "As he was dying, Father Gaspard focused on only one thing. He took my hand and gripped it with all his might. He kept repeating *'Rentrer'*—French for 'to return' – It has the connotation of going home. He was trying to get me to see what he meant."

"He thought you were Valerie, who had come home from America."

"Yes, that's what I thought too. I told him that 'I had returned' but he shook his head. He meant something else." She shook her head in defeat. "I have no idea what he wanted me to understand. *Rentrer* was his last word."

Father Albers tone was soothing. "At least you were there to give a dying man comfort."

Murph stood up and began to pace, "He was dying, but it didn't have to be then. Brother Almaric killed him because he was talking. There was something that Almaric was afraid that the priest would tell us." He smacked his fist into his palm.

Father Mahoney piped up, "Who was this Brother Almaric?"

"He was in charge of the assisted living facility for the retired priests, monks and nuns. He ordered the nurses around like they were his slaves."

Father Albers held up a finger. "The police have identified Mathieu Almaric as neither Italian nor a Rosminian monk. He began serving at the abbey only two years ago. By his fingerprints, he is actually a Slovenian Jew, who is well known to Interpol."

"What?" Murph stopped in his tracks.

"It will take some time to trace his history further, but for now, Interpol believes that he began impersonating a monk to hide from authorities."

"It appears that he succeeded." Mahoney commented lightly but then turned his attention to his Danish pastry when Albers glared at him.

Murph began pacing again. "There is something bigger going on here." He stopped and faced the group. "When he was balancing on the ledge, he said, '*You do not know what you do not know—and your searching will come to nothing*' What puzzles me is that we went to see Father Gaspard to find out more about the involvement of the Catholic Church in the Holocaust. That shouldn't be controversial—or at least not worth killing over."

Father Albers considered this seated at the table, hands together, index fingers tapping the sides of his nose.

Murph continued, describing a vision that would haunt him for years. "Right before he threw himself off of the tower, he looked me in the eye and said, *'From evil comes a greater good'*"

"That is very strange." Father Albers's eyes were closed.

"By itself, that's an odd phrase." Murph approached the table and placed his hands on the surface, leaning in to the group. "What has me concerned is that Cyrille Bastien used that exact phrase when he was threatening me in D.C."

Albers's eyes snapped open.

Carli made it clear and connected the dots for the group. She and Murph had realized the link on the drive from Turin the night before. "That phrase connects the false President with Father Gaspard."

Father Albers rose from his chair. "Alas, it has always been one mystery … Rocco, would you care to share your part of the tale?"

Speechless, Murph sat down next to Carli.

Rocco opened a file and set it on the table in front of him. "Since Franklin Buchanan began as Acting President, the only observable change in US policy has been in its relations with Israel. During the eight years of the Obama administration, US policy was the most pro-Arab that it had ever been. Relations with Israel became increasingly strained, to the point that many analysts were openly concerned that Israel would have to conduct a pre-emptive strike on Iran to prevent the Arab world from getting a nuclear weapon."

"Since the Israelis feared the US would not support or defend them if attacked by the Arabs?" Murph wanted to be sure he understood the situation.

"Exactly. Israel felt increasingly alone, surrounded by countries that were plotting their demise. In Europe, leaders were expressing concerns that the Middle East was becoming increasingly unstable. Rather than act militarily, some in Tel Aviv charted another course.

"During the campaign for the 2016 election, Super PACs began pouring millions of dollars into TV ad campaigns supporting the candidacy of then Vice President Biden and his new running mate Franklin Buchanan. It was an easy sell—an affable old man and a young war hero running mate. As they were Democrats, the media were happy to see them succeeding and declined to investigate the source of the money. It was a close election, but the Biden/Buchanan ticket was elected.

"The sudden death of the likeable President Biden shocked the country. It has only been since President Buchanan has consolidated his power that a shadowy figure has emerged. The source of the Super PAC funds is a Jewish billionaire—Simon Cohen."

Chapter 52

Murph sat at the table, mouth open in utter disbelief. He shook his head to clear it, so many questions swirling in his brain that he couldn't pick one to start.

Carli was first to come out of shock. "So we now know who may be behind things, but we don't know what they are planning—or why?"

Rocco shrugged. "That about sums it up."

"But we have a place to start." Murph was coming around, a plan forming in his mind. "We need to see my patient, Valerie David, and ask her more questions. Now that we can connect Father Gaspard, Louisa, and Simon Cohen, a more focused interview may reveal more in her memory. She also may be in danger if they know that we know who she is."

Father Albers said, "I may be able to help with that. Take Father Foa with you when you meet her. If you sense Valerie is in jeopardy, have him take her to the Apostolic Nunciature —ah, the Vatican Embassy, in Washington, D.C. We can provide protection for her there."

Rocco cleared his throat. "There is one more thing. When we were following the threads on Simon Cohen, we discovered something else. While he is an American, he has close ties to Israel. He has recently invested a large sum of money, millions really, into a museum south of Haifa."

Carli raised an eyebrow. "Where people spend their money often reveals what they care about. What kind of museum?"

Rocco read from his file, "The Altit 'Illegal' Immigration Detention Camp Museum teaches the story of the more than 122,000 people (known as ma'apilim—illegal immigrants) who between the years 1934-1948, were transported from Europe and Arab countries to British Palestine. At the end, many were survivors of the Holocaust. Once they arrived, they were detained in camps, much like the NAZI concentration camps they had escaped, on the very land they had risked their lives to reach."

"Interesting." Carli ran her fingers through her ponytail. "We met the Israeli ambassador and his wife at the White House dinner. Maybe we should pay them a visit and see what they know."

Murph shook his head. "Politicians are too likely to be involved. There's too much risk in that direct of an approach. A billionaire can have a very long reach. I have a better idea. I've treated a former Mossad agent for TMJ problems, and we have become good friends. He may have some contacts in Israel that could get us information without raising any alarm."

Rocco agreed. "I like that plan. Let me know what you find out."

Rocco pushed his chair back and got up from the table. "I don't know about the rest of you, but I still work for a living and I need to get out of here without being seen. The earlier I get going the better."

Murph and Carli thanked him for all his help. Father Albers had Father Mahoney escort Rocco from the Vatican.

Father Albers checked his watch and nodded approvingly. He motioned to Ferdinand and the butler went to the front door and locked it, then disappeared into the galley. Murph exchanged glances with Carli, but she simply shrugged.

"Father?" Murph asked, indicating the locked entry.

"Before you leave, there is one more person who would like to speak with you."

A gentle knock behind them gathered the librarian's attention. He moved quickly to a small door at the rear of his office. He opened it and a small bespectacled man entered the room. He wore a white Mozzetta, short shoulder cape, over a simple white cassock. A white zucchetto, skullcap, covered his head. A simple silver crucifix on a chain from his neck was the only adornment he wore. Peace radiated from his warm smile and the kindly glint in his eyes.

"Thank you, Lawrence." He shook hands with Father Albers and turned to the dumbfounded Murph and Carli.

Murph practically rolled out of his chair to kneel on the brocade carpet as Carli positioned herself beside him. Murph looked up into the kind, smiling face of the Pope.

"Your Holiness!" Murph bowed his head.

The pontiff reached out and placed a hand on each of their shoulders. "Caroline and Michael, please rise and sit with me."

Father Albers offered a leather armchair for Pope Francis as Murph turned a dining chair around for Carli and then seated himself.

"That's so much better."

Murph had heard that Francis was less formal than most Popes, but this was a surprise.

The Pontiff began simply, speaking slowly. "Father Albers has informed me of the disturbing events at Sacra di San Michele and told me of your involvement in preventing a greater tragedy."

They both moved to object, minimizing their involvement but the Pope raised his palm to ward them off. "Caroline, to comfort a person at the time of death is to be as an angel—to ease them from this life into paradise. Thank you for caring for Father Gaspard."

She bowed her head in appreciation.

"And, Michael. This is not the first time that you have faced evil—at great risk to yourself. God has a plan for you both, of that I am certain. There are powerful forces on the move. We do not know their plan but it may fall to you to stop them. I will do all I can from here."

"Thank you, your Holiness."

"I am going tomorrow to Sacra di San Michele to celebrate the funeral Mass for Father Gaspard and Father Falcone. The murder of two priests is a terrible thing and the faithful need to be comforted in their time of sorrow. You have uncovered a link connecting an old story with a current mystery. Often provoking the enemy is a useful tool, as it may bring them out of the shadows.

I am bringing the majesty of the Vatican to shine the light on the abbey and the pilgrim road through the Alps. I send you into the shadows to find the heart of the evil."

The Pope reached out and placed his hands on top of Murph and Carli's heads as they bowed. "Remember, The Lord is my shepherd, I shall not want. Though I walk through the valley of the shadow of death, I will fear no evil—for You *are* with me."

Pope Francis removed his hands and made the sign of the cross over them, blessing them. "As a shepherd, I must go to tend my flock. I am sending you to find the wolves—and to protect us from them. God be with you!"

Chapter 53

Murph had called ahead and informed Derek Whitman of their departure plans. As he had expected, Derek tried his best to sound crestfallen that his Roman holiday had been cut short, but Murph wasn't buying it. They were going home sooner than expected, but it felt good to be moving. Murph felt energized with the sense of purpose.

Arriving early at Ciampino Airport, Murph and Carli made a point to seek out the customs agent who had interviewed them on their arrival. They were actually pleased to see her come out of the office when they asked for her.

"Capitano Liriano, it's good to see you!" Murph smiled broadly.

Her face was expressionless as she surveyed the two travelers. "You are leaving sooner than expected?"

"Sadly, yes." Murph shrugged his shoulders. "Our time in Rome is always too short."

"But exceedingly eventful." The Customs supervisor reached down and took their passports from the agent who had cleared them. "I was advised to alert the American White House of your movements. You have been in Italy for two days and have been involved in a triple murder."

Murph took in a quick breath but her dark eyes narrowed, glaring at him. He closed his mouth and let her continue.

"You traveled more than six hours from Rome to the French border. Your visit to a medieval abbey resulted in the deaths of two Catholic priests and a monk"

She took a long moment to examine them, first looking Murph then Carli up and down.

"Amazingly, the Carabinieri not only immediately cleared you, but credited you with saving the life of the Abbot and preventing further disaster." She shook her head.

Murph was apologetic. "The local police took our statement and were most understanding. It was a tragic day at Sacra di San Michele." Murph took Carli's hand and squeezed. "One we will not soon forget."

Liriano's eyes softened. "I imagine so." She handed Murph their passports. "I usually recommend that foreign tourists return to Rome soon—but I am not so sure in your case."

Murph thanked her for the passports. "We will return to Rome, but I don't know when. I feel drawn to the power of the ancient city, but lately I am seldom relaxed when I am here."

"What would you have me tell the White House?"

171

Murph thought a moment. "Please tell them we are returning directly to Washington DC—the truth shall set you free."

Liriano nodded. "It is always the best policy. Travel safely, my friends." She turned and walked slowly away.

Murph and Carli collected their bags and quickly covered the distance from the terminal to the waiting Gulfstream. The jet taxied out and was airborne in minutes, heading west toward home.

Chapter 54

Murph and Carli found the quiet time soaring across the Atlantic a useful experience. Carli's investigative instincts had her hot on the trail of information and she wasn't about to let go.

"That patient of yours that was the Israeli agent—he's the guy you became friends with during your rehab, right."

Murph looked up from his computer. "Yes. Gabriel Levi was a member of the Mossad until he emigrated from Israel to the US two years ago. When I was recovering from my shoulder wound and couldn't run, he suggested bicycling as exercise. He helped me find the proper bike and taught me how to do things right. We rode together every couple of days and got to be really good friends."

Carli was eating a yogurt, waving a spoon at Murph as she talked, "Did you learn he was former Mossad when you were riding?"

"No. I found out before I got to know him well." Murph closed his computer and turned his chair to face her. "It was the strangest thing—he came in as a patient with terrible headaches and pain in front of his ears. I did a complete exam and diagnostic workup for his TMJ problem. I noticed a scar on his chin, right on the point of his jaw. I asked him if he had been in an accident in which he had struck his jaw. That's a common cause for TMJ problems."

"What, like a bike accident? Going over the handlebars and hitting the ground face first?"

"That's what I expected. Boy, was I surprised when he told me what struck his jaw!"

Carli took another spoonful, "What hit him?"

"Rifle butt."

"Really!"

"Yeah. An answer like that will always get a follow-up question! So we got to talking about his past. It's amazing what you can learn about people if you just listen."

"That's really what you do best," Carli observed. "People love you because you care more about what they are saying than yourself."

"And I thought it was my magnetic personality?"

She shook her head, "Naah," then laughed when he pouted.

Carli put down the yogurt and sat in his lap. "What's your plan when we land?"

"I'll call Gabriel and invite him for a bike ride. I can explain everything we know and see if he wants to help. If not, then we'll take your approach and call the Israeli Ambassador —what was his name?"

She tapped the side of her head with the spoon. "Shimon and Sarah Perski."

"I'm glad you remember. There's no way I could come up with those names!"

"That's why you keep me around." She giggled. "See— not just a pretty face!"

Murph pulled her closer but she whacked him lightly on the nose with the yogurt spoon. "Not so fast. We still have work to do."

As if on cue, Murph's phone chimed with a text. Looking down, they both saw that it was from Bernie Foa. Murph looked at his watch and calculated their arrival time. "We can meet him for dinner."

"Yes. I don't think we want to talk to him on the phone or by text. They're still probably tracking our phones."

"I agree. We'll have to see if we can use that to our advantage." Murph answered the text and told Bernie that they would pick him up at the Jesuit residence in Georgetown and take him to dinner.

His response was excited like a little kid.

"I think we made his day!" Murph laughed.

* * * * * * *

The Gulfstream G-550 landed at Reagan National Airport in the early afternoon. Murph and Carli quickly cleared customs and took the Metro subway into Washington DC. They went first to the Center for Esthetic and Restorative Excellence and checked in with Margaret and the staff.

Ever efficient, as soon as Murph had announced their return, the team had scheduled the rest of his week. Carli went into Murph's office and touched base with her program director at Georgetown. The defense of her thesis was looming in November but she was on schedule with her plan.

Margaret had been in contact with their legal team during Murph's absence. She took Murph into her office and called Billy McGinty, putting him on speaker.

"Hey, Doc! Welcome home." Came the raspy voice over the phone.

"Hi, Billy! Glad to be back." Murph noticed that Carli had slipped back into the room as he was speaking. "What's the news?"

"Well, they say you measure a man by the quality of his enemies. If that's true, you really have moved up in the world."

Murph frowned. "I don't like the sound of that!"

"Yeah. I don't either. You've really picked a tough one here. We traced the cyber attack to the Executive Branch— NSA or somewhere in the White House. My hackers went as far as they could, then got scared about a visit from the IRS or something." Billy chuckled.

"Yeah, I get it."

"We tried to set up the best firewalls we could on your computer network and phones, but I don't think I would trust them. Don't email anything you wouldn't want to see as the headline in tomorrow's Washington Post."

"Understood."

"I even had a team go over your condo—we took out the bugs, well at least the ones they found anyway."

"So I should consider myself on tape at all times, like on a reality TV show?"

"Probably a smart idea. These guys are good, Murph! And they mean business."

"Okay."

"You be careful out there!" Billy sounded grave.

"Thanks for the warning, Billy. You be safe too." Murph touched the speaker, and the line went silent.

Carli moved further into the room. "Well, that's cheerful news."

"Nothing we didn't expect, I guess." Murph sat down heavily in one of the armchairs.

Margaret took half-glasses off her nose and set them down on the desktop. She pushed back her chair and spread her hands wide, palms up. "So what are you going to do?"

Carli perched on the arm of Murph's chair. "It's good we still have the phones and iPad from Rocco that are probably off the grid as far as tracking is concerned."

Murph folded his hands in front of his face and tapped his fingers on either side of his nose. "True. We'll take Bernie Foa out to dinner tonight—someplace noisy so we can talk safely. Margaret, have Laurie call Gabriel Levi and have him come in for an examination and adjustment on his TMJ appliance this week."

"Got it." Her pencil was scratching immediately.

"Let's see if Rocco has found out anything interesting?"

Murph reached into his backpack and pulled out the iPhone that now had Carli's smiling face as the wallpaper. Touching the contact for Ed Eagle, the phone rang.

"Yello!"

"Uh, Hi!" Murph was suddenly at a loss for words. What if someone is listening?

175

Remembering the bookie act from when they received the phones, Carli leaned over, "Hey, do you have any info on those horses we asked about this morning?"

"Oh, yeah!" There was a cough on the other end, and they could hear Rocco moving to a quieter spot in the bar. "About that horse Cyril—I wouldn't bet on him. He's French, but other than that, I don't know nothin'. It's really very mysterious. He's got no record, but he's really tough."

Murph nodded to himself. "That's what we thought too."

"The other horse has made a ton of dough. Like billions! Began slowly but growing fast lately. Racing most where you are these days, but also in the Middle East. His home stable is here in Susa, up north near Turin."

"That's interesting."

"He's the one I'd bet on."

"Got it. Thanks!"

The phone went dead from the other end.

Murph put away the phone slowly. "Nothing really surprising there."

Carli nodded. "Probably no coincidence that Cohen has an estate in Susa. That's in the Valley of the Abbeys at the foot of the Cottian Alps, just west of where we were in Avigliano at Sacra di San Michele. It's right on the French-Italian border."

"You know I don't believe in coincidences. They're both on the pilgrim trail to Rome. After we have dinner with Bernie, we need to take him with us to interview Valerie David. She's the key to this somehow."

"I agree." Carli jumped up. "But, first things first. You promised dinner!"

Chapter 55

Murph and Carli grabbed the Mustang and drove through the ever-present Washington traffic to Georgetown. Stopping briefly at her house, Carli ran in and dropped off her bags. She changed quickly into a floral sundress and lavender sweater. Dashing back out to the car, Murph held the door for her, but she slipped into the back seat. Murph inclined his head and raised an eyebrow.

"I know Bernie will love the chance to ride up front with you! He loves cars as much as you do."

Murph leaned in and kissed her on the cheek. "I think you may be right. Let's see!"

They picked up Bernie Foa at the Jesuit residence, standing excitedly outside at the curb. Murph eased the Mustang to the curb as their guest noticed Carli in the back.

"Caroleen-a! You are so nice to-a me." The little priest slid in the passenger seat, grinning from ear to ear.

Murph nodded and glanced at Carli in the rearview mirror. Her satisfied smile spoke volumes. He mouthed, *"I love you."*

She simply said, "I know."

Murph answered Bernie's questions and explained the features of the Mustang as he drove the short distance to the restaurant. Murph and Carli had selected one of their favorites. *Café Milano* was on Prospect Street NW in the Georgetown neighborhood of Washington.

Murph pulled up and let the valet take the car. They made an interesting trio for dinner. Murph and Carli were their usual stylish but understated selves, instantly drawing attention in spite of their efforts to remain unnoticed. Bernie looked like their geeky little brother, probably a grad student somewhere in D.C. He had correctly ditched the priestly collar for the evening, but his blue polo shirt and pleated khaki slacks with penny loafers were woefully out of date.

Carli fluffed her skirt and took Murph's hand as they went to the hostess. In the summer, *Café Milano* had a beautiful sidewalk patio, with the floor-to-ceiling front windows of the restaurant open, flooding the street with warmth. The smell of fine Italian cuisine and the sounds of music brightened the neighborhood.

Murph was temped to sit outside, as would have been their usual choice, but he elected a table inside. They gave up the ambiance of the streetscape for the noisier confines inside the restaurant. For their purpose tonight, louder was better.

The hostess seemed a bit surprised, but led them past framed designer scarves adorning the walls. It was a creative homage to Italian fashion, giving the appearance of a stylish Milan boutique. The café was known for its Southern Italian cuisine, with a coastal flair, served with European excellence.

Murph ordered a crisp Pinot Grigio for Carli and opted for a glass of Barolo Seghesio Nebbiolo for himself. Bernie seemed a bit at a loss, so Murph came to his rescue and ordered another glass of the red wine for their guest.

"Thank-a you." Bernie began to settle in and relax. "It is so-a nice here. So much to see."

Murph laughed. "*Café Milano* is one of the best places in Washington for people watching. It's always fun here."

Murph took care of ordering for them, just simple salads—a house specialty of butter lettuce tossed with lemon vinaigrette, candied walnuts, and gorgonzola cheese—and the signature pizza: tomatoes, imported fresh mozzarella, baby artichokes, seasonal mushrooms, ham and Gaeta olives.

As dinner was served, they reluctantly got down to the business at hand. Murph and Carli filled Bernie in on the events at the Sacra di San Michele. Bernie had met Father Falcone on several occasions and was saddened by his death. The little priest was stunned that Murph and Carli had met the Pope.

Murph summed up their concerns that the false President and Simon Cohen were obviously connected. "We now have a close advisor to the President who witnessed the murder of his family at the hands of a serial killer. Who knows what psychological damage that trauma caused in such a young boy?"

"I hate to think what he might be capable of." Carli shook her head. "What concerns me even more is that whatever they are planning has been in the works for a very long time."

Bernie took a bite of pizza and waved the crust at Murph, "I found-a that Cohen and a group of children came to the

178

United-a States right after the war in 1945. Major Arnold went to Rome and-a worked with Father MacLaughlin to secure the rights for the children to emigrate as refugees. They came-a to Washington and were adopted to families near here."

Carli's eyes widened. "Do the adoption records exist that we can follow them? Some should still be alive and may remember something valuable."

"Sadly, no." He looked down at his plate, sadly. "The adoption records were sealed at that time to protect the children since they were considered orphans."

"That's OK, Bernie. We think we may already know the name of one of those orphans. We are going to interview her later this week and we would like you to go with us." Bernie brightened noticeably at Murph's invitation.

Carli put down her fork and pressed the issue. "What else did you find out about Major Arnold and Father MacLaughlin?"

"Father Mac returned from Roma and was assigned as a parish priest in-a McLean, Virginia. He passed away of a heart attack in 1950 when he was only 60 years-a old. There is nothing more to know."

He finished his pizza crust, took a swallow of wine, and continued, "Major Arnold is-a more interesting. He retired from the Army almost immediately but stayed on as a civilian working at-a the Pentagon until he retired. He died only eight years ago. He also lived in McLean."

Murph shrugged, "So what's so interesting in that?"

Bernie pounced, "Ah-Ha! For a man who retired on a government pension, Fred Arnold lived-a very well. His house was far too nice for his salary. There had to be some other source of money than just his government-a job."

Murph rubbed his chin. "That's all circumstantial, but it does give us something to search. If you follow the money, it leads you…"

"To see the light!" Carli lifted her wine glass and touched it to Murph's.

Chapter 56

Murph was pleased that his staff had scheduled Gabriel Levi at the end of his day. He found treating TMJ patients both physically relaxing and intellectually stimulating. Where most dentistry is reconstructive, repairing the damage done by decay or wear, TMJ treatment is medical in nature, involving physical therapy techniques. It appealed to Murph's abilities to interview people and get them to realize how external stresses were negatively impacting their health as well as how their muscle physiology was causing pain and loss of function in their body.

Gabriel had come to Murph by a path that was fairly common. He had been treated unsuccessfully for migraine headaches for years. After a thorough examination, Murph determined that bite interferences and muscle spasm in his jaws were causing his pain. By creating a bite appliance that relaxed the overworked muscles, the pain resolved, and Gabriel was eternally grateful for getting his life back. Chronic pain had sapped him of his ability to cope with life. Providing relief had freed him to be the father and husband that he wanted to be.

Murph examined his TMJ patients on a regular basis, because treatment was a balancing act. Life stresses or another injury could easily send a patient spiraling out of control. Gabriel was pleased to see Murph again. Like most of Murph's TMJ patients, they had become good friends during the numerous visits to gather the data to correctly diagnose the problem and fabricate the treatment appliance. After verifying that the appliance was continuing to work well and provide comfort for Gabriel, Murph took off his mask and gloves. He pushed back his chair and then turned on the high volume suction.

Gabriel looked puzzled as the vacuum hissed loudly in the background. He sat up in the dental chair and swung his legs around to face Murph.

Where Murph was tall and lean, Gabriel Levi was compact and powerfully built. The strong, square jaw with heavy jowls was common for a heavy tooth grinder. He sensed the anxiety in Murph's actions and began to squeeze his teeth together, his cheeks bulging out.

Murph reached out and patted him on the cheek, handing him his appliance case. "Why don't you put this in your mouth? When you clench like that—it's how you got in trouble in the first place." Murph laughed.

Gabriel chuckled, but scratched his wiry, black hair. His coal black eyes fixed Murph with a stare. "You turned on the suction like you are worried the room is bugged—what's going on?"

Murph rolled his chair in closer. "I need your advice. When we started talking about your case, I noticed that scar on your chin."

Gabriel rubbed the point of his lower jaw with his fingers, thinking, "You were the only person to notice and ask about it. That's how you know that I was Mossad before emigrating to America, right?"

"Yes. I need to know if you still have contacts in Israel and would be willing to gather some information for me."

"What kind of information?"

Murph had decided that honesty continued to be his best friend, so he laid all his cards on the table. He explained how they had found out that the President was an imposter, how the pilgrim trail to Rome had assisted Jewish children in avoiding the Holocaust, and how all the trails seemed to lead to Simon Cohen. "The only change in US policy since President Buchanan was sworn in seems to be in relations with Israel. Simon Cohen has come out of the shadows and appears to be a significant player in Washington politics. He is a US citizen who was granted refugee status when he came here from Italy after World War II. His original birth citizenship was probably French, but his documents were created by the Vatican and list an Italian birth."

"Why me?"

"Cohen is a billionaire. His holdings span the globe, but he has invested extensively in Israel only recently. My informant said he was a major contributor to the Atlit Illegal Detention Center Museum near Haifa. I believe that people invest in causes that are close to their heart."

Murph rolled closer and looked Gabriel in the eyes. "We know that something's terribly wrong, so much so that Carli and I have been threatened. Three men are dead. Two men have looked straight at me and said, "From evil comes a greater good." Those were the last words of a monk who threw himself off the tower of a medieval abbey. I don't know what *greater good* they envision, but I am deeply concerned about the *evil* they are capable of."

Gabriel nodded slowly. "I understand—what do you expect to find?"

Murph sat back in his chair and exhaled. "That's the problem. I have no idea." He rubbed his eyes, suddenly fatigued. "We know who is involved. We know that the President is phony. But we have no idea why. I feel something powerful moving, but I can't stop what I can't see."

Gabriel reached out and clasped Murph's arm in a grip of iron. "You noticed the scar on my chin caused by the blow from a rifle. That was the spark that grew into the pain that nearly took away my life. If your assessment of Cohen is right, witnessing the murder of his family may be the seed that has blossomed into whatever he is planning now. That's 70 years of horror and seething hatred. That can motivate a great evil."

They both sat in silence for a moment, the suction hissing loudly, before Gabriel stood up.

"I will see what I can learn." He reached over and turned off the suction. "Thanks, Doc! Let's plan on bike riding Friday. I could sure use the exercise." He winked and walked out the door.

Chapter 57

Murph debated how to contact her, but decided to save Rocco's secret phones for emergencies only. He picked up his office phone and called Valerie David. He told her that he was going to be in Virginia to go to a farmer's market and wanted to stop by to see how she was doing after the root canal.

"Oh, Doktor. Thank you zo much for your conzern." Her accent was thicker on the phone. "I vill be home all day."

"Great. I will have Carli with me too. I want you to meet her!"

"Sank you for telling me! I will be sure to bake cookies."

They set the time and Murph picked up Carli and Bernie Foa. They made sure to go to the farmer's market. They needed the fresh produce anyway—Murph was excited to get some really excellent local bicolor corn—and they picked up some ripe tomatoes to give to Valerie.

They arrived right on time at her home. It was just as he expected, a tidy suburban bungalow in McLean. They pulled up on the street and walked to the door. She greeted them in a pale pink suit, skirt and low heels. She had dressed in her finest to honor her guests.

Valerie set them at the kitchen table and made coffee to go with the cookies. She had also made an excellent peach cobbler. The cups and saucers were fine bone china, white with purple flowers. The entire house was perfectly preserved from another era – and suited her precisely.

Murph made small talk for a while, introducing Carli and then Father Foa. Bernie was accurately named as a friend who was in the US visiting from the Vatican. Valerie was pleased to be entertaining a priest, and the fiancé of her favorite dentist.

Murph asked about how her tooth was feeling.

"Oh, excellent. It looks so goot. Thank you, Doktor."

"Mrs. David, do you remember the story you told me that day—about when the Nazis came to the convent?"

"Oh, yes." She averted her eyes. "I am so embarrassed!"

"Please don't be." Murph patted her arm. "I think that you were meant to tell me that." He held her hand. "I think it is very important."

Murph looked closely at her. "Who was the priest who saved you?"

"Father Henri."

"Gaspard?" Carli reached over and held her other hand.

"Yes… How did you know that?"

Murph considered how to proceed. "We were asked to look into an old mystery by an old friend who is a Jesuit priest working for Pope Francis." He paused a minute for that to sink in. "Your story is part of a bigger puzzle. I think this may be the most important piece of all. Can you tell me everything that happened after the Nazis left?"

Valerie closed her eyes. Murph and Carli could feel her squeeze their hands, the emotions rushing back as she returned to that day. Tears began to roll down her cheeks, dropping onto the back of Murph's wrist.

"Father Henri held us down in the basement. He wouldn't let us look, but we could hear the nuns screaming. The guns cracked, then it was silent. The trucks started up and roared away into the mountains, leaving behind the crackling of the fire. We could smell the wood of the sanctuary roof burning.

When night fell, Father Henri led us out into the forest. He took us into a cave that he had prepared for such an emergency. There was food and water, along with blankets, hidden there. I started to cry about my sister but he took me aside. He told me that I was the oldest girl and I needed to be strong. If I panicked, then all the others would too.

He made me in charge of the girls. The oldest boy, Simon, was made boss of the boys. There were 20 of us. Father Henri left us there while he went to make sure it was safe. We waited in the cave for a week then he came back. He led us over the mountains, traveling mostly in the moonlight. We stopped in some churches, where they hid us for a few days each time. It was hard to avoid the German patrols but we made it to Rome several months later. We were given sanctuary at the Vatican. It was good to feel safe for once, but Father Henri had to leave. He said he had work still to do in the mountains.

The war ended soon after. One day, Father Henri came back and we were all brought together again. He introduced us to an American priest, Father MacLaughlin. He took our names and stories. He wrote them in his book and said he thought he could bring us to America. We were excited, but nothing happened for months. Finally, Father MacLaughlin came back and brought an Army officer with him. Then we were put on a ship and brought to Washington D.C. I was adopted by an Italian-American couple who couldn't have children."

Valerie took a silk handkerchief from out of the sleeve of her blouse and wiped the tears from her cheeks as she opened her eyes.

Carli held Valerie's hand in both of hers. "Do you know what happened to any of the other children?"

"I think they were all adopted, too. The only one I know of is Simon. He went to live with Major Arnold here in McLean. I saw him a couple times during high school, but I have not seen him since." She looked drawn.

Murph hated to push the issue, but he had to know. He reluctantly asked, "Where was the convent in the mountains?"

"It was right on the Italian border with France." She considered a second. "In Susa."

Bernie Foa's eyes widened, but Murph waved his hand to hush him.

"Mrs. David, what was your sister's name?"

Her answer was so hushed they could barely hear it the first time. "Louisa—it was Louisa."

This time, Bernie audibly gasped.

Murph reached out and took Valerie by the shoulders. "I think that Louisa may have survived the war."

Valerie pulled her hands up to cover her mouth. "How?"

185

"I don't know. Carli and I were with Father Henri this week when he died. His mind wasn't completely clear. He thought Carli was Louisa at first."

"My God."

Carli squeezed her hand. "When I told him I was from America, he called me Valerie and was happy that I had *returned*. He said that we needed to go tell Louisa! He passed away right after that, but he was happy that I—or really, you—had come home."

"Louisa?" She sobbed.

Murph moved around and cradled Valerie in his arms. After he allowed her to cry quietly for a few minutes, he sat her up. She looked lost. She had believed for 70 years that her sister had died. Murph could tell she was struggling to process the information.

"Mrs. David. We are going to try to find Louisa. There is something else going on now, but we don't exactly know what it is. It involves Simon in some way. I'm concerned that you may be in danger. I want you to pack a bag and come with us now. Father Foa will take you into protection at the Vatican Embassy, here in Washington."

Her face was blank, but she nodded. Carli took her into her bedroom and helped her gather her things.

Murph and Bernie picked up the coffee and washed the dishes, setting them carefully to dry on the rubber mat next to the sink. Murph packaged the peach cobbler in Tupperware to bring along. They arranged the house and prepared for Valerie to leave for a while. As Carli helped Valerie out to the car, Murph took her bags and put them into the trunk. Carli and Bernie climbed into the back seat and Murph closed the door on Valerie in the passenger seat.

Murph went back to the trunk, bent down and reached into his backpack. He drew out his secure iPhone and turned it on. He selected Rocco's contact and sent a simple a text message.

"Search Simon Cohen as Simon Arnold."

Chapter 58

Murph finished a long, productive day at work before changing quickly into his bicycling gear. He was looking forward to the exercise. It was a beautiful evening in Washington and, for summer, a relatively cool 80 degrees. He mounted his Bianchi road bike and pedaled off. Traveling through the National Mall, rather than on the congested streets surrounding it, dramatically reduced his travel time. He quickly reached the Lincoln Memorial, 15 minutes early for his scheduled meeting with Gabriel Levi.

Murph walked his bike up the steps and leaned it against one of the 36 Doric marble columns. He walked into the shadowed hall and gazed up at the peaceful face of Abraham Lincoln. As he always did whenever he visited the memorial, he read aloud the Gettysburg Address.

"…that this nation, under God, shall have a new birth of freedom—and that government of the people, by the people, and for the people shall not perish from the earth."

"Nicely done!" The deep voice came from right behind him, but Murph didn't flinch. He had heard the slight shuffle of Gabriel's shoes on the marble. "You should consider TV?"

Murph chose to ignore the jab and stay in the moment. "There is such power in the language. So few words, but expertly chosen—each one perfectly placed for maximum effect. We just don't talk like that anymore. Oratory is a lost art, I fear."

"You may be right, but I like to think that there is still a place here in Washington for someone who speaks from the heart."

"Exactly!" Murph turned and shook Gabriel's hand. "What makes the Gettysburg Address so powerful is that I feel that President Lincoln truly believed those words. And the country did too! Now, I'm not so sure we know what we believe."

Gabriel shrugged. "It is tough to know, my friend."

"That's why I come here. Whenever I feel unsure, I return to these granite and marble memorials and read the words, remembering a time when things seemed more clear."

"Ah, my friend, I have a feeling that the future was anything but clear to President Lincoln in 1863 when he wrote those words. It was as much a prayer—a hope for the way he wanted things to be—as a statement of facts."

"True. He found the strength of will to lead the country out of the wilderness of war. I guess it looks clear to me through the benefit of 150 years of hindsight."

"Then we should ride, for we have much to discuss." Gabriel led Murph over to the bikes. "Perhaps, we can find clarity as well."

They carried their bikes back down the steps to the street. Gabriel led Murph at a brisk pace across the Arlington Memorial Bridge, banking right onto the Jefferson Davis Highway until they reached the US Marine Corps War Memorial, the 78-foot tall bronze and granite re-enactment of the flag raising on the island of Iwo Jima. There, five Marines and a Navy corpsman perpetually raise a 60-foot bronze flagpole, the Stars and Stripes waving proudly.

Murph and Gabriel parked their bikes and walked onto the grassy knoll that overlooks the memorial. With sun descending in the sky behind them, the monument began to glow with a golden sheen, silhouetted against the darker eastern sky beyond. They sat down and had some water, Murph pulling a pair of granola bars from his pack to share.

Gabriel scanned the small crowd to be sure they were alone. There were the usual tourists taking pictures on the monument. A couple of 'old salt' marines were there, as well, wearing camouflage pants and red t-shirts with the Marine globe and anchor logo. The Marines were answering questions from a visiting group of middle-school-aged Boy Scouts.

Confident they were alone, but still cautious, Gabriel continued looking at the Memorial and remarked casually, "Simon Cohen is a powerful man. He has interests all across Israel and extensive investments in Western Europe."

"Did you find out how he made his fortune?"

"It appears that he began with a small start in the 1950's as a very young man. There is nothing suspicious or criminal in his business dealings. He was exceptionally shrewd and took risks in oil, gas, transportation, and later communications companies."

"He made his money the old fashioned way!"

"Just so!" Gabriel took a bite of his power bar. "Recently, he has become heavily invested in real estate in Western Europe, especially Italy, France, and Germany."

"Given the population explosion, it would make sense that real estate there would be poised for growth." Murph considered for a moment. "But how does that business positioning benefit from controlling the American Presidency?"

"As a billionaire businessman, controlling US government policy is of incalculable value for everything. The Buchanan administration has dramatically changed policy relative to Israel and the Middle East."

"I know what that feels like here. How does Israel see that?"

"The pro-Arab policies of the Obama administration were the source of great anxiety in Tel Aviv. The leaders in Egypt, Jordan, Syria, Lebanon, and especially Iran were emboldened. Israel was forced to plan her own defense, since she felt alone in the region."

"Yes. It did seem that the area was becoming increasingly unstable with every passing month. With the increased support of Israel now, there is more balance and a level of calm seems to have been achieved."

"That is really an illusion more than a reality." Gabriel shook his head. "The Arab states see Israel as a crusader kingdom, perched precariously on the coast. Without the support of the Western powers, especially the US, the Arabs believe that they could easily push the Israelis into the sea."

"They are probably right."

"Oh, there is no doubt of that," Gabriel admitted easily, "which is why this fragile balance is so important. The conventional forces of the Arab states could over-run the Israeli Defense Force without much effort, so the Israeli government understands that if they fear attack, they cannot wait for the Arabs to strike the first blow. Israel is already surrounded and is a very narrow country. They must make a pre-emptive strike to disable the Arab forces arrayed against them. The Israelis also understand that they must consider using nuclear weapons for self defense."

Murph turned to face Gabriel, shocked, "Could it really come to that?"

"There have been many war-games scenarios played out over the years. The use of tactical nuclear weapons in the region is a very real possibility."

Murph looked down at his lap. "I have heard every President since I was a kid talk about working to achieve *peace in the Middle East.*"

Gabriel laughed coldly. "My friend, there has not been peace in the Middle East for 10,000 years. Initially, wars were fought for access to water. Conflict over ideology alone is a recent development, at least the last 1,000 years or so. There will never be *peace* in the Middle East. What we hope for is *stability.*"

"It would seem that to a man like Cohen, stability would lead to predictability in his investments. If he can create a balance of power between Israel and its Arab neighbors, brokered by the US, that would be the best for him."

"That's a goal that would benefit everyone! Jew and Arab alike."

"Does that seem to be what he's up to?"

"It is very difficult to tell. All of his investments seem to point that way—except for one."

"The museum?"

"Precisely!" Gabriel handed Murph a description of the Atlit Illegal Detention Camp Museum. "This museum reminds Jews that persecution did not begin and end with the Nazis. The camp was built by the British Army, as Palestine was a British possession from 1920 through World War II and after.

Jews came to the Holy Land by boat as refugees and were seen as illegal immigrants to the region. It was an act of the United Nations that created the state of Israel out of British Palestine in 1948. This led to a flood of Jewish immigrants from Europe to the new Jewish state, which infuriated the Arabs."

"Highlighting those events in a museum would increase the tensions between Jews and Arabs." Murph continued scanning the document as Gabriel spoke.

"But what really concerns my contacts is the construction of the museum. The money actually spent far exceeds the publicly stated figure and is not evident in the outward appearance of the museum."

"What do you mean?"

"Simon Cohen and his people put more money into the museum than is widely known. It appears they built something *under the museum*."

Murph looked up suddenly. "So the museum is an elaborate cover?"

"Make no mistake, it is a well-done museum that commemorates something that needed to be remembered. However, there is something happening there—and we need to find out what is!"

"How do *we* figure it out?"

"I'm making arrangements to meet my old team in Israel later this week. I need to be on the ground to see for myself."

"How can Carli and I help?"

"I'm afraid that you will need to come to Israel as well." Gabriel frowned. "The fact that the United States government is involved by proxy, I would like the help of Americans. The tentacles of this seem to go up highly in the Israeli government. I cannot access as much information as I would expect, so there is some degree of interference. You will be at risk if you come…"

"…but we can also give you cover if we blunder into something official at Atlit. Carli and I would create a low level diplomatic incident and be expelled from the country."

191

"Something like that—I hope."

Murph got up from the grass. "Then we need to start planning! You have to reconnect with your team in Israel. I need to transport Carli and me into Israel without causing suspicion."

"That may be difficult. I haven't come up with an idea yet." Gabriel put on his bike helmet.

"Don't worry about that. I'll contact you when I have the details arranged. I think I may have just the thing. I have to talk to an old friend—and then see if I can convince Carli that we need to go help with another archeological project."

Chapter 59

Murph watched as Gabriel pedaled back across the Potomac River into Washington DC. Taking his cell phone, he quickly texted Carli:

YOU HOME?
YES JUST GOT BACK
BE THERE IN 15

Murph climbed aboard his bike and headed north through Rosslyn, Virginia, selecting the Key Bridge as his path across the Potomac into Georgetown. Traffic was in gridlock, but he moved swiftly on the bike. In less than ten minutes, he was carrying his bike up Carli's steps, locking it against the porch railing.

Murph was removing his helmet when Carli opened the front door and let him in. She was dressed for yoga, and by the way her skin glistened, she had just returned from her hot yoga class. He kissed her on the cheek. "Salty!"

She laughed. "I thought you liked it that way!"

He swept her up in his arms and kissed her again.

"If you put me down, I'll get us some iced tea."

"I suppose that will have to do." He set her gently back on her feet. "We have work to do anyway."

The kitchen was small but efficient. Murph went to the bar and pulled over a stool. She filled two large glasses with ice as Murph poured the tea from the pitcher on the counter. He sat down heavily on the barstool. Carli jumped and pushed herself up with her hands, sitting down on the bar, facing him at eye level.

"So what did you learn from Gabriel Levi?"

"If we want to learn what Cohen is up to, we'll have to go to Israel."

"That's good. I've always wanted to go there!"

"Well, that was an easier sell than I was expecting!"

"Come on, Murph. Neither one of us expected Gabriel to come up with the answers long distance."

"I know – but I was hoping, just for once, that it was going to be easy."

"Silly boy!" She leaned forward, framing his face with her hands, "we're in this together, no matter what it takes."

"OK then, here's what we have to do." He took her hands in his and held them on her knees as he began to explain. "Gabriel is leaving for Israel right away to reunite with his old team. The museum at Atlit seems to be the one part of Cohen's empire that doesn't make sense."

"Really? Why?"

"The amount of money spent on the museum is way too much for what it should have been. There are rumors that some construction was done under the museum that is not apparent to the outside."

"And we're going to pay the museum a visit—together with Gabriel's team. Probably after hours."

"That way we won't need to worry about buying tickets." He laughed. "I need to meet with the Vice President before we go—just in case we spark an international incident."

"That's an encouraging thought!" She took a sip of tea. "How do we get into Israel in the first place?"

193

"Israel?" Carli's roommate Jane walked into the kitchen in a t-shirt and shorts, freshly out of the shower, unwrapping her blonde hair from a towel and fluffing it out with her hands, "My brother's going to be in Israel next week!"

As Jane padded by them, flip-flops slapping, and grabbed a water bottle from the fridge, Carli asked, "Peter? I thought he was on the ship?"

"He is. The *Dixon* is scheduled to make a port call in Haifa for a couple of days."

Murph looked at her in disbelief, "Navy ship movements are supposed to be classified."

Jane stood at the bar, across from them, "They are. Peter and my Dad worked out a code. Peter embeds numbers in his emails and Dad can decode the message and follow him. They wouldn't do it if they were on some secret mission, you know."

"Good thing." Murph tried to sound relieved. "I guess some sailor could post a picture of themselves on Facebook and everyone would know where they are anyway."

"Yeah. Anyone who really cares already knows where all the Navy ships are. All this secrecy just makes us feel better back home."

Murph took out his phone and opened the electronic notepad. "Actually, Jane. That information could be really helpful. What ship is he on and what does he do?"

Jane's pride in her brother shone brightly, "Lieutenant Peter Mitchell is a helicopter commander on the *USS George Dixon*, a guided missile destroyer."

Murph was making notes as Carli leaned in closer. "How does this help us get into Israel?" she whispered.

"Not IN – I'm looking for help in case we need to get OUT in a hurry!"

Murph collected as much information as he could from Jane, and then she went back into her bedroom to finish getting ready for her evening. He turned back to Carli and shared his plan.

"Here's how we do this! Remember, a couple of months ago, I got an email from the Dean at the Case Western Reserve

University School of Dental Medicine asking us to go with their team of dental students to Israel on an archeological dig."

"Oh, yeah. Someone was digging a sewer line for a housing project and fell into a cave where they found a bunch of bones."

"That's the one. The dental school is sending another team of two dozen students and some faculty back to Israel this month. My Dad thought it would be a great idea for us to go—you being a famous archeologist and all—and suggested it to the Dean. Jerry Goldberg and my dad have been friends for years, and I know him pretty well, so it was tough to say no. I told them that you were so busy with your Ph.D. defense that we couldn't make the trip. I'm sure if I call him back, they could add us to the expedition at the last minute."

"That's perfect!" Carli sat up straight, her mind racing. "Just tell them that I'm ahead of schedule, and we would love to be a part of the project."

"Once we're in Israel, we could get away for a day and meet with Gabriel to go see what's up at Atlit, then go back to the dig. The CWRU team will only be there for ten days anyway. They have to get back by the start of school."

"I don't want to put the students in any danger."

Murph's eyes hardened. "I know. I want to keep them as safe as possible. That's why we need to see the Vice President."

Carli arched her eyebrows. "He did say to let him know if we needed anything."

"Well, now we do." Murph snapped his fingers. "If anything happens at Atlit, we won't go back to the dig. I need to see if we can arrange a *get out of jail free card* in advance."

Carli tried to smile, but it was forced. "Do they play Monopoly in Israel? They seem kind of obsessive about their security."

Murph had to be honest. "There's no sugar coating it. The Israelis are uptight about security—because for them it is a matter of life and death. If we screw up, there's little Brooks Borlon—or anyone else for that matter—can do to help us."

"That's reassuring!"

Murph held her hands tight and looked straight into her eyes. "All kidding aside, we need to be very sure we want to do this. We're really not directly threatened, and we do face being locked up in an Israeli prison—or worse, if we go."

"Three men are dead already and we were powerless to stop it then. We're committed. Whatever the cost."

Murph smiled and pulled her close, kissing her tenderly. "That's my girl. I just needed to be sure that you were with me."

"You're not getting rid of me that easily! Let's set up that appointment with the VP and see if we can get some protection. Were you thinking of having him alert the top level of the Israeli government that we were there, in case we are arrested?"

"Not really. I don't know whom to trust, so I don't want to tell anyone what's up." Murph stood up and lifted Carli off the counter and put her on the ground. "I want him to contact the Captain of the *USS Dixon* and make sure the US Navy will be there to pull us out if we need to get away in a big hurry."

"It would be nice to know that the cavalry is there."

"Let's just hope we don't need them." Murph took her by the hand. "Now what do you pack for an archeological dig and clandestine break-in, while on vacation in Israel this time of year?"

She laughed and all the tension evaporated. "That's a tough one. Let's start making a list."

Chapter 60

Murph called the Dean of the Case School of Dental Medicine in Cleveland, Ohio and was pleasantly surprised to find that Dr. Goldberg remembered him well. He was happy to add Murph and Carli to the team for the dig. Case would take care of registering them with the Israeli government, which resolved the Visa concern that Murph had secretly worried about. Case was happy that Murph could fly them to Tel Aviv on the Gulfstream, since the dental team already had their flights settled. Murph and Carli would join the Case group at the airport in Tel Aviv and take a van to the site.

Murph did tell Jerry Goldberg that he and Carli would leave the dig for a day. He made the excuse that Carli had to follow-up on one of the details for her thesis. He felt bad lying to a friend, but the less that the Case team knew, the better. In this situation, ignorance was safety.

With their entry settled, Murph contacted Gabriel Levi and informed him of their plans. Using the secure iPhone, Murph was able to reach Levi just before he left for Israel.

"The dig is near a place called Manot. Does that help us?"

Gabriel answered quickly, "Manot is north, in the mountains—very near to the Lebanese border. Not the most stable place on earth, but it could be worse. The museum is in Haifa, which is also in northern Israel. It will be just less than an hour's drive."

"When do you want to meet us?"

"I want to arrive at Atlit at 2:00 a.m. Plan to meet us outside the entrance to the kibbutz at Kabri at 1:00 a.m. That will be a couple of miles south from your camp at Manot, which should provide some safety for the other Americans. Travel light. I will confirm with you the day before. Shalom."

Murph said, "Understood." But the phone line had gone dead.

* * * * * * *

Murph considered how to meet the Vice President. Running around the Naval Observatory again was an option, but Carli had agreed that it would seem rather suspicious. In the end, Murph selected the conventional method and called Mr. Borlon's chief of staff, Maeve Corrigan. It was lucky that she was an old friend of Murph's from high school and he had her private number. While waiting for her to pick up he worried.

197

How are we going to meet the Vice President through all the West Wing security? It seems too much like going into the lion's den.

But, Maeve had good news. Brooks Borlon had not yet had enough time to move from his old office in the Capital. The former Senator from Ohio was still using his office in the Senate Office Building.

Murph and Carli presented themselves at the entrance of the Senate Office Building and were quickly whisked through security. Brooks Borlon greeted them warmly and made sure his security detail was out of earshot. He was clearly in the process of moving, with his office filled with file boxes stacked along the walls. He cleared a stack of papers off of one of the two chairs in the room and seated them facing him at his desk. Brooks appeared nervous, fidgety, twisting his wedding ring around his finger.

Murph went straight to the point. "Mr. Vice President, you said to ask you for help when we needed it. Now, we do."

Borlon nodded. "What can I do?"

"We followed the trail of influence and it leads to Simon Cohen." He let that hang there for a moment. "When we followed a lead to northern Italy, it led to the death of two Catholic priests at the hands of a monk, who then killed himself."

"After losing a fight with Murph," Carli added. "The monk's last words were *from evil comes a greater good.* We don't know what that means yet, but it certainly sounds ominous."

Murph summarized. "We have been held at gunpoint and told to forget everything we know, and then I was told that whatever I think I know is wrong. We still have more questions than answers, but we now have a plan."

The Vice President was having a tough time keeping up. "Cohen is the billionaire who is an advisor to the President. What does he have to gain in this?"

"We're not sure. But that's what we are going to find out!"

"What are your plans?"

198

"We are following a trail, and it leads to Israel. We leave for Tel Aviv in a few days."

Borlon looked troubled. "What do you hope to do?"

"We're not completely sure, but poking around directly can sometimes get a response that makes things more clear."

"Once again, what can I do for you?" He leaned on his elbows, extending his hands, palms up.

"Before Carli and I go to swat a hornet's nest, I need to know that I have a way out." Murph reached into his pocket and took out a note card. He handed the card to Borlon. "The guided missile destroyer *USS George Dixon* is docked in Haifa, showing the flag in Israel. I would like you to contact the Captain. His name is John Rayburn." Murph pointed to the card. "And ask him to give us whatever assistance we need."

Brooks let out a low whistle. "That's a tall order!"

"We will visit the ship personally when we arrive and see if we can get his support, but I need you to open the door for us. The Captain of a US Navy ship won't see us without some form of recommendation. We need your help."

The question sat heavily in the air.

Murph sat back in his chair, calmly holding Brooks Borlon in his gaze, not backing down. It was now or never. Either the Vice President believed them and was committed to help, or not—and Murph needed to find out.

Brooks's smile broadened, and he laughed. He stood up, walked around his desk, and sat on the front edge, patting Murph on the shoulder as he went by, and then launched into an impromptu speech:

"What we're all looking for in a CEO, in a business partner, in a candidate, is formidability—someone to be reckoned with—not necessarily someone with all the answers —because no one has all the answers. No, we want someone who seems to be magic about to happen. That's the electricity around the star quarterback. People aren't attracted to him because he's a solid, reliable, by-the-book kind of guy. No, it's the feeling that he can create lightning.

199

"They don't teach formidable in school. They teach the opposite—compliance, taking the easy or safe route, avoiding risk. A friend of mine, business guru Seth Godin turned me onto a book by Paul Graham, and he gets credit for coining the term. 'A formidable person is one who seems like they'll get what they want, regardless of whatever obstacles are in the way.'

"There are two critical traits in the choice to be formidable," the Vice President ticked them off on his fingers. "Skill—to understand and master the details necessary to make your promise come true—and passion—the willingness to see it through, finding a different route when the first one doesn't work.

"Formidable leaders find the tough questions and then eagerly seek out the answers, taking on a problem and not letting go until they solve it. They bite off more than others can chew, getting results that seem impossible. I guess the best way I can put it is to say, 'It's not a dream if you can do it!'"

Murph and Carli sat there, stunned. Murph opened his mouth then realized he had nothing to say.

Brooks returned to his desk and pulled open the center drawer. He removed the tools of his office, taking out a page of letterhead and writing a personal letter of introduction to Captain Rayburn, ending it with his bold, flowing signature. He placed warm wax below his signature and then imprinted the brass seal of the Vice President of the United States. He folded the document and sealed it again, handing it to Murph.

"I will contact Captain Rayburn and ask him to give you every assistance in your mission. The President may rue the day when he engaged such formidable adversaries as you. I'm betting on your ability to figure out what is going on here and to stop it if needs be."

Murph stood and shook Brooks' hand. "Thank you, Mr. Vice President. I don't know what to say."

Carli gave him a hug. "We appreciate your support—and we won't let you down."

Brooks Borlon's blue eyes still twinkled, but his smile faded. "The Middle East is a very unstable place and people are easy to take offence. Please be careful. There is only so much I can do to help you if something goes wrong. It's nice to be the Vice President, but a billionaire can have a long reach and a heavy thumb, as well. In fact, the Israelis are known for being a bit touchy all on their own."

"Yes, Sir. We understand the risks we are taking." Murph took Carli's hand. "But we intend to get to the bottom of this, one way or the other."

Chapter 61

The next two days passed in a flurry of preparation. Murph and Carli arrived at the executive terminal at Reagan National Airport and found Derek Whitman prepping the Gulfstream G-550, whining as usual.

"Everything's a rush with you guys. Why can't you take a leisurely weekend in Vegas or something?"

Murph clapped him on the shoulder. "That's why you get the big bucks!"

"Oh, yeah. Now I remember!" Shaking his head, he opened the cabin door, extending the stairs to let Murph and Carli in.

Derek took the small pack from Carli, hefted it and looked at Murph's. "Traveling awfully light this time."

Carli smiled sweetly. "I hear that the dig is very remote and that the kibbutz where we are staying has very few creature comforts. I've been on enough rustic expeditions that I don't care, but Princess Michelle over there may miss his hair dryer."

Carli and Derek laughed, but Murph could only protest, "Hey, I can rough it as well as the next guy!"

"OK, then." Derek closed the stairs and headed for the cockpit. "Let's get this show on the road. I hate flying into

Israel. You have to call ahead for a reservation, and they get so annoyed if you don't arrive on time."

Murph grabbed Derek's arm. "I want you to drop us off and take off immediately. You'll need to rest, so fly wherever you want to spend the night and refuel. Just wait there for me to call you."

"OK, Boss." Derek pulled Murph into the forward galley, his voice dropping to a whisper. "This isn't just a simple week's vacation digging for bones, is it?"

"No, it's not." Murph frowned, his voice low. "The less you know, the better on this one. Just take off, and go somewhere a couple of hours away where you are safe. I'll call you when you can come pull us out."

Derek nodded. "No unnecessary risks for you. You're engaged now. You have to be respectable." He ended with a laugh then added, loudly, "Well, I guess we'll go to Barcelona. I've heard the food is great there."

"And the siesta seems to be your style."

"That's true!" He entered the cockpit and closed the door.

Murph returned to the main cabin to find that Carli had arranged their seats and had the coffee brewing.

He picked up her backpack and judged the light weight. "Looks like you took my advice."

"Don't bring anything you would be upset to leave behind." She deepened her voice and mimicked his tone, laughing. She pointed to his more stuffed bag, "Looks like you didn't listen."

He opened his backpack, "It looks worse than it is, but I picked up a few special things that may help us."

The Gulfstream accelerated and they took off for the flight back across the Atlantic. Settling in for the long flight, they took stock of their situation.

Murph had the secure iPhone, and Carli had the iPad mini she had received from Rocco. Murph had reluctantly decided to leave his MacBook computer in the safe at the Center. He felt naked without it, cut off from the world. They both were wearing lightweight hiking boots, military weight cargo pants, and running shirts and pullovers. They had packed changes of clothes, toiletries, and a small camera.

Carli had brought a reference manual on the Neanderthals that were the subject of the dig. "Looks convincing, don't you think?"

She reached over into Murph's bag, seeing the worn blue binding of a book. She pulled out a Bible and looked at Murph, raising an eyebrow.

"When traveling to the Holy Land, bring the Good Book. I felt that The Word would comfort us." He took the Bible and placed it back at the bottom of his backpack. "Father Albers gave me that copy when I graduated high school from Ignatius. Somehow, it just felt right."

Carli squeezed his hand in agreement. She went to repack her bag. A small manila packing envelope slipped out. Murph pointed to it.

Carli pulled it out and the front was addressed in a flowing feminine script to Lt. Peter Mitchell. "I had Jane make this for her brother. It was his birthday last week, so I had her put in a card, some pictures, and a book for him as a present. I thought it would give us some reason to go to the ship."

"That's a great idea. I'm sure the Israeli customs officers will ask us what we are going to do in Israel. I have all the information about the dig at Manot, but I was going to be honest and tell them we were going to visit the *USS Dixon* in Haifa. I hadn't figured out a good excuse why—and this is perfect!" He leaned over and kissed her, "Thanks!"

Carli tapped her temple again. "See—not just a pretty face!"

Murph took out a pair of strange hooded sweatshirts and handed one to Carli. She held it up. It was light and soft, with a faint metallic sheen. She pulled it over her head. The end of the sleeves had a thumbhole, with the fabric covering most of her hand. She turned around, allowing him to admire the fit. "Not exactly the height of fashion. What gives?"

"I got these from a guy named Adam Harvey. He's a professor at the School of Visual Arts—and a creator of 'stealth wear.' This reflective, metallic fabric is designed to reduce the thermal footprint of the wearer. In theory, this limits one's visibility to aerial surveillance vehicles employing heat-imaging cameras to track people on the ground."

"Drones?"

"Yes, Manot is less than four miles from the Lebanese border. I've heard that the Israeli Defense Force uses drones to watch for activity along their borders. We have a couple of miles of night running to do to meet Gabriel and his team. I don't want to take any chances."

"I hope you're just being paranoid." She pulled the hoodie off. "But I'm afraid that it's a good precaution." She shuddered.

Murph took the reflective hoodies and rolled them up tightly, placing them at the bottom of his pack. He went to the coffeemaker and poured a mug for each one of them. He placed cream and sugar in hers, preferring his black.

She savored the aroma then took a sip. "Mmmm. Perfect, as always."

"You're welcome." Murph sat down and turned his chair toward her. "So, what's up with this dig? How did the dental school at Case get involved?"

"Well, I talked to Dean Goldberg and the dig coordinator for the dental school, a really nice dentist named Roma Jasinevicius. She told me they believe the excavation will contribute to the knowledge of human evolution and its connection to modern dental problems, such as malocclusion (crooked teeth), cavities, and periodontal or gum disease."

"The site is in a cave?"

"Sort of." Carli grabbed a pen and started to draw on her napkin. "Manot is on the top of a mountain. When they wanted to run a sewer line to a group of houses, they started to dig a trench. Right away, the hole collapsed into a cavern. The workers shined a light down and they saw bones. They stopped and called the police. The first object they found, 30 meters down on the cave floor, was a skull. It was clear that this wasn't a crime scene, so an anatomy professor from the

University of Tel Aviv rappelled down. He found a large cavern and two smaller rooms on the side. At first, Dr. Hershkovitz thought the skull was 20,000 years old, but he's since determined it to be a 58,000 year-old Neanderthal skull."

"When did they discover the cavern?"

"2008," she said matter of factly.

"2008? What has the poor guy been doing that wanted the sewer?"

"Still going to the outhouse, I guess?" Carli seemed surprised at his question. "This is really important, Murph. The ground of the cave is covered with bones and tools. The fire pit, which served as a kitchen area, has charred animal bones and other debris that provides evidence of how the Neanderthals lived. The Neanderthals were the first hominids to bury their dead, and they did it in their living spaces. We may be there to help uncover skeletal remains under the layers of sediment that have filled the side chambers. We could be part of the discovery of further evidence of the evolution of the human form."

Carli was rolling, so Murph decided to go along with her passion. "I guess that the shape of the human face has changed the most during this time period. I remember being told in school that humans are the only adult animals that cannot eat and breathe at the same time. Human babies at birth can nurse and breathe simultaneously, but when teeth begin to appear, changes occur in the structure of the jaws and the larynx, closing off the throat. It was an evolutionary advantage for us as we stood up straight and walked, rather than being hunched over on all fours, sniffing the ground like a dog."

"Really. I guess that makes sense."

"It also means that humans now struggle with snoring, sleep apnea, and choking due to our shorter jaws. We also don't have room for three sets of molars, so most people have their wisdom teeth taken out."

"See! That's why the dental students are there."

"But I still feel bad for the poor guy who has been waiting ten years for the sewer line to be connected to his house!"

"You're impossible!" She wadded up the napkin and threw it at him.

Chapter 62

Simon Cohen was irritated. He paced across the suite, leaving a path in the plush carpet in front of his desk. He wasn't afraid. He wasn't even concerned, but he remained, well, piqued.

Reaching onto the desk, he picked up his phone and dialed. "Cyrille?"

"Yes." The bass tone was flat, expressionless.

"I am annoyed."

"How can I be of service?"

"The dentist and his fiancé have proven to be persistent. They refuse to see the folly of continuing to meddle in our affairs."

"Through Buchanan's mistake, they suspect him. They have found Valerie—and Gaspard. They have collected a few pieces, but they cannot see the puzzle."

"They may stumble onto something. They have met with the Vice President."

"It is of no consequence."

"I do not want to take any chances."

"There is no risk." Cyrille was firm.

"Still, I am annoyed." Cohen sighed heavily, "They are flying to Israel as we speak."

"I am aware."

"I no longer have patience with their interference. Take a team and collect them. It was their mistake to travel where it is easy for us to eliminate them. Let us make them sorry for that error."

"As you wish."

Chapter 63

The Gulfstream crossed from the brilliant blue of the Mediterranean Sea to the tan of the Israeli desert, broken only by low shrubs and high-rise gray cement buildings. To an American on their first visit to Israel, it looked and felt a lot like the desert southwest, maybe Arizona or New Mexico, in climate. They were arriving in late August, so the skies were clear blue dotted with puffy white clouds, and not a hint of rain. The temperature would range from near 90 degrees to lows in the 60's—perfect weather to visit the Holy Land.

The G-550 taxied to the terminal and stopped. Derek came back and wished Murph and Carli good luck. They bounded down the stairs and immediately put on their sunglasses, squinting in the brilliant sunshine. Murph waved at Derek and they walked toward the terminal building and were met instantly by officials of the Israeli Ministry of Foreign Affairs. After a brief introduction, two officers continued on to meet with Derek at the airplane, while the remaining two escorted Murph and Carli into the terminal.

Presenting their passports, the customs officers verified that their documents were valid. Murph was relieved to see that their entry visas were recorded as part of the Case School of Dental Medicine team.

"What is the purpose of your visit to Israel, Dr. Murphy?" The face on the man who had introduced himself as Officer Litvak smiled, but his tone was icy. The presence of an additional guard behind him, with an assault rifle hanging at his side, added to the tension.

Murph knew that now was the time he had to be confident. Since everyone always told him he was a bad liar, he led with the truth.

"We are here to support the dig at Manot with the dental students from Case Western Reserve University in Cleveland, Ohio, USA."

"How long do you intend to stay?"

"Our part of the dig is scheduled for two weeks, but my work schedule may require that I leave early. I'm not a professor. I work for a living seeing patients," he shrugged. "So we didn't schedule a commercial flight with the rest of the students. I'm lucky that my office has access to the corporate jet, and I can have it return and get me sooner if needed."

"Are you going to Manot with the dental team?"

"No. We arranged a car for us." *Or really, Margaret had thought ahead and arranged it*, Murph thought.

"Are you going anywhere else, other than Manot during your stay in Israel?"

"Yes. Since we will be going north along the coast anyway, we plan to stop in Haifa today."

"Why is that?" Officer Litvak was gradually unpacking their bags and laying the contents out on a table.

"Miss Chamoun's roommate's brother serves on the *USS Dixon*, which is in port."

Carli chimed in, "It was his birthday last week, and he's been at sea for six months. She sent along a birthday card, and a present, I think." She pointed out the pouch.

Litvak shook the yellow padded packing envelope. He reached into his pocket and removed a knife, snapping open the blade and slipping it quickly into the end, looking closely at Murph and Carli for a response.

"Do you mind if I open this?" He asked casually.

Carli smiled sweetly. "Well, I don't mind. Jane and Peter might be annoyed, but then, they're not here."

He tensed his wrist, the knife blade straining against the tape closure. Seeing no reaction, Litvak pulled out the blade and put the package down.

"I guess that will not be necessary." He continued to rummage through the packs. He examined the Neanderthal text. "What do you expect to find at the dig?"

Carli was ready. She launched into her dissertation on the evolution of man and how a site like this could reveal a series of settlements over time, possibly thousands of years of human bones.

Sensing she was just getting started, Litvak raised his hand quickly to cut her off. "That is good. I hope you find the evidence you are seeking. Dr. Murphy, are you here to examine any teeth they find?"

"As interesting as that would be, I'm here more for pushing a shovel; manual labor, this time. She's the archeologist." Murph opened his arms and shrugged. "I just feel bad for the poor guy whose sewer line has been delayed for ten years since they found the bones in his hole!"

The armed guard laughed, but stopped short when Litvak glanced at him sternly.

Carli huffed, "Men!"

Litvak removed the Bible from the pack and ran his fingers along the worn binding. He fanned the pages, noting the post-it notes and papers wedged inside.

"You have as many pages noted in the Old Testament as the New. That is unusual for a Christian."

"The entire book contains the Word. Jews and Christians begin at the same point. We have more beliefs in common than those that differ. After all, we pray to the same God, if in different languages. In the end, we seek the same things."

Litvak regarded Murph for a moment—then set the Bible down.

"Everything is in order." He stamped their passports and gave them their visas. "Welcome to Israel. Shalom."

Murph took the papers. "Peace be with you also. Thank you."

Chapter 64

They quickly refilled their backpacks and headed out of security into the main terminal. Murph quickly spotted their driver and in minutes they were speeding out of Ben Gurion airport. Their route led through the middle of Tel Aviv then proceeded north on Highway 2 along the coast. It was a beautiful hour and a half drive, with the blue Mediterranean on their left and the spine of mountains inland on their right.

It didn't take long in Israel to understand how small a country it is. To an American, living safely in the US, the idea of trading land for peace made perfect sense. To come to Israel was to see the difficulty in that negotiation technique. There just wasn't much land to begin with, and for the Israelis to make their country smaller was long-term military suicide.

Tel Aviv looked like any other modern metropolis, with glittering high-rise towers and wide highways, crowded with cars. The blue road signs with titles in English looked like home, until you noticed the line of Hebrew characters. With the lack of land to spread out the population, the coastal plain was filled with cream and gray apartment buildings that stood out clearly against the backdrop of the earthy brown of the mountains behind them.

Their driver was skilled, if not much of a conversationalist, and they arrived promptly in the port of Haifa.

Carli leaned in toward Murph, whispering, "I was worried Officer Litvak would find the letter from Brooks and become suspicious."

"So was I—so I took precautions." He reached into his pack, removed the Bible, and handed it to Carli. "A great man recently quoted Psalm 23 to us. I feel the need to remind myself of that often."

Carli opened the Bible to the Book of Psalms and found Psalm 23, reading aloud, "The Lord is my Shepherd, I shall not want…" She turned the next page and found the sealed letter from the Vice President as a bookmark.

"Hidden in plain sight!" Her eyes were wide with amazement.

"That's often the best way."

He reached over and plucked the letter of introduction from the Bible, placing it in his pocket. In the midday heat, Murph had removed his jacket and elected to go with an open-collared white polo shirt and pants. Carli looked dazzling in a light gray sweater and tank top, a tangerine scarf and oversized sunglasses. It was as formal as they could get to meet the Captain of a Navy warship, given what they had brought in their light packs.

Their driver negotiated base security and pulled up as close as he could to the dock. The *USS George Dixon* was berthed in the distance, standing out among the patrol boats of the Israeli Defense Force. Murph confirmed that their driver would wait for them and they began the long walk down the quay.

The *USS George Dixon* (DDG 117) was an Arleigh Burke-class destroyer, one of the newest commissioned in the US Navy. It was named for the Civil War Confederate Captain of the ill-fated submarine *CSS Hunley*. Lieutenant George Dixon had led his crew in successfully torpedoing a Union warship blockading the Confederate port of Charleston, South Carolina. Returning from the mission, the Hunley was lost with all hands when it sank in the channel near Fort Sumter. Lieutenant Dixon is remembered for his bravery and leadership in a hopeless cause.

While Carli had worked on the Neanderthals, Murph had done his research on the *Dixon*. He explained to Carli as they walked closer that the ship was over 500 feet in length and could sail at over 30 knots. It had a crew of 290 officers and men and was armed with an array of guns, missiles, and torpedoes. According to Jane, Peter Mitchell was the aircraft commander for one of the two Seahawk helicopters carried onboard. The *Dixon* had been serving in support of the operations to stop pirates from hijacking ships in the Arabian Sea. They had recently entered the Mediterranean to support the *USS George H.W. Bush* and Carrier Strike Group 2. They

211

had been deployed for more than six months and were due to rotate home soon.

Murph walked boldly up to the uniformed officer at the bottom of the boarding gangway and introduced himself and Carli, asking to speak with Lieutenant Peter Mitchell.

Here was the moment of truth. Had Jane gotten word to Peter to expect them? Had Brooks Borlon contacted the Captain? Murph stood there in the sun as the duty officer picked up the phone to contact the officer of the watch. The young ensign spoke quietly then nodded several times, placing the phone back.

"Sir, Lt. Mitchell is unavailable."

Murph stood still, but his heart sagged.

"Interestingly enough, Captain Rayburn will see you." He handed his clipboard to the sailor next to him. "I am to escort you and Miss Chamoun to the Captain's cabin to meet him. Please follow me."

The sailor stood there holding the clipboard, his mouth hanging open, as Murph and Carli walked by, heading up the ramp onto the USS Dixon.

Chapter 65

"Welcome to the USS Dixon, my name is Ensign Samuel Mark." They reached the top of the ramp and stopped. The sentry on duty saluted, and Ensign Mark returned his salute. They were allowed onto the deck of the warship. The heat of the sun baked down on the gray surface and reflected back up at them in waves.

Ensign Mark had obviously not been on duty long, as his khaki uniform shirt was still pressed, and only the slightest spot of sweat was beginning to show between his shoulder blades. He turned to Carli and warned her to be careful of the ropes on the deck. They reached the entrance to the superstructure of the destroyer. The Ensign undid the latch and pulled open the hatch.

"Mind your head; the bulkheads are low." He turned to Carli as he spoke, looked down at her and laughed, realizing she was only 5-foot tall. "Well, at least you don't have to worry about hitting your pretty head."

Murph bent over as he entered, his 6'2" frame clearly a disadvantage here on ship. "Don't worry, I'll be careful," he said to no one in particular, since the young Ensign scarcely realized he was there.

The Dixon was not a large ship, but there was still a maze of passages that led to the officer's quarters. Ensign Mark led them down a narrow passageway, ending at a door emblazoned with the brass nameplate: CAPTAIN. He knocked crisply and a deep voice said, "Enter!"

Mark turned the knob and pushed open the door, leaning his head in. "Dr. Murphy and Miss Chamoun."

"Thank you, Ensign. That will be all."

"Yes, Sir." Ensign Mark opened the door fully and let Carli and Murph enter, closing the door behind them.

The room was quite small, since space is precious on a warship. Captain John Rayburn rose from his desk and came around it to greet Murph and Carli, shaking each hand. He was a stocky man probably in his late forties, though his sandy hair was beginning to gray prematurely in the temples. His large hands and forearms gave him a powerful grip.

Captain Rayburn clasped Murph's hand for a moment, sizing up his guest while Murph returned the grip with equal force. The Captain offered two chairs facing his desk and returned to his seat, keeping the desktop as a barrier. Murph held Carli's chair for her and then seated himself.

A career Navy officer, Captain Rayburn seldom had a meeting like this one. He rested his elbows on his desk and spread his hands. "This is new for me, so I'll get right to it. Please explain to me how a dentist can have the Vice President of the United States contact the captain of a US Navy destroyer and put that ship and its crew of 290 at his disposal."

Murph took a deep breath. "Captain, we appreciate your taking the time to meet with us. We have a story to tell that sounds so fantastic that I have a hard time believing it when I hear myself speak. But, with your indulgence, I'll start at the beginning."

"That sounds like a good place to begin." Captain Rayburn stopped at a faint knock on the door. "Ah, yes. One thing first." He raised his voice in command. "Come in, Lieutenant!"

The cabin door opened and another khaki-clad officer entered and snapped smartly to attention. He was six-foot tall, broad shouldered, with dark brown hair cut short, off the collar and over the ears. He had brown eyes and a sly smile. *He looks just like Jane*, Carli thought.

"At ease, Lieutenant."

Peter Mitchell relaxed slightly. Murph turned and rose to greet him. He shook hands warmly with the pilot.

"Hi, Peter. It's been a long time. You were a senior when I…"

"…was a freshman at Ignatius. You've changed a bit since then, Murph, and grown almost a foot."

"I was so short as a freshman!"

"Yeah, I never pictured you as a volleyball player, but I get it now."

Peter walked further into the room and leaned down to hug Carli. "Jane's told me so much about you. You two really have hit it off!"

"Thanks, Peter. Living with your sister has been my pleasure." Carli reached into her pack and gave him the manila envelope. "This is from Jane. Happy Birthday!"

"AHEM." Captain Rayburn was frowning.

"Sorry, Sir." Peter returned to attention. "These two are who they say they are. I haven't seen Dr. Murphy in more than ten years, but that's him."

"Thank you, Lieutenant. Why don't you stay by the door and see that we are not disturbed—while we deal with this matter vital to national security." His voice dripped sarcasm.

Murph sat back down and continued. "Several weeks ago, while attending a dinner at the White House, we were called to the private residence of the President. He had bitten down on a popcorn hull and fractured a tooth. President Buchanan was in excruciating pain, so he was taken to my office immediately. I took x-rays and then removed the broken tooth, relieving his pain. The extracted tooth was very unusual, so I took a picture of it, which you can see here."

Murph had his iPhone prepared, so he quickly called up the image of the extracted, pink molar.

Captain Rayburn examined the picture. "I'm no dentist, but that tooth looks pink to me."

"Excellent observation. What would you say if I told you that the one thing that makes a tooth have that particular coloration is a chemical used only in root canals done by Russian or former Soviet Bloc dentists?"

Rayburn's frown deepened. "That's not possible. The President is a decorated pilot who was shot down in Afghanistan, but…" He shook his head, continuing, "What you are suggesting is impossible! Mitchell, come over here and look at this."

Peter left the door and stood over Captain Rayburn's shoulder, bending down to see the phone in Murph's hand.

Murph had no choice but to continue. "Yes, Sir. I know it's impossible—or at least I don't want to believe it, since the implications are too terrible to consider." Murph swept his fingers across the screen and changed to the next image. He had prepared the side-by-side images of the panoramic x-rays. "To be sure, I obtained the x-rays of Colonel Buchanan in the armed forces medical database. The image on the left is before he deployed to Afghanistan. The image on the right is the one taken in my office three weeks ago."

Murph let them study the films for a minute. "Captain, you could go to Afghanistan and have a root canal done by a Russian dentist. Not very likely, but it's possible. But you can't grow wisdom teeth back after you had them removed in high school."

215

The Captain sat back in his chair, the color draining from his face. "Holy Shit."

"Yes, Sir. We are left with only one conclusion—that the President of the United States is an imposter. He was probably substituted after his deployment but before he ran for office. There was a time when Colonel Buchanan was in a coma in a military hospital and then in a private hospital back in the states, before he apparently made a full recovery."

The Captain was stunned, but his brain was looking for a way out of the fog. "So why are you in Israel?"

Carli jumped into the story. "In trying to solve the questions as they came up, we began looking for who would stand to gain the most from controlling the President. We followed several leads, which led us to northern Italy. Two Catholic priests were killed and a monk committed suicide after losing a fight with Murph. All the trails lead to a billionaire, Simon Cohen, who contributed millions behind the scenes into TV ads that helped the Democratic ticket of Biden/Buchanan get elected. Cohen has come out of the shadows as a frequent visitor at the White House since President Biden's death."

Murph laid out the plan. "The most significant change in US policy since Buchanan became President relates to our foreign policy in the Middle East."

The Captain rubbed his chin, "That's true. In the previous administration, we were far more pro-Arab. We would never have made a public relations visit to Israel like we are now. In a few short months, this administration has gone a long way to solidify our relations with the Israelis."

Peter nodded. "On our last cruise, they were very nervous. We've come into port now, and it's been really relaxed. I'm sad that we're leaving tomorrow."

Murph's head snapped up. "Tomorrow??"

Captain Rayburn noticed Murph's surprise. "Yes. The crew is returning to the ship now, and we are getting underway at dawn tomorrow. We have to be in Charleston,

South Carolina for the commemoration of the burial of the remains of the CSS Hunley crew."

The blank looks on Murph and Carli's faces were immediately apparent.

Rayburn turned to Peter. "Lieutenant?"

"Yes, Sir." He leaned his hands down on the desk, bending over to get closer to their bewildered guests. "This ship is named for the captain of the Confederate submarine CSS Hunley. The Hunley sank with the loss of all her crew in 1864 after the first successful torpedoing of a ship by a submarine. The wreck of the Hunley was found in 1995. The submarine was raised in 2000 and has been carefully studied since then. The remains of her crew were removed from the wreck and are being buried with full military honors in Charleston. We are to be there for the ceremony to provide a symbolic navy presence, which is why our cruise here in the Mediterranean is being cut short."

"We sail at dawn tomorrow." Captain Rayburn placed his palms on the desk and pushed himself up. "So how can we be of service to you?"

Chapter 66

Floored by the news, Murph was scrambling, his mind whirling. He stood up to meet the Captain, using his superior height for all he could. Murph took the Vice President's letter out of his pocket and handed it to the Captain.

Captain Rayburn broke the seal and quickly read the document, handing it to Lieutenant Mitchell. "So?"

"Simon Cohen has invested extensively in the Middle East, but his support of the Atlit Illegal Detention Camp Museum here in Haifa makes no sense. The amount of money spent is too high and there are rumors of extensive construction done below ground at the site. We are going to visit the museum at night with a team of Israelis to get answers to our questions."

Murph stopped. He wasn't really sure what he needed after all, anyway. "I guess what I need from you is an assurance that if something goes wrong with the raid…" He swallowed hard. "…that you'll let us on the ship when you go."

Captain Rayburn stood, silent. "I will not endanger my ship and crew for you. I will not cause an international incident. If you reach the ship before we sail, I will allow you to board and take you home." He locked eyes with Murph. "If you are arrested, you are on your own. That becomes an issue for the State Department. For now, I will give you what assistance I can, but my ship and its crew are my primary concern. Your story is compelling, and frankly, it scares me to death, but for now, I take my orders ultimately from the Commander in Chief—whoever he is!"

Murph reached out his hand and shook the Captain's firmly. "Thank you, Sir. That's the best I could hope for, given the tale I have told you."

"Lieutenant Mitchell, please show our guests off the ship. We have to prepare to sail."

"Yes, Sir."

Carli stood up and shook the Captain's hand and they followed the pilot out of Rayburn's cabin. Peter led them out and down the gangway back to the dock. He gave Carli a hug and shook Murph's hand.

"Sorry I can't be more help."

"That's OK, Peter. I understand your Captain's reluctance to risk his ship when even I'm not sure what is at stake here."

Peter took out his phone. "Give me your number so I can recognize it when you call. Here's my cell number. Call me after the raid and let me know you are OK—or warn me that you're coming, and I'll do my best to hold the ship—if I can."

"Thanks, Peter. I hope that won't be necessary. Maybe the museum is just a museum." Murph put on his sunglasses and took Carli's hand. "Talk to you soon!"

"Great. I've got to get back and prep my aircraft. We're flying tomorrow when we sail. It looks impressive to have both helicopters up when we leave port."

Peter turned and headed back to the ship. Murph and Carli walked briskly down the quay toward their waiting car.

They had barely made it out of sight of the Navy guards when Carli turned to Murph.

"They're leaving tomorrow??" The veins were popping out on her neck.

"Just keep walking, like we're out in the park." Inside the wheels were spinning, but he was fighting to look calm. "I'll call Gabriel, and tell him we have to go tonight."

"This was already tight, but now—I'm not sure we can pull it off."

"We'll do the best we can. That's all we have ever been able to do."

They reached the car and pulled out, returning to the highway for the 45 minutes remaining to Manot. As the car wound its way toward the mountains, Murph had to risk a phone call. He dialed Gabriel, and the phone was answered immediately.

"The ship is leaving tomorrow. We have to go tonight."

Gabriel swore. "That makes it complicated."

Murph had nothing to say, so he allowed the silence to deepen.

"I will arrange the team for tonight. Come to the Kibbutz at Kabri at 1:00 a.m. Wait in the trees by the entrance, and we will find you."

"Understood."

Murph put away the phone, and they rode the rest of the way in silence, lost in their own thoughts.

Chapter 67

Their car pulled up to a narrow road, lined with oak and juniper trees. Attempts were being made to grow olive trees in

this climate as well. The dig was based near the peak of the mountain, with the headquarters in a cement block building with a brown tile roof.

The living arrangements were spartan, with a large bunkroom for the women and a separate one for the men. Each wing had a pair of showers, and there was a central gathering space and kitchen. The best part of the accommodations was that they were very close to the cave.

Murph and Carli were welcomed by the dental students and their supervising dentists. Eager to be working, Murph and Carli saw to the preparations of dinner, with Murph improvising an excellent pasta sauce from local olives, as well as tomatoes, garlic, onions and basil.

Fatigued from travel, the camp was early to bed soon after the sunset, knowing that dawn would bring a heavy day of work at the Neanderthal site.

Chapter 68

The phone rang. A harsh chime that resonated against all of the hard surfaces in the subterranean space, cement floors and cinder block walls. The guard stubbed out his cigarette with distaste and walked over to the phone, slinging his machine pistol further over his shoulder.

"Shalom." He held the phone in a greasy hand.

"Ashram!" The deep voice was commanding.

"I'll get him." The bored guard dropped the handset onto the table and shuffled off to another room. "Ashram! Phone—it's *him!*"

Ashram jumped off the couch and shoved the guard out of his way, running to pick up the phone.

"Yes?"

"That's better. You know I do not like to be kept waiting."

"I am sorry. Jaffet is useless." Ashram spat in the general direction of Jaffet, who shrugged and lit another cigarette. "What do you require?"

"The dentist has come to Israel. We need to see to it that he is entertained."

"Yes, Master." Ashram licked his lips. He reached across the table for a pencil and an envelope covered with greasy fingerprints. "Where can I find him?"

"He and the girl are at the Kibbutz in Manot. Take a team there and bring them back to Atlit. I will be there tomorrow to find out what they know."

"Yes, Mr. Bastien. It will be done." He wrote Manot down. "How will I know them?"

"He is over six feet tall and very athletic. She is barely five feet tall and very beautiful with brown hair. They should easily stand out in any crowd."

"I'll bring them here for you."

"Do not underestimate them. They are not easily frightened and may provide more of a struggle than you anticipate."

"It will not be a problem, master. I will make them sorry they came to Israel."

"You will do *nothing* except bring them to the base. I will send you pictures of them so that there will be no mistake on whom you are to capture."

"It is not necessary, master. I can handle this task."

"Ashram—do not take Jaffet with you tonight. I will deal with his insolence when I return."

"Yes, Sir. We will leave immediately."

Ashram cursed when he realized he had been speaking to a dead line. Cyrille had hung up on him. He went into the guard's break room and turned off the television, kicking the sleeping form of a guard on the couch.

"Get up, you dogs. There is work to do!"

221

Chapter 69

The staff and dental students were all snoring away when Murph and Carli crept out of the building, meeting in front of the house at midnight.

"Hello, my dear. Beautiful, night for a run, don't you think?" Murph whispered.

"Breathtaking!" She leaned over and kissed him on the cheek.

The cloudless sky was an inky black. The absence of lights on the mountain allowed them to see stars that were invisible in the US. At home, the light pollution created by too many parking lots and streetlights obscured all but the brightest stars. Murph and Carli stopped for a moment in awe of the panorama twinkling in the heavens above them.

A faint sliver of waning moon provided the slightest of background light. The darkness masked their movements, but would make travel down the mountain treacherous. They pulled on their stealth sweatshirts and adjusted the hoods. Each of them placed a baseball cap on, Carli pulling her ponytail through the back of the hat, and then put up the hood. They put on their packs, crouched down and listened. Assuring themselves that all was quiet, they decided to accept the risk of running on the road to take the relative safety of not breaking an ankle going straight down the mountain. There was only one road from Manot to the highway. They would be more exposed to any traffic, but they also wouldn't get lost. They really had no choice, so Murph led off down the gravel path that passed for the road at this height, remembering from their trip up earlier that they would reach asphalt paving fairly soon.

Murph set an easy pace. As the distance runner, Carli could have covered more ground at a faster pace, but she knew that Murph was saving their energy, in case they had to sprint to safety. In spite of the cool air, they soon were sweating freely. Murph had estimated the distance to Kabri at about five miles. Luckily for him, it was mostly downhill.

Chapter 70

The white Chevy panel van was old and overused, making it the perfect, nondescript vehicle for the task at hand. Ashram rode in the passenger seat, as befit his station as commander of the mission. His driver, Palti, was a small, swarthy thug with greasy black hair tied back with a red bandanna. He drove up the coast road from Haifa like a man possessed. The night was dark, and the van had one headlight out, but that did not deter Palti from his breakneck pace.

In the back of the van, the remainder of the team, if you could call this gang of mercenaries a team, readied their weapons. Discharged former members of the Israeli Defense Force, they had difficulty finding jobs that suited their surly nature, so they had become soldiers of fortune, selling their talents with weapons to the highest bidder. The five were at best comrades, but certainly not friends. Ashram was nominally the leader, only because Cyrille had named him so.

The mercenaries all held Ashram in contempt. Tall and scrawny, without enough muscle to stand up to any of them, Ashram was in charge because they all feared Cyrille Bastien more than they hated Ashram.

Bastien was a mean one and very quiet. He was so quiet that it made them nervous. They were accustomed to soldiers boasting of their prowess with guns, or their fists, or with women. It was the quiet ones they feared. They were truly dangerous—not needing any attention, being confident in their abilities.

Ashram had described the mission. Drive to Manot and capture a dentist and his girlfriend. Ashram showed them the photos Bastien had emailed him. The mercenaries passed around the prints. The dentist was confident, smiling, his headshot taken from the website for The Center. The image of the girl wasn't as clear. It was a grainy picture—a screen shot from a video—with her dancing with Elvis.

"Americans!" they muttered with contempt.

This was so easy that they were insulted. All this job needed was a taxi, not trained soldiers. Ashram should have done this by himself, but Bastien had insisted that they take a team, at least that's what Ashram had said.

Now they were bouncing around the back of this dirty van as Palti drove like a madman. Instead of sleeping at the base, it was midnight and they were barreling through the mountains. What a waste of talent! Enoch lightly oiled his cloth and wiped the barrel of his shotgun. He looked at his watch. 12:15. They should be in Manot soon; then they could get this over with. As Ashram had said, the girl *was* beautiful. That sounded promising. Enoch whistled softly to himself and considered the possibilities.

Chapter 71

Murph looked down at the luminous dial of his watch. 12:15. They were making good time, coming down the mountain and reaching the main road. Murph heard a faint buzzing sound, pulling back the hood of his sweatshirt slightly and cocking his head to one side. There it was again. This time, Carli heard it too.

Murph pulled her off the pavement and into the bushes on the side of the road. They crouched down, showing their backs to the sky, faces to the ground.

Carli whispered, "Drone?"

"I don't know. I'm not really sure what one sounds like, but let's stay here for a minute to be sure."

Murph had them lie down on the ground as the noise became louder. More familiar somehow, then the sounds of tires squealing on the pavement gave it away completely. A white van roared around the corner, tires screaming, one headlight bobbing like the eye of the Cyclops. The van barely stayed on the road and charged up the hill past Murph and Carli.

As soon as the van was out of sight, Murph got Carli up and started running quickly down the road, away from the van.

"I have a bad feeling about that. They were going somewhere in a big hurry."

Carli nodded. "And the only thing up there—was us!"

Murph lengthened his stride. No time to save energy now. They needed to get to the rendezvous at Kabri as quickly as possible.

Twenty minutes later, the road they were on enlarged to four lanes as they neared a major crossroads. There was a traffic light and the entrance to the Kibbutz was on their left. Murph jumped the guardrail and led Carli into the scrub brush and below a line of junipers. The green road sign proclaimed Kabri in English and Hebrew.

They sat down, and Murph took his phone and called Gabriel.

"We're here."

"Good. We will be there in three minutes."

Several cars passed quickly, but Murph stayed hidden. Finally, a white van with the royal blue Hebrew lettering proclaiming the Israel Electric Corporation pulled off to the side of the road in front of them. The door opened and the passenger, in the blue coveralls of a repairman, looked up at the power lines overhead. He looked into the trees and said loudly, "Four score and seven years ago."

Murph grabbed Carli by the wrist and pulled her up. "Come on, it's Gabriel."

"How?"

"We both share a respect for President Lincoln—and a love of oratory."

He led her to the edge of the trees. He looked around and made sure that no other cars were coming. He helped her over the black and white striped metal guardrail and to the back of the power company van.

Gabriel came to the back door and rapped twice on it. The door opened and another blue clad employee came out. He moved to the passenger seat, allowing Murph, Carli and Gabriel to climb into the back of the van. They had barely shut the door when the van lurched forward and turned sharply, accelerating back down the road toward Haifa, leaving Manot far behind.

Chapter 72

Ashram and his band of thugs arrived at the entrance to the neighborhood at Manot. Palti pulled the van off the side of the road and shut down the engine. He opened the driver's door with a grating CREAK and slid out of the seat to the ground.

Ashram hissed, "SILENCE!"

Palti waved his arm, panning the darkened buildings, "They sleep like babies. What difference does it make?"

Up the street, a dog began barking. Ashram glared at him. "That's why, fool!"

Another creak announced the opening of the rear doors and the five remaining mercenaries piled out and stretched. Though they had been highly trained soldiers in the past, months of boring guard duty had made them lazy and un-disciplined. They collected their weapons and walked around the side of the van to join Palti. They stood in a loose circle, Enoch idly chewing on bubble gum.

Ashram had gone ahead to look at the layout of the street. He returned in a few minutes and bent down to one knee on the gravel. As the team gathered around him, he took out a knife and quickly drew a map of the street in the dirt beside the road.

"They are in a house at the end of the street. We will spread out and encircle the building then go in together. Palti and Shet will remain outside to prevent anyone leaving."

Tall and gangly, Shet had a baby face, which made him look younger than 18. He nodded enthusiastically, being the newest to the job. Palti just shrugged and grunted, "Whatever."

Ashhram cursed to himself at being surrounded with such incompetents, but continued his briefing. "When we go in, there are wings on the right and left that look like bunks. Rafe and Gilead will take the bunkrooms. Samuel and Alva will come in the back, as there may be small single bedrooms there. I will enter the front. Gather all the sheep into the common room in the middle, and I will identify Murphy and Chamoun. Then Palti will get the van, and we will go."

The thugs nodded, reluctantly seeing the wisdom of his plan.

Ashram took his boot and wiped out his map. "As little noise as possible. And no shooting! We need them alive—for the boss."

Ashram looked at his watch. "Spread out and get into your positions by 1:30. Wait and watch to make sure no one is outside. We go in at 1:45. Understood."

They all nodded again, each pulling a bandanna up over his mouth and nose. Their identities hidden, they spread out, crouching down and moving from one spot of cover to another. Their old training had reawakened with the adrenalin of the mission.

Chapter 73

Gabriel Levi helped Carli to sit on a box and smiled warmly. "Welcome to Israel. What do you think of my country?"

"In the twelve hours I've been here, I'm very impressed. The coast is strikingly beautiful." She grabbed the side as the van made a hard turn. "I just wish we had the time to enjoy exploring, rather than running around in the dark."

"You will have to come back soon, and I will show you everything. I dream of a time when there is less stress here. There will never be peace, but I hope that the next generation, both Arab and Jew, will be more tolerant."

Murph agreed. "You told me that you left the Mossad because you...well, why don't you tell it. It's your story."

Gabriel sighed. "Like all Jews, I entered the army as a very young man, doing the mandatory two years of service. I enjoyed it and moved into military intelligence and then was recruited into the Mossad. I have done special operations for more years than I would like to admit."

"I'm sure there are more stories there too."

"Yes, Murph, things that I will never be able to discuss. But in order to do that job, you have to make someone your enemy. Your side is good—right? And the others are evil. The only way you can perform in that world is to make it absolute, black and white. A few years ago, I began to see gray."

Carli cocked her head to one side, "I'm not sure I understand."

"I was in the Golan Heights on a mission, chasing a group of young Arabs, boys really. When I caught one, I tackled him and rolled him over in the dust, clutching him by the throat with my pistol against his cheek. I saw myself reflected in his eyes—and I saw a monster."

Gabriel stopped and swallowed hard.

"Don't get me wrong. Israel is surrounded by enemies who would wipe her off the map if they could. Someone has to do the dirty jobs to keep my people safe. It just can't be me anymore." He rubbed his eyes. "The fear in the eyes of the Palestinian kid troubled me, but I know it's necessary. To keep the peace, Israel must be strong. The Arabs respect Israel because we are so strong. If we become weaker, then we are finished."

Murph bounced along with the speeding van, reflecting on how they got here. "How does Cohen figure into this? I don't see it. He could change the policy of the US to support Israel without replacing the President. It's too much work for too little gain!" Murph flexed his fingers together, cracking his knuckles. "There must be more to this than we can see."

"I agree. And that's why I'm dressed as an electric company repairman, and we are going to Haifa in the middle of the night. So, we have serious business to attend to." Gabriel turned to Carli. "Have you fired a gun before?"

Her eyes widened. "No. I, uh…"

"That's alright. I intend that it not come to that." He faced Murph. "What is your experience with firearms?"

"My uncle took me with him to a shoot when I was in college. It was a gathering of Thompson submachine gun owners at a range outside of Columbus."

"So you have fired the Thompson?" Gabriel was impressed. Carli just looked shocked. This was news to her!

"Yes, the local Sherriff's department also brought some other guns to the range so we could try them out—handguns, a Glock, I think, and an MP-5."

Gabriel reached into a chest next to him, drawing out a compact assault rifle, carefully keeping the barrel pointed up at the roof of the van. "The Heckler & Koch MP 5, just like this one?"

Murph nodded and reached for the gun.

Gabriel pulled it back. "I sincerely hope that won't be necessary. I have a team of professionals that will be carrying this, including myself. Adding you at this time would introduce a level of uncertainty that—well, let's say that any benefit of you shooting one of the bad guys is outweighed by the risk of hitting one of us. Nothing personal."

"Oh, I agree!" Murph shook his head enthusiastically. "I was hoping there would be no gunfire at all."

"Me, too, but we have to be prepared. The research by my team this week has indicated that there are as many as 20 mercenaries at the Atlit compound, though not all at one time. They are all former IDF, Israeli Defense Force, troops. They are well armed and extremely dangerous." Gabriel stopped and looked deeply into the eyes of both Murph and Carli. "Are you sure that you wish to continue? We can call this off now."

They both answered immediately, "NO!"

"We need to find out where this goes," Carli insisted. "We have seen friends killed over whatever they are hiding."

Murph admired her strength, supporting her completely, "We understand the risk, but we can't walk away now. We are in this to the end."

"Very well." Gabriel reached into the cabinet again, this time removing a heavy handgun. He handed this one to Murph. "For extreme emergencies, this is the Heckler & Koch VP 70 M. It is a semi-automatic weapon. Just pull the trigger and it fires. The blowback chambers a new round, and you can fire again. The M means this is the military variant. It has a selective fire switch that allows you to fire a three round burst with one pull of the trigger when it is set like this."

Gabriel showed Murph the selective fire settings, placing it on single for now, and made sure the safety was on. He reached down and removed two additional clips of ammunition.

"Firing a 9 mm round, it holds an 18 round magazine. It has a polymer frame, so it's fairly light. With the three shot burst, even an amateur like yourself can hit something, if you need to."

"That's comforting!" Murph commented dryly. He took the clips of ammunition from Gabriel and stowed them in his backpack.

Gabriel gave Murph the pistol. He held it pointed at the back doors of the van. Gabriel quickly reviewed how to hold it in his right hand, index finger off of the trigger, pointed forward until he made the conscious decision to shoot. Left hand palm up under the bottom of the gun, fingers up to wrap around the right hand, supporting the right wrist, hand, and gun.

Murph was smiling slyly. "I almost hate to admit it, but it feels good!"

"I know. Let's just put it away and hope the first time you fire, it will be on a firing range at a paper target." Gabriel patted him on the back. "Just remember, when you pull the trigger, aim at the largest part of the body. None of this Hollywood, *I'll just try to wound him* bullshit. Shoot to kill—because the other guy will be."

Murph's smile vanished. He tucked the handgun inside his belt, in the small of his back, and placed his sweatshirt over it to cover it. It felt cold and hard against his t-shirt, a fitting reminder of the dangerous game they were playing.

"I have something that is more suited to your talents." He pulled a pair of hypodermic syringes out of his pocket. "These are filled with Ketamine. It's an animal tranquilizer that will knock someone out for several hours."

Murph took the syringes and put them in his pack. "If you're a really big guy, a dose like this of Ketamine will only make you sleepy."

"Yes, but that may be better actually. Your victim would be still able to walk, but look drunk and be easily controllable."

"Sounds good. Just inject it in their neck for fastest results?"

"If you can, but I would settle for anywhere in the body unless we have the subject restrained. In a pinch, just jab him wherever you can and I'll be happy."

Gabriel again reached into the chest and selected a brown envelope, removing an aerial photograph of Atlit, placing it in front of Murph and Carli.

"This is the Atlit Illegal Immigration Detention Camp Museum. Between 1934 and 1948, more than 122,000 people came from Europe and Arab countries to the shores of British Palestine. They were known as ma'apilim or illegal immigrants. They weren't wanted here, so they were detained in camps like this."

Carli shook her head sadly. "They survived the Holocaust and were imprisoned in camps just like the ones they had escaped."

"Precisely. This museum reminds Jews and the rest of the world that the modern country of Israel has only been around since 1948. It was a struggle to make it happen in the first place, and the continued existence of Israel is not assured."

Murph was carefully examining the photo. "Where is the recent construction?"

Gabriel pointed to the entrance first. "Near the outer gates, here, there are reconstructions of the barracks originally built by the British Army in the 1930's. This dirt pathway, lined by palm trees and barbed wire fencing is the Promenade. This strip divided the detention camp between women and men. It was the only meeting point between married couples."

"How sad!" She could feel the pain of their separation.

Gabriel pointed to a low, square building. "This is the Disinfection Room. When immigrants arrived, this was their reception center, for processing and 'disinfection.' Eerily similar to what you see at the Nazi concentration camps, it's the only original structure to survive. The museum was built around it."

"The irony here is so tragic." Murph had been to Buchenwald and Auschwitz. The evil there was palpable. It was something he would never forget.

"Exactly so!" Gabriel tapped the image with his finger. "This building, near the water, houses a multimedia exhibit tracing the journey of a Jewish immigrant boat, the *Haim Arlosoroff*, which allows visitors to follow the voyagers' experience in coming to Palestine. The museum has set a goal to find out the stories of the immigrants who risked everything to come to Israel before 1948. They are collecting the oral histories of the survivors. There also is a memorial to the ma'apilim, honoring the 3,000 immigrants who lost their lives trying to reach the Jewish homeland."

Gabriel looked up from the map. "There is a door on the side of this building that faces the sea. It is cordoned off from the museum and appears different than the others."

"What do you mean?" Murph studied the building in the photo.

"There is more security on that door. This building also has more electrical connections than would be expected for its apparent purpose. It also has several satellite dishes concealed on the seaside face. There is even a covered loading dock at the end of the building, shielded from any cameras."

"I see that now."

"It is this area that we will explore tonight. We need to finish our preparations."

Gabriel helped Murph and Carli apply camouflage facial makeup to darken their faces. Their dark thermal-masking sweatshirts and black cargo pants would work well. Gabriel shed his electrical company coveralls to reveal a black fleece top and combat pants. Then, he applied his camo makeup.

The pitch of the engine changed, and the van began to slow. They could feel the tires leave the paved road surface and crunch to a stop on the gravel shoulder. The front doors opened, and they heard the scraping of a ladder being taken down off the roof of the van. Gabriel shut off the lights in the back of the van, allowing their eyes to begin to adjust in total darkness.

Then one of back doors opened, and the van was flooded with the cool night air. The scent of the sea was on the air. Murph could taste the salt and smell the fish. The open rear door of the van shielded their exit from the road. Gabriel led Murph and Carli deeply into the shadows beside the van, and they crouched down.

The faint moon glistened off the undulating surface of the Mediterranean a scant quarter mile away. Murph regarded the barbed wire fence and palm trees in front of them, and quickly recognized the barracks. They were perched against the fence beside the museum at Atlit. Murph settled his backpack between his shoulders and adjusted the pistol in his belt.

Gabriel considered them, looking for confirmation. Murph reached out to Carli and she squeezed his hand.

He nodded firmly and inched closer to Gabriel. "Let's do this!"

There was no turning back now.

Gabriel touched the earpiece of his headset and checked in with his team. Everyone was in place. Gabriel motioned to the man up the ladder on the electric pole. He drew Murph and Carli to him.

"Stay close to me!" Gabriel then spoke quietly into his microphone. "GO!"

With a snap like a shot, the agent in coveralls cut the main power line to the museum and the camp went completely dark. Gabriel led them through the fence and into the main yard, racing at a full sprint across the promenade.

Chapter 74

Ashram stood in the shadow of an oak tree, across the street from the house. So far, his plan had gone off flawlessly. The house had been surrounded and the perimeter quietly secured. He checked his watch for the thousandth time as the minutes ground slowly along. He had overestimated how long it would take to get into position, so they had all been waiting for more than a half an hour. He had no way of communicating with his team, so they had to all sit tight until the time he had set.

His watch finally clicked to 1:45 a.m. He walked purposefully out of the shadows and across the street. He heard a scream, and the lights flashed on in the back. Cursing the noise, he lifted his leg and kicked at the lock. The front door burst open, and he charged down the hall, brandishing his machine pistol in the empty hallway.

Shet heard the commotion and began to move forward, but Palti motioned for him to stay put, as he had been ordered. With stealth out the window, Palti took out a cigarette and lit it. He surveyed the yard casually, smoking and waiting in case anyone would try to escape.

Ashram stood in the common room as his accomplices herded the stunned dental students in. Enoch ran up to Ashram, whispering, "They are not here!"

Ashram cursed. "Search the compound!" he hissed.

The leader of the dig started to shout, "What is the meaning of this?" but fell silent when Ashram aimed his rifle at him.

"Where is Dr. Murphy?" Ashram shouted. Enoch, Rafe and Gilead disappeared back into the hallways, turning on every light, opening every closet.

It was immediately clear that the Case dental students had no information and were of no use to Ashram. In their haste to enter the building, Ashram's thugs had erased any footprints that would have been useful.

Ashram howled with rage. His team grinned to each other, secretly wondering how Ashram was going to explain to Bastien that he had let the dentist get away.

Ashram's phone buzzed. "Yes?"

"Ashram!" The voice was excited, whispering. "It's Jaffet! The power just went out! What should we do?"

"Shit!" Ashram whirled on his heel, looking to the sky for advice. "Turn on the generator and set the defenses, you fool! We will be back as soon as we can."

"Did you capture them?"

"Do not bother me with stupid questions. You have work to do!"

"So you didn't get them." Jaffett chuckled. "How unfortunate!"

Ashram launched into a tirade of profanity, but the call ended. He shouted for his team to return to the van. They left the students with their mouths open, shaking, standing in the common room.

As they reached the van, Ashram shoved them into the back, slamming the door. He climbed into the passenger seat, yelling at Palti to get moving.

"Trouble at home?" Palti sneered as he put the van into gear.

Ashram looked at his watch then stared blankly out the front window, fuming.

"Two a.m." He thought. *" It will take us an hour to get back to Atlit. I have over half of my forces out here in Manot. I'm so screwed!"*

Chapter 75

Anticipating that the museum would have a back-up generator, they sprinted, fully expecting the lights to go back on at any second. Gabriel led Murph and Carli to the target building, successfully covering the distance in the safety of darkness. The other members of Gabriel's team had entered the museum complex from the other sides, arriving simultaneously with Gabriel.

As planned, two soldiers covered the loading dock, as the other four joined Gabriel at the highly secured door to the building. When they reached the door, they could hear the roar of the auxiliary generator kicking on. They were bathed in light, and shots rang out. Murph pushed Carli to the ground and covered her with his body. The cement block retaining wall over Murph's head exploded with two bullets, showering Murph with stone and dust.

Gabriel called out the shooter's location, and Murph could hear the pop of gunfire, but he couldn't see the soldier returning fire. The shots aimed at the door stopped, so Murph assumed success.

One of Gabriel's agents placed an explosive charge on the door lock and stepped back. Another shot rang out; the bullet whizzing past Murph's head. The explosive detonated, blowing the door off its hinges. The agent kicked it in, and he and Gabriel tossed canisters as far into the hallway as they could. The flash-bang grenades were aptly named. The noise was deafening and the flash would blind anyone using night vision goggles. The Israeli team rushed into the hallway as soon as the last grenade exploded.

Another shot impacted in the dirt, spurring Murph and Carli right in behind the agents, rushing to try not to get separated from Gabriel. The lights in the hallway suddenly snapped on, momentarily blinding them. Murph could see one of Cohen's guards down near the doorway, felled by the explosives. Gabriel was in the lead, with two of his agents flanking him. Ahead of them, the passage abruptly ended, with stairs leading down.

Gabriel headed down the stairs. Murph and Carli trailed behind. Reaching the bottom of the stairs, Murph could see a cement floored hallway extending away from them, lit by bare light bulbs hanging down from the ceiling. On either side of the corridor were doors, spread every 20 feet or so. Gabriel checked the doors on the left as his partner checked the ones on the right, moving slowly and carefully down the hall.

Murph noticed a slight movement on his left. A door knob turned slightly, then the door cracked open, swinging slowly toward Murph. He was shielded from view, being behind the door as it opened. The barrel of a rifle began to appear. Murph lunged, slamming his shoulder into the door, pinning the guard between the door and the frame. Murph had caught his assailant across the shoulders, and the sudden force of his attack had broken at least a collarbone. The guard shouted in pain, beginning to fall forward. Murph reached out and grabbed for the barrel of the gun. Murph pulled on it, yanking the guard into the hallway.

Murph gripped the rifle with both hands, careful not to point the barrel at himself, and drove it into the guard. The guard spun around and crashed to the floor with Murph on top of him. He could feel the crunch as the stock of the rifle pressed against the chin of the guard, smashing his head against the concrete floor. Murph could see his eyes roll back as the guard lost consciousness.

Murph started to roll off his victim, looking back over his shoulder for Carli, just in time to see another guard coming out of the door, the barrel of his gun a black hole growing ever larger in Murph's eyes.

BANG! BANG! Two shots rang out in quick succession. The second guard slowed, then tipped forward, falling onto Murph, blood pouring out of his mouth. Gabriel had turned, firing over Murph's prone form to kill the guard before he could shoot at Murph.

Murph pushed the dead body off and quickly got up, wiping the blood off of his hands onto the shirt of the dying guard. He waved thanks to Gabriel. Murph kept the gun from the prone guard, checking the safety to be sure it was on. He felt better with the assault rifle in his hands, even if he had no intention of firing it.

The team moved further down the hallway, finding a passage branching off to the right. Gabriel sent his two agents forward on the main corridor, while he led the way up the side path with Murph and Carli. The hallway ended at a metal desk and chair, sitting beside another doorway.

Murph quickly rifled the desk, finding several magazines and a half-eaten bag of pretzels. A garbage can was nearly full of wrappers and an empty bottle of water. He noticed the knob on the door. Something was strange. Then it dawned on him.

Murph whispered to Gabriel. "This looks like a guard station. And that door is locked from *this* side."

Gabriel agreed. "We'll go in together. You unlock the door and push it open. I'll go in first. Follow me in. Find the switch and turn on the lights as soon as you can."

Murph nodded agreement. He opened the sliding bolt lock and grasped the doorknob lightly, tensing his hand and turning until he could feel the latch open.

Gabriel mouthed, "NOW" and Murph shoved. They burst through the door and Gabriel fell over a kitchen chair that had been placed just inside of the arc of the door. He collapsed to the ground as Murph jumped over him, reaching the light switch on the wall. Murph threw the switch, and light flooded the room.

They had changed from the cement block hallway into a cozy condo with cream-colored carpet and plush armchairs. Murph panned his weapon around the room, but didn't see the

238

club swinging behind him until it was too late. The shadow crossed his peripheral vision and he ducked, rolling forward. His quick reaction saved the back of his head, but he was hit in the back and sent tumbling to the floor. The blow was absorbed by his backpack, the loud CLANG indicated that the spare magazines for his handgun had taken the brunt of the force.

Murph rolled over and popped up, raising his gun at his assailant. He squeezed the trigger, but it wouldn't fire—the safety was still on!

Faced with the barrel of a gun, Murph's assailant raised his hands over his head, still holding the frying pan that had been his weapon of choice. Carli came in and disarmed him, then dropped the pan in shock.

"Oh, my God!" She covered her mouth with her hand.

Murph knew the face in an instant, though he could hardly believe what he was seeing. "Mr. Pre—uh, I mean—Mr. Buchanan, are you OK?"

"And just who the hell are you?"

"Well, that's a rather long story—and we really don't have time for introductions now."

Gabriel had run past Murph and moved through the room to check it out. He came out of the bedroom. "Room's clean. We need to get going!"

"Exactly." Murph was surprisingly calm. "Sir, it will have to suffice for now to say that we are Americans here with Israeli help to rescue you. Please get anything you need and come with us. Now!"

"I haven't got anything of value here. Let's go." Buchanan was fully dressed. He grabbed a black half-zip jacket and pulled it over his head as they ran out the door.

Gabriel spoke into his mike. "Four coming out now."

They ran out the hallway, past the bodies of the guards, up the stairs and into the night air. Gabriel stopped them, and they crouched down, backs against the cinder block wall of the building, panting. They hid in the shadow of the wall, taking stock of the situation.

This was indeed an unexpected surprise. Now they had the real President. That was bound to ruin the night of the current occupant of the White House—and Murph smiled inwardly at the thought.

Chapter 76

Gabriel led them out of the Atlit compound, staying in the industrial district along the waterfront just north of the museum. Haifa was a mixture of construction—million-dollar highrise hotels with beachfront access sitting next door to a seedy waterfront with worn down dockyard buildings. The soldier leading Gabriel's team found a low-roofed steel and concrete building, where they could hide the Electric Company van out of sight in the loading dock.

The team forced the lock open, and Murph, Carli, and their guest quickly entered. The Mossad team set up a perimeter and secured the building. Murph found several steel folding chairs and a grimy card table in the business office, which he quickly set up for them.

Gabriel walked up to the President and introduced himself. "Colonel Buchanan, it is an honor to meet you. I am Gabriel Levi, formerly of the Mossad."

"Buck Buchanan," was the simple reply combined with a firm handshake.

Gabriel turned to Murph. "I need to set up my team. Eliazar told me that there was evidence of at least twenty guards, and we dealt with only six. I expect reinforcements to arrive soon. They will no doubt begin to search for us. I will return and we can plan."

Murph nodded in agreement and Gabriel left, walking swiftly to the front of the warehouse.

Murph turned to Buchanan, "Allow me to introduce my..."

"I figured that out already. You're that dentist from the *Dental Apprentice*. Mike Murphy."

"Guilty!" Murph shook his extended hand and indicated to Carli, "This is Carli Chamoun, my fiancé."

"Pleased to meet you." He took one of the folding chairs and sat down heavily. "Now, will you please tell me what the hell is going on? Gabriel is Mossad, so I'm in the Middle East somewhere. You two certainly aren't CIA."

Carli frowned. "One thing puzzles me. How did you know Murph? "

"Several times a week, a woman came in and talked to me about seemingly useless things about my past—people that I knew—stuff like that. When my interrogator visited unexpectedly this week, she was asking if I knew a Dr. Murphy and whether he had taken out my wisdom teeth while I was in the Air Force? It was really odd. I remembered that my wife had enjoyed that *Dental Apprentice* TV show… and that's where I knew you from."

Murph smiled, fondly remembering his fifteen minutes of reality TV fame, then got back on point. "Did you have your wisdom teeth removed in the military?"

"No. I had them taken out in high school. What's all this about?"

"We don't have all day, so I'll give you the short form."

"Wait a minute! Are my girls OK?"

Carli patted him on the arm. "They are in South Carolina, living with your in-laws outside of Columbia. They are doted on, beautiful and seemingly well adjusted, in spite of everything that's going on."

Buchanan's eyes began to mist over as he gave in to the emotions he had banished for over a year. "What is happening?"

Murph sat down and looked Buchanan directly in the eye. "I don't know where to begin, so I'll just give it to you straight. In Afghanistan, you were wounded and went into a coma. You were transported to the hospital at Ramstein Air Base in Germany. You have been held captive, probably here in Haifa since you were in the coma."

Buchanan agreed. "I woke up here. I remember the mortar blast as I was getting the Marines in the chopper, then nothing else until I was in that condo, where you freed me."

"Good. That confirms one thing." Murph ticked off one finger. "While you were here, an imposter was substituted in your place."

Buchanan's eyes widened, and he started to speak, but Murph waved him off.

"For your actions in saving the Marines in the firefight with the Taliban, you were awarded the Congressional Medal of Honor. You returned to Congress and ran for Vice President on the Democratic ticket with Joe Biden."

"What??"

"With your star power as a wounded military hero, you won the election and became Vice President." Murph began to speed up, worried that Buchanan's head was about to explode. "Five weeks after the inauguration, Biden had a stroke and eventually died. You -er, your imposter—is now the President of the United States."

"Unbelievable!" Buchanan shook his head in disbelief. "What happened to my girls?"

Carli squeezed his hand. "When you retuned to Congress, before joining the campaign, you remarried. That is, your imposter married the nurse who watched over 'your' recovery from the head injury. Jane is her name. They sent the girls to live with their mother's parents to 'spare them the stress' of living in the White House."

Murph added, "We suspect it really was because the girls would have been able to spot the imposter. We know that billionaire Simon Cohen is behind the switch, though haven't figured out what his end game is. It has something to do with US foreign policy in the Middle East. That's why the team of Israelis is involved."

"How did you get involved? " Buchanan fixed Murph in an icy stare. "Are you really just a dentist? I mean, no offense and all. I'm glad to be rescued, but, a *dentist?* "

"No offense taken. It's a fair question." Murph smiled sadly. "Carli and I were at a State dinner at the White House celebrating the inauguration of the new Vice President, an old friend of ours, Brooks Borlon. The President broke a tooth on some popcorn and was in excruciating pain. We took him to my office and had to extract the tooth. The tooth was pink, which is characteristic of root canals done by only Russian dentists. I became suspicious and had a friend pull your x-rays from before you deployed to Afghanistan and compared them to the ones I took that night of the President. He still has his wisdom teeth. They were gnarly impacted ones. Yours have been gone since high school."

Buchanan was amazed. "So you get suspicious of a tooth, and now you're in Israel on a Special Forces op, faces painted camo green and carrying a rifle?"

Murph shrugged. "If you suspect that the most powerful man in the world is an imposter, whom do you tell?" He walked over and put his arm around Carli's shoulders. "We had no choice but to figure out the mystery ourselves and gather the incontrovertible proof to make the case."

Buchanan shook his head. "That's the damndest story I've ever heard. Which means it has to be true. No one could possibly make *that* up."

"Well, Mr. President…"

"*No.* I'm not that guy, and I didn't earn the title." He stood up. "Just call me Buck."

"Well, Buck. Now that we have you, we need to figure out a way to unmask the imposter without causing a crisis of faith in the American government and chaos in the rest of the world!"

"That's going to be a tall order!" Buck rubbed his temples, still in disbelief.

Carli laughed. "Tell me about it!"

Murph suddenly smiled; a light bulb had just gone on. "We specialize in the unbelievable! So let's go do the impossible." He started walking to the doorway, shouting for

Gabriel. Turning back, he winked at Carli. "Don't go anywhere. I think I have just the solution!"

Chapter 77

When Ashram arrived at the compound in Atlit, his worst fears appeared to be confirmed. The main power for the museum was out, casting the compound in complete darkness. He could see the emergency lights surrounding the low building against the docks, but there was no evidence of movement.

At his command, Palti shut off the light of the van and rolled quietly to a stop near the gate. The team disembarked and readied their weapons. A much higher level of alert replaced their previously casual attitude. Leaving Palti to guard the van as their means of escape, they moved cautiously toward the gate.

Ashram stopped and surveyed the hole in the fence and the power line lying on the ground. He turned to his team. "Professionally done. Spread out and move quietly. I don't see any movement. Jaffet and the others aren't answering my calls. If we move quickly, we can catch the intruders still in the building."

No words were needed. They set off quickly, crossing the compound in stages, moving one by one from shadow to shadow, covering for each other. Reaching the back door of the classroom building, Ashram swore bitterly. The security door had been blown off its hinges and he could see the body of Joachim, face down on the floor. He sent Samuel and Alva to the loading dock, while he and rest entered the main door.

They passed another body and went down the stairs. In the middle of the hallway, Ashram found the bodies of Seth and Jaffet. Seth was face down in a pool of blood. Ashram rolled him over, finding two bullet wounds to his chest. Jaffet's jaw was clearly broken and his shoulders lay at a contorted angle. His face was spattered with blood. Ashram pushed himself up, leaning on the body.

Jaffet moaned. Ashram jumped in surprise, his feet tangling and he fell backward back in a heap. Enoch couldn't suppress his laugh as he stepped out of the way of the tumbling Ashram.

Enoch looked down at Ashram. "I will check for the prisoner," his voice dripping with contempt.

Enoch and Gilead moved on down the hallway, as Ashram climbed back to his feet. He walked over to Jaffet and kicked him in the side, a groan coming with the contact of his boot.

"Wake up, dog!" Ashram bent down, his nose inches from Jaffet.

The prone guard's eyes opened slowly, as he found it difficult to focus. The haze began to clear, and he found himself staring into the black eyes of Ashram.

Jaffet gasped in shock, tried to push Ashram away, and screamed at the searing pain in his shoulder and chest. Panting, he finally found his voice, "Welcome home, Ashram."

Ashram raised his fist to strike, but held the blow as Enoch trotted back.

"Well?"

Enoch's face was impassive. "The prisoner is gone. The rest of the guards are dead. At least one of the attackers is wounded. There is a trail of blood leaving the building through the loading dock."

Ashram grabbed Jaffet by the collar. Jaffet grimaced, but would not give Ashram the satisfaction of hearing him moan. Ashram pulled Jaffet up so they were face to face. "So what do you have to say for yourself?"

Jaffet managed a pained smile, "They were Israeli Special Forces. We were outnumbered, because you had left us undefended. They over-ran the building."

"I can see that!"

"While you were at Manot, I saw him. The American was here!" Jaffet spat it out in triumph.

245

Ashram let go, and Jaffet dropped to the concrete floor, moaning in pain.

Ashram stood up, swearing. He swung his fist to punch the wall, then thought better of it. He turned around, looking for answers, but the faces of his team remained blank. It was his problem alone. Gilead bent down and began to care for Jaffet.

Enoch shifted his assault rifle, slinging it back on his back, the immediate danger past. The raiders were clearly gone. "You must call Cyrille and report."

"I know. I need to gather all the facts before I report."

"You know the facts." Enoch spoke slowly. "The prisoner is gone. The Americans are gone. Five of us are dead. *You* have failed. Those are the facts."

Ashram whirled, facing Enoch with fire in his eyes, coiled to strike. He took a quick breath and opened his mouth to shout a sharp retort, then stopped. The air escaped with a rush and he slumped defeated. Accepting his fate, he walked toward the entrance and pulled out his phone. When he had sufficient cell service, he dialed Bastien.

The deep voice answered with a question. "You have the Americans?"

"Well, there was a…"

"Ta Gueule!" Cyrille's French fell on deaf ears with Ashram. "Shut up! I want the FACTS. NO excuses! Now begin!"

Ashram took a deep breath. "I took a team to Manot, but the Americans were not there. While we were at Manot, a team of Israeli Special Forces cut the power to Atlit and invaded the classroom building. The Americans were with the Israelis. They have taken the prisoner. Five of my guards are dead. One is wounded."

"Merde!"

It was the first time Ashram had ever heard Cyrille Bastien swear. This was bad, very bad.

Bastien instantly regained his composure. "Ashram, listen very carefully. This was not an official operation of Israeli

Special Forces. We know of all the activities of the IDF. This is some small group of private forces under the direction of the Americans. There cannot be many troops, and they cannot move through Israel with impunity. They also cannot move the prisoner out of Israel easily. I am coming to Haifa immediately."

Ashram's blood went cold. This wasn't *bad*. This was a *disaster*.

"You are to take your men and find them. They cannot have gone far. The usefulness of the prisoner is at an end. When you find them, KILL HIM and the Americans, too. I grow weary of their interference."

"Yes, Sir. It will be done."

Once again, Ashram was speaking to a dead line. Cyrille was gone, but Ashram had been given a chance to redeem himself, one that he dare not squander. He raced back into the building to motivate his team. They were on the hunt and their quarry had nowhere to go.

Chapter 78

Murph ran back into the business office and found Buck telling Carli about his children and the sad story of his wife's battle with cancer. Both of them had tears in their eyes. Gabriel came in right behind, speaking into the microphone against his cheek.

"Yes, that is what we are looking for. Observe it for a few minutes and make sure it is safe. We will be out soon." He turned to Murph. "Eliasor has found one."

"Excellent!" Bursting with newfound energy, Murph turned to Buck and Carli. "Here's our problem…"

"Well, that's a great place to start," Carli said dryly.

Murph gave her a mock frown, and continued. "We have to get Buck out of Israel, but he has no passport and is immediately recognizable. We can't have Derek fly back in and pick us up, so that's out."

"True." Both Carli and Buck nodded in agreement.

"We could cross Israel and try to get him out through the desert border with Egypt, but that area is so unstable and we may have even more trouble sneaking him out of Egypt."

The Mossad agent was stone faced. Whatever Murph's plan was, Gabriel clearly was not a fan. "You have no friends in Egypt now—nor anywhere else in the Arab world. And I cannot help you clear Israeli security here. To smuggle out the President of the United States? Madness!"

Murph's faith was warming the room, in spite of the gloom. "We can't reach the USS Dixon before she sails. The time is too short—and we couldn't get Buck past security, especially in a rush. There will be too much activity in the port and both the US Navy and the Israelis will be on high alert."

Carli couldn't wait any longer, "So…"

Murph was grinning like the Cheshire cat. "So we steal a boat!"

"What??"

"Eliasor has found a suitable fishing boat. We sail into international waters and let the Dixon come to us. If needed, Peter Mitchell can pick us up in the helicopter with minimal risk."

Buck was quickly assessing the risks. "International waters are 12 miles out! That's a long way!"

"But it could work!" Carli stood up. "When we make it to the ship, we are on US soil again. Peter said the Dixon was sailing straight from here to Charleston."

The realization that he could finally go home was starting to give Buck strength. "That's great that the ship is going to the States, but how do we get me into the US? I still don't have a passport, remember?"

Murph was ready. "I still don't have the answer to that one, but we'll have at least a week sailing on the ship to figure it out. Anyway, US border security is much more porous than

248

the Israelis. Getting out of here is much tougher than getting home will be."

Carli came over and hugged Murph. "Sounds like a plan."

Buck rose as well. "I'm in!"

"Good." Murph looked at Gabriel with a *see, I told you so* smile. "I'll go get ready for our run to the boat. But a couple of things first." Murph took off his baseball cap and tossed it to Buck.

Buck regarded the block O on the front of the black cap. "Ohio State?"

"That's THE Ohio State University to you!" Murph laughed, breaking the tension. "Carli, we need to darken his face and put him in my sweatshirt. When he goes onto the ship, I want his head covered so no one can see his face. I'll have Peter tell the Captain to pass the word that Buck is our prisoner—like this is some sort of CIA operation. We've captured a terrorist and we're taking him back to the US for questioning."

Buck considered that for a second. "That's a good idea. There are enough stories out there about the CIA taking prisoners for rendition. Plus, if you mention the CIA, guys in the military will give you a wide berth. They hate the CIA and all their black-ops stuff."

"My thoughts, exactly." Murph took off his sweatshirt and handed it to Buck. "We're all agreed then. It's risky, but it's the only way I see for us to get out."

Seeing the determination in their faces, Gabriel said, "Then it's settled. Let's get moving."

Carli took the camo makeup from Gabriel and began obscuring Buck's features as best she could.

Murph stepped out of the office and dialed Peter Mitchell.

"Peter?"

"Murph?"

"Yes. I need your help, and the help of Captain Rayburn! We need to get out of Israel fast, and not by normal channels. We have three for pick-up. Repeat: three for pickup."

"I don't know. We're powering up to sail now. I told you we sailed at dawn, and the Captain told you he wouldn't wait or risk the ship." Peter felt really sorry, but there was only so much a Lieutenant could do.

"I know. But here's the plan. Let me outline it for you and then you can see the Captain. Call me back to confirm when you talk to him." Murph proceeded to go over his plan with Peter in detail.

"That's just crazy enough to work!" Peter was shocked. "Let me go see the Old Man, and I'll call you back."

Gabriel had been standing beside Murph. He pulled off his black nylon jacket and had Murph put it on. It was a bit tight on his tall frame, but the material stretched and moved well, providing darker concealment for Murph.

"My friend, I admire your courage." He grabbed Murph by the shoulders. "This plan is audacious enough to succeed. Good Luck!"

Murph embraced Gabriel. "Will your team be OK?"

"Oh, yes. We will blend in and disappear as soon as we send you off. I will remain here in Israel for a while to see what happens. Taking back the President should send shock waves through whoever is behind things here, and nervous people do stupid things. I will let you know what I observe."

"Thank you for all you've done."

"I've done nothing more than my duty. You have uncovered a plot that, well, we still do not know what is going on. But you are about to shake the world to its foundation. We will all have to see this through."

Carli and the heavily camouflaged Buck came out of the office. "We're ready."

"Good." Murph looked at Gabriel, who checked his watch and nodded. "It's time."

Then Murph's phone buzzed. "Yes."

"I understand your plan." The voice was Captain Rayburn. "If you make international waters, the Lieutenant will pick you up. Nothing more."

"Understood."

Murph put the phone back into his pocket and looked at his friends, his jaw set with grim determination. "Then we better get going!"

Chapter 79

Murph and his merry band left the warehouse and followed Gabriel to the docks. The faint moonlight cast a ghostly pall across the pavement. This was the edge of the industrial port with well-worn roads and buildings that had seen heavy use. It was just past 4:00 in the morning, so there was little movement in the area. They only had to avoid a few passing trucks and quickly reached the quay where Eliasor waited.

The object of their search was a 28-foot sport fishing boat with a fiberglass hull and fully enclosed cockpit. The fishing gear was attached to a full tower above the transom. Eliasor's head popped up from the cabin as they approached.

"There are two gas engines here, but I can't figure out how to start them." He was clearly frustrated.

Gabriel went down on one knee on the dock. "I would imagine you need the keys!"

Buck jumped onto the boat and patted the young Eliasor on the back. "Keys? City boys! I grew up on the shore in Charleston. I can hot-wire a boat easily enough. Just get ready to cast off!"

Eliasor handed Buck his flashlight in defeat and climbed out of the boat.

Murph reached out and helped Eliasor onto the dock.

"Thanks. This is a great find. This boat will be perfect—although the yellow color of the hull is rather ugly. But, beggars can't be choosers!"

Eliasor smiled. "Shalom!" He trotted up the quay to take up a position as a sentry for protection.

Carli had been considering the stern of the boat then Murph helped her over the rail. She set her pack against one of the fish boxes. She stood, hands on her hips, slowly rocking with the waves. "She's called the '*Alley Cat*,' and I'm good with that!"

The engines began to rumble, indicating Buck's success. He popped his head out of the cabin and gave a thumbs-up, moving to the wheel. He checked the instruments and looked back to Murph.

"We're in luck. Tanks are full of gas!"

"Thanks for checking. I hadn't thought of that!" Murph grinned sheepishly. He turned to Gabriel. "Thank you again."

They shook hands and Gabriel handed Murph one of the assault rifles they had taken from the guards at Atlit. "I hope you won't need this, but I think you've earned it!"

Murph stepped over the aluminum bow rail, and Gabriel untied the bowline and tossed it to Murph. He stowed it and moved to the stern, taking the stern line from Gabriel as well.

Murph faced his friend and waved. "Shalom!"

Gabriel ducked down into the shadows and moved back off the quay, toward the road. Buck advanced the throttles and the *Alley Cat* moved slowly into the channel. He aimed them at open water, unable to mask the guttural roar of the engines.

Carli moved down into the cabin as Murph stood next to Buck, keeping a sharp eye for any movement along the docks.

252

Buck looked over at him, smiling. "Just relax. We can't hide, so we'll try to act natural. Like we do this every day."

Murph grinned. "Then why do I feel so naked?"

Carli stuck her head up from below, "Besides, what's more natural than two guys going fishing with their faces blackened with camo paint?"

Murph pushed down on her head, shoving her back into the vinyl seat. "That's enough out of you!"

Buck just added more power as they began to work against the swells, the waves of the Mediterranean pushing against them as they fought their way out to sea.

Chapter 80

Cyrille Bastien had raced to Orly Airport in central Paris, boarding the LearJet that had been waiting at his command. The plane took off immediately and was streaking to Israel. Events were moving rapidly—and in an unexpected manner. Cyrille valued order in his life. Michael Murphy had been a randomizing influence since his appearance and Cyrille despised that effect.

Opening his computer, Bastien began to search for the thread of Murph's plan. He could not have just blundered upon Buchanan. To be worth freeing the prisoner, there had to be some preparation to get him out of Israel and back to Washington.

Where could they go? Murphy had access to the private jet of the Center for Esthetic and Restorative Excellence, but the G550 was still in Barcelona, according to Bastien's latest reports. He placed a call to his man in Spain to recheck the location of the Gulfstream.

Israeli border security is very tight. Bastien thought about their options. The only weaker borders were with Syria and Egypt. Entering Syria would be through the Golan Heights, and Syria is so unstable that there was no benefit to that route.

The Gaza Strip and the smuggler's tunnels into Egypt would offer a possibility. Bastien considered calling his contacts in Egypt but waited. His research into Murphy and Chamoun had revealed that they would have few friends in Egypt, especially with the new government. They would need to be desperate to go there.

What would I do? He sat, tapping his fingers to his forehead, sipping bottled water. He never drank alcohol and didn't smoke. In fact, he had no vices that anyone could name. His associates, for he had no friends, considered him a monk.

His phone buzzed with an email. The word from Spain was that the crew was prepping the G550 to leave immediately. The flight plan was for Washington, DC.

Puzzled, Cyrille decided on a big picture approach. He called up the satellite images of Haifa and the area around the museum at Atlit. *Where could they go?* The border with Lebanon was near, but crossing there would be impossible, especially with the President of the United States.

His finger traced idly over the images, stopping suddenly. He magnified the image, squinting, then leaning back. *Yes! I see now what you are up to!* Cyrille picked up his phone and dialed.

A quarter of the way around the world, a stern female voice answered. "This is not a good time."

"I don't care." Bastien's deep bass was slow, even, and commanding. "I need answers, NOW."

"Wait a moment." There was shuffling and then a whisper, "What could be so important? You will jeopardize everything!"

"I understand the stakes far better than you. The prisoner has been freed."

Cyrille heard the phone clatter to the floor, then the voice slowly returned, wavering, "What do you mean?"

"Murphy has rescued the prisoner and is trying to get him out of the country. I need information. NOW!"

Her voice shook. "What do you need to know?"

"There is a Navy warship in the port of Haifa. What is it? When does it sail?"

"I will find out and call you back." She pleaded. "You must deal with this!"

"Yes. Personally!"

He ended the call and sat quietly for a moment. Then he called Ashram again.

"How can I be of service?" The mercenary tried in vain to sound calm and in control.

"Ashram, have you found the Americans?" His voice was cold as ice.

"No, Master. They appear to have gone into the warehouses near the docks. We are searching each building."

"Listen to me. There is a US Navy warship in the port of Haifa. The Americans will try to take the prisoner to the ship and leave Israel by that route."

"Yes, sir. I will bring my men back and move to block the entrance to the naval base."

"Very well. Do not let them reach the ship!"

Having covered his bases, Cyrille sat back to await more information. He closed his eyes, not to sleep, but to allow more clarity in his meditation. Less than a half hour later, his phone rang again.

"What the hell is going on?" The President raged. He was not used to hearing bad news. "You are paid handsomely to make sure things like this don't happen!"

"Events happen in spite of meticulous planning—especially when someone gives into tooth pain and makes a poor decision." Bastien's tone continued even. "I will deal with it. Do you have the information I require?"

"The ship is the destroyer USS Dixon. She sails from Haifa this morning, returning to the US."

"Remain calm. Your panic is unbecoming of your office. This changes nothing. Continue with everything as planned."

"You will keep me informed!"

"YOU do not command me." Cyrille's voice slashed like a razor. "You must maintain your schedule as if nothing is going on. I am in consultation with Simon. You and I will have minimal direct contact, as we had always planned."

The President began to shout, but Cyrille ended the phone call.

Moving quickly, he dialed Ashram again.

"Where are your forces now." Cyrille seldom bothered with pleasantries in his conversations.

"Um—we have gathered—back at the base. They—um— just left for the naval base." Ashram was clearly scrambling to keep control of his team.

"Stop." Bastien knew he had to exert more direct control. "Gather them around you and put the phone on speaker."

"But they—um—just left."

"Ashram. I know they are still there." He sighed. "I will speak with them, NOW!"

"Yes, Sir." Ashram put the phone on the table and turned on the speaker.

Enoch began. "We are here." And there was general grunting to announce their presence.

"Very well." Cyrille began his briefing. "The Americans have freed the prisoner and intend to get him out of Israel. The US Navy destroyer docked in Haifa sails this morning. They do not have time to get to the ship before it leaves. The Americans will sail out to meet the ship. They will have a small boat docked near Atlit and will be moving very soon. Take boats and find the Americans. DO NOT LET THEM REACH THE WARSHIP. They must be stopped, no matter the cost. DO YOU UNDERSTAND?"

"Yes." The response came as a chorus.

"Do not attempt to recapture the prisoner. Eliminate them all, and dispose of the bodies in the sea. Leave no trace behind."

Chapter 81

There was less pageantry than he expected. Peter Mitchell stood on the flight deck at the stern of the USS Dixon as a small contingent of Israeli stood on the dock waving. The commander of the IDF naval forces in the port shook hands with Captain Rayburn, saluted, and left the ship. The gangway was withdrawn and lines released. The guided missile destroyer slipped out of her mooring and entered the channel at a sedate pace, a faint wake streaking the deep blue of the Mediterranean.

Peter finished his walk-around and confirmed with his crew that they were ready to launch. For this mission, they were carrying a crew of four. As aircraft commander Lt. Mitchell was responsible for his copilot Lt. j.g. Nick Bradshaw and their two enlisted sailors, Petty Officer Marcus Williams and Airman Charlie Piper. Peter and the Captain had personally briefed the crew, so Airman Piper was already in his wet suit. He and Petty Officer Williams were readying the winch, litter, and harness for the water rescue of their targets.

Lt. Bradshaw sat in the left seat, finishing the pre-flight on the SH-60R Seahawk helicopter. He tapped his helmet, nodding. He received the message and leaned out the window of the helicopter. He motioned for Peter and pointed up toward the bridge.

"Lieutenant. Captain wants to see you."

Mitchell waved and ran into the hangar bay and up the stairs to the command bridge. He entered and saluted, remaining at attention until the Captain returned his salute.

"At ease, Lieutenant."

Mitchell spread his feet the width of his hips and relaxed slightly. "Sir?"

"Just to confirm—we'll launch you as soon as we clear the harbor into the Med. Make it look like a routine safety patrol around the *Dixon* until radar spots our target. If they are safely out of Israeli waters, you can go get them."

"Yes, Sir."

"I'll take your cell phone now, Lieutenant. Then I can stay in contact with them while you are flying." The Captain extended his palm.

Reluctantly, Peter handed over his iPhone, first disabling the password then setting it in the Captain's hand. "Yes, Sir."

"And, Lieutenant. Take no extra risks. Understood?"

"Shall I have Petty Officer Williams guard the prisoner?"

That had the desired effect. Peter was happy to see all the heads of the bridge crew snap around and look at him. He tried not to smile when the Officer of the Deck mouthed *"Prisoner?"* at him. Peter frowned slightly to silence Lt. Cortell.

"No. Our guests must care for their own prisoner. I'm picking them up under protest as it is." Captain Rayburn turned to his Officer of the Deck. "Lt. Cortell."

"Yes, Sir." He snapped to attention.

"Prepare the cabins in the forward pilot ready room area for guests. There will be three. Two men and a woman. After they arrive, station an armed guard to secure the passageway."

"Yes, Sir."

"Now get to work, both of you." The Captain waved them out. "Good hunting, Lieutenant. No international incidents, please."

Peter grinned and left the bridge, a dumbfounded Bill Cortell trailing behind.

The entered the passageway and headed aft, toward the flight deck. Peter could feel the deepening vibration of the engines as the ship began to accelerate. Cortell caught Mitchell by the shoulder of his flight suit.

"Peter, what the hell's going on?"

"C'mon Bill. You heard the Old Man. We're having guests for lunch." He continued walking purposefully toward the stairs down to the waiting helicopter.

"Why the big rush? And all the secrecy?" Cortell stood scratching his strawberry blond hair.

Peter started down the stairs, calling over his shoulder, "I've gotta go. It's not every day I get to pick up two CIA agents and their prisoner!"

Bounding down the stairs, two at a time, Peter smiled to himself. He could have sworn he heard Cortell's jaw hit the floor.

Chapter 82

Ashram and his band of thugs moved purposefully through the docks, quickly finding two suitable boats. Ashram commandeered the first, a zodiac rigid inflatable boat. Capable of high speed, it was a lightweight, inflatable hull with a powerful motor. Ashram took command in the bow and put Samuel at the wheel. Alva climbed in the stern for balance, and they took off at high speed.

Enoch boarded a larger, deep V-hulled fishing boat. Manning the center console himself, he placed Shet, Rafe, and

Gilead with him as they cast off. The V-hulled craft was slower than Ashram's zodiac, but still significantly faster than the transom sport fisher that Murph had taken. With the outboard motor running wide open, they roared into the shipping channel, a few minutes behind Ashram.

Murph had a lead, but he was moving slowly in order to be inconspicuous. The Americans didn't know it yet, but the race was on!

* * * * * * *

Now that *Alley Cat* had cleared the mouth of the harbor, Buck pushed the throttles forward and the boat rose on her hull, straining against the swells, forcing her way into the open Mediterranean Sea. Murph was constantly scanning the horizon for threats, but was relieved to see the sleek gray form of the USS Dixon following them out of the anchorage.

Tapping Buck on the shoulder, Murph pointed behind them. "Cavalry's coming!"

"Now that's a sight for sore eyes!"

Murph marveled at the increasing speed of the destroyer, white foam rising from her bow as the ship cut through the deep blue water. The sun was rising in the east, and the water's surface began to glitter like gold.

Murph took out his phone. "Looks like they are going to catch up with us soon. Let's see if I can get an early pickup." He dialed Peter's number and the phone picked up immediately.

"Captain," was all the voice said, but Murph immediately recognized Rayburn and not Peter.

Murph considered the open line and said, "We are the fishing boat *Alley Cat*. Requesting permission to approach for boarding."

"Negative. Keep to the original plan. Your identity cannot be verified. If you approach my ship, we will blow you out of the water."

"Understood." Murph put away the phone.

Carli shouted up from below. "That went well! Someone got up on the wrong side of the bunk today."

Buck shook his head. "No. I agree with the Captain. Since the terrorist attack in Yemen on the USS Cole in October, 2000, the Navy has been understandably touchy about security. The terrorists used a small boat loaded with explosives to strike a destroyer just like the *Dixon* there. The suicide bombing killed 17 sailors and wounded another 39. I wouldn't let any boat come within a half mile of my ship. He's just being smart. If he picks you up by helicopter, then he knows exactly what he's bringing onboard."

The *Dixon* was turning away from the *Alley Cat*, opening the distance as they both ran for international waters. Buck and Murph could see the stern of the destroyer, where a Seahawk helicopter sat on the flight deck with its rotors turning. The *Dixon* returned to a straight course, heading out to open sea. The rotors spun faster and became a blur, then the gray helicopter jumped from the ship. It gained altitude and began a slow turn, surveying the harbor.

Peter Mitchell sat in the right seat, marveling as he always did at the beauty of a sunrise at sea. The sunlight sparked golden on the water, the deep blue of the sea cut by the white wake of the speeding destroyer. He could see a small fishing boat turning to run parallel to the *Dixon*, but carefully not closing the distance. Scanning back into the harbor, Peter was shocked to see two other wakes exiting the harbor mouth.

The lead was a zodiac inflatable, moving at reckless speed, bouncing across the waves, aimed right for the fishing boat. Another speedboat was following the zodiac, about a mile further behind. Extending the lines of their wakes, it was clear that they were trying to intercept the slower fishing boat from two sides.

Peter keyed his mike, calling the *Dixon* to report. "Rebel, this is Moonshine 508."

Rebel was the call sign of the USS Dixon. The helo was from Helicopter Maritime Strike Squadron (HSM) 87, *The Moonshiners.*

"Moonshine 508—this is Rebel. Your target is a sport fishing boat named the *Alley Cat.* Please identify."

"Roger."

Peter flew past the Alley Cat at 500 feet. Murph and Carli waved. The man driving kept his head down, trying to urge as much speed as he could from the boat.

"Rebel—Moonshine 508. Lead boat is our target. Crew of three. Positive ID on two passengers." Peter rose to 1000 feet and hovered over the *Alley Cat.* "We do have a problem."

"Go ahead 508."

"Two targets approaching at high speed. They look to be trying to cut off the *Alley Cat*. Requesting orders."

"508. This is Rebel One."

Lt. Bradshaw looked at Peter, his eyes widening. The both recognized Rayburn's voice.

"508—Awaiting instructions."

"You are to proceed with Rebel until we are Hot Dog Yellow. Observe but do not intervene."

"Roger."

Bradshaw keyed his intercom so only the helo crew could hear. "Hot Dog Yellow! That's 15 miles off shore. Hot Dog Red—international waters—is 12 miles."

Peter answered. "I know." He studied the oncoming zodiac. It was gaining fast. "They'll never make it."

Peter changed to the main frequency again. "Rebel—This is 508."

"Go ahead, 508"

"You have to warn them. They will never see the zodiac that is the lead pursuer. They will catch the *Alley Cat* before they are Hot Dog Yellow."

"Roger. We will inform."

Peter and his crew were left to watch as the wakes of the speeding boats came ever closer to intersecting. The helo moved ahead to mark the finish line—rooting for the lead horse, but knowing that the wolves were going to run him down before he could get there.

Chapter 83

Murph's phone rang, so he answered without thinking, "Hello?"

"This is the Captain. You are being pursued by two boats. The lead is a zodiac, which is very low to the water and will be tough for you to see. It is rapidly approaching on your port side. The other is slower, though still faster than you, and is on your starboard side."

"I understand."

"The helo is stationed at the line you must reach. That is your target. Good luck!"

Murph put away the phone. He called Carli up from the galley so that he could talk to them both.

"We have company. Two boats approaching. A faster zodiac to port and a slower one to starboard." He pointed to the hovering helicopter in the distance. "The Captain was so nice as to station the helo at the finish line, so we know how far we have to go."

Carli snarled. "How sporting of him. I suppose they are just going to sit there and watch!"

"That's about how this is going to go. We are on our own until we reach the chopper."

Buck considered the situation. "Do the thugs following us know who we are?"

"They know who you are. I'm not sure if they know who Carli and I are."

"We may have the element of surprise working for us. If they underestimate what we can do, we have a chance."

Murph nodded. Buck positioned Carli at the wheel and showed her how to keep the heading straight for the helicopter and at maximum speed. Murph and Buck each took an assault rifle and crouched down in the stern, peeking over the rail to look for the zodiac. It only took a few minutes until they saw it fly up over a wave, visible for a second. The speedboat was far closer than they expected.

Buck crawled over to Murph.

"The controls are in the center console. Aim for the guy at the wheel. He's the key. If we take him out, the boat might capsize at the reckless speed they are moving."

All Murph could do was nod in agreement. He had nothing to add.

"Just wait until I shoot and fire everything you have. We will only get one chance at this." He patted Murph on the shoulder and moved to the stern rail. Murph stayed on the side, resting his arms on the bait locker.

With the way the boat was bouncing up and down on the four-foot swells, Murph wasn't concerned about hitting the guy at the controls. He worried he wouldn't hit the boat at all.

* * * * * * *

From his perch a thousand feet up. Peter and his crew had a bird's eye view of the chase. He was pleased to see that the V-hulled boat that was trailing was actually no faster than the *Alley Cat*. They were out of the race as long as Murph kept moving.

The zodiac was another matter. It was almost within striking distance of the fishing boat. Peter watched as two people on the *Alley Cat* had moved to the stern and taken positions on the rail. He couldn't see into the cockpit, but assumed that Carli was at the controls.

The black-hulled zodiac was bouncing across the waves like a stone skipping on a pond. They closed to within 50 yards; then, Peter saw two gunmen in the zodiac open fire. Fiberglass pieces in the structure of the *Alley Cat* splintered and the cockpit glass shattered.

"Rebel. This is Moonshine 508. The *Alley Cat* is taking fire. I say again, they are taking enemy fire. Request permission to intervene."

"Negative 508. Hold your position."

Peter slammed his fist against the door.

* * * * * * *

Carli had ducked down at the last second, then the world above her exploded. Fiberglass splinters and shards of glass picked at her. She held on to the wheel from below and kept the boat angled toward the helicopter in the distance. She looked back at Murph and gave him a thumbs-up and a weak smile.

Murph's face was a mask of concern. He motioned for her to stay down, peeking over again and realizing that the zodiac

264

was angling for another pass. He turned to Carli and made his hand into a flat blade. He chopped to the left with his hand, indicating for her to turn the *Alley Cat* to the left, closing the range with the zodiac. She nodded in agreement.

Buck reached out and squeezed Murph's arm. He mouthed, NOW, over the roar of the engine. Murph glanced at Carli and inclined his head to the left. She swung the wheel a half-turn and the fishing boat heeled to port.

Buck stood up and raised his machine gun. Murph was astonished at his bravery. *I guess that's how you earn a Medal of Honor*, he thought. Murph stood up as well, and they both opened fire at the zodiac, each one emptying the 30-round magazine at the maximum rate of fire. At 800 rounds a minute, it didn't take long.

When the *Alley Cat* suddenly veered to the left, closing with the zodiac, Ashram realized his mistake. Unfortunately for him, it was too late. He saw the two Americans rise up from the stern and begin to fire. He pulled the trigger on his assault rifle, but the zodiac was an unstable firing platform and his bullets went high.

The Americans' aim was true. Standing at the center console, Samuel was hit first. The force of the bullets threw him to the left and his grip spun the wheel with him as he fell. At the high rate of speed, the zodiac couldn't make the turn and rolled like a car on the highway. As the boat flipped, Ashram and Alva were thrown from the craft, their bodies flying through the air like rag dolls. In seconds, it was over.

The *Alley Cat* continued on as the zodiac disappeared, disintegrating into flotsam, scattered across the waves.

* * * * * * *

Peter and his crew looked on, dumbfounded.

Keying his intercom, Peter said, "Well, I'll be damned."

From the back, the pilot heard, "Holy Shit, Lieutenant! They took out the zodiac!"

"Pipe down back there! Let's get ready." Peter got down to business. "They did their part. I think they're going to make it. Now we have to pick them up!"

His headphones crackled again.

"508—This is Rebel. Report!"

"The *Alley Cat* returned fire and took out the zodiac. They are approaching Hot Dog Red. We are preparing for standard rescue."

"Roger." There was a short pause. "Moonshine 508. You have permission to assist as soon as they are Hot Dog Red. Go get them."

"Roger! 508 out."

Peter checked on the V-hulled pursuer. It was still several miles away, but closing. They would need to work quickly to extract the three occupants of the *Alley Cat* before the other boat could interfere.

Peter keyed his intercom. "Petty Officer Williams. Prepare the litter. We'll put Airman Piper in the water and bring up the girl and one of the guys in the litter. Then we'll pull up Piper in the rescue strop with the last passenger."

"Roger that."

Peter began to descend to 500 feet in preparation for the water rescue. He pushed inside the 15-mile line and crept closer to the 12-mile international boundary. He glanced at the approaching V-hull and shook his head. This was going to be close. Very close!

Chapter 84

Murph's phone rang again.

"Well done, *Alley Cat*. You have reached the boundary. When the helo is above you, stop your engines and wait. They will drop an airman into the water. He will assist you in the rescue."

"Thank you. We're not out of the woods yet. There is one more speedboat out there."

"We should be able to complete the rescue before he reaches you."

"Understood."

Murph put away the phone and passed the word. Carli had found an old plaid shirt in the cabin. She gave it to Buck.

"You'll need to cover your face with this. The sailors can't see you. It would be such a shock! I'd love to see their faces—but we can't let that happen."

Buck reluctantly agreed.

Murph was thinking aloud. "You are our prisoner, but we can't tie your hands. You need to be able to swim if you fall in the drink."

Buck frowned at Murph. "Thanks. I've come this far, I'd rather not drown now."

Their conversation was drowned out by the approaching helicopter. Murph cut the throttles to idle and the *Alley Cat* sat down in the water as she slowed.

Fifty yards downwind, Peter established a stable hover. Moving slowly forward at 10 knots, Peter masterfully placed Airman Piper fifty feet from the fishing boat. He jumped from the helicopter, dropping straight down into the water, popped up and gave a thumbs-up to the pilot. Swim fins on, Charlie Piper swam powerfully toward the *Alley Cat* and Murph pulled him aboard.

The helo rose to 70 feet and engaged the hover coupler, sitting in a stable position above the *Alley Cat*. The force of the rotor blades pounded the passengers down into the boat. Buck sat in the stern, his head wrapped in the plaid shirt, hands in his lap.

Airman Piper was about 5 foot 6, so he reached up and pulled Murph down to yell in his ear.

"I'm Airman Piper. I'm here to help you! They will lower the litter and I'll put the girl and the prisoner on and up they'll go."

Murph nodded.

"After they are in the helo, then they'll send down the strop—it's like a sling. I'll put you in it and ride up with you. Once they have us moving up, they can move away from that other boat with us swinging below."

Murph patted Piper on the shoulder. "Sounds great, Airman. You're the boss!"

Up in the helo, Petty Officer Williams was already lowering the litter. Careful to be sure that it touched the water first, to dissipate any static electricity from the rotors, he awaited Piper to guide the basket. The litter was used to bring up injured people, lying flat. In an emergency, it could be used to lift two people if they weren't too heavy. Tiny Carli hardly counted, so the litter was an ideal choice to limit the rescue time to just two trips up.

Piper dove into the water and swam the short distance to corral the litter, bringing it back to the boat. Murph turned the *Alley Cat* into the waves and kept enough power on to keep her position stable under the helicopter. Piper lifted the litter into the fishing boat and quickly helped Buck and Carli in. He adjusted their positions for balance and waved. Williams began the slow lift, working hard to keep the load from swinging too much in the wind.

Peter was pleased at the quick work of his crew. He stole a glace at the approaching V-hull—and was shocked to see how close it had come. Peter looked down and found Murph staring up from the *Alley Cat* through the shattered transom. Peter leaned through the window and aggressively pointed at the V-hull, racing in over the horizon.

Murph climbed onto the foredeck to get up higher. He could see that the V-hull would get there too soon. He figured that Buck and Carli weren't even halfway up yet. He jumped down, ran to the stern, and picked up his MP-5, grabbing a full magazine and jamming it in place.

Airman Piper came over and stood beside Murph.

"Airman, we've run out of time."

"Yes, Sir. I kinda figured that."

They both looked up, willing the winch to move faster, and regarded the approaching boat, riding high on its hull, slicing quickly through the water.

* * * * * * *

Enoch had seen the disaster with the zodiac and realized immediately what had happened. *Ashram was such a fool... rushing in, underestimating his opponent.* He had made those mistakes all day and paid for it with his life.

Enoch was smarter than that. He didn't need to risk his life. His orders were to kill the prisoner and the Americans. There they were in front of him, hanging in a basket like a clay target. All he had to do was get close enough to shoot them.

He ordered his men onto the bow of the boat and took the wheel himself. No need to get within range of the *Alley Cat*. Just close enough to fire at the helicopter and its winch.

Enoch slowed the V-hull and worked to keep her steady in the waves so his gunmen could do their job. Their rifles were on their shoulders, aiming.

"Wait a bit longer!" He shouted to them. "Ready!"

* * * * * * *

Murph saw the bow of the V-hull fall as it slowed. He could see the three thugs on the foredeck, rifles pressed to their shoulders. His eyes widened as a sickening realization flooded over him. His blood turned to ice.

Piper saw it too. "What are they doing?"

"They don't need to risk coming close to get us. They can stand off, out of range, and shoot them in the air."

Murph waved at Peter, crossing his arms over his head and then waving the helo off, back away from the V-hull. He turned to Piper and suddenly shoved him in the chest, throwing him overboard, falling backward into the water with a splash.

Running to the cockpit, Murph shouted at the stunned Piper as he swam, "Sorry, Airman. Gotta go!"

Murph had left the engines on idling, so they responded immediately when he slammed the throttles forward. The *Alley Cat* leaped ahead, and Murph turned the wheel to set a course straight for the V-hull. They were only fifty yards away, so he began closing the distance quickly.

Murph wanted to distract them, so he began firing over the bow as he drove. There was little chance that he would hit anything, but a few bursts of gunfire did seem to make a point. He charged straight at the V-hull, aiming for the middle of the boat.

Enoch was forced to move the V-hull and Murph made him turn away from the helicopter. The three gunmen on the foredeck began firing at the *Alley Cat*. Murph could feel the slugs slam into the hull when the bow was up. The angle of the boat saved Murph from attack, but the holes were below the waterline and Murph could feel the boat begin taking on water.

The V-hull was faster and more nimble than the sport fishing boat to begin with, and the increasing weight from the water made the *Alley Cat* sluggish. Murph was struggling to keep his boat between the V-hull and the helo. So far, he had been able to occupy the gunmen.

The *Alley Cat* staggered through another turn, but Enoch cut off the fishing boat and crossed behind her. Murph could see the gunmen begin to train their guns on him, so he dove down into the cabin, alarmed to find four inches of water in the lower compartment. The machine gun fire tore through the cockpit, shattering the instruments as the V-hull flashed astern. A four-foot hunk of countertop crashed down on Murph's back.

Murph shook off the cabinet and rose from the water, wiping his soaked hair from his forehead. He ran back to the wheel and turned the *Alley Cat* to follow Enoch. The fishing boat was wallowing, bow down with the flooding and laboring to move forward. Murph willed it to stay in the chase, but he knew it was a losing proposition.

"Come on, Baby. Hold it together!" He implored.

Enoch whirled the V-hull and closed in on the *Alley Cat*, then slowed the boat, lowering the bow and giving his shooters a clear line of fire.

Murph saw Enoch's smile and knew it was the end— then Enoch's eyes widened and his smile became a silent scream, lost in the roar of the Seahawk helicopter.

Peter slid the helo over from behind the *Alley Cat* as Petty Officer Williams opened up with the door mounted 50- caliber machine gun, tearing the V-hull to pieces. Murph drove the sinking fishing boat away from the stricken V-hull, heading back to where a smoke and die marker indicated the position of Airman Piper, now treading water and waiting.

Williams made sure the V-hull was destroyed before Peter followed the *Alley Cat*. With its engines flooded, the fishing boat lost power and foundered. Murph patted the ship goodbye, thanking her for great service. He grabbed his bag and dove into the water. Glad he had done so much swimming in rehabbing his shoulder, Murph reached Piper with a few minutes of strong strokes.

Peter re-established his hover and Williams lowered the winch. Piper fastened the strop around Murph and attached himself. The two rode quickly up as the *Alley Cat* slipped below the surface.

It was a tired dentist who was dragged into the chopper, flopping like a tuna onto the floor at Buck's and Carli's feet. Airman Piper detached himself and gave a thumbs-up.

Williams hit the intercom, "Lieutenant, we have all the passengers secured."

Lieutenant Bradshaw answered, "Roger."

As Peter banked the helicopter to chase after the *Dixon*, now just a spot receding on the horizon, he called in. "Rebel— This is Moonshine 508. We have our guests—all of them. Returning to base."

"Roger. Well done, 508."

Buck leaned down from his seat and patted Murph on the shoulder. "Show-off!"

Murph pushed himself up on one elbow, realizing as the adrenalin was ebbing just how much he was hurt. He pulled a two-inch splinter of wooden cabinet door out of his leg and held it to stop the bleeding.

Carli took a towel from Piper and wrapped it around the wound, tying it tight. She bent over and kissed him, wiping away the tears.

Williams secured the machine gun and helped Murph up onto the bench. "We'll have the medic meet the helo when we land. Sir, that was the bravest thing I've ever seen. I'm honored to shake your hand."

Murph managed a pained smile and said thanks, shaking both Williams' and Piper's hands. He leaned his head back into the quilted padding and gradually slid down until he was pressed against Carli. Murph closed his eyes, but Carli continued the ruse of intently watching Buck, since he was supposed to be their prisoner.

It was a short ride to the Dixon, but by the time they arrived, the word of the battle with the "terrorists" had spread throughout the ship. The Seahawk helicopter landed with the fanfare of conquering heroes returning from battle, and the tale would continue to grow as the chopper crew would tell and retell it.

The crew of the USS Dixon looked upon the hooded prisoner with disdain, but Murph and Carli were accepted with the adulation that can only come for the victors. They were escorted from the flight deck to the waiting cabins, exhausted and soaked, but triumphant.

They were back on US soil—and only 6000 miles from home!

Chapter 85

Murph and Carli had been given a pair of rooms that were adjacent to the pilot ready room. This gave them a confined space that included a small conference table, refrigerator, microwave oven, and coffee maker, as well as a couple of recliners and a TV. The staterooms each contained a pair of bunks and a bathroom (the Navy called it "the head"). The rooms were small, but perfect for their needs, especially since they had to keep Buck under wraps until they got him off the ship.

Fortunately, Buck had been uninjured and arrived on the *Dixon* simply tired and wet. Carli had small cuts and abrasions from the shattering glass in the cockpit of the *Alley Cat*. These were easily treated by the medical corpsman with antiseptic and a couple of small Band-Aids. Murph had not been as lucky, as his tattered clothing clearly indicated.

Several lacerations on his arm and legs were large enough to require treatment, but they were not deep enough to need stitches. Several steri-strips later, the corpsman was finishing cleaning and bandaging the wound where a bullet had grazed Murph's chest, just under his left collarbone.

Peter Mitchell knocked and entered the ready room, assessing Murph with a long look. "What the hell happened to you?"

Murph shrugged. "Boat had a bad case of termites… and I got splinters."

The corpsman laughed and pointed at the bullet wound. "Lead mosquitos?"

Murph shook his head, "Nah, don't be silly. Jellyfish— big one!" He gestured with his hands two feet apart.

The corpsman packed up his kit, still chuckling.

Murph stood up stiffly and shook the medic's hand. "Thanks, Petty Officer Ramirez. I owe you one!"

"Not at all, Sir. It's an honor to help. I don't get many combat wounds."

"Which is a good thing, by the way," Peter quickly added.

"I agree, Sir." Ramirez walked to the doorway. "I left you a bottle of ibuprofen in the head. Take some. You're going to need it!

Ramirez left, shutting the door tightly behind him. Murph limped slightly as he walked to the door and locked it. He came over and shook Peter's hand, slapping him on the back. Carli came over and gave Peter a hug as well, kissing him on the cheek.

"Thanks for coming in and fishing us out!" Murph's smile was thin as his chest was beginning to burn with each breath.

"You're welcome!" Peter smiled broadly. "You do know how to make an appearance! Very heroic stuff!"

Murph coughed. "Yeah. Right up until I had the boat shot out from underneath me and Airman Piper tossed me into the helicopter like a tuna."

"You did flop around a bit!" Carli made a face like a fish, then walked over and opened the stateroom door. Buck stepped out. "Lieutenant Peter Mitchell, please meet our guest of honor…"

"Jesus!" Peter was incredulous, then snapped to attention, saluting.

Murph patted him on the back. "We *were* in the Holy Land, but no—that's not who it is."

"Mr. President!" Peter stammered.

Out of respect for military tradition, Buck stood tall and returned Peter's salute. "At ease, Lieutenant." He extended his hand and shook Peter's. "Someone else was elected to that office. For now, just call me Buck."

Before Peter could answer, the door lock rattled as someone tried to open it. There was a sharp pounding on the door and a loud voice shouted, "Murphy! Open this door!"

Carli whispered, "Captain Rayburn" and ushered Buck back into the room, pulling the door nearly closed.

Murph stood and turned to face the door. He nodded at Peter, who unlocked and opened the door, stepping back at attention to allow his commanding officer to enter.

Rayburn burst through the door and reached Murph in two strides. He came within inches, but had to look up slightly, as Murph had at least three inches on him. Realizing the disadvantage, the Captain stepped back and shouted, veins popping out on his neck.

"You are the craziest sunnavabitch I've ever seen. Heroic as Hell, but crazy enough to nearly get four of my men killed. And I've got a $28 million helicopter with bullet holes in it! What the Hell were you doing?"

"Captain, I want to express our thanks for pulling us out of the water and bringing us here." Murph spoke firmly and evenly. "I understand the risk that I put your men in."

"Do you? DO YOU?" Rayburn poked a finger into Murph's chest. "I have the port commander of the Navy of the Israeli Defense Force on the radio now looking for an explanation. Just what do you think I should tell him?"

Murph had been expecting that, so he calmly answered, "I think you should tell him that you dispatched your helo when your radar indicated what appeared to be a ship in distress. When the helicopter arrived to provide assistance, you found several boats involved. Your sailors were fired upon as they attempted to rescue swimmers in the water. Your men returned fire in self-defense and left the boats as they were. In your opinion, this appeared to be some kind of drug deal gone bad. Your sailors were not wounded and you are continuing on your mission. I'd thank the Israeli for his concern about the health of your crew and thank him again for his hospitality while you were in port."

Rayburn stood there for a moment, finger touching Murph's chest, mouth hanging open.

Peter added, "Good one!" but shut up instantly when he was subjected to Rayburn's withering glare.

The Captain folded his finger back into his fist and stepped over to the conference table. He leaned down and rested his hands on the dark wood surface.

"That just might work. " He turned and regarded Murph. "You're too good of a liar."

"Lot's of practice lately. It's not something I'm really good at, but I'm working on it."

"I've got to answer the Israelis, but just don't think this ends it with us. I'll be back and, Mister, you have a lot of explaining to do!"

"Captain?" Murph stopped Rayburn in mid turn. "I think you should know why this is so important—Carli!"

She opened the door and walked in, leading Buck behind her.

"Jesus H. Christ!"

Buck looked at Murph and regarded Rayburn, now standing stiffly at attention. "I'm getting that a lot lately."

Murph just shrugged, grinning as Buck returned Rayburn's salute.

"At ease, Captain. Thanks for helping us out back there. I'm so glad to be back on US soil, even if it is on water."

"Mr. President! Welcome to the USS Dixon."

"Thank you, Captain. But please just call me Buck—or Colonel Buchanan if you must. Until we sort this out a bit more, yes?"

Carli jumped in, "If he's the President, does that make the ship Navy One now?"

All four men glared at her.

"Or, maybe not?" She backtracked.

Murph walked over to the Captain. "Go answer the Israelis. Something tells me that our friends out there on the boats are not directly connected to the Israeli government, and they won't want to ask too many questions. If you give the commander a plausible way out, he'll take it and we can sail on. Let's use the value of bureaucracy!"

Rayburn agreed. "That's probably right. They really don't want to challenge us. I'll try your bluff."

"Then come back down here, and we can talk about where we go from here." Murph slumped into a leather easy chair. "I imagine we have some time—how long is the crossing of the Atlantic anyway."

Peter answered, "From here in the eastern Mediterranean, ten days, give or take a day."

Murph shook his head, "Not nearly enough time to figure this all out!"

Chapter 86

Cyrille Bastien seethed with rage as his Learjet landed. He stalked down the stairs onto the tarmac, oblivious to the heat waves that radiated off the blacktop. He barged through customs to enter the country, his eyes wide with anger. Few made any effort to impede his progress. He entered Israel with the ease of a seasoned diplomat. Even as he had landed in Tel Aviv hundreds of times before, his connections had made smooth his path. He forced himself to appear calm then burst from the airport terminal. He berated his driver for the traffic, as though he had personally caused the morning rush hour that blocked their path.

Arriving in Haifa, Cyrille went directly to the shambles that now represented their carefully designed plan. He wandered through the bunker underneath the classroom building, looking for clues about the team who had infiltrated the prison. His trained eye easily discerned the force that had penetrated these defenses was not a group of amateurs, but a professional team. This was not the work of the dentist, yet he clearly was involved.

The fact that a meddling dentist had been able to disrupt his carefully orchestrated plans angered Cyrille. He was the professional. He would overcome this. He would see to it that the plans succeeded—and that Murphy paid the price.

Cyrille heard the van pull up on the gravel outside the loading dock. Drawing his Glock pistol, Cyrille flattened himself against the wall of the passageway. Hiding in the shadows, he waited.

A scraggly middle-aged man entered, sweaty bandana around his forehead. He peered in, but his eyes were not adjusted to the darkness.

Remaining in the shadows, Cyrille spoke quietly, "Come in Palti. I would know what you know."

Standing in the sunlight, Palti froze. He considered running, but realized he would never escape. Accepting his fate, Palti stepped into the darkened hallway. He described the ill-fated expedition to capture the dentist and his girlfriend. He told of how they had arrived here only to find their base destroyed and the prisoner gone. Palti had been left behind to guard the van while Ashram and the others pursued Murphy in two boats. When they did not return after several hours, Palti returned here to await Ashram or any of the other mercenaries.

Cyrille considered all that he had heard. He knew Palti was not exceptionally bright and, in his heart, Cyrille knew that Palti spoke the truth. Cyrille thought of the dentist, anger rising again with bitter bile in the back of his throat.

Cyrille extended his arm suddenly and the gun barrel was only inches from the back of Palti's head when he fired. The body stumbled forward, ending face down on the cement floor, a pool of dark liquid expanding rapidly.

Cyrille searched the loading dock and quickly found what he wanted. Grabbing a gasoline can, he doused the compound, covering well the room where the prisoner had been held. He struck a match against his belt and tossed it onto Buck's bed. The flames caught then roared. Cyrille left the building, walking slowly into the sunlight as black smoke poured out of the doorway, staining the sky with a dark smudge.

An icy calm had returned to Cyrille. His driver noticed the menacing look on his face and thought *I was safer when he was cursing me.* Cyrille sat down in the back seat of the Mercedes sedan.

"Airport," was all he said.

Cyrille withdrew his phone and called.

"The prisoner is gone and all of our team in Haifa have been eliminated." Cyrille waited while the screaming subsided on the other end of the phone. "I have destroyed the compound at Atlit. I shall proceed with spreading an explanation for the damage. Where is the USS Dixon bound for?"

The President continued his ranting, profanity-laced tirade against the dentist.

Cyrille cut him off. "I will deal with the dentist—personally. Where is the ship going NOW?"

Frank Buchanan stopped to take a breath. "South Carolina. The ship is crossing the Atlantic and is scheduled to go directly to Charleston. There are no other stops."

"Excellent. I will finish here and fly to Charleston to meet the ship. They can't get off before making port. They've trapped themselves, and I'll make them pay for that error. A team can meet me there, and we'll prepare an appropriate welcome for them."

Cyrille's smile was growing, but it was a smile without any trace of mirth. Frank continued cursing. Cyrille ended the call and left the President yelling by himself. *Yes,* he thought, *At last they have made a critical mistake—and I have them!*

The driver looked back in the rearview mirror and instantly regretted it. The sight he saw would haunt his nightmares for years. The killer's face was a mask of pure evil, eyes unfocused, staring into the distance, smiling at the prospect of revenge.

Chapter 87

The USS Dixon sailed swiftly across the blue waters of the Mediterranean. The sailors returned to the routine tasks of running a warship at sea, the excitement of the rescue beginning to fade as the anticipation of returning home began to grow. Rumors continued to spread about the identity of their mysterious passengers.

Murph and Carli had been given free run of the ship. Lieutenant Bradshaw was similar enough in size and build to Murph so that he could wear one of Bradshaw's spare flight suits. Carli was a bit more of a problem, but the crew managed to find her a change of clothes. She was able to hem a pair of khaki uniform slacks and an officer's khaki shirt looked only a bit too large for her. The overly bloused outfit did little to reduce her attractiveness, so the sailors were more than happy to be helpful. Carli had an escort anywhere she wanted to go onboard the ship.

Buck was unfortunately trapped in the ready room. At Carli's suggestion, he was allowing his beard to grow in an effort to hide his identity. Captain Rayburn had continued to have the door to the room guarded 24 hours a day, which added to the mystery.

Peter had introduced Murph to the other officers on the ship. He had quietly led them to believe that Murph was both CIA and a dentist. It was the consensus that this was a fantastic cover. Who would suspect that a celebrity dentist was really a CIA agent? Murph was beginning to get the usual dental questions from the crew at meals or on deck. *"Hey, Doc…I've got this tooth that…Is that serious?"* He laughed and would offer whatever advice was appropriate. It felt good to be part of the ship's company. It made him feel useful and passed the time.

Murph and Buck were sitting at the conference table when there was a light knock on the door. Buck ducked into the head before Murph unlocked the door. Carli and Peter Mitchell slipped in.

Buck returned to the table and sat down. Murph sat across from him, and Peter took another chair. The Lieutenant had brought along his laptop computer, opening it and waiting for it to connect to the ship's network.

Carli poured herself a glass of ice water and stood behind Murph, walking her fingers up his arm and shoulder.

"A strange thing happened while I was out on deck today," she began, slyly. "The sailors were helpful as usual, but they seemed to be keeping their distance from me. Why do you think that would be?"

She looked straight at Peter and he blushed.

"Well," Peter looked down at his hands, "Murph and I were observing the effect that you were having on the crew, so I…"

"So you what??"

"Well…I kind of let slip that while Murph is a big, strong guy, he still really is just a dentist."

"Uh huh…" She waited to pounce.

"But you…well, you are really beautiful…and, you're the really dangerous one." He hurried along, looking sheepish. "Ok, I told Bradshaw that there were a hundred ways you could kill him and throw him over the side before he knew what happened."

She smacked Murph in the back of the head. Buck just burst out laughing and eventually they all were laughing as well.

Carli put her hands on her hips, looking hurt. "So, suddenly I'm this CIA killer?"

"Something like that…" Murph managed between laughs. "I mean, there are worse reputations to have."

"Thanks a lot!" She couldn't keep the pouty face going for long, but she did punch him in his sore shoulder.

"Ow!" He moaned through the laughing.

"Don't you get uppity with me," she grinned. "I'll just throw you overboard anyway."

Murph reached out for her, but she ducked under his arm and flopped into one of the recliners.

There was a sharp bang on the door. Before Buck could disappear, a voice barked, "Rayburn! Let me in!"

Murph went to the door and admitted the Captain. As more time on the ship had passed, Murph had begun to win over the taciturn commander. Murph respected his concern for the crew and the ship that had been entrusted to him. It was a heavy burden, but Rayburn had been well trained. He was a Naval Academy grad, having spent his entire career as a surface warfare officer. The *Dixon* was his first command, and he ran a tight ship.

Murph waved Captain Rayburn to his seat at the table and grabbed another chair, turning it backwards, and placing his arms over the back of the chair. They had been meeting as a group daily, trying to figure out a plan. Finding Buck in Israel had been unexpected, and now Murph and Buck had to decide what to do with this bargaining chip. They were safe on the Dixon, but landfall was coming soon.

Rayburn immediately took command of the meeting. "Let's review again where we stand. Now that you have found the Pres... I mean Colonel Buchanan, you need a plan to protect him once off the ship."

Murph spread his hands, "We still don't know what *their* plan is. They were keeping Buck as a source of information to keep the false President appearing genuine."

Buck agreed. "The woman who repeatedly talked to me. was always asking about my friends and family members, stories about my childhood. At the time, I had no idea what she was doing, since her questions had nothing to do with military secrets or US defense. I can see it now. She was filling in the President on who I knew on Capitol Hill so he could act like me." He swore bitterly. "How stupid of me!"

Murph patted him on the shoulder. "No point beating yourself up. We can't turn back time."

Buck looked up at them, pleading. "I really want to see my girls! It's been so long—and they won't know me!"

Murph could understand his pain. "We know. That's a high priority, but your safety comes first!"

Buck nodded, understanding but not really pleased.

Carli stood up and began pacing, pulling absent-mindedly at her ponytail. "We have to be very careful. If the country suddenly finds out that there are two Presidents, it could cause chaos in Washington and around the world." She suddenly stopped pacing and stared at them. "Do you think that's the plan? That kind of shock could destroy confidence in the government and bring America to a grinding halt."

Murph shuddered. "I don't think so. I just don't see what could be gained from that kind of chaos." He snapped his fingers. "But I think you are on to something."

"How's that?" She stood behind him and put her hands on his shoulders.

"We need to force their hand. Being passive and waiting for them to make a move serves no purpose. They already know we have Buck."

Buck was encouraged, "So how can we use that to our advantage? I hate just sitting around like a target."

Murph smiled. A plan coming together. "We take the fight to them. We force a confrontation, bringing Buck and the President together at a place of our choosing."

Peter whistled. "Man, that's risky!"

Rayburn nodded. "I agree. What do you plan to do when they face each other?"

"I, uh…well, I'm not really sure. We'll just see what happens and then react, I guess."

"Not your best plan, Stan." Carli patted Murph on the shoulders. "We live there, but they *own* Washington. We would be at a huge disadvantage."

"True. Is there any way we can get the President out of DC?"

Peter began typing rapidly on his computer. "Actually, there is!"

All eyes turned to the Lieutenant. "What do you mean?"

Peter turned the laptop around so they could see the screen. "That's why I came down here in the first place. I was going to see if I could get Buck to place a wager on the football game with me!"

They looked at the computer screen, Murph's smile growing from ear to ear.

Peter explained in triumph. "This year they are playing the game for the Commander in Chief's Trophy on Saturday, September 16th. It's the Navy Midshipmen against the Falcons of the Air Force Academy…"

"And it's in Cleveland!" Murph finished his sentence. "That's perfect!"

Buck nodded in agreement. But Carli and Captain Rayburn remained unsure.

"I'm not sure I see your play here." Rayburn drummed the table with his fingers.

Murph was rolling now. "The President always attends that game. As the Commander in Chief, he'll sit for one-half with the Naval Academy midshipmen, then he changes sides at halftime and will sit with the Air Force cadets. Except this year will be special, because…" Murph extended his hand to Buck as an invitation to jump in.

"I'm an Air Force Academy alum?"

"Precisely! And you were the quarterback of the football team for your junior and senior years, if I remember right."

"Yes. And my old coach is still the head coach of the Falcons. Bobby Malone will know which one of us is the real one!"

Murph's enthusiasm was contagious. "Plus, the game is in Cleveland, which gives us the home-field advantage. I know First Energy Stadium well, and one of my Dad's best friends is the Director of Ballpark Operations. If we can find out what the schedule is for that day, it's possible that we could set up a confrontation on our terms and record the event as evidence."

"Is there any chance we could substitute Buck for the President? I'm thinking crazy but…switch them back?" Carli bit on her fingertip.

"That's asking a lot." Murph wrinkled his brows. "However, that would be ideal. Let's see if there is any possibility of a switch as we plan. If the opportunity presents itself, then we'll be ready to jump on it!"

"I hate to be a kill-joy, but there's something you all should know." Captain Rayburn set his palms on the table and pushed himself up, standing facing the now silent group. "I've just been on a secure line, video conferencing with the President of the United States."

Chapter 88

Franklin Buchanan shut down his computer and regarded his guests with a self-satisfied smile. Sitting at his desk in the Oval Office, he closed the lid of the laptop and patted the case.

"That should take care of it," he said smugly. "Cyrille Bastien will control the team of NSA agents, but, Paul, I want you to go to Charleston and take direct control of the situation."

Paul Ramon, the President's Chief of Staff, nodded in agreement, then took out his phone to order his staff to make his trip arrangements.

Simon Cohen stood calmly beside the desk. "Mr. President. I'm concerned this dentist is much more resourceful than we have been willing to admit. I think your solution is a bit simplistic."

"Nonsense! When the *Dixon* docks in Charleston, Captain Rayburn will hand over the prisoners to our NSA team. They will in turn give them to Bastien. What could be simpler than that?"

Cohen continued evenly, "But what shall we do with the prisoners?"

"What prisoners?" Buchanan responded flatly. "Bastien will eliminate them immediately."

"Very simple, indeed."

Chapter 89

A heavy silence descended on the pilot's ready room. The fans of the air recirculation system hummed as the group stared at Captain Rayburn. He let the gravity of the situation set in with them all.

"Murph, you are correct in your assessment of a number of things. The President is aware that you are on the *Dixon* and that you have Buck. He told me that you are all part of a plot to replace him. He ordered me to arrest you and to turn you over to a team from the NSA as soon as we make port in Charleston."

"That's preposterous!" Murph started to rise out of his chair.

Rayburn held up his hand for silence. Murph sat down, biting his tongue.

"I can't disobey a direct order, so I told him that I had you confined under guard." He pointed at the door and smiled. "And that's technically true, since the sailor outside that door is armed."

"Yes, he is." Murph could feel the room becoming warmer again.

"Murph, when you warned me that the President would probably contact me, I listened very carefully. And when he did, I listened very carefully to what he said, and his story just doesn't ring true. If you were plotting to replace the President with an imposter, this is a really lousy way to do it. Why would you escape Israel and have a US Navy warship pick you up so that you could illegally enter the US? Just walk from Mexico across the border in Arizona, for Christ's sake. This is way too convoluted. Right now, you're trapped."

"I understand, Captain. And we appreciate your support." Murph stood up and shook his hand. "I'll ask you to leave now, so you don't have to know any more of what we are planning. When the ship makes port, and we are nowhere to be found, you can honestly say you have no idea what happened."

"You have the assistance of my ship and crew. Crazy as it seems, you may pull this off!"

Buck walked over to the Rayburn and shook his hand. "Thank you, Captain. We'll do our best."

Rayburn went to the door, reached out for the handle and turned back to the group. "IF it were me, I'd figure out a way to get off the ship before we reached the port. Once we dock, my authority drops, and I can't help you. Lieutenant Mitchell, I'd look to the schedule of events for that day for inspiration."

Rayburn winked and opened the door.

Peter's eyes widened, as a light bulb went off. "Yes, Sir!"

Leaving quickly, Rayburn shut the hatch behind him, and Murph locked the door.

He returned to the table. "Peter, what did he mean by that?"

Peter was calling up an image on the computer, zooming in on an aerial view of Charleston harbor. "Just a minute… Ah, here it is!"

Peter pointed at the map. "We arrive on Friday morning, the 15th of September. The ceremony for the internment of the CSS Hunley crew is at 10:00 a.m. at Fort Moultrie. The *Dixon* will pass in review in the channel between Fort Sumter and Sullivan's Island. The crew will line the rails on deck in their dress whites."

Buck considered the image. "That's an impressive sight for the crowd on shore."

"You bet." Peter agreed. "To add to the show, we are launching both helicopters while we are still out at sea. The *Hunley* went down near the channel, so we are going to fly both helos over the spot in formation, then pull one of them up in a kind of 'missing man' formation."

Murph tapped the screen. "If you flew close enough to the shore on that pass, we could drop into the water and swim ashore. I visited Ft. Moultrie when I was a kid. I don't think you can see that beach from the fort."

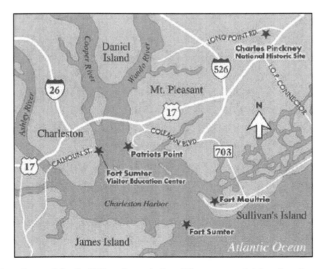

Buck nodded. "You're right. The trees hide the beach, so we could come ashore unseen, then walk into the fort complex up the path. The only problem is the currents in the channel are very strong. There's a reason they post signs prohibiting swimming on that end of Sullivan's Island. The undertow claims at least one person a year. But, if Peter could drop us in just the right place, we could do it."

Peter looked hurt. "I'll put you on a dime. I'll get the charts for the currents and plan the drop for you. I'll also see about getting you wet suits and a waterproof bag to keep your gear dry while you swim."

"Excellent." Murph took out a pad and began making notes. "We'll need some help when we come ashore. We'll have to rent a car. I don't want to steal one, and I'm afraid to use our credit cards. That would put us back on the grid."

Buck scratched the growing stubble on his chin. "You guys have done all the heavy lifting so far. Now is the time for me to help. I think I can call in a favor and get us some help. In fact, I think it's time to call in the Marines!"

Chapter 90

Buck had requested access to the military database and scanned it, quickly finding the people he was seeking. "We're in luck! Four of the guys I need are together, stationed at Camp Lejeune. I just need to have Captain Rayburn request them for a temporary duty assignment. I'll have him cut orders for them to report to Charleston to meet the *Dixon* when she makes port."

"Sounds good." Murph took the names and added them to his list. "I'll talk to the Captain now."

"You don't need to tell them why. The less we say, the better. Orders are orders, and they will obey them. When we get in range, I'll call Lieutenant Scharver and explain. It will make more sense live. I don't know how I would go about explaining this in writing."

Murph snorted. "It's no easier in person. Lord knows. I've tried!" Murph consulted his notepad. "I've got to explain what I need to people in Cleveland. I think I'm just going to contact my Dad and see if he can put it together for us. We won't have much time after we land. It's an 11-hour drive from Charleston to Cleveland. I've done it enough times to know!"

Carli was working on the computer with Peter. "We should get to your parent's by midnight Friday. According to the Internet, the football game is a 3:30 kickoff on Saturday."

Murph shook his head. "We can't stay with my parents. I'm sure the NSA guys will be watching their house. I'm hoping to get some help from friends when we get there, but I can't make those calls while we're out at sea."

Peter tapped the keyboard, then jumped up to high-five Carli. "Yes! The Lord helps those who help themselves!"

"What is it?"

"The pregame show with the Academy bands is including local high schools. The Saint Ignatius marching band is one of them!"

Murph clapped his hands together. "That's fantastic!"

Buck was confused. "Why's that so important."

Carli was ready to help him out. "Murph's younger brother Brian is a senior at Saint Ignatius. He's part of the drum line for the Wildcat Marching Band."

"And my Dad is a big band booster. He was in the band when he was in high school and college, so he helps them out. Since the Iggy band is going into the stadium, that means an equipment truck and large cases for drums, xylophones, tubas, and conductor's platforms. That could help us get into the park, or back out."

"Sounds good." Buck finished writing the script for the orders he wanted and pushed it across the table to Murph.

"Thanks. It means more people involved, but that gives us greater flexibility, depending on what happens when we meet the President."

"Right now, I just want to punch him in the nose." Buck spoke through clenched teeth. "We can go from there, but I've got a score to settle with that guy!"

Murph nodded in agreement. "Amen to that!"

* * * * * * *

The *Dixon* knifed across the Atlantic, swiftly making the crossing. They arrived off the East Coast a half-day early, allowing Murph and Buck to make the cell calls they needed. By dawn Friday, all the preparations were in place. Captain Rayburn joined the group one last time in the ready room.

Rayburn was in his dress whites, prepared for the day's ceremonies. "Good luck today and in the future with whatever you have planned. I'm going to be following what happens from here."

Murph shrugged. "I'm hoping that you won't notice anything. If we do this right, no one will know that there was ever a problem."

Rayburn chuckled. "That's what I'm praying for!"

Buck shook Rayburn's hand. "Captain, it's been an honor to be on your ship. Thanks for bringing us safely home. I haven't been in the States for a long time. It feels great to be almost home."

"Mr. President, it will be my honor to serve you as the Commander in Chief when you get back to Washington." Rayburn stood at attention and saluted, then turned to Carli. "You are welcome on my ship anytime, even if you are a trained killer." He laughed and gave Carli a hug.

"Captain, you and your crew have been wonderful. It's been my pleasure to be here." She kissed him lightly on the cheek.

Rayburn looked at Murph. "You, however, have been a pain in the ass!"

"I try, Captain."

"I hope you go ashore and become a bigger pain for the other guys." He laughed.

"I'll do my best. With your help, we have a chance. Thanks again."

"If anyone can pull this off, I think you guys can. Just come to our home base at Mayport, Florida and tell me about it. Drinks are on me!"

"You're on!"

Peter came in the door in a hurry, flight suit on, looking stressed. "Time to go!"

Buck pulled a hood over his head and masked his face with a bandana. Murph picked up their waterproof bags and they followed Peter out the door and down to the flight deck.

Rayburn watched them as they left, shook his head, and turned. His purposeful steps quickly led him up to the bridge. He assumed command of the *Dixon* and began barking orders. Looking aft, he could see the rotors turning on the helicopter. He aimed the ship toward the channel and focused on the task at hand. He couldn't help them any more. They were on their own.

Chapter 91

Peter led the team to the flight deck, where his Seahawk helicopter sat with rotors turning. The other helo had already been launched and was trailing the *Dixon* about a half-mile away. Murph waved at Lt. Bradshaw, seated as the copilot in the left seat.

In keeping with their cover story, Murph led the group, carrying the waterproof bags. Carli led Buck by the arm, his face hooded again. Buck held his hands together as if he were restrained.

The same crew had requested to be on the helo for this mission. Airman Piper and Petty Officer Williams helped their passengers into the cabin, securing them and their gear. Peter Mitchell settled into the pilot's seat and completed the preparations for takeoff.

With a salute to the deck crew, Peter advanced the throttle and pulled back on the collective, which increased the speed and lift of the rotors. When the lift of the rotor exceeded the weight of the helicopter, the Seahawk lifted easily off the deck. Using his foot pedals to adjust the tail rotor to counteract the torque of the main, Peter smoothly nudged the cyclic forward and eased the helo away from the speeding *Dixon.*

"Moonshine 508 away." Lt. Bradshaw called in his southern drawl.

Peter keyed his intercom and had Piper give Murph a headset. When he was set up, Peter asked, "Murph. Any last messages for Rebel One?"

Murph shouted into the microphone over the engine noise. "Tell him…"

Peter said, "Let me patch you in and you can tell him yourself."

Petty Officer Washington had been listening in on his headset and quickly scrawled on a white dry-erase board, "We're Moonshine 508. The *Dixon* is Rebel."

Murph heard, "This is Rebel, go ahead." He struggled to think of a good Navy saying and was relieved when a thought popped in his head.

He gave Washington a thumbs-up and spoke, "Rebel, this is Moonshine 508. Thanks for all your help. Fair winds and following seas to you all, until we meet again."

Piper was grinning and Washington clapped Murph on the back, so he figured he had gotten the old Navy salutation right.

"Thank you. It was our pleasure. Rebel One says good luck and good hunting! Rebel out."

Peter smoothly slid Moonshine 508 in position slightly behind and below the other helicopter as they followed the *Dixon* toward the channel. Murph, Carli, and Buck had shed their borrowed navy clothing and sat there in black wet suits, pulling on swim fins.

Murph clicked his mike and patted Washington on the shoulder. When both sailors looked over, he said, "Guys, I just want you to know what this was about. It's top secret but you've earned the truth."

Murph reached over and shook Carli by the arm, indicating that she should uncover Buck's head. She looked at him with alarm but he mouthed, "It's OK." She untied the wrapping on Buck's head and showed his face. He turned to smile at the sailors.

Piper's mouth dropped open. Washington spoke and Murph couldn't miss his southern accent on the intercom.

"Jaysus Christ!"

Murph laughed. "We're bringing him home to set things right in Washington."

"Damn! That's one hell of a big job to do!"

"Thanks to you guys, we have a chance!"

"We better get you all ready. We only get one chance to do this."

Washington opened the side door of the helo and helped Murph up. They both leaned out and took in the sights.

It was an overcast day, with heavy gray clouds that foretold of rain. There were no showers now, much to the delight of the crew lining the deck of the *Dixon* in their dress white uniforms. Murph could see the ship heading for the low mass of rock that was the island of Fort Sumter.

During the Civil War, the Union Navy had shelled Fort Sumter for three years, blasting the three-story brick fortress into one level of rubble. However, the Fort never fell and Charleston harbor remained open to Confederate raiders while the Union Navy could only sit outside the harbor mouth in blockade. Murph's target for the day was easily visible on the shore opposite Fort Sumter.

The first shots of the Civil War had been fired by Confederate guns at Fort Moultrie, shelling the Federal garrison on Fort Sumter. When the Union troops vacated Fort Sumter in 1861, they ceded control of the port of Charleston to the Confederate government.

The light gray sides of the *Dixon* were defined by the dots of white sailors standing in review at the edges of her deck and the phosphorescent wake cut in the gray-green water of the ocean. The two helicopters had dropped to fifty feet of altitude and were closing in behind the destroyer, flying close together on a parallel course.

Murph pointed to the tan strip of sand; the thin beach below Fort Moultrie before the channel narrowed forming the mouth of the harbor. The edge where the sand met the Atlantic Ocean was flat for a short distance then became increasingly dominated by large rock boulders. Carli leaned on Murph and pointed to the boulders with alarm, the white breakers crashing against the rocks. Murph pointed to the rocks and shook his head no, then indicated the flat sand. Carli's eyes were still wide with concern.

Murph sat her back down and leaned in close to Carli and Buck. "The tide's running high and the waves are breaking on the rocks below the fort. We have to swim hard for the sandy beach, or we will be sucked into the channel by the undertow. We'll drop quickly one after the other and stay close together. Got it!"

They both nodded and stood up, tightening their fins and masks.

Murph turned to Petty Officer Washington. "We need to drop as a group, before we get too far into the channel."

Peter heard and clicked in, "That's the plan. Now get ready, this will go quick. Washington, be ready to push them out!"

Murph called up front, "Peter, thanks for your help. I owe you!"

"Not at all. When this is over, I'm going to buy you a beer!"

Murph, Carli, and Buck sat down on the edge of the open door of the helo. Murph put their waterproof bag on his back and took off his headset, handing it to Washington. Both sailors shook Murph's hand and Piper positioned himself behind the passengers.

Murph could see the water get closer and the helo dropped down to ten feet and the pace picked up as the two helicopters sped up to catch the destroyer. He reached out and took Carli's hand, squeezing it for luck.

The roar of the helicopter prevented any conversation, so the three were left each with their own thoughts. All Murph could think of was the shepherd's prayer; well, astronaut Alan Shepard's prayer—"Oh Lord, please don't let me screw up!"

* * * * * * *

The crowd gathered on the shore for the ceremony pointed at the approaching guided missile destroyer. They were impressed by the crew lining the rails of the ship in review, brilliant in their dress whites. The rake of the bow cut the gray water, forcing the ocean aside in a white frothing wake. The hull number 117 proudly announced the *USS Dixon* returning to Charleston harbor.

The ship had barely cleared the narrows in the channel when a pair of blue-gray camouflaged Seahawk helicopters came flying in at low altitude, skimming the surface of the water. As the helos neared the beach, the lead chopper's engine roared and it shot up in a missing man maneuver.

People pointed, gaping at the precision. The lead helicopter soared up and away, while the second continued straight on into the harbor, chasing after the *Dixon.* The crowd cheered and clapped, all eyes on the lead Seahawk when it lifted up and away.

The maneuver was executed flawlessly. And no one noticed the three black objects that dropped from the trailing helo into the water. At that low altitude, the rotors turned the water's surface frothing.

Had the crowd been paying attention, they would have seen three heads pop up in the channel and begin to struggle to reach land, but they were all too preoccupied with the spectacle of a guided missile destroyer and its helicopters passing in review only a hundred yards off shore. It had been quite a sight. One that the assembled crowd would not soon forget!

Chapter 92

As the helicopters approached the channel, Airman Piper had closed the door facing Fort Moultrie and opened the other side. Murph and his band had been sitting on the edge of the doorway looking at Fort Sumter, with the lead helicopter closer to the Carolina shore. When the time approached, Petty Officer Washington had signaled them with a thumbs-up, then the go signal.

Buck went first, then Carli, with Murph last. Peter dropped down at the last minute to about six feet, but falling feet first into the cold water was enough of a shock to take your breath away, especially since they didn't do this every day.

Piper leaned over and made sure to see three heads pop up. Murph gave a thumbs-up, but the helo wasn't sticking around to see how they were.

Washington keyed his mike, "Passengers away."

Peter Mitchell acknowledged the news. "Roger that."

Washington couldn't resist asking, since they were still isolated on the chopper. "Was that really the President?"

"Yes." Peter couldn't think of anything else to say.

"Holy Shit!"

"That's about the size of it, Petty Officer." Peter looked back, but couldn't see Murph in the water. "And the best thing you can do is forget you ever saw them."

"Yes, Sir!"

Peter said a prayer for their safety and turned his attention to the task at hand. He flew close to the shore at low altitude, making sure to draw as much attention to his helicopter as possible.

* * * * * * *

Murph began treading water instantly, and then swam over to join Buck and Carli. The channel had over 4-foot swells, and visibility in the water was very poor. The current was churning the bottom, leaving a brown sandy cloud in the gray water. Murph pointed at a large palm tree on the far right border of the beach and established that as their target.

He urged Carli, "Don't swim straight in at the beach, the current will carry you onto the rocks. Aim for that palm tree, and you'll probably end up right in the middle of the beach."

She nodded in agreement and they set off swimming with smooth, deliberate strokes. All three were in excellent shape, but fighting the current and the swells was hard work. Buck and Carli made excellent progress, but burdened by the weight and bulk of their waterproof sack, Murph was having a tougher time. He was glad that so much of his rehab for his shoulder wound had been done in the pool.

Realizing that Carli was now more than 50 feet ahead, Murph began to increase his pace. The muscles in his shoulders were on fire. The current grabbed the pack and pulled him further into the channel. He felt the beginnings of panic, so he consciously slowed down. Re-establishing his target, he began even, long strokes aimed at the tall palm tree in the distance.

Murph could see Buck and Carli reach the beach. It was a miracle that it was deserted. Murph hoped that their luck would continue to hold. Buck helped Carli out of the surf. As they had planned, they immediately ran for the cover of the tree line, in case the beach was being observed.

In spite of his efforts, Murph was being dragged further into the channel. He worked his legs in slow strokes for maximum effect with the swim fins. His attention was focused on the palm tree and he became lost in the rhythm of his strokes. It wasn't until the edge of one of the rocks under water cut at his wet suit that Murph realized that he had reached the shore.

Murph was at the opposite end of the beach from Buck and Carli, but he managed to drag himself onto one of the cement blocks that had been placed to minimize the erosion of the beach. He pulled up out of the water and leaned on his back, his breath coming in ragged gulps. Turning over, he reached out and grabbed a signpost to pull himself upright.

Looking at the sign, he laughed. It had the red circle with a line through it over the drawing of a man swimming and huge red letters.

DANGER
NO SWIMMING ALLOWED
STRONG CURRENTS

I'll agree to that! Murph thought to himself.

He eased himself to the edge of the rocks and looked across the beach, waving at Carli. He could see the concern on her face even at this distance. Murph looked up at the fort, but saw no signs of movement. He settled the waterproof bag on his shoulder and started out across the beach. His tired legs refused to behave normally. He weaved and staggered across the sand until he reached Carli.

As Murph ducked under the tree branches, Buck took the pack. Carli helped Murph as he collapsed onto the sand.

"I didn't think you were going to make it there. You had me worried!"

He smiled weakly, "I wasn't so sure myself!"

Buck opened the pack and took out their clothes. They all shed their wetsuits, changing quickly into their combat pants and pullovers. Carli had her yoga pants and top. She squeezed out as much water as she could from her hair and pulled it back into a ponytail.

Murph filled the waterproof bag with their wetsuits and fins, and then buried it in the underbrush.

"I hate to litter. We'll come back someday and pick that up."

Carli looked around the beach to remember the area. The sun was trying to break through the clouds. "It's so pretty here. I can see why you like it."

Murph stood up, stretching. "Charleston is one of my favorite places. The food is fantastic, the scenery is amazing, and the people are warm and inviting. I'd love to retire here someday!"

Buck peeked around the trees. "Well, now's not the time. We have a lot to do! Let's get moving."

Murph checked his watch. "You bet. We're late. Somebody must be a slow swimmer!"

Buck led the way off the beach, through a sandy path between the lines of trees. The path led them onto a grassy plain facing the brick and stone walls of the fort. As they left the beach, they could see the muzzles of the cannons peering out of the battlements of the fort, pointed at them. It was clear that the purpose of the fort was to prevent exactly this: intruders coming in from the sea.

Chapter 93

Murph took Carli's hand, walking up the worn path to Fort Moultrie like they had not a care in the world. He knew they would arouse suspicion if they tried to crouch down and not be seen. He pointed to the tower that was the highest point of the fort.

"Fort Moultrie is part of the Fort Sumter National Monument, administered by the National Park Service, so we'll see uniformed rangers when we get up there." Murph took the lead. "Where Fort Sumter was destroyed in the Civil War, Fort Moultrie was in use from the Revolutionary War through the end of World War II. That observation tower was used to direct ship convoys entering and leaving Charleston Harbor during WW2. They have the park set up so you can see what the fort looked like in all of the time periods between 1776 and 1945."

They were approaching the outer wall of the fort. The brick and earthwork walls towered over them, but the gates were open, welcoming them in. There were a number of tourists wandering around, with little children climbing on the cannons and their mothers yelling at them to get down.

Carli smiled. "Some things never change."

Murph led them across the main parade ground to a group of yellow brick buildings set against the outer wall of the fort. He indicated for Buck and Carli to go in.

Buck raised an eyebrow. "The powder magazine?"

"It's dark and quiet, and few people come over here. Even with the scruffy beard and sunglasses, you still look too much like the President."

Carli had to agree, but she was concerned about leaving Murph's side. "I hate to split up. How will you know Buck's friends when you see them?"

"We can't risk Buck wandering around here any more than necessary. Besides, I think I can spot a Marine lieutenant when I see one."

Buck nodded. "About my height, but thinner. Sandy brown hair and blue eyes."

"Got it. I'll be back soon." Murph tried to sound confident. "Hopefully."

Murph crossed the parade ground again, heading for the rendezvous that Buck had arranged. He climbed to the battery of 5-inch naval guns that had protected the fort from the German raiders that never came. Murph studied the board that explained the type of gun and its use, and then looked out over the barrel at the beach. The *Dixon* and her escort helicopters were long gone.

Turning around, Murph was face to face with a young man, slightly shorter than he was, but with sandy brown hair sticking out from a baseball cap. The man studied Murph then took off his sunglasses, revealing penetrating blue eyes.

"Lieutenant Schuster?" Murph asked quietly.

"Who wants to know?" The voice was a deep, low growl coming from behind Murph.

Murph started to snap his head around, then forced himself to turn slowly. He faced a bulldog of a man, 5'6" at best. The flat top haircut and globe and anchor tattoo on his massive forearm gave him away instantly as a Marine.

Murph turned back to Schuster. "I'm Michael Murphy. A mutual friend of ours sent me to find you and take you to him." Murph extended his hand and Schuster shook it.

"First Lieutenant Jeffrey Schuster. My bodyguard here is Staff Sergeant Ron Covrett."

Murph turned to shake Covrett's hand. His massive paw enveloped Murph's hand, and the grip was a vice. "Pleased to meet you."

Schuster waived his sunglasses, casually indicating around the fort. "The rest of my team is watching us, so no funny business, OK?"

"Agreed." Murph began descending the steps to the parade ground. "Follow me."

As they walked, Schuster continued, "I receive orders from a Captain I've never met, calling for my team to join the

301

USS Dixon in Charleston Harbor. Then I get a cryptic phone call from an old friend asking me to meet him here. Then you show up. This is all very cloak and dagger."

"Lieutenant, you don't know how tired I am of cloak and dagger," Murph shook his head sadly, "but that's the only game in town now."

They arrived at the powder magazine, and Murph whistled softly. Carli stepped out of the shadows. The two Marines looked her over and considered this development.

Covrett observed, "Very nice!"

He was disappointed when Carli wrinkled her nose in his direction and went to stand with Murph, taking his hand.

"Lt. Schuster and Sgt. Covrett. May I introduce Miss Carli Chamoun?"

Schuster shook her hand, and then indicated that Covrett should guard the entrance, making sure they wouldn't be disturbed.

Carli led Schuster and Murph into the guard office that was the outer chamber of the magazine. Sunlight filtered in through the dirty glass windows.

Buck stepped out of the shadows. "Lieutenant. Thank you for coming."

Schuster regarded Buck guardedly. "You're welcome."

Buck seemed taken aback by the Lieutenant's distance. "Do you have something for me? I'll take it back now."

A broad smile split Schuster's face and he reached out, hugging Buck. The two men held on, patting each other on the back for a long time.

"Colonel! It really is you!" Schuster stood back, reached into his pocket and handed Buck a locket on a chain.

Tears streamed down Buck's face as he opened the locket. The two pictures inside were his girls. "When I was wounded in Afghanistan, I gave the locket to Lieutenant Schuster. He was the commander of the Marine unit I had been shot down trying to help. When I was hit, I was concerned I wouldn't make it and I wanted to be sure my girls got the locket so they would know how much I loved them."

302

Carli took his hand. She was crying too.

Schuster's eyes were moist, but he looked angry. "I was supposed to give the locket back the first time I saw you. Right after the election, Vice President Buchanan came to Camp Lejeune. I met him and went to hand him the locket. He dismissed the gesture and me as if he didn't even know who I was." Schuster slammed his fist into his other palm. "Now I understand why!"

Murph patted Schuster on the shoulder. "Now you know how we all feel—betrayed! But we can catch you up on how we got here at another time. For now, we have to get out of here." Murph looked Schuster in the eye. "Are you with us?"

"Yes."

Murph could see the determination in the young Marine's face.

Schuster was adamant. "Whatever it takes, we need to get that guy!"

Buck hugged Schuster again. "Did you bring what I asked?"

"I've got two rental cars, some food and drinks in coolers, a couple of prepaid cell phones and some cash."

Murph took the lead. "Good. Thanks for taking the leap of faith with us. We're going to Cleveland to meet our destiny … or his. We have to stay off the grid. We'll drive through town and get on I-26 to Columbia then take I-77 to Cleveland. It's eleven hours. I know. I've driven it enough times. Let's get moving."

Buck put his sunglasses and hat back on, and the group left the powder magazine. They went toward the main gate. Schuster and Covrett walked out first, heading across the street to the parking lot. Murph, Carli and Buck followed a few minutes later. As they reached the lot, the remaining members of Schuster's team had arrived.

Schuster introduced the remaining Marines. Sergeant Nate Lobas was a stocky weapons specialist with wavy black hair, beard and moustache. He was dark and quiet, the exact opposite of the tall, lanky kid of the group, Lance Corporal

Jason Wick, who was grinning from ear to ear and shaking hands like he was on an adventure. Private Warren Myles completed the group, a Californian who looked like he would be more at home on a beach with a surfboard than in the Marines. They all were combat veterans, tested and confident in their abilities.

Murph quickly laid out the plan. "We need to stay off the grid. That means no texting or phone calls. There are tolls on the West Virginia turnpike. Pay them with cash, not a credit card. We buy gas with cash as well. No speeding. No more than five miles per hour over the limit. We can't afford getting stopped. Got it!"

They all nodded in agreement. Schuster was going to drive the gray Ford Taurus. Murph assigned Buck to him, so they could catch up on old times. Covrett and Myles would ride in the back seat. Murph was driving a black Chevy Impala, with Carli up front and Lobas and Wick in back.

Murph considered Schuster. "Follow me into town. I'm hoping that the bad guys will assume we are going to Washington. We've left enough clues to make them think that, so they'll focus on I-95. That's the straight route to DC. We have to get west of I-95 before they close the net on us."

Schuster handed Murph one of the prepaid cell phones. "I programmed the numbers of the other cell phones on these so we can call each other easily."

"Great thinking. You keep one, give one to Buck, and I'll take this one. Let's get moving!"

They climbed in and left Fort Moultrie with Murph in the lead. He had made the drive from Charleston to Cleveland probably twenty times. He knew the route like the back of his hand, but now he was seeing threats behind every bush. It was going to be a long trip.

Twenty minutes into the drive, they were crossing through the diamond-shaped towers of the Ravenel Bridge, leading into Charleston where they would pick up I-26 to Columbia. The bridge was high and long, providing a panoramic view of Charleston harbor. Murph and Carli

304

scanned the docks, easily finding the silhouette of the *USS Dixon*. Murph turned to point out the destroyer to his passengers, but like good Marines, they were sound asleep.

"Never miss the chance at a good nap!" Murph tapped Carli on the shoulder, pointing in the back seat.

"They've got the right idea." Carli scanned the horizon, pointing at all the church steeples. "What a beautiful skyline."

"They call Charleston *The Holy City* since there are so many churches. Some of those date to the 1700's. Most of the old buildings have cannon and bullet holes in them from the Civil War. It's a great place to visit, but, as usual, we don't have the time."

"One of these days, Murphy, you're going to stop all this running around and take me on a real vacation." She nestled against his arm.

"I can't wait." He kissed her on the top of her head. "But for now, I've got to make sure that Schuster sticks with me when we make the next turn."

Murph looked back for a last glimpse of the *Dixon,* but the support wires of the bridge obscured his view. His turn signal clicked, indicating the change onto I-26. Looking in the mirror, Murph was pleased to see the gray Taurus right on his tail. At this rate, they would reach Cleveland before midnight. *Perfect!*

Chapter 94

Paul Ramon, the President's Chief of Staff paced back and forth on the concrete steps of the Custom's House. The old building had a clear view of the docks as the *USS Dixon* eased in to port. He was supremely uncomfortable in this role. He was in Charleston to supervise, but he had no authority to actually make anything happen. That left him as a reluctant observer.

Ramon could see that the NSA had stationed agents to restrict the space on the dock around the berth of the destroyer. Cyrille Bastien had his own team of goons but they were out of sight.

The *Dixon* docked in an efficient, professional manner. The gangway was secured and the armed watch was stationed on the dock. Lieutenant Cortell had drawn the short straw again, or so he thought as he descended the gangway with his clipboard. He led the armed sentry to his post and then settled in, open for business. The crew prepared for their first liberty in the US in six months and they were itching to get off the ship.

Paul's phone buzzed. "Mr. Ramon? It's Agent Krantz." *Ugh, the lead NSA agent.* "We need you to give us authority to board the ship."

Paul thought a minute, feeling old and tired. "I'll be right there," he sighed.

Paul walked down the steps of the customs building and stepped briskly along the dock. With the temperature 89 degrees, he looked very out of place in his charcoal gray pinstriped Armani suit and pink silk tie. He could feel the stares of the tourists in shorts and flip-flops as he walked by. He stood tall and tried to walk with an air of command.

As he approached the gangway, he was joined by four NSA agents in black suits, small headsets in their right ears with a mike along their cheek.

Lieutenant Cortell glanced up from his podium at the approaching group. "Good afternoon. How can I help you?"

"Captain, ahh," Ramon stared down at the nametag. "Cornell. I need to speak with your commanding officer."

"Sir, I'm Lieutenant Cortell. I'm the officer of the watch of the *USS Dixon*. Whom may I say is calling?" His tone was polite, but not overly helpful.

"Cortell! You will admit me to see Captain Rayburn immediately. These agents and I need to get on this ship, or no one is getting off! Got it!"

Bill Cortell was not one to be easily intimidated and to the silent approval of the armed sailor, he deliberately laid down his clipboard and called the bridge. "Officer of the Day. Yes. Lt. Cortell here. There is a rather impatient man here with a team of 'agents' who want access to the *Dixon*. He wants to see the Captain but won't tell me who he is."

Paul went ballistic. "You idiot! I'm Paul Ramon, Chief of Staff to the President. These men are agents from the National Security Agency. Get your butt in gear and get me on that ship, or I'll have your ass in Afghanistan so fast you won't be able to pack!"

Cortell was preparing a response but was interrupted, luckily for his career. "Lt. Cortell, thank you for the information. This is the Captain. I was rather expecting Mr. Ramon, or someone of his ilk. Please bring him to my cabin. The NSA agents may stay on the deck."

"You heard the man." Paul Ramon began heading for the gangway.

"Not so fast, Sir." Cortell extended his clipboard, pen in hand. "You all need to sign in—please."

* * * * * * *

Bastien stood on the dock, fuming. Paul Ramon and the NSA agents had boarded the ship more than an hour ago. No one had left the ship, of that Cyrille was sure. Paul Ramon walked down the gangway to the dock, looked left and right, then spotted the bald head and big eyes of Cyrille Bastien, lurking in the shadows. He walked toward the spot, passing Bastien, rounding the corner of the building, stopping only when he was out of sight.

As Bastien approached, Ramon said, "I don't think we should be seen together."

"I do not give a damn what you think."

Paul shivered in spite of the heat.

""What did you learn from the Captain?" Bastien's words were clipped.

"The dentist and Colonel Buchanan were on the ship."

"Idiot! I know that." He reached out and grabbed a handful of silk tie, lifting Ramon off his feet.

"They are not on the ship now. No one seems to know where they are or how they got off." Ramon could feel the tie constricting on his neck. He rushed to finish. "But the good news is that no one knows that the prisoner was Colonel Buchanan. For some reason, Dr. Murphy kept his identity secret."

Bastien released his hold, tossing Ramon against the wood-sided building. Paul collapsed on the ground, the back of his suit ruined by the paint rubbing off where he hit the whitewashed boards.

"Dr. Murphy kept the secret because he is much smarter than you are!" Cyrille hissed. "If the word were to get out that there are two President's, it would cause global chaos. None of us wants that. He will try to confront the President in Washington, hoping to resolve the problem without anyone knowing."

Bastien turned in a slow circle, thinking rapidly. "There is no way that they could have gotten off the ship, unless they dove overboard and swam to shore. Nothing left that ship today except—the helicopters!"

Paul Ramon lay bathed in sweat, glad to be alive as Cyrille Bastien ran off. He could hear the assassin swearing in a foreign language, but he neither knew nor cared which one. Paul knew only one thing. He was done with this.

He stood up and smoothed the wrinkles out of his suit. He walked off toward his hotel, planning the exact words he would use in his letter of resignation.

Chapter 95

Murph was pleased. They had reached Columba, SC without incident and were now moving up I-77. He knew the path well: Charlotte, Lake Norman, Mt. Airy, Wytheville, Ft.

Chiswell, Princeton, Charleston, Marietta, Canton, Akron, and then Cleveland. He should be tired. Everyone around him was asleep. But his mind was racing, planning what they had to do. And the Navy-Air Force game was tomorrow!

In the end, the faster they got this over with, the better. Murph went over the plans again in his mind and made another couple of phone calls to confirm the details. *Honestly, this plan probably has less than 20% chance of success, but it's the best we can do.*

When Murph had called Derek Whitman to request that the Gulfstream be positioned near Cleveland, just in case, Derek had been thrilled. Murph had forgotten that he had been out of contact with his people since arriving in Israel. Derek was pleased just to know that Murph and Carli were alive. With any luck, Murph would see them soon.

* * * * * *

It took Bastien and his team more than a half an hour to cover the distance to Fort Moultrie. They went flying across the Ravenel Bridge but were stopped when the swing bridge leading to Sullivan's Island was open to allow a large sailboat to pass. All Cyrille could do was sit and stew as the lumbering boat inched across the channel.

Arriving at the fort, Bastien had his men fan out, interviewing as many people as were still in the area. Bastien went to the office and demanded to see the Ranger in charge. Threatening the authority of the NSA, Cyrille was given access to the surveillance video. Having a good idea of the time, it didn't take long before Bastien had a glimpse of Murph and Carli in the fort, making contact with another group and leaving in two cars.

Bastien shoved his chair back and stalked out of the ranger's office, whistling loudly for his men to return. The prey had eluded the net and were on the run. Now he had to catch them before they reached Washington and caused more trouble.

As his men ran to load up the van, Cyrille took out his phone and made a call.

"Cyrille, I trust you have good news for me?" Cohen had had several days to regain his composure.

"No, Sir. The dentist and the prisoner have entered the US. I believe they are in cars heading to Washington. They obtained help here in Charleston. Surveillance video leads me to believe that a team of soldiers has arrived to assist them. They are in a gray Ford Taurus and a black Chevy Impala. Their only reasonable course would be west on I-26 then north on I-95. We should use the NSA capabilities to alert the authorities to apprehend them."

"That is an interesting recommendation, coming from you. That means that I have to tell the President that you lost them and need his help." Cohen was goading Bastien.

Cyrille answered coolly, "My only concern is for the mission at hand. If the President can offer assistance, we should take advantage of it."

"Very well." If Cohen was surprised, he didn't show it. "Are you aware that Paul Ramon has submitted his resignation."

"An excellent choice."

"You don't like him?"

"That is irrelevant. He lacks the stomach for what is necessary. Therefore, he should resign and find a more suitable line of work."

"What is your plan now?"

Bastien considered this a moment. "My team and I will follow Murphy and drive him into the trap. If they stop, we will catch them. When the police detain them, we can take over and make sure there are no loose ends."

"Excellent." Cohen actually felt elated. "The end is near. Whether we capture Murphy or not may not matter after all. The chess pieces are in place. In a few days, all our work will bear fruit."

"Yes, Sir. I will see you tomorrow."

* * * * * * *

Murph and Carli stood apart from the cars as Corporal Wick filled up the tank for the last time. Buck and Schuster walked over.

"Almost there?" Schuster was obviously tired of sitting and driving.

Murph nodded slowly. "Yes. We just crossed the Ohio River. It's less than three hours now. We've made great time so it will be before eleven when we get there."

Buck furrowed his brow. "Then what?"

"They'll be watching credit cards so we can't go to a hotel. I figure they may be watching my father's home so we can't go there either. For tonight, we bunk with my father's good friend, John Kinsley. He was one of Dad's dental school classmates and has a house big enough."

"Sounds good. I've gone over the plan for tomorrow and it's risky—but that's why it has a chance to succeed."

"I'm glad you feel that way, Buck. I feel like we have to be bold here. If we sit back and let them tell the story, we're done." Murph put his arm around Carli's shoulders. "I think I've called in every favor I have in Cleveland!"

"And all of your Dad's, too." Carli snuggled against his ribs. "I'll be glad to get this over with. I'm tired." She yawned broadly.

"Stop that." They all said together.

"You'll get us all doing that now." Murph stifled a yawn himself. He looked at the young private who grinned as he put the gas cap back.

Murph made a rotating motion with his finger in the air. "Wind her up. Let's get going!"

They were back on the highway in minutes, racing through the dark toward Cleveland and the rendezvous. Murph hoped that getting Buck and his presidential doppelganger together in the same place wouldn't just turn out like some sort of matter-antimatter reaction that detonated and destroyed the world.

311

Chapter 96

After crashing for the night in the Kinsley basement, the morning of Saturday, September 16, 2017 dawned clear and bright. It was a day full of promise and risk. Murph was awake when the sun was beginning to lighten the eastern sky. He padded up to the kitchen and took John at his word, making himself at home. Murph found the coffee maker and began to brew a large pot of the aromatic liquid. The smell was a powerful draw. Murph had poured himself a cup when Dr. John Kinsley came down the hall. Murph filled another mug and gave it to his host.

"Thanks, Dr. Kinsley, for letting us use your house."

John scratched his tousled brown hair, dismissively. "Murph, you are always welcome at the home of your Buddy Kins. Your Dad and I go way back, so it's the least I could do."

"I wish I could tell you what's going on, but the less you know, the better for you in the long run."

"I get that." Kins took a big gulp of coffee. "Your Dad, Sean, dropped off a bunch of stuff you asked for before you got here. Looks like clothes. I'll let you take it down as soon as they wake up."

"Thanks. I've got to get everyone up pretty soon. We have so much to do before noon."

"Let me know if there's anything you need. Otherwise, Jackie and I will just stay out of your way. There's bacon and eggs in the fridge. Help yourself!" John refilled his mug and headed back upstairs. "Good luck, whatever's going on, I'm sure I'll read about it in the paper someday."

Murph waved at him, thinking, "*I'm hoping it doesn't make the papers. That would be the worst thing possible.*"

Carli poked her head up from the basement, rubbing her eyes. "Smells good!"

Murph filled a mug for her and finished it with cream and sugar.

She sipped the coffee and pronounced it "Perfect."

"John said there were bacon and eggs in the fridge."

She smiled at him over the coffee mug, the wisps of steam floating across her face. "You know the deal. I've got the eggs, but the bacon's yours. I don't do spatter!"

Murph loved the sound of her laughter. It made his heart light, and he needed that more today than ever. "OK, you're on. I suppose the smell of bacon will wake them up."

"No, the sound of you clattering pans will wake them up. You couldn't cook quietly to save yourself. Either way, they need to get up."

Murph walked over and pulled her to him, squeezing her against his chest. "I love you!"

"I know." She patted him on the tummy. "Now let's get cooking."

* * * * * * *

There's nothing like a good breakfast to start the day off right. After everyone had eaten, they devoted themselves to their jobs with gusto. Murph sent Buck up to shower and shave. A hair stylist friend of his mother was coming over to trim Buck's hair. Murph downloaded several pictures of the President from earlier this week as a target for her work.

Murph's parents had done the shopping for them. Buck was in jeans and a t-shirt, with an Ohio State baseball cap. Murph was now in khaki slacks and a navy blue polo shirt. Carli looked fabulous in jean capris, navy flats, and a white blouse over a navy camisole. Her auburn hair shined with a fresh shampoo, but was still pulled back in a ponytail for convenience.

Sean Murphy and his friend, the VP of Operations at First Energy Stadium, had provided tickets and passes for everyone. Murph, Carli and Buck had field passes, which would allow them limited access to the area below the park. Timing was everything, so they all set off early to be at the ready when the stadium opened.

Sean Murphy was going in with the Ignatius Marching Band as he always did, helping with the equipment truck. It was a short drive from the campus of Saint Ignatius High School, taking only ten minutes to reach the stadium. The vans were admitted by security and took their places below and behind the park. Sean helped unload the percussion equipment and flags. The busses with the band members pulled in and unloaded. The band formed up and marched into the stadium, Sean Murphy and other dads trailing behind, dragging the conductor's podium.

Murph was concerned about Buck being recognized at the security checkpoint. He was relieved to see that the focus was clearly on any bags people were carrying and not on the person. Murph and Carli sailed through security, even though they were leading the President of the United States and Murph had hidden the two syringes of ketamine tranquilizer in his pants pocket.

Not stopping to celebrate, Murph led them down to the field then back up the tunnel toward the locker room. Murph approached the door labeled Bobby Malone, Head Coach, USAFA. He took hold of the handle and turned to face Buck and Carli.

"Are you ready?"

Buck nodded immediately. "Bobby Malone was my coach twenty years ago, but he also is one of my closest friends. If there's anyone I can trust, he's the guy."

"OK, then. Let's do it!"

Murph pushed down on the latch and the door opened with a heavy click. It stuck slightly, so Murph forced it with his shoulder. He half stumbled into the office, looking up in surprise.

Chapter 97

The heavy door creaked open, allowing Murph to practically fall into the room. He righted himself quickly, scanning the room as Carli stepped gracefully in behind him.

Murph realized that the Coach's private office was only a small space with a desk and two side chairs. There was a large dry-erase board on one wall and an old-fashioned chalkboard on the other. The coach was a short, stocky man in his early seventies. His steel gray hair was cut close to his head. His black nylon slacks set off the sky blue of the Air Force Falcon half-zip windbreaker that was his game day uniform.

Murph's eyes were still adjusting to the darkness, but he quickly apologized for barging in. "Coach Malone, I'm sorry for interrupting, but…"

A deep baritone cut him off, "Murph?"

"Agent Collins?" Murph couldn't believe his luck. "I'm so glad to see you."

Coach Malone was irritated. "Who are these people? I have a game to play and hardly have enough time to sit here in a briefing with you guys in the Secret Service."

Darnell Collins shrugged his broad shoulders. "Sorry Coach. This is Dr. Michael Murphy and Carli Chamoun. They are, well … old friends of mine."

Murph stepped forward and shook Bobby Malone's hand. "But that's not why we're here. Coach, I have an old friend of yours who wanted so much to see you."

Buck stepped into the office and closed the door. Collins took in a sharp breath, and then let it out slowly in a low whistle.

Bobby Malone wasn't surprised. "Buck Buchanan! Why, if it isn't mister all high and mighty politician. So good to see you!" The tone was mocking.

"Thanks, Coach! You haven't changed a bit." Buck tried to put a good face on things.

"Now you're a damned liar." Bobby laughed. "Both of us know how worn out I look. That's why this is my last year."

Murph sensed something wrong in the Malone's approach. "Coach, have you met the President since he was came back from Afghanistan?"

315

"Oh, yeah. He came to Colorado Springs while he was campaigning." The old coach's voice caught in his throat. "I guess a coma will change a man."

"A-ha." Murph stepped close to the Coach and lowered his voice a bit. "Please ask Buck something that only the two of you would know?"

"Fair-nuf." Malone faced Buck directly and barked, "The Notre Dame game your senior year. Fourth and goal from the 4-yard line. I called an off-tackle blast to the right. That touchdown won the game for us."

Buck shook his head. "Not a chance. We lost that game by three touchdowns. You called the off-tackle blast, but I changed the play at the line. I faked the hand-off and ran the ball in myself."

Bobby Malone's face brightened a bit. "Exactly. That's why I said you're such a natural leader!"

"Like Hell!" Buck laughed heartily. "You ripped me a new one for not running the play you called. You even told my commanding officer that I'd never amount to anything since I couldn't take orders."

Tears started building in the eyes of the old Coach, his face softening. "You told me then that you had been following my orders all along."

"That's right. Your order was to score a touchdown. Handing off to the running back was…"

Bobby Malone finished the sentence with him, "…just a suggestion." The tears began to flow. "Buck, it is you!"

The two men embraced, hanging on to each other for a long time. When they parted, ten years had fallen off Bobby Malone. "I feel like a new man again. There's got to be a reason why you're here; tell me what do I need to do?"

Murph stepped over to shield Buck and the Coach. "Buck will explain it to you." Murph fixed his gaze on the bewildered Secret Service Agent.

"Darnell, the last time we were together, I took out a pink tooth on the President."

"I remember."

"Well, since then, I have secured x-rays that prove that the man in the White House is not the Colonel Buchanan that served in Afghanistan. This one is." Murph gestured over his shoulder at Buck with his thumb. "We've been to Italy and Israel. We've been threatened and shot at, and we have the scars to prove it. Something terrible is about to happen. You can help us, or stay out of our way. That's your choice."

Darnell didn't hesitate, his deep voice strong and confident. "I've known for a long time that something was wrong. I just didn't know what I could do about it. Whatever you need, I'm with you—all the way."

"Thanks, Darnell. Here's what I need you to do!"

Chapter 98

The first half of the football game passed quickly on the field. The Air Force Falcons were leading the Midshipmen 17-7 as time expired. Murph had found a way to play the Armed Forces Radio broadcast to pass the time as they hid in the cramped office. With the end of the half, it was show time, so Murph, Carli, Buck, and the Marines—Schuster and Covrett, took to their hiding places, waiting in silence.

The Falcons arrived in the locker room in an excited rush. Bobby Malone had a few words for his team, congratulating them on a successful half, but reminding them that the most important part of the game was yet to come. The Falcon players couldn't put their finger on it, but Coach seemed to be a new man and they were riding high on the wave of his energy. Bobby entered his office and closed the door. He sat down heavily in his chair, waiting. There was nothing to say, so they all sat, brooding in silence.

The President had been seated with the Navy Midshipmen for the first half and was moving to the Air Force side for the second half. Since he was a former AFA quarterback, President Buchanan had been invited to stand on the sidelines with the Falcons. After coming to the locker room, he would run out onto the field with the team after the conclusion of the marching band shows.

There was a rap on the door, and then Darnell Collins stuck his head in and examined the room. Satisfied that it was clear, Agent Collins entered the room and let in the President. Agent Ron Kerner followed him in and closed the door.

"Great half of football, Coach." Buchanan came over and shook Malone's hand vigorously.

"I agree. The ending was just like the drive you led before halftime of the game against Notre Dame your senior year, don't you think?"

Buchanan backed off a bit. "I guess I don't really remember that game so well, Coach. That concussion in Afghanistan really scrambled a few things, you know!" He had mastered the art of using his injury to dodge dangerous questions.

Malone stood up and walked around the desk. "I know. I have senior moments now too." He tapped the side of his head with his finger. "I called for an off-tackle run, but you changed the play and ran it in for a touchdown. "

"Oh, yeah, now I remember." His broad smile was a reflex.

"That's when I knew you would be successful—you could improvise."

"That's always been my style!"

"Except it's not *my* style, dirtbag!" Buck stepped out of the shadows facing the President.

Agent Kerner reached for his gun, but Sgt. Covrett whacked him in the back of the neck with a leather bag filled with metal ball bearings. The blackjack was designed for just such a purpose and it performed admirably. Kerner slumped to the floor, unconscious. It would take a while, but he would wake up with a severe headache.

The President turned to Agent Collins. "Shoot him!" He pointed at Buck.

"I don't know who *you* are," Collins answered calmly, "but *that's* the real Buck Buchanan. Personally, I think you have some explaining to do, Mr. President!"

Buchanan broke for the door, opening his mouth to yell. Murph jumped out from behind the chalkboard, clamping his hand over Buchanan's mouth and jamming the syringe in his neck. The President collapsed almost as soon as Murph depressed the plunger. Murph supported his weight as he slumped to the ground.

Murph rolled the prone man on his back and made sure he was still breathing. "We really don't have time for too much talking. Get his clothes off and make the switch. Everything changes—underwear, socks, jewelry, nothing missing."

In just a few minutes, Buck stood where the President had—a perfect match. Murph and Carli scanned him carefully, trying not to overlook anything.

Murph clapped him on the arm. "You've got this. Nothing to it, just be yourself—well, sort of."

Carli leaned up and kissed him on the cheek. "Take a page from the imposter over there. He's got the right idea. Try to get hit by a ball or run over by a player while on the sidelines then claim it re-aggravated your concussion symptoms."

All the guys nodded in agreement. "She's good," Schuster said.

"Hey, not just a pretty face!" Her laughter broke the heaviness of the moment.

Buck hugged her. "Thanks. You're right. I can do this."

Murph stepped close. "Just play it cool, and let Darnell Collins help you. I trust him. Once I get these guys out of here, I'll be back to join you. Look for me!"

Buck looked over at Collins and the Coach. Standing tall, he straightened the collar of his white polo shirt and settled his Air Force windbreaker. "Gentlemen, let's go win that game!"

Bobby Malone led Agent Collins out the door. When Buck entered the locker room, they all could hear the cheers. Murph could see Buck shaking hands and high-fiving players.

He was in his element. Murph thought, *This just might work, after all.*

Murph closed the door then assessed the dressing Schuster and Covrett had done on Frank Buchanan. The former President was now clad in the camouflage fatigues of a Marine enlisted man. They stood him up and supported him, his head hanging low, chin on his chest. Murph turned up his collar and put a cap on his head. With Schuster and Covrett supporting him between them, Frank looked exactly like what they were trying to pass him off as, a Marine too drunk to walk, with his buddies trying to hide his identity from the Military Police.

Murph sized up the situation. "OK, now that we have all committed treason, let's try to get out of here in one piece. Stick to the plan, and we'll be fine."

"Yes, Sir." The Marines were ready.

"You two carry sleeping beauty here down, and Carli and I will try to run interference for you."

Covrett nudged the body of Kerner on the floor with the toe of his boot. "What about 'im?"

Murph knelt down and felt for a pulse. Kerner was alive, thankfully. Murph took the handgun and radio from the Secret Service agent. He used the butt of the gun to smash the radio then tossed it in the trash. Murph handed the gun to Schuster, who tucked it into his waistband.

"We leave him here. Someone will find him eventually, and hopefully it will be too late to hurt us. I just can't justify anything else." Murph couldn't bring himself to add another victim to the story.

"Agreed. He was just doing his job." Schuster adjusted the weight of Buchanan, draping his shoulders over theirs while holding his belt loops with their inside hands.

"Ready." They all nodded at Murph. "Good. See you in the transport area under the park."

Murph opened the door slightly to verify that the team was gone. He pulled back the door fully and they went out into

320

the hallway. Murph and Carli were in the lead, with the drunken sailor and his friends staggering along behind.

Chapter 99

Thanks to an exciting football game, the crowd was happily in their seats, cheering on a winner. Murph and company met little in the way of traffic as they negotiated the distance from the locker room to the parking area under the north stands of First Energy Stadium. The Ignatius Marching Band had dropped off their equipment after performing and had returned to the stands to watch the end of the game. As Murph arrived, his dad and the rest of the crew of parents were finishing loading the conductor's platforms into the equipment van.

Murph went over to Sean Murphy and gave him a big hug. "Thanks, Dad, for all your help."

He laughed, "Someday you'll have to tell me what this was all about!"

"We'll do that, but for now, the less you know, the better." Murph walked his Dad up to the front of the navy blue van. "Carli's going with you now."

Murph glanced over his shoulder and saw Schuster and Covrett half-dragging Buchanan toward the van. They quickly covered the distance, moving through the open parking lot and lifting the President like a sack of mulch, tossing him in the back. Sgt. Covrett jumped in and stowed the body in a trunk, lightly closing the lid. Lt. Schuster came around the van and walked up to Murph.

"So far, so good, eh, Murph?"

The color drained from Murph's face. "Kerner!" Without pointing, he indicated the Secret Service agent and two other men in black military style fatigues running out of the building, scanning the lot.

Murph grabbed Carli's wrist and pulled her close. "Wait a couple of minutes then get out. Follow the plan, and meet Derek at the plane. I'll call you later." He kissed her quickly. "C'mon Lieutenant, we've gotta go!"

Murph grabbed the back of Schuster's collar, yanking the camo fatigue jacket so hard it pulled up over his head. Murph ran, dragging the stunned Lieutenant across the parking lot toward a line of taxis awaiting fares. The commotion of Murph forcefully jerking the Marine, his arms waving, running across through the parked cars and trucks had the desired effect. He could hear the shouts as Kerner and his partners spotted them.

Murph made it to the first taxi in line as Kerner had reached the middle of the lot, bellowing for him to stop. Murph opened the door of the cab and tossed Schuster in the back, following him in. The driver had his headphones on and was oblivious to the armed agents running across the parking lot.

Murph leaned up to the window in the Plexiglas divider. "Let's go. West Side Market!"

The cabbie just grunted and put the car in gear, heading out of the lot and up the hill from the stadium. They turned on Superior Avenue quickly crossing the Cuyahoga River on the Veterans Memorial Bridge. Murph scanned their trail out the back window and was pleased to see another cab racing after them. *C'mon. Stick with me!* Murph leaned forward and had the driver slow down a bit.

The street was nearly deserted with the game going on, and Murph made sure that Kerner saw them turn left onto W 25th Street, racing toward the Ohio City neighborhood. Traffic was congested here and the trailing taxi quickly caught up.

Murph felt at home, less than two blocks from the campus of Saint Ignatius High School. This was his neighborhood in the heart of the city of Cleveland. When the 137-foot tall spire of the clock tower at the market soared above them, Murph had the cabbie stop and stuffed a $20 in his hand. They piled out at the corner of Lorain Road and W 25th Street, running for the sanctuary of the massive building.

The bricks of the market glowed with an orange, sand-stone color. The West Side Market dated back to the 1840's, but the current building was dedicated in 1912. A Cleveland landmark for more than a century and home now to over 100 vendors of great ethnic diversity, the market offered, not only fine meats and fresh vegetables, but also fresh seafood, baked goods, dairy products, and even fresh flowers. There were booths selling ready-to-eat foods, herbs, candy and nuts. Tourists from all over the world toured the market every year, drawn by television programs produced by the Travel Channel and Food Network featuring segments on the West Side Market. Last year an estimated million plus people visited the market.

On a sunny Saturday afternoon, it always felt like the million people were here at the same time. Murph was counting on it now. He glanced back, pleased to see Agent Kerner and friends jumping out of their cab and running toward him. Murph grabbed Schuster and pulled him through the green metal doors into the maze of stalls and press of people.

As their eyes adjusted to the relative darkness inside, Murph whispered to Schuster, "We need to keep them occupied for a few more minutes to let Carli get away cleanly. When I signal, I want you to take off your camo jacket and leave, going west on Lorain Road. In two blocks, you'll be at St. Ignatius. Meet the van at the music room, behind the Breen Center for the Performing Arts. It's a big, red brick auditorium. You can't miss it. Just like we planned, they'll take all of you to meet Derek Whitman and the Gulfstream at the Lorain County Airport. He knows where to go from there!"

"Got it." Schuster adjusted his cap lower on his head and hunched up his shoulders. "Here they come!"

Murph led Schuster into the throng of shoppers, weaving among the glass cases of steaks, pork chops, chicken, fish, cheese, and pastries. The ceiling was arched, a high vaulted arc of subway tile, which gave the crowded room a feeling of space.

323

Down below, it was tough going for Kerner to force his way through the crowd. Little old ladies with their wheeled pull-carts blocked his path. Their hair tied up in babushka's, they shouted at him in Old World languages, no doubt swearing at him under their breath. He tripped over another baby in a stroller, turning to the black-clad men behind him.

"Kozlowski. Taylor. Spread out and find them!" Kerner spotted a dark green camouflage cap bobbing along in the next row. "There they are!"

Murph had sent Schuster ahead a bit, to flash the camo. When Kerner bit on the bait, he was waiting. Kerner and Taylor came around the corner, passing a butcher's stall, closing on Schuster.

Murph had wedged himself behind a display rack of olive oil, shoving hard with his legs as they approached. With a crash, the bottles came tumbling down on the two, knocking them to the floor. They slithered around for a bit, fighting to get up, covered with the slippery yellow-green liquid. It was such a waste of excellent olive oil, Murph thought, but it did slow them down immensely.

Murph dashed to catch up with Schuster, just in time to see the Marine surprise Koslowski with a sharp uppercut that laid him out cold. The crowd of shoppers was beginning to sense that something was wrong here, murmuring and moving away from the oil slick.

Taylor was up first, spotting Murph. He drew his gun, which led a woman next to him to shriek at the top of her lungs, "He's got a gun!"

A general panic was beginning to brew.

Murph noticed a butcher walking idly through the stalls with an uncut side of pork ribs on his shoulder. It was the size of a suitcase, probably weighing in excess of 60 pounds. Murph caught the butcher in two long strides, grabbing the meat with both hands. He pulled it off the shoulder of the butcher and swung it at the charging Taylor with all his might.

Taylor tried to stop, but the oil on his combat boots denied him any grip on the tile floor. The side of pork struck him squarely in the jaw, slamming him to the ground. Murph lifted the pork ribs as a shield as Kerner fired two shots. The slugs slammed into the meat, losing their power while passing through.

Schuster entered the scene, with his head down, face hidden. "Help!" he croaked, running toward Kerner with ragged steps, acting like he was trying to reach safety.

Murph moved to intercept the President. When Kerner turned to face Murph again, the agent was surprised as Schuster tackled him instead of hiding behind him. Kerner and Schuster crashed into a glass case filled with gourmet cheese.

Kerner's gun was knocked out of his hand, landing in the shattered case next to a wheel of Gouda. He shoved Schuster away and reached back for his pistol. Many of the display cases in the market were over fifty years old. The glass shards had cut the insulation off of the wires to the fluorescent light bulb in the case.

Kerner kept his head up, eyes on Murph as he reached into the display case for his gun. He found the weapon and gripped it, but his oil soaked jacket touched the bare wire. It arced—the current racing through the agent, his body twitching as he screamed. The oil ignited and he burst into flames, his cries silenced as he fell in a heap next to the cheese vendor. In seconds, the entire stall was involved in the fire, black smoke beginning to rise to the ceiling.

Murph lunged forward to help Kerner, but Schuster jumped up and held him back. "He's gone. There's nothing you can do!"

Murph agreed, whispering a silent prayer. "We need to get out of here. Take off that camo jacket."

Murph took the jacket from Schuster and tried to smother the growing fire, with little results. "Time to call for the pros"

They both began yelling, "FIRE!" inciting a general panic and a flood for the doors.

Murph took Schuster by the shoulders. "GO. Meet up with Carli and get out of here."

Schuster shook his hand. "Where are you going?"

Murph yelled over his shoulder as he began to run, "Back to the stadium. I have a plane to catch!"

Chapter 100

The commotion created by the fire was the perfect diversion. Lieutenant Schuster left the West Side Market with a flood of people. With them running, no one noticed one more person sprinting down Lorain Road. Schuster spotted the blue Ignatius van and ran up as they were finishing moving the unconscious President. Sgt. Covrett had Buchanan over his shoulder in a fireman's carry, setting him in the back of Sean Murphy's Ford Explorer.

Schuster trotted over and took command. "Mount up. Let's get out of here."

Shoppers with bags were running down the street, away from the market. The garage doors of the firehouse down the block from Ignatius rolled up, letting the engine and rescue squad out, sirens blaring.

"What the hell happened?" Carli stood there with her hands on her hips, her lips a thin, taut line. "Murph?"

"We led Kerner into the West Side Market. We took out two agents. Kerner was electrocuted, which started a fire. In the chaos, Murph sent me here with orders for us to meet Derek at the plane." Schuster sighed. "He went back to try to help Buck."

Her eyes followed the flashing red beacons as the emergency vehicles clustered at the market. "We've got to go. There's nothing more we can do here."

Sean Murphy closed the equipment room and locked the door. He started the SUV and headed west for the Lorain County Airport. Carli, Schuster, Covrett and the former President also had a plane to catch.

* * * * * * *

Murph ran out the other side of the market, exiting into the back alley. He crouched down to let his eyes adjust to the bright sunlight. He was in the loading dock, surrounded by debris: wooden pallets, torn cardboard boxes, lettuce leaves, and tomatoes that had escaped and rolled here. It was a haven for birds and the pigeons regarded him with disdain.

He could hear the sirens of the fire trucks as they converged on the West Side Market. The fire damage would close the market for several weeks as they repaired and modernized the display cases and repainted to resolve the smoke damage. Though a few witnesses would report they heard gunshots, the official story was that faulty old wiring had led to an electrical fire in one of the stalls. It burned quickly, igniting cooking oil, which caused a smoky fire. The body of Ron Kerner, charred beyond recognition, was quietly removed. The other two agents disappeared in the panic and were never reported.

Murph needed to get away from here. Scanning the rear of the vegetable stalls, he spotted a bicycle leaning against the brick wall. *What's one more crime today?* He grabbed the bike and began pedaling the faded red Schwinn out of the parking lot. The market was close to the Lorain-Carnegie Bridge, which led into downtown Cleveland at the Indians ballpark. Murph knew the area well, turning left on Ontario Street, passing the Horseshoe Casino and heading toward Lake Erie.

The traffic was approaching gridlock status, so having wheels that let him use the sidewalk was a blessing. In ten minutes, he had returned to First Energy Stadium. The game had ended with a 38-17 win for the Air Force Academy. Buck Buchanan had taken his time signing autographs and shaking hands on the sidelines after the game. He kept scanning the crowd, looking for Murph.

Darnell Collins caught Buck's attention and tapped his watch lightly. Buck nodded and resigned himself to the fact that he was leaving alone. They said their goodbyes. Buck embraced Bobby Malone then left the field with Collins.

327

A tight group of Cleveland police officers and Secret Service agents surrounded Buck as he moved through the tunnel into the lower levels of the park. They exited the stadium into the garage, where the Presidential limo was waiting. Buck stopped to thank the policemen who had protected him, shaking hands with them before heading off.

"Mr. President!" The booming voice echoed against the low, cement ceiling and pillars.

Buck turned and saw Murph trotting towards him. The cops whirled to face the threat, but softened when Buck recognized him. "It's OK, guys. It's just Dr. Murphy."

Buck waved Murph over, and they shook hands, embracing like old friends. Chatting with pleasantries about Murph being a dentist from Cleveland and having taken a tooth out of the President. They talked football, how exciting the game had been. Even the cops laughed along when Buck showed them the huge grass stains on his pants. He had been on the sidelines next to Coach Malone, when a wide receiver caught a pass and was tackled into Buck. It was sure to make ESPN Sportscenter that night, with footage of the President being run over while attending a football game.

Darnell Collins tapped his watch, "I hate to break up the reunion, but…"

The President shrugged, looking at the cops, "He's such a kill-joy." They all laughed.

Buck took Murph by the wrist. "Why don't you go with me to the airport, Doc? I could use a quick exam. Since I got hit, I feel a little fuzzy, if you know what I mean."

"Sure. I've got no plans." Murph followed the President to the waiting limo, getting in the back with Darnell and Buck.

The motorcade had barely left the garage when the story of *the President being tackled and needing looked at by his doctor because he felt funny* hit the Twitterverse. Buck's public approval rating was sky high, with the American public hoping for his success and worrying about his health. News like this spread quickly, with people praying that their popular President had not suffered a setback with his head injury.

Arriving at Cleveland Hopkins International Airport, the motorcade rolled across the tarmac to the waiting blue and white 747. It required some talking, and bullying, but the President being the President, he got his way. Murph had a recent security clearance check, since he had been a guest at the White House dinner, and Agent Collins could independently vouch for his identity. The staff didn't like sudden changes in plans, but Murph was admitted to the travelling party and boarded Air Force One for the return flight to DC.

The President's physician gave him a quick exam and pronounced him fit, with no negative effects from the sideline collision at the game. The MD informed the press corps that the President had sustained a collision on the sideline. He had a slight headache, for which he was given a couple of Tylenol. The doc was quick to mention that for people with a history of severe head injuries, there was always a risk of another trauma causing problems, so they would be observing the President for a few days. However, he reassured them, there was no cause for alarm. As the President's dentist, Dr. Michael Murphy concurred and reported no dental injuries from the accident. The flight left without further incident and was soon on its way back to Washington.

* * * * * * *

Sean Murphy arrived at Lorain County Airport to find the red and white Gulfstream G-550 standing ready—engines warm and door open. Sgt. Covrett helped, or rather carried, the still groggy Frank Buchanan onto the plane and secured him. Schuster boarded, as well.

Carli hugged Sean, "Thanks for all your help!"

"Glad to." He looked at her hand for the first time, admiring the ring. "Congratulations. If you two ever stop running long enough to sit, we'd love to have you for dinner."

"I can't wait." She smiled a wan smile. "When this is over, you have a date."

He let her run to the jet and watched as Derek retracted the stairs, waving.

In minutes, the G-550 taxied out and was gone. They were bound for Washington, too, and rushing to beat Air Force One into the area. The arrival of the President slowed down traffic, both in the air and on the ground. And the G-550 had a different purpose for its drugged cargo.

Chapter 101

Air Force One touched down gently onto the tarmac at Andrews Air Force Base in Maryland. As the giant blue and white Boeing 747 taxied to a stop, there was a flurry of activity as staffers and journalists prepared to deplane. The President had returned, and it was a Saturday night. No more news to cover, they were hurrying to get off the clock and on to their lives.

Murph pulled out his iPhone and dialed the Vice President.

"Senator—um, Mr. Vice President?" Murph fumbled when Brooks answered. "Sorry, Sir. I still can't get that right."

"That's OK, Murph. That's why I keep asking you to call me Brooks." He laughed. "Where are you?"

"We just landed in DC—well, Andrews actually."

"Andrews??" Brooks was aghast. "That means…"

Murph cut him off before he could say it. "Yes. We went to Cleveland and met the President at the Navy-Air Force football game."

"Genius!"

"Well, that remains to be seen." Murph was feeling very vulnerable, a traitor sitting on Air Force One. "I need you to come to the White House immediately. We need all the support we can get."

"I'm on it. I'll meet you there." Brooks yelled to have his car brought up. "Murph, be careful. Talk to as few people as possible!"

"Believe me, you don't have to tell me twice."

Murph hung up and dialed Margaret Farouk.

Her sweet voice answered on the first ring, "Hi, Murph. Where are you?"

"DC." He didn't want this to last long and she was way behind in the storyline. "I just landed at Andrews with the President."

"Oh, my God."

"It's OK. Please have Murray bring you to the White House in a couple of hours. I'll have security expecting you. We need your knowledge of DC and its people."

As always, Margaret was quick to pick up on things. "I understand. I'll see you in a few hours, with my teacher's cap on. How's Carli?"

"I'm not sure. She's got the easier job today. She's delivering a package for us. I'm hoping it's a breeze."

Murph hung up and dialed Carli, "Hey, beautiful. How's it going?"

"Just about to take off again. I've got everyone now."

Murph could hear some commotion in the background, then a young voice chipped in, "Hi-ya, Murph. How you doin?"

"Great, Bernie. Glad you are there. Take care of Carli for me, will ya?"

"No problemo! Miss Caro-lina is-a safe with me. Like-a the Swiss Guard, but-a without the striped suits."

Murph laughed as Carli took back the phone.

"How are you? Schuster told me about Kerner." Her voice was filled with concern.

Murph tried to sound confident, more so than he really was. "It was too bad about him, but there was nothing we could do. We're safely here. The President had a collision on the sidelines, but his doc says his brain is only a little rattled."

"Good. Are you OK?"

"It's a bit dicey." He took a deep breath. "I don't know whom to trust. But I'm going on instinct and hoping for the best. It's like walking into the kitchen in the middle of the night. We've turned on a bright light. Now we have to watch where the roaches run—and then exterminate them."

Carli shuddered at the image. "I'll call you when we get settled."

"Excellent. Rocco will meet you when you land. He'll take care of you." Murph could feel her passing out of his grasp. He hated sending her away, but it was the only option. "Remember, I love you!"

"Love you, too. I'll see you soon!" A ding sounded in the background and the engine noise increased. "We're taking off. I've gotta go." She kissed the phone and signed off.

Murph looked down at his phone, Carli's smiling face winking up at him from her contact picture. He set his jaw in determination. *Time to go to the lion's den.* He didn't know what traps might be waiting for them, but the road led through the Oval Office. They had no choice but to take it head on. He stood up and joined the crowd flowing off the jumbo jet.

Chapter 102

The phone rang, shattering the serenity in the darkened study. Johnson, the butler, reached over and picked it up. He handed it to the old man.

"It's Bastien, Sir."

Simon Cohen opened his eyes and reached for the phone. He set down the tumbler of scotch he had been nursing and tapped the screen to answer.

"I trust that you have apprehended the dentist. It has certainly taken you long enough."

"Agent Kerner is dead."

"What?" Cohen jumped to his feet, knocking over the table beside him, scotch spilling all over the brocade carpet and his silk pajamas. "That's impossible—The President?"

"Murphy went to Cleveland instead of DC. I believe they confronted the President there." Bastien's tone was even, dispassionate. He was reporting the facts. "The President has returned to Washington. Murphy was with him on Air Force

One, so we must assume that Colonel Buchanan is in the oval office now. The Gulfstream jet of the Washington Center for Esthetic and Restorative Excellence…"

"The what??" Cohen yelled in agitation.

"The G-550 owned by Dr. Murphy's practice flew from a small airport outside Cleveland to Reagan airport. It took on fuel and passengers and is now on a flight plan for Rome."

"What are you saying?" The old man sputtered, fighting to regain control.

Bastien spoke slowly and clearly. "It would appear that Dr. Murphy has successfully swapped Colonel Buchanan for our President. The dentist is with Buchanan at the White House. An aircraft flying to Rome most likely has our President as a prisoner. Murphy has many contacts in Rome, so they may be able to hide him there. I still believe that Murphy does not want to expose the fact that there has been a false president in the White House."

The line sat silent for a few minutes as both men collected their thoughts.

Bastien spoke first. "I will return to Washington—and deal with Murphy once and for all, myself."

"No. He is not the primary concern now. Wednesday is all that matters now. You will take direct command of the operation. Make sure there are no problems. When the goal is achieved, we no longer need worry about the American President. The wheels are turning, and Murphy cannot stop them now."

"Yes, Sir." Bastien sounded relieved. "I will alert a team in Rome. What shall we do with Murphy?"

"Leave him to me." Cohen's eyes sparkled with fire. He felt more alive than he had in years. "It's time that I meet this dentist myself. He has shown himself to be smart and resourceful, which is more than I can say for most of my own people. I admire that."

"Yes, Sir." Bastien was forced to agree. Murphy had proven to be a worthy adversary.

"However, it is time to put an end to this for the greater good." He shut off the phone and glared down at Johnson, blotting the scotch and water on the carpet. "Leave that. Inform the White House that I will visit the President in the morning. Make the arrangements for my car."

Cohen turned on his heel and headed for the bathroom. Johnson noticed a spring in his step and thought he heard whistling.

The butler stood up and walked over to the desk. He opened the calendar and turned to the next week. *Wednesday? What's so important about Wednesday?* He traced his finger to the day. September 20. *Rosh Hashana.*

Chapter 103

Buck Buchanan looked well rested after his nap on the flight. The media on the plane were glad that the President appeared healthy as he chatted with them as they left the plane. With several years in Congress, Buck knew many of the reporters and they seemed happy that he was delighted to talk to them.

Buck called Murph over, putting his arm around the tall dentist. "Come with me. We have a helicopter to catch." He pointed to the trio of olive drab helicopters sitting with their rotors turning slowly.

"Not another one of those! I'm about helicoptered out." He shook his head.

Buck clapped Murph on the back and led the way, with Darnell Collins in tow. Saluting the Marine guard, standing at attention in his dress blues, Buck boarded Marine One and they were off. Flying with multiple helicopters as decoys was routine procedure, sometimes as many as five identically painted choppers. For today, the routine three for DC operations were in use. The noise made conversation difficult so they all sat in silence for the journey to the White House.

Setting down on the South Lawn, the President bounded down the stairs first, accepting the salute of another Marine guard. He stopped and crisply returned the salute.

"Welcome home, Sir." The young Marine shouted over the engine noise.

"Thank you, son. It's good to be home!"

The Marine's eyes opened wide. *The President's never spoken to me before!*

The President was joined by his party and moved toward the open door of the White House. A sudden thought exploded in Murph's brain. He angled over and gripped Darnell's shoulders, pulling the taller man's head down enough to speak in his ear.

"Where's the First Lady?" Murph asked in panic.

"Europe, why?"

"She'll know the difference!"

The light dawned and Darnell shook his head. "She's on a trip meeting with European Union leaders' wives. The press has dubbed it the 'Fashion Summit.' She won't be back until next weekend. The President seemed pretty happy she was going to be gone."

Buck had been putting on a bold face, shaking hands and greeting the staff. As soon as he got in the White House, his shoulders slumped and he looked tired. He asked to go to the private residence to relax.

When they arrived at the Treaty Room, Buck had the prime time college football game put on and ordered a light dinner of sandwiches for everyone. When only Murph and Collins were left, he stopped the tired act and brightened up again.

"I don't know how these James Bond types do it. Staying in character is hard work!"

"And you're impersonating yourself! That should be easier!" Murph patted him on the back. Murph had told Buck about asking Brooks and Margaret to come over. Brooks arrived first, greeting Buck with some reservation. They knew

335

each other from their time in Congress, though Brooks had been a Senator and Buchanan serving in the House.

Buck and Murph quickly filled in the Vice President on what had happened. Unfortunately, they had little to go on for the future, other than to play out the scene and see where it went.

Margaret arrived and was escorted straight to the Treaty Room. She was dressed impeccably in black slacks and heels that accentuated her long legs, with a cashmere sweater set in raspberry. Her shoulder length brown hair was pulled back over her ears by her glasses, sitting on top of her head. The look on Buck's face confirmed that her sexy librarian look was working.

Murph made the introductions and explained the reason for the meeting. This was a crash course in Washington people. Brooks was there to prep Buck on the White House staff and current political climate. Margaret was connected to the social scene. She made sure that Buck was informed on the non-political intrigue in the Capital city.

When they were ready, they called in the President's personal secretary and asked what was on the schedule for tomorrow.

Marcy Sims smiled sweetly. "There's only one thing scheduled. You have a meeting with Simon Cohen at 11:00 a.m. His staff called and requested that just over an hour ago."

When Buck frowned, she asked, "You know he always gets priority scheduling. Is everything OK, Mr. President?"

He smiled warmly. "It's OK, Marcy. You did the right thing. I'll just be up and ready to see him then. Thanks, that will be all for now. Enjoy your night."

"You, too, Sir."

She left quietly and the group eyed each other over the table.

"They know!" Murph voiced their thoughts.

"Well, it's probably better to get it over with." Buck pushed back his chair.

336

"We're pushing them to see what they're up to. We provoked them into a direct meeting. That's progress." Murph stood up and began to pace. "After all this time, I really want to meet that guy."

Murph's phone buzzed and he stepped away to answer it. "Yes—that's excellent! Keep a sharp eye out. Thanks for letting me know. I'll pass the word along."

He came back to the table, the group sitting in rapt attention. "That was Sergeant Lobas. I sent him on a special mission early this morning." Murph paused for effect.

"Oh, just spit it out already!" Buck was getting tired.

"OK. The three Marines, Lobas, Wick and Myles, are in position around the house, securing your daughters. The girls and your in-laws are fine and well protected now. The guys made great time, driving back to Columbia in nine hours."

Buck had no words. He hugged Murph, nearly beginning to break down.

Murph stood him up straight and shook his shoulders. "You are the most powerful man in the world. Now act like it. Have a secret service detail fly down and pick up Gayle's parents. Bring Laura and Blakely here to the White House. Get the reunion started."

Buck looked determined. "Yes. It's been far too long. Darnell, can you help with that?"

Collins smiled. "With pleasure, Sir."

Murph put his hand on Collins shoulder as he started to leave. "When you set up the pickup, Sgt. Lobas and his team have orders not to release the family without the proper password."

Buck tilted his head. "Password?"

"Yes. For security, the identification phrase is 'I have your locket.' Without that, the kids stay put—and I wouldn't try those Marines. They're battle tested and smart."

"I'll make the call now. The pickup will be in the morning, but they should be able to be here by mid-afternoon."

"Then tomorrow can't come soon enough." Buck smiled in exhaustion. "Murph, I can't thank you enough."

Brooks pushed up from the table. "You seem to have thought of everything, my friend."

Murph scratched the stubble forming on his chin. "That's what worries me."

Chapter 104

Murph had decided not to leave the White House. Afraid of not being allowed back through security in the morning, he had slept on the couch in the Treaty Room, the imposing figure of William McKinley staring down at him. It was a restless night.

Murph was still bothered by the fact that he had no idea what the endgame was for Cohen. They had successfully replaced the faux President with the correct one. Murph thought Israel somehow played a role in Cohen's plan. Cohen clearly had a connection to northern Italy. There was still a piece of the puzzle missing. Murph tossed and turned, going over every piece of information he could remember, searching for a link. He awoke tired and frustrated—and no closer to an answer.

Murph decided to get up, crossing the hallway to the restroom. He washed his face and rubbed the bed-head out of his hair as best he could with his fingers. He found individual bagged toothbrushes with toothpaste in the medicine cabinet, so he was able to brush thoroughly. Feeling much better, he returned to the Treaty Room.

The White House staff delivered coffee and pastries. The aroma of the coffee helped banish the cobwebs, and Murph began to function, planning for the meeting with Cohen.

Murph felt that it would be advisable to meet with him in the Oval Office. Using the full power of the Presidency seemed to be a good idea. Buck agreed. The plan sounded so good over coffee and biscuits with strawberry jam that their mood was positively joyous when Darnell Collins came on duty at 10:00 a.m. with the news that the Secret Service protection detail had arrived in Columbia to take over for the Marines.

Murph quickly called Sgt. Lobas and confirmed that the Secret Service had the correct password. The girls were safe and preparing to travel to the airport for the flight on a military Learjet transport to Washington. They would be at the White House for the reunion by mid-afternoon. The Marines would be returning to Camp Lejeune as soon as the Secret Service team headed for the airport.

All the joy evaporated when the door behind them opened and a white-haired man in a tailored gray suit stepped in. His blue eyes were icy cold. His skin had the texture of parchment. A slight smile was fixed on his face. And he was an hour early!

"Good morning, gentlemen." His voice was strong, clear and precise. "Allow me to introduce myself. My name is Simon Cohen. Agent Collins there will be happy to confirm my identity."

Cohen walked slowly into the room as the door shut quietly behind him. Murph and Buck had risen to their feet immediately upon his arrival. Cohen walked up to them as they stood beside the table.

"Colonel Buchanan, we have met before, but I know you have no memory of that. In fact, you have no memory of a number of things. Please understand that I meant you no harm. I simply needed to borrow your identity for a while." Cohen sounded truly sorry. "It is unfortunate that you escaped and have come here. That forces me to deal with your presence more directly."

Buck's hands closed into fists. "You cost me two years of my life. Two years of my daughters' growing up that I'll never get back."

Buck made to lunge at Cohen, but Murph reached out his hand, grabbing Buck's wrist and stopping his fist moving forward. Buck stepped back stiffly.

Cohen turned to Murph and extended his hand. "Dr. Murphy, it is truly a pleasure to meet you. I have dealt with many people over these long years, but rarely have I met anyone with the resourcefulness and tenacity that you have shown. I wish that you could have worked for me, rather than against me."

Murph reached out and shook the old man's hand. The grip had strength and power. "I'm intrigued to meet you, as well. I want to know how an orphan who survived the murder of his family by a French physician and escaped the Holocaust with the help of a Catholic priest came to America and became a billionaire."

Cohen stepped back and tapped his nose with his finger. "Ahh. You do know my story better than almost anyone alive. You met Father Gaspard?"

"Carli and I were with him when he died."

Cohen's eyes fell. He walked over to the couch, unbuttoned his jacket and sat down. "Father Henri was a great man. I owe him my life." The old man's voice cracked.

Murph was shocked that he felt sorry for the man. He poured a glass of water and took it to Cohen, who accepted it with thanks. Buck Buchanan, still seething, sat back down at the table, watching the two men carefully.

Murph chose a chair opposite Cohen and waited in silence. After a while, Cohen spoke.

"My father was a banker. He was a smart man, but not very imaginative. We were not wealthy, only comfortable. When the Nazis came, my father thought, like many Jews, that if they were quiet and made no trouble, they would be left alone. My father was well liked and had many friends who were not Jewish.

It took time, but the Jews realized their mistake. They thought it was impossible for Hitler to be as dangerous as people warned. They were wrong. Hitler was a monster. But by the time they woke up, it was too late.

A French doctor let it be known that he could get Jews out of Paris to the safety of Spain. Fearing what he heard about the

340

death camps, my father gathered all the money he had and bought our passage. Dr. Bloch killed them and would have killed me, if…if not…" Cohen choked on the words.

Murph leaned forward, "…if not for the fire, you would have been murdered, as well."

Cohen looked up, his eyes wide, "How do you know about the fire? Only two people got out alive that night!" His voice was a hoarse whisper. "Myself and . . ."

"Dr. Bloch kept a diary of sorts—a ledger of all the people he murdered—names, dates, addresses, occupations, possessions. I have the diary. When this is over, I am turning the list over to a museum in Germany that is specializing in the records of Jews lost in the Holocaust. I hope that this document can provide closure for families who wondered what happened to their loved ones. Dr. Bloch had over 300 victims."

Cohen dabbed his eyes with a handkerchief. "I had no idea he kept records. That will provide comfort for many families."

"So, you ran from the burning house and found Father Gaspard?"

"In reality, Father Henri found me. I was curled up on a street corner, in the gutter under a gas lamp. Cold, wet and scared—I could barely speak. He took me with him as he made his way out of Paris. We followed the pilgrim trail to Rome."

"You met Valerie at the convent?"

Again, Cohen was surprised. "You are remarkably well informed. Yes, Valerie and I were part of the band of refugees that Father Henri shepherded to Rome. Valerie and her…well, we were the oldest, so we worked together to help Father Henri keep the children together. After the war, Valerie and I came to America."

"Yes. Major Fred Arnold brought you here and adopted you out to families. Valerie has been very successful. She spoke highly of you!"

"You have spoken to Valerie?"

341

"Yes, she is a patient of mine. She still has vivid memories of when the Nazis captured the convent and took her—sister!" It was as if someone had lifted a veil.

Cohen moved slightly. It was a tiny twitch, but Murph could sense him beginning to squirm.

"You returned to Italy after the war with Major Arnold. With Father Gaspard, you went to Susa and found Louisa, Valerie's sister, didn't you?"

Cohen spread his hands wide, palms up. "Well, she wasn't quite right in the head. The Nazis had—used her—then made her a slave. We took her in to help her."

Murph's tone became sharp, cutting at the old man. "But she still could remember where the cave was that held the Nazi treasure." It was a guess, but Cohen's grimace told Murph he was right. "You used her to get the Nazi hoard and that became the start of your fortune. Your wealth came from loot stolen from the Jews of Europe."

"No! Well...yes...really, it was Nazi gold, but I used it for good causes. From out of that evil came a greater good, you see."

"All I see is profiteering from the misery of the Jews in Europe."

"No. I need you to understand." Cohen was pleading with Murph. "I chose to take the fortune and grow it into something I could use to benefit all the Jews. I want to leave a mark that will set things right."

"So what do the Israelis have to do with this? The museum at Atlit celebrates the struggles of the Jews in finding a place in Palestine. The creation of the state of Israel leaves quite a mark."

"Bah! There is no lasting mark in Israel. Within another generation, the Arabs will conquer the Jewish state and the sands of the desert will wipe away any trace of its existence." Cohen's eyes burned with inner fire. "Israel is a political creation by the United Nations. It sits on the coast like a giant boil on the skin. It has been more harm than good from the start."

"But you are a Jew. How can you say that about Israel?"

"There is your ignorance. Indeed, I am a Jew." Cohen spoke like a teacher to his pupil, slowly so that Murph would see and understand. "I am a French Jew by birth and an American Jew by choice. I owe no allegiance to Israel."

Murph sat back in his chair, stunned. "I'm beginning to understand."

Cohen leaned forward. "Dr. Murphy, do you know what percentage of the United States is Jewish?"

"I have no idea really, a couple of percent?"

"Over 2%—2.2 % to be exact. That's 6.7 million Jews, as of the last census. In the Israeli population, it is 75.1 %—slightly over six 6 million Jews. What percentage of Europe's population is Jewish?"

"I would have to guess that it's fairly low, since the Holocaust anyway."

"Precisely right. The Jewish population across the European Union is 0.18%—a total of 1.4 million Jews in a total population of 815 million. It is a shame. It's time for them to come home!" He sat back, triumphant.

"*Rentrer.*" Murph said it in a whisper. "Of course!"

Cohen's eyes opened wide, bushy eyebrows flaring, his forehead a sea of wrinkles. "What did you say?"

"*Rentrer!*" Murph said it louder. "Carli said it was French for 'to return.' We had no idea what it meant, but it makes sense now!"

Buck came over and asked, "Where did you see the word?"

"*Rentrer,*" Murph smiled at the President. "It was Father Gaspard's last word. We knew he was trying to tell us something important." Murph stood up and regarded Cohen coldly.

Murph pointed down at the billionaire, "Just like before, he is trying to make a fortune while appearing to be a saint. Cohen has been buying up rental property all over Europe. Apartment buildings and condos in France, Germany, Italy, Austria, Switzerland, Romania, you name it and he owns it."

Cohen stood, looking indignant. "I am merely providing a place for the Jews to come home to, and be welcomed. Not like Atlit. Not like the prison camps they were herded to in Palestine while the superpowers haggled at the UN over what bone to throw to the poor Jews." He spat out the last words.

"I see a hypocrite here in front of me." Murph threw up his hands.

"You see, but you do not understand!" Cohen inhaled to continue speaking, but his phone chirped. He withdrew the device, considered the number, and looked at Murph. "Michael, I think this call is for you."

Cohen handed Murph the phone and touched the screen to put it on speaker.

"Mr. Cohen?" The female voice was familiar. Murph fought to place it.

Cohen did not speak, but waved his hand that Murph should answer.

"Mr. Cohen is here, but this is Michael Murphy."

"Ah, Doctor Murphy, so good to speak with you again. This is Capitano Dalia Liriano, the commander of the Italian customs desk at Ciampino Airport. I'm sure you remember me."

Murph's heart sank. "Yes...I remember you."

"Good. Well, I have several friends of yours who have tried to enter Italy illegally. I have been forced to detain them. I will not turn them over to the Carabinieri, the Italian Police. They have been taken where you cannot reach them...for their safety while you consider your options. For the record, your fiancé is quite a feisty one. She has been difficult to restrain. The little priest and the old lady were a surprise gift. I had not expected to see them."

Murph squeezed the phone, his fingers white. "I need to speak with them, to know they are OK."

"As you wish." He heard a struggle, then Carli's voice, panting with exertion.

"Murph, whatever they want—don't do it. We'll be OK."

Then Liriano's voice, "OK? We will see who is OK."

Then gun shots and screaming,

"Oh, God." Carli's voice, choked with fear. "They shot Schuster!"

Liriano's silky voice returned, calm and measured. "Your friends are OK for now, but their fate is in your hands. Just do as we say, remain quiet for a few days and no one will be harmed."

"Wait!" Murph yelled at the phone. But they were gone. The phone went dark as the connection ended.

Chapter 105

Murph looked up from the phone at Cohen, but found the barrel of a handgun aimed between his eyes. Cohen's face was impassive, jaw set in stone.

"So, you see. I still hold all the cards." Cohen flicked the gun in the direction of the table. "I want all three of you close together, where I can see you. And Agent Collins, please place your pistol on the ground, and kick it over to me."

As Collins slowly drew his SIG Sauer from its holster, Murph watched Cohen's eyes stay on the agent and his gun. Murph still held Cohen's phone in his right hand.

Seizing the opportunity, Murph threw the phone at Cohen and charged. The old man ducked as the phone whizzed past his head. It was only three steps, and Murph lowered his shoulder, hitting Cohen in the chest like a linebacker sacking a quarterback. Murph could feel the rush of wind as the breath was crushed out of Cohen's lungs.

Cohen's hand dropped, his finger squeezing the trigger, firing one round with a BANG. Murph felt a sharp pain in his leg. Cohen was lifted off his feet by Murph's diving tackle, hitting the back of the couch, but bouncing upright.

Collins fired twice. An excellent shot, both bullets struck Cohen in the chest and the old man slumped to the floor, the red stain on his white shirt expanding to consume his torso.

Murph crawled to the billionaire, slapping the gun out of his hands. Cohen tried to speak, so Murph leaned over to hear the words.

"From evil, comes…"

Then his eyes became fixed, his pupils dilated and his head rolled back.

Murph slammed his fist on the carpet then jumped up, turning around in a fruitless search for someone or something to strike.

"From evil, comes death and more evil! Arrgh!!" Murph screamed. "Nothing good comes from evil!"

He let out the cry in frustration, breathing heavily. He squeezed his hands together, nails of his fingers biting into his palms. *Think. Calm down and think.*

Murph took a deep breath, held it, and then let it out slowly, forcing his heart rate to slow. He walked to the window and opened the blinds. The morning sun shone on the White House lawn. The Washington Monument stood silently glistening in the sunlight. Across the reflecting pool, Murph knew the statue of Thomas Jefferson stood on its pedestal, staring at him. Murph began to mumble to himself.

Buck put his hand on Murph's shoulder, "What was that you said?"

"*Malo periculosam, libertatem quam quietam servitutem.*"

Buck turned Murph to look him in the eye. "I think you got hit in the head. You're not making any sense."

"It's a Latin phrase that was a favorite of Thomas Jefferson's. It means 'I prefer dangerous freedom over peaceful slavery.' I can't sit here and do nothing."

The sound of gunfire had brought the remaining Secret Service team to the Treaty Room. Collins and the President went to assure them that the crisis was over. Simon Cohen had tried to kill the President but Dr. Murphy had foiled the assassination attempt. Agent Collins had shot and killed Cohen after Murphy had disarmed him.

Murph took out his phone and began making calls.

"Rocco! What the hell happened?"

346

"Murph, I don't know. We had bribed our usual immigration officials and had all the right paperwork to get your party into the country. Suddenly, Liriano shows up at the plane and takes them all at gunpoint before they reach customs. Carli, the Marines, the little priest and the old lady were shoved in a van and driven off the airport before we could react. My men are following them now. They didn't go into Rome."

"I can tell you where they are going." Murph was certain of this one. "They are going to a former convent in Susa. It's on the French border with Italy. Cohen owns the property. It's at the foot of some big mountains. I want you to follow them and then do reconnaissance on the facility. I want to know everything—number of guards—how they patrol. See if you can get a drawing of the buildings. I'll be in touch soon."

Murph spotted Cohen's phone on the carpet, sitting against a bookcase. He went over and picked it up, slipping it into his pocket. He went to Cohen's body and searched the pockets of the jacket and pants for any clues. Nothing appeared unusual, but when Murph settled the body back to a reclined position, the head fell back, opening its mouth. Murph's eyes widened in surprise.

He leaned forward and examined the billionaire's teeth, then snapped a photo with his iPhone. He dialed another number as Buck regarded him with surprise.

"Margaret! I need your help, quickly."

"Sure, Murph. What's wrong?"

"They have Carli and the others. They captured them when they arrived in Italy. Cohen's dead. Shot at the White House. He's plotting to have Jews return to repopulate Europe."

"How is he going to do that?"

"I haven't figured that part out yet. They have taken Carli to threaten me to keep quiet for a few days. Is there anything big going on in the world this week?"

"Let me look at the calendar." Murph could hear her nails click on a keyboard. "Wednesday is Rosh Hashanah. That's the Jewish New Year. Wait, Thursday is Ras as-Sanah al-

347

Hijriyah. That's the Islamic New Year. If I were planning something, those are good target dates."

"It has to be. He has something big planned for either Wednesday or Thursday. I just don't see what yet."

"Keep working the problem, and it will become clear."

"Hey, Margaret. Can you research the First Lady, Jean Buchanan?"

Buck glanced over again, wondering what Murph was up to.

"Sure, why?"

"It's a wild hunch, but Cohen is congenitally missing his upper lateral incisors. When we met Jean and Frank Buchanan at the state dinner, the President made a big fuss about ridiculing his wife for having 'expensive teeth.' She had just finished having implants to replace missing lateral incisors." This was sounding more outlandish with each word. "I know that congenitally missing teeth have a genetic component. Is it possible that the First Lady and Simon Cohen are related?"

"I'll check it out and get back to you!"

Murph hung up the phone and returned to Buck and Darnell. They noticed him limping, a trail of blood following his movements around the room.

Collins bent down and tore his pant's bottom. There was a neat bullet hole in Murph's calf, entering from the outside front and exiting in the back of the leg. He pushed Murph onto the couch and called for a medic, binding the leg with a cloth napkin to slow the bleeding.

Murph thanked Collins for his help. "Darnell, where exactly is the First Lady today?"

Collins consulted his government issue Blackberry. "Today, she is in Italy. They changed her itinerary yesterday. She's now in Turin, to be exact."

Murph shot up from the couch. "I need to get to Italy, pronto!"

This time Buck shoved him back down. "Easy now. I'm working on it. You just relax and let us bandage your leg, and

348

then I'll get you over there to rescue Carli. Even heroes need a Band-Aid now and then. Just sit there, and let me help you."

Murph leaned back as the White House physician arrived. He was a young Army doctor, who informed Murph that he was very lucky. It was a clean, through-and-through wound. The bullet had torn muscle but had missed the bones. He injected some anesthetic, cleaned the wound, and stitched the entry and exit points closed. The doc protected the stitches with cotton gauze pads and wound the leg tightly with a compression wrap. He offered Murph a painkiller, but Murph refused, instead accepting a couple of Advil.

When he struggled to his feet, his left leg didn't hurt anymore, thanks to the local anesthetic. But it was difficult to walk on a leg that he couldn't control.

Buck hung up the phone and approached Murph. "You saved my life, and I'm going to repay you by sending you back out."

"That's OK." Murph managed a smile. "I laugh in the face of danger!"

"Good thing!" Buck set a pad of paper in front of Murph. "Here's the plan."

Chapter 106

His leg was beginning to throb as the anesthetic wore off. Murph sat alone with his thoughts in the back of a Marine helicopter heading back to Andrews Air Force base. He closed his eyes, working to visualize what he had to do. Pope Francis had told them, "Be not afraid, for the Lord was with you." Murph's faith was strong; however, this was to be a severe test. *Lord, if it is your will, let me be the instrument of good. Give me the vision and strength to save them.*

Turning into the wind, the helicopter slowed and settled gently to the ground. The wheels had barely touched when he was ushered across the tarmac, limping slightly, arriving at the operations building for the 113ᵗʰ Wing. Operated by the District of Columbia Air National Guard, the 'Capital Guardians' provide air sovereignty forces to defend the Nations Capital.

Out of the jet engine noise on the base, Murph removed his headphones and handed them to the airman leading him. "Thank you!"

"Welcome to the 113ᵗʰ, Sir. I know you are in a rush, so I'll take you right to Colonel Shaw."

"I appreciate that." The airman walked swiftly through the maze of corridors. Murph was struggling to keep up, while trying not to favor his leg.

They arrived at a drab gray door with the nameplate *Col. Lawrence Shaw*. The soldier rapped on the door and opened it. "Colonel. Dr. Murphy to see you!"

Murph was led into a spartan office—metal desk, corkboard on the wall with papers held by thumbtacks, computer monitors on the desk, and metal file cabinets along the wall. This was all business.

Colonel Shaw was a bull of a man—in his fifties, at least six inches shorter than Murph but with massive forearms and hands. His grip enveloped Murph, forcing him to squeeze back with all his might, smiling to mask the pain. Shaw's hairline was receding and a hint of gray was touching the temples of his brown, close-cropped hair. The corners of his brown eyes were creased with wrinkles from squinting in the sun. They added to the playfulness of his smile, broad white teeth grinning as he looked Murph up and down.

"Son, you look like shit!"

"Thanks, Colonel. I'm trying my best to hide it." Murph laughed and disengaged his hand from the vise.

"I just got off the phone with my old wingman, who happens to now be the Commander in Chief. He thinks the world of you. And that means a lot. He didn't give me many details, but I'm under orders to FedEx you to Italy."

"Well, I absolutely, positively have to get there overnight." The determination in Murph's face made an impact.

"I understand." Shaw called for his adjutant. "I'm going to fly you to Aviano Air Base myself. They're prepping an F-15 E Strike Eagle for us. You'll be in the weapons officer's seat in the back. Lieutenant Jordan, here, will get you all geared up and go over the emergency egress instructions."

Jordan smiled as Murph tilted his head. "Emergency egress?"

Jordan patted Murph on the back. "Ejector seat. But don't worry; it's easy enough."

Shaw studied Murph. "Are you sure you're up for this, son?"

"Yes, Sir. I'm in this all the way."

"Buck tells me that you are joining a Delta Force team when you get there. You sure don't look like a Special Forces guy."

"No, Sir. I'm a dentist."

Shaw and Jordan burst out laughing, but stopped when they realized that Murph was not. He was simply standing tall, feet spread apart, hands on his hips—determined and ready.

Shaw nodded. "Very well then, whatever is going on, it's serious. The President trusts you implicitly, and so will I."

"Thanks, Colonel. Thanks for flying me. There is more at stake here than you know."

Shaw started for the door, "Jordan, get him in a flight suit, and get him something to eat."

Murph called after him, "Is there anything you suggest before flying?"

"Bananas!"

Murph was surprised. "Bananas help prevent air sickness?"

"No – but they taste the same coming up as going down."

Chapter 107

Murph was geared up and ready to fly. He carried his flight helmet and walked with the bow-legged gait of the pilots, flight suit and tight-fitting anti-g force trousers restricting the movement of his legs. They approached the twin tailed F-15 E Strike Eagle. Its menacing appearance in dark gray camouflage paint and the sheer power of its twin engines were beautiful and terrifying all at once.

The ground crew helped Murph up the ladder and into his seat behind Colonel Shaw. They attached all his electronic connections and communications. Murph learned each man had to eject himself—the pilot couldn't punch Murph out if he had to go. After going over the instructions for emergency egress, Shaw's voice rang out in Murph's helmet.

"Last chance to get off the roller coaster."

"No, Sir. I have an appointment in Italy, and I can't be late."

"Then let's light this candle. Next stop, Mach 2."

The ground crewman tugged on Murph's flight harness to make sure he was strapped in tight. He patted Murph on the shoulder and gave him a thumbs-up. The canopy closed. He was committed now. Murph could feel the raw power of the engines behind him. In mere moments, the ground disappeared beneath them, and they soared out over the Atlantic.

Settling in at cruising altitude, streaking across the ocean at Mach 2, Murph heard Col. Shaw's voice on the intercom.

"OK, now that it's just us up here, why don't you tell me what's really going on."

"Well, it's a rather long story…" Murph was trying to be evasive.

"It's not like we're going anywhere for a while." Shaw wasn't irritated, but simply curious. "Look at this from my perspective, I've flown combat missions over Iraq and Afghanistan. I'm now in command of the air defense of Washington. I get a phone call from the President and you show up on my base. Suddenly, you have a full Colonel ferrying a dentist non-stop to Italy at Mach 2, diverting aerial refueling tankers to support us as we cross. I think I deserve an explanation!"

"Colonel, you certainly do." Murph sighed. "So here's the story, from the beginning, with nothing left out. You tell me if you think this is important."

Murph began the tale. By the time they landed, Shaw was impressed and deeply disturbed.

"That story is so crazy, it has to be true."

The pilot landed and taxied to a stop, opening the canopy. Murph allowed the ground crewman to disconnect him from the jet, setting his flight helmet on the dash in front of him. He moved to get out and found that his legs had stiffened. It was a challenge but Murph managed to climb down without falling. Standing on firm ground again, he stretched his back, his neck popping.

Colonel Shaw placed his helmet on the cockpit rail and climbed down. He shook Murph's hand.

"It was my pleasure to fly with you. You're a great storyteller. You should write a book sometime!" Shaw grabbed Murph by the shoulders and led him toward the base operations office. He acted like he didn't notice Murph's wobbly gait.

"Thanks, Colonel. The pleasure was mine. That certainly was an e-ticket ride!"

"Son, you're too young to know about e-ticket rides. But thanks for trying!"

Shaw was smiling broadly when they entered the operations building. A pair of tall, slim Army officers jumped up and saluted. Colonel Shaw returned their salutes.

"Hello, Colonel. Welcome to Italy!" The leader had close-cropped black hair and a large nose, with a hump in the middle indicating a previous break. "I'm Captain Sam Wells. My partner is Lieutenant Rick Neven." He indicated to his twin, a redhead with a freckled faced.

Col. Shaw shook hands with both officers. They were young, but highly competent Army Rangers. They exuded the easy confidence of men who were comfortable with their capabilities. Murph respected that and was glad to have them on his side.

Colonel Shaw indicated Murph. "Gentlemen, this is Dr. Mike Murphy. He's the toughest dentist I've ever met! I think you'll find that he will turn out to be an asset to your team."

Both Rangers raised an eyebrow, but shook his hand warmly.

"Glad to have you, Sir. Considering the source of our orders, you come very highly recommended." Captain Wells looked him over.

Shaw laughed, reaching over to shake Murph by the shoulder. "Murph may look like shit now, but get him a couple hours of sleep and he'll be ready to go."

Murph's iPhone chirped. He reached into his flight suit and pulled it out. "Two voicemails."

The Colonel pointed to a small office. "Go check those out. I'll brief the Delta Force team here on what you have told me."

Murph nodded thanks and entered the room.

The first voicemail was from Rocco. He had emailed the plans for the convent and the results of his reconnaissance. He had seen Carli, Bernie, Valerie, and Lt. Schuster all taken into the compound. Schuster was limping, but everyone else looked OK.

The second email was from Margaret. She confirmed Murph's suspicion. Jean Buchanan was Simon Cohen's granddaughter. Cohen had married Fred Arnold's daughter, but their children kept the surname of Arnold. Murph hit himself on the side of his head. *How did I miss that??*

Murph asked the airman manning the counter if he could use a computer. He opened his email and printed the drawings from Rocco and the descriptions of the guards.

He came out of the office and found Col. Shaw and the two Rangers sitting in a small conference room. When Murph walked in, the soldiers regarded him with new respect.

Lt. Neven got up. "Coffee?"

Murph smiled. "I'd love a cup—black—thanks!"

He took the mug and downed a gulp. "It appears that Col. Shaw has been telling tall tales."

Wells pointed at the leg of Murph's flight suit. "That blood stain indicates he speaks the truth. We'll need to have a medic dress that bullet wound again. The g-suit probably opened the stitches."

"First things first, we have planning to do." Murph closed the door tightly and spread out the papers he had just printed. "Here are the plans for the convent in Susa. These notes detail the number of guards my sources have seen and how they seem to be patrolling."

Lt. Neven pulled satellite images out of his file and laid them next to Murph's architectural drawings.

"Jesus!" Capt. Wells shook his head in disbelief. "Where did you get that information?"

Murph shrugged. "Friends in low places."

"At least now we know what the interior of these buildings look like." Neven was tracing the corridors with his finger. "That's huge!"

Murph nodded in agreement. "Our objective is to rescue five people and assess the nature of the threat from this group." He took photos out of his pocket and set them down one at a time.

"Valerie David, age 87. She survived the Nazi takeover of the convent in 1944 and escaped to America. I refuse to let it end for her back there after all this time.

"Father Bernardo Foa, pronounced Fo-wah. He's a Jesuit priest who works for the Vatican. He speaks Italian and excellent English.

"First Lieutenant Jeffrey Schuster USMC. He may be wounded, possibly in the leg. He was seen limping severely when he entered the compound.

"Sergeant Ron Covrett USMC. Both Marines have combat tours in Afghanistan so they know what to do.

"Carli Chamoun, PhD candidate in Archeology at Georgetown."

Neven whistled. "Her, I would rescue anytime!"

Colonel Shaw whacked him lightly in the back of his head. "That's Murph's fiancé, dummy!"

355

"Sorry. No offense!"

Murph laughed. "That's OK. I'm rather partial to her as well."

Wells rubbed his chin. "What's their game here?"

Murph tapped the maps with his finger. "That's the big problem. We don't really know. They went to a lot of trouble to substitute the President, but I really can't figure out why. That's one of our goals here—and we're likely to find a man who looks exactly like President Buchanan. We captured him in Cleveland on Saturday. What day is it now?"

"Early Monday morning." Neven offered.

"I sent him to Italy to be held by my contacts here until we could figure out what was going on. Sadly, the organization headed by billionaire Simon Cohen controlled the Immigrations office at Ciampino Airport in Rome, and all of these people were captured."

"Unfortunate." Shaw was following closely, thinking.

"Another possible problem is that the First Lady is somewhere in Italy. There is a chance that she will be in Susa as well. I have just learned that Jean Buchanan is the granddaughter of Simon Cohen, which makes her part of this conspiracy."

Wells let out a low whistle. "This just keeps getting better and better."

"I know." Murph could appreciate their concern. "The one positive is that we have speed on our side. They believe that I am still in Washington, being watched by Cohen himself. They have something big planned for Wednesday or Thursday —Rosh Hashanah or the Islamic New Year. If we strike quickly, we may take them off guard."

Murph sat down heavily. "Guys, I need your help. I've gone as far as I can alone."

"Doc, you have brought enough intel to make this much easier to plan." Capt. Wells waved a hand over the table. "You see the medic about that leg, then get some sleep. My team will plan this operation. That's our job."

"I know you're the best at it. I just want to go along, if you'll have me."

"You know the players, and we'll need you to explain it at the briefing."

Neven grinned at Murph. "Never had a dentist on an op before!"

Col. Shaw grabbed Murph by the collar. "Not too many dentists who have crossed the Atlantic at Mach 2 either. Let's see the flight surgeon and let these professionals do their thing. You've had a long day already, and I think it's going to be an even longer night."

Chapter 108

Murph was sitting in his boxers as the flight surgeon was finishing dressing the wound on his calf, still sipping the coffee as it gradually became cold.

Doctor Korn, an Air Force Major in his fifties, shook his head sadly. "I've done the best I can, but it won't be pretty. It'll heal fine, but your girlfriend had better like scars. That one will be impressive."

"That's OK, Doc. I haven't exactly been the best patient." Murph reached for his shirt. "It's been a tough couple of days."

"More than that, from the look of it!" Captain Wells came in behind Murph. "How many scars do you have? At least three of those are bullet wounds. What the Hell were you doing Doc?"

"Maybe you should consider putting your patients to sleep before you work on them?" Lt. Neven chimed in, carrying black combat clothing and boots for Murph.

Doc Korn tapped Murph on the shoulder. "That one's a knife wound. He's seen more combat than you have, Rick. I'd make sure he has your back tonight."

Murph pulled on a black t-shirt and combat trousers, uncomfortable with all the attention. "Hey, you guys are the

357

pros. I'm just going along to ID the bad buys. I hope I stay out of your way."

Capt. Wells handed Murph a pistol. "I don't like giving a civilian a weapon, but I'm worried about you being unarmed. Have you handled one of these before?"

Murph accepted the SIG Sauer P229, the standard issue handgun for the Army Special Forces. He smoothly released the magazine, checked its load, slammed it back into place, chambered a round, and set the safety. He carefully pointed the pistol away from everyone, up at the ceiling, cradling the handgrip in his left palm, supporting his right hand around the grip, finger off the trigger along the side of the barrel, just as Gabriel Levy had taught him. "Nice weight. I haven't fired a SIG before, but I like the feel."

Neven's mouth hung open, his jaw resting on the table, eyes wide. The doc burst out laughing.

Wells patted Murph on the back. "You'll do, Murph. You'll do fine!"

"Just trying to be prepared." He set the gun down on the table.

"Rick will help you gear up, then let's go over the plan. We've decided that speed is an asset for us."

Neven stood up. "No sleep for you!"

Murph laced up his combat boots. "The sooner we get this over with, the better. They're holding the Americans as hostages to keep me quiet and pinned down in DC. But, at some point, they won't need them anymore, and they've shown they have no problem eliminating people." He pulled on the nylon combat shirt, then placed his holster across his chest and set the pistol in place, a determined look on his face. "C'mon Rick. Let's go."

They left the flight surgeon's office and returned to the briefing room. Captain Wells was briefing the Delta team. As Murph entered, Sam indicated to him. "Dr. Mike Murphy. He's the reason for this little show. He will be in charge when we get to the rescue."

358

Murph threw up his hands. "No way, Captain, you're the boss! I'm just an observer."

"Don't let him fool you." Wells grinned. "Like the guy in the beer commercials, Murph is the most interesting dentist in America! He handles a SIG like he knows what to do with it, but I don't want him doing any shooting."

"That makes two of us!" Murph leaned against the wall.

"We have five targets to rescue. Two are active duty Marines. An 87-year-old woman, a priest, and Murph's fiancé. Carli's little, right?"

"Five foot one. She's a leader. She'll be in charge of the hostages."

"Murph, who are the bad guys you want captured, if possible?"

"A guy who looks just like the President. He goes by Frank Buchanan." That got the attention of the Delta team. "We may find the First Lady, Jean Buchanan, as well. The dangerous one is called Cyrille Bastien."

Rick Neven looked up from his clipboard. "French national?"

"I really don't know. He is in command of their mercenaries. Pale skin, shaved head, big buggy eyes, small head, huge torso and arms—kind of a troll. You won't miss him."

Neven scratched his head. "How do we know it's not really the President?"

"I left the real Buck Buchanan in Washington yesterday. If we meet one here, the fake one is missing a lower right molar." Murph tapped his lower jaw. "I took out the six-year molar on the guy a couple of weeks ago—and that started all this mess. But that's hard to check while he's conscious."

"Got it. We'll check the teeth when he's horizontal, but if you see him here, assume he's an imposter." Wells wrapped up the briefing. "Gear up. Choppers leave in 15."

Murph looked surprised. "We're flying?"

Wells nodded pointing at the map. "Aviano is here, northeast of Venice. Susa is west of Turin on the border with

France. That's a five-hour drive in the mountains, through Padua, Verona, Milan and Turin—too hard to keep the element of surprise for that long."

Neven grabbed his pack and shouldered it. "Besides, you've got connections! The President—the real one— called the Italian Prime Minister and got permission for us to run an American op here in Italy. You're *spay-shal*."

"Thanks, guys. I appreciate it!"

Wells looked Murph in the eye. "We'll get her back, man. Count on it!"

Murph shook his hand firmly. "Let's roll!"

Chapter 109

The heavy iron bolt on the door slid open with a shot, and the ominous creak of the wood dragging against the frame told them that someone was coming. Sgt. Covrett struggled against the chains. Manacles at his ankles and wrists bound him to the iron ring in the wall. He was restrained in the same manner that prisoners had been held for nine hundred years. Valerie David was huddled in the corner, shivering with the damp cold. Father Foa nestled against her to keep her warm, thinking of Father Gaspard and Father Falcone, praying silently.

Lt. Schuster rested on grain sacks that they had pulled over on the floor to make as comfortable a bed as possible. He smiled through the pain, but Carli could see from the beads of sweat on his forehead that the fever had begun. He had been shot in the leg, just below the left knee. A local doctor had been dragged into their prison. The doctor did what he could to stabilize the fractured bone and dress the wound. His bandage had stopped the bleeding but proper treatment would require surgery. The more time passed, everyone knew that the chances of saving the leg were fading quickly.

Carli pushed back her hair and dabbed the sweat of Schuster's brow with a damp cloth. The only light was from two partially burned candles they had been given. It was small comfort that these were altar candles. Bernie assured them that they would intensify his prayers, the smoke drifting straight up to Heaven.

The arrival of light, in the form of a halogen lantern, momentarily blinded the prisoners as their guards descended the stone steps. Carli had correctly discerned that this was an old storeroom under the Convent. The doorway opened onto the main courtyard, surrounded by high walls.

Carli stood up defiantly, hands on her hips to face their captors.

"It's about time you got here. We called for room service hours ago!" She taunted.

"Still feisty. I like that." The voice was familiar. "However, I wouldn't be so quick to anger my associates here."

Frank Buchanan stepped out from behind the lantern, where everyone could see him. He had changed into khaki slacks and a navy blue windbreaker with the seal of the President of the United States.

"How are you enjoying our hospitality?"

Carli snorted. "Hello, Frank—or whatever your name really is. I wouldn't get too used to wearing that logo. You haven't earned it."

"On the contrary," his voice was even and conversational. He was in complete control. "I was elected Vice President and then sworn in by the Chief Justice Roberts after the death of the President. You cannot get more legitimate than that."

Carli had to admit he had a point, but she wasn't ready to concede anything. "But you were elected under false pretenses. You're not Buck Buchanan."

"Ahh, but there you are wrong." He smiled broadly, perfect teeth gleaming in the halogen glare. "In the eyes of the world, I am Franklin Buchanan."

"Murph will expose you. You have to know that!"

"He will do nothing of the sort." Frank folded his arms across his chest. "He is in Washington, biding his time with the—other guy. They will not risk global chaos by coming

361

forward. In a couple of days, it will not matter anyway. Dr. Murphy can declare himself President for all I care."

The halogen lantern served as a spotlight on Carli, standing protectively in front of the other prisoners. A guard held the light and Frank Buchanan stood in front of him, so that the light illuminated his face. Carli could sense that there were others behind the guard with the lantern, but they were completely in shadows.

"Murph and Buck can have a press conference and foil any plans you have."

"An excellent idea, Miss Caroline, but you are forgetting several important facts." Frank's tone was of a teacher scolding an annoying student. "For one, Simon Cohen owns most of the media outlets in the metro DC area. If you own the cameras, you control the message."

Another figure stepped out of the shadows and moved toward Frank, eventually holding his hand. Jean Buchanan tossed her hair and smiled, "Besides, the two of us trump any dentist and his presidential impersonator friend, don't you think?" She smiled sweetly.

"Why Mrs. Buchanan," Carli spat out the words, "you've been in this from the beginning!"

"Oh, my Dear. I've been in this since before the beginning." She took three steps to stand directly in front of Carli, wagging a finger in her face. Jean stood a head taller than Carli. "You have no idea how long this was planned. Intricate steps in years of waiting—building, then you and your meddling boyfriend stumble in and make things difficult."

Carli smiled, "I'm so glad we were able to ruin your little coming-out party."

Jean's hand swung suddenly, striking Carli on the side of the jaw, the slap ringing like a shot in the stone cellar. Carli was knocked to the floor by the savagery of the attack.

Carli leaped to her feet and lunged at Jean, but a guard caught her and pinned her arms behind her back. A trickle of blood escaped the corner of her mouth and traced the line of her jaw.

Frank Buchanan laughed as Jean was massaging her sore hand. "Now, now, girls. No point in fighting. Dr. Murphy has accomplished nothing. He still has no idea what is going on. I guess it's dumb luck. He has managed to kill a few of my men and make us chase him around the globe—but, in the end, it has no significance. From evil will come a greater good!"

Jean Buchanan's eyes narrowed, glaring at Carli, who struggled against the guard, stamping down on his instep. He staggered a bit, but did not release her. Walking toward the stairs, Jean yelled up at the door, "Franz!"

A giant of a man, nearly seven feet tall stooped down and descended the stairs, carrying a bundle in his arms. His long strides carried him quickly across the room. He knelt down and laid the roll of blankets at Carli's feet.

Frank smirked. "Since the end is so near for you, I thought you would like more company. We are tired of caring for her. You have nothing else to do, so we'll leave her here."

The bundle of blankets stirred and began moaning as Franz stood up and backed away. The guard released Carli and she ran over. She lifted the blankets and found the face of an old woman, fear in the brown eyes staring up at her. Carli cradled the woman in her arms and she felt the grip of the bony hands as she sought Carli's protection. Carli helped the woman sit up and face the light.

"Louisa?" Valerie stood up with the little priest's help. "Louisa is that you?"

The hunted brown eyes turned and then began to fill with tears. "Valerie?" Her voice was little more than a croak. "Ho pensato che erano morti."

Valerie moved as quickly as her legs would allow, Bernie supporting her as she staggered across the floor. "Dead? No I'm not dead. I went to America years ago." She knelt down and took her sister's hand. Tears flowed as they embraced.

Frank Buchanan turned and led the guards toward the stairs. "I do love a good reunion, but her mind is so far gone that this should be a short. Enjoy the time you have!"

363

He helped Jean and then ascended the stairs himself. The last guard turned out the light, returning the cell into near darkness. The door slammed shut and the bolt slid closed. Carli stamped down on the stone floor with frustration and sat down, alone with her thoughts.

Chapter 110

The three Army Blackhawk helicopters moved smoothly through the Alps, setting down outside of the quaint Italian town of Susa, situated at the foot of the Cottian Alps, 32 miles west of Turin. Founded by the Gauls in the first century BC, Susa has remained important as a hub connecting roads from southern France to Italy. It's population had remained fairly constant, and the current 6,743 residents slept peacefully, unaware of the arrival of the Delta Force team of US Army Rangers.

Moving swiftly, they fanned out and encircled the former convent at the edge of town. Crossing a small park, Murph could see the three-story stone façade of the building silhouetted in the moonlight, with the shadow of the Cottian Mountains in the background. The attack team crossed the river, *un fiume*, Dora Riparia, and dodged from shadow to shadow along the Via Brunetta until they reached the base of the wall.

Captain Sam Wells knelt down and surveyed the building. So far, there was no apparent response. He contacted his group leaders and confirmed that they were all in positions around the building.

Wells turned to Lt. Neven and Murph. "Rick, you follow me in. Murph, stick to Rick and stay behind him, out of his way."

"Roger."

Neven leaned in to Murph. "Last chance to wear the night vision goggles."

"No thanks. I've never worn them before, and I'm worried that it would make things worse. I'll just attach myself to you and hope they turn the lights on sometime."

"Let's hope not. We do our best work in the dark!" Wells patted Murph on the back. "Let's do this!"

Wells gave the order, and snipers dispatched the guards in the watchtowers. Wells, Neven, and Murph ran across the street and hugged the base of the wall. The element of surprise had gotten them safely this far, but that cover evaporated in a flash when a Ranger blew open the double wooden door. Wells and Neven charged through the opening with Murph right behind. The assault was under way. A bullet whizzed by Murph's head and impacted the stone archway behind him, spraying him with chips.

This is getting really old! Murph thought to himself as he ducked.

The raiders fanned out across the cobblestone yard. Murph could hear the reports of other units safely accessing the building, securing the convent room by room. Wells was leading the frontal assault, taking the shortest route to the quarters of the former Mother Superior of the convent. It was the largest apartment in the complex and the likely base of operations for the leadership—and also the most probable place to find their targets.

A searchlight blazed to life on the corner of the wall, sweeping the courtyard. Wells and Neven separated to avoid the beam of light. As they scattered, Murph was passing too close to Neven and tripped over his leg, crashing to the ground. Momentarily blinded, Wells and Neven removed their night vision goggles, shouting, "Someone get that light!"

Murph rolled over, coming back up to his knees. Without night vision goggles, his eyes were more accustomed to the light. He drew his pistol, extended his arms, and aimed the SIG at the searchlight. Murph fired three shots in quick succession, and the searchlight swung away from them.

Rick grabbed Murph by the back of his collar and pulled him to his feet, tugging him forward. As they continued running across the now darkened courtyard, Neven grinned as he questioned Murph, "You were aiming to take out the searchlight, right?"

Murph nodded. "Yeah, why?"

"Well, you missed the light—but you dropped the guy manning it, so I guess that's all that counts!"

They reached the far wall of the courtyard. It was lined with a series of wooden doors with iron banding. Wells pointed at the doors then moved on with other members of the team, running toward the main office. Murph started to move, but Neven grabbed him by the arm.

"No. We have to check these doors, one at a time." He motioned for three other Rangers with them to cover him. "Just keep your head down, and try to remember you're a dentist!"

Chapter 111

Valerie and Louisa sat in the corner, huddled together like little children. Valerie's Italian was obviously rusty, since she hadn't used it in seventy years. Bernie Foa sat cross-legged with them, assisting with translation.

Lieutenant Schuster had drifted off into a tormented sleep, tossing and turning, occasionally moaning. Carli could feel his temperature rising as the infection took hold. Sgt. Covrett sadly watched, as there was nothing he could do to help. His restraints were too firmly attached.

Louisa's brain initially appeared to be addled, but seeing her sister seemingly broke the fog. Carli joined the group, squatting down and supporting the old woman as she told her tale.

As the Nazis left the convent, Louisa had been taken by the SS officer as his prize. The trucks had gone into the Cottian Mountains, finding a narrow entrance to a cave off of the main pass. The Nazis unloaded the trucks, filled with the plunder of occupied France. A massive hoard of gold, silver, jewelry, artwork, and currency was secreted away in the mountain. The Nazi troops obscured the cave entrance and set up living quarters in the rear of the cave.

The Nazi SS Colonel, Gerhard Metz, was fanatically loyal to Hitler. He was also supremely efficient. He cataloged and prepared the vast wealth for future use by the Fatherland. Louisa was kept, initially as his prisoner, then his servant, and finally as his lover.

The troops moved on to other tasks in the defense of Italy, but Metz remained with Louisa. He kept the cave completely provisioned for a long stay. Metz would leave occasionally for a few days at a time, but always returned. Weeks passed, then months. Louisa's world shrank until it consisted only of Metz and the cave.

When Colonel Metz left for the last time, he told Louisa to remain and to keep the cave clean and prepared for his return. When he failed to come back, Louisa lost track of time. She maintained the apartment in the cave and conserved her food. The cave had a spring, fed from the river, she thought, so water was never an issue.

Louisa had no idea how long she waited, but when she ran out of food and became hungry, she knew she had to leave the cave for help. The world she found shocked her. None of the people she had known were around. The war had ended, but the order of Nazi occupation had been replaced with complete chaos.

Frightened, Louisa first stole some bread. She continued to steal food, finding a way to survive. She wandered aimlessly for a while, and then was found by Father Henri. She seemed like a lost child to him, though she was now nearly seventeen. The priest took her in and gave her a purpose in life. She felt ashamed of her time with the Nazi SS officer. She confessed her sins to Father Henri and repented. She gave her life over to God and became his assistant, supporting him in his ministry as a Nun, even though she had no formal religious order.

Years later, Simon Cohen returned to Italy and found Father Henri. Cohen was surprised to see Louisa. He remembered her from the convent and told her the terrible news that her sister Valerie had died on the trip to America.

At this, Valerie became incensed at his lies and the pain they had caused. She started to curse Cohen, but Father Foa intervened, instead choosing to bless the fact that they had been reunited.

Carli's eyes widened, turning to Bernie. "Ask Louisa if Cohen wanted something."

The little priest translated the question. Louisa began to cry again. "She says that he was very interested in where the Nazis had gone after leaving the convent. When she showed him the entrance and led him into the cave, he told her to never tell anyone."

"Why not?"

"He said that if anyone found out about the cave, they would call her a collaborator." Bernie squeezed her hands. "After the war, what they did to people who were accused of collaborating with the Nazis was terrible. Women had their heads shaved and they were shunned. Some of the women and most of the men were lined up and shot as traitors. It was horrible, in France and Italy—really in all of the occupied countries. The victorious members of the resistance were nearly as vicious as the Nazis had been. Cohen told her to keep the secret for her own safety."

Carli hugged Louisa and kissed her on the forehead, wiping away her tears. She stood up with clenched fists. "Now we know how Cohen made his fortune!"

Valerie looked up in disgust. "And he destroyed Louisa's mind in the process. The guilt she has carried for years has consumed her."

There was an explosion outside. The stone walls shook slightly, and dust drifted down from the rafters. Every head turned, their eyes fixed on the doorway. Several popping noises followed, then a whistle blowing.

Sgt. Covrett was on his feet, straining against his chains. "Gunfire! Possibly a rescue."

Carli scanned the room for the thousandth time looking for something to use as a weapon, disappointed to find that nothing had appeared. "They may come for us—to eliminate us before we can be found. We have to get ready."

Recognizing the sound of gunshots, Louisa struggled to her feet and staggered toward the back of the room, leading Valerie by the hand.

"Where is she going?" Bernie asked and then clapped his hands with joy when she spoke. "She knows a way out!"

Louisa chattered away, pointing at the back wall. Bernie ran ahead. Carli grabbed a candle and followed him. "This is the main store room for the convent. There is a passage out the back that runs outside the wall to the field, where grain was brought in."

Louisa reached the corner of the room. The flickering light of the candle revealed a stack of barrels on the floor with bags of flour sitting on top of them. Louisa began to tug at the top bag, but her feeble efforts were of no use against the fifty-pound bags.

Carli had Valerie pull her aside and hold her. "I sure hope she's right!" She set her feet and tugged, toppling the first bags of flour onto the floor, falling backward as the top bag split open. The white powder exploded, turning her white and

369

leaving them coughing. Carli didn't stop to brush herself off. She and Bernie set themselves to their task, working to clear a path. There was no guarantee of a door, but there was no other way out!

The sound of the iron bolt sliding free on the door announced that they were out of time. Carli doused the candle and turned to face the threat as the door swung rapidly open.

Chapter 112

The sharp crack of gunfire continued sporadically around them, indicating that the convent was yet to be secured. The Rangers moved methodically from door to door along the courtyard.

They blended into the shadows beside each archway, backs pressed against the wall. The ancient wooden doors had wide oak planks held together with iron bands. At each chamber door, one by one, a Ranger pulled back the bolt and pushed the door open. Then, a second Ranger panned his flashlight across the room while the remaining Rangers were prepared to fire on any threat in the room.

They had entered three chambers already, finding nothing but empty storerooms. The team approached the fourth door with the same care as the previous ones.

Throwing back the bolt, the Ranger shoved with his shoulder. This door gave way easier than the others and he nearly fell into the room. There were stairs down to a lower floor level. The flashlight beam cut through the dark, and then was obscured by a white fog. A Ranger began to descend the stairs, his assault rifle tracking possible threats. The flashlight beam transfixed a ghostly white figure in the corner, and the shooter raised his weapon.

"Wait!" Murph shouted, coming down the steps two at a time. "I'd know that figure anywhere!"

He flipped on his flashlight and ran across the room, sweeping Carli up in his arms.

"Oh, Murph!" She wrapped her arms around his neck. "They said you were in Washington."

He winked. "I'm like a bad penny. I always turn up." Murph trained his flashlight around the room, shocked by the condition of his friends.

Murph yelled over his shoulder, "Rick, they're all here. But we need a medic and some other help."

Neven assigned a Ranger to guard their exit, called in that he had secured the prisoners, and requested additional help. His long strides took him quickly to Murph. "Looks like you got the girl, but she looks a bit worse for wear!"

Murph shrugged. "She looks fantastic to me." He tugged her close to him. "Carli, please meet Lieutenant Rick Neven, US Army Rangers. He and his Delta Force team are our way out."

Carli took Murph over to Schuster. "Murph, the Lieutenant's slipping away. They never really treated his leg wound."

Murph felt Schuster's head. "How long has he had the fever?"

"It really only started today, but he's getting worse quickly."

"Rick, he needs medical evac quickly."

Neven nodded. He called in to Sam Wells and returned to Murph in a second. "Wells says the convent is secure. The medevac chopper is coming in now."

"Did they find Buchanan?"

Carli slid out of Murph's arm, "Jean Buchanan is here too."

Murph reloaded his pistol. "I was expecting that. At least they're all together."

Neven listened to his com link then answered. "Wells got to the Mother Superior's quarters, but Buchanan escaped out some sort of passageway. It led out the back of the building,

371

running underground. The passage came out in a field, but beyond where we had set up the perimeter around the convent."

Murph shoved his gun into the holster in frustration.

Carli grabbed his tunic. "I know where they are going! Or at least Louisa does!"

Murph furrowed his brow. "Louisa?"

"I'll tell you everything as we work, but Louisa is Valerie's sister! She knows where the cave is. We have to move these barrels, then there is a way out!"

Bernie Foa was nodding vigorously in agreement. Murph trusted Carli implicitly, so he waved to two of the Rangers. "Help me move these!"

With Murph and the Rangers working, it only took minutes to clear a path, finding a wooden access door in the corner. Murph kissed Carli on the forehead. "Perfect!"

The medics arrived and began caring for Schuster. Members of the Delta Force team began working to release Covrett.

Murph ran over to the Marine Sergeant, gripping his shoulder. "Ron, look after the Lieutenant!"

"You've got it!"

Murph came back over to the wall, lifting the panel that acted as a gate. "It's a bit low. Going to be a tight fit! Do the women have to go?"

Carli shook her head. "Louisa is the only one who knows the way. And Valerie insists she is going."

Murph wasn't happy, but he could see the determination in her eyes. "I know. You lost her once, and you're not about to lose her again!" Valerie nodded.

He turned to Bernie, who was bending down, sizing up the five-foot tall passage. "What's your story?"

"I have-a to go as the interpreter. Louisa speaks Italian, not too much English."

Murph grabbed him by the shoulder, pulling him back from the tunnel. "You're forgetting that I speak Italian."

"I was-a hopin' that you would-a forget." Bernie had the giant puppy-dog eyes.

"Alright. You can come too."

Murph assigned Bernie to look after Valerie and Lousia, helping them to keep up. "Rick, let's get moving. The sun will be up soon!"

Neven radioed in their intention to follow the Buchanans, and the team headed down the passageway. Carli was concerned whether Louisa would remember the way, but she bit her tongue and kept her thoughts to herself.

Chapter 113

The first glimmer of dawn was lightening the eastern sky as the team pushed aside the wood planked barn doors and emerged into the grassy field facing the Cottian Mountains. The grain passage had proved to be mercifully short, ending in the stable connected to the outer wall of the convent. For years, a small herd of cows had provided milk and cheese for the nuns. The ancient cow path was worn through the field, extending toward the base of the mountain. It took very little imagination to follow the trail, as Louisa confirmed to Murph that they were on the right track.

With Lt. Neven and three Rangers in the lead, the group moved cautiously, yet as swiftly as they dared, into the mountain pass. They were aware of the possibility of ambush. Captain Wells and his troops had assessed the number of casualties on the part of the defenders of the convent. From the assessments provided by Rocco Meroni, there were only a handful of mercenaries unaccounted for, but Murph agreed they should proceed with caution.

A heavy mist obscured vision, reducing visibility to only a few hundred feet. It also muffled the sounds. No one spoke. Murph followed closely behind Neven, with Carli beside him. Bernie Foa helped Louisa along, proving to be much stronger than he at first appeared.

After nearly thirty minutes, the pass steepened into a significant climb. The asphalt road, cracked with years of disuse, wound through the narrow valley between the peaks. A sharp bend in the road was closely bordered with pine trees. Louisa pointed off the road, into the forest.

Murph tapped Neven on the shoulder. The lead Ranger was thirty feet ahead on the edge of the road. Neven stopped the team, and Murph examined the roadside. They could see where the pine branches had been disturbed. It was also apparent where moisture had dropped and accumulated into small puddles on the pine straw and grass where someone had brushed against the branches. This was the place.

Murph huddled with Louisa, speaking quietly for a moment, then returned to Neven. "Only one way in—a narrow entrance. There's a metal door and a sentry station just inside the rock opening of the cave. Manmade construction from there—the Nazis smoothed the floor and walls. Near the entrance is the warehouse area. The living quarters are in the back."

Neven quickly considered the options. "Dangerous, but we have to go in the front door. My Rangers will lead. After we secure the guard station, Murph, you keep the civilians there at the entrance until I tell you it's safe."

Sergeant Wolfe, the lead Ranger, had been scouting through the pines, coming back from his point position. He joined Neven and Murph. "Not too many footprints, Sir. Hard to be sure, but I'd say only four or five people came this way."

"Thanks, Sarge. Take the lead. The longer we wait, the more time they have to prepare."

The rocky face of the mountain wasn't far. Murph held his band of amateurs back while the professionals did their job. The sun was rising. Murph could see the sky through the filter of the pine boughs as it shifted from navy to golden orange, heading for the icy blue of another spectacular morning in the Alps.

His earpiece clicked and Rick Neven's voice said, "Sentry station is unmanned. Bring them up."

"Roger." Murph led Carli and the old women forward. Bernie brought up the rear. They moved through the forest and arrived at the cave entrance. From the road, it appeared to be a solid wall of rock, covered with green moss in places. It looked like it had been undisturbed for centuries. Louisa pointed them around to the right, where a fissure opened up, allowing them to enter the musty, dark mouth of the cave. Murph hooded his flashlight with his hand and used it to illuminate the path for the others as they crept forward.

The fissure widened to a circular room where a metal door stood, painted dark gray to match the stone, hidden to the left side. There was an obvious position for a sentry, but the flagstone base was covered with lichen. On the opposite wall, another soldier could hide behind a low outcropping of rock to protect the primary sentry.

The Rangers were examining the door. The lock was solid, but the frame was showing signs of rust. Sgt. Wolfe tried the handle, but to no one's surprise, it was locked.

"Blow it." Neven gave the order. "We go in now."

Murph consulted with Louisa again. "Beyond the door is a short corridor that opens into the store room of the main cave."

Neven and the Rangers nodded their understanding. The explosive charge was quickly placed, and the lock on the door disintegrated with the force of the C4, the blast echoing in the narrow chamber. Wolfe kicked in the door, and the other Rangers tossed in flash-bang grenades. They charged in as soon as the concussion of the grenades passed.

The hallway was ten feet in length, and then opened into a fifty-foot room, now largely empty. There was a sharp crack of gunfire. The Rangers quickly dispatched their quarry, and Neven called Murph in.

He found Sgt Wolfe down at the end of the hall with a bullet wound in his left arm. Murph quickly knelt and examined the Ranger. The bullet had entered high in the shoulder but appeared to have missed the bone. Bernie Foa tore a sleeve off his shirt and handed it to Murph. He wrapped the wound in the black cloth of the priest's vestment and tied it tight to stop the bleeding. Bernie crouched down to assist the Ranger.

Murph guided Louisa and Valerie behind Bernie and indicated that they should stay put. Motivated though she was, it was amazing that Louisa had made the trek with them this far. In her frail condition, it took sheer will power, but she seemed committed to see this through.

The remaining Rangers were disarming three mercenaries on the far side of the room. One was down and not moving. The others stood with their hands behind their heads, assault rifles down on the ground. The gunfight had been short but savage. The training and skill of the Rangers had been too much for the hired guns, who had quickly lost interest in the cause.

Murph moved to Rick Neven's side, whispering. "That's three down. Two still unaccounted for." Neven nodded, pointing at the back of the cave. There was a wall of wood paneling, with a door in the middle. In front of the wall, to the far right side of the cave, an area had been converted to an office. There was a metal desk and gunmetal gray filing cabinets. To the left of the door was a kitchen with a sink, hand pump to bring water to the spring, hot plate and pantry cabinets. A round table and folding metal chairs completed the setting.

Rick Neven inched forward, crouched down, his Hechler and Koch MP 5 machine gun ready. Murph followed behind, with Carli on his left hip. Murph spotted the knob on the door begin to turn. Neven saw it as well, and they both froze.

The door creaked in its frame, opening slightly inward. Jean Buchanan peaked around the corner of the doorframe, smiled and then ducked back, flinging the door open wide.

Sgt. Wolfe pushed Bernie away and began to rise, reaching for his weapon, standing in front of the priest and the women. The other Rangers turned, but Neven and Murph blocked their line of fire.

Murph drew his pistol and shoved Carli to the ground, stepping in front of her. Neven took two strides and raised his rifle, aimed at the doorway, closing the distance quickly. Out of the corner of his eye, Murph saw Frank Buchanan step from behind the filing cabinet, appearing from the shadow with an assault rifle in his hands, barrel coming up toward level, aimed straight for Neven.

Murph yelled, "RICK" and went to one knee. He extended his arms, right arm straight out, left arm bent, left palm supporting his grip on the SIG Sauer. Without thinking, Murph fired as quickly as he could squeeze the trigger. His aim was true. Three bullets slammed into Frank Buchanan, his torso shaking with the impact of the 9 mm rounds. The former President was thrown backward into the filing cabinet, the rifle clattering to the ground. His legs collapsed, and his body slid down the face of the cabinet, ending up sitting on the floor, mouth open, eyes staring at Murph.

Rick Neven charged through the open doorway into the bedroom. There was a small dresser and nightstand. The thin mattress was on a metal bed frame with a brown military blanket carefully done up on the bed. Jean Buchanan was sitting calmly on the edge of the bed, her hands folded in her lap.

Murph ran over to Buchanan, kicking the rifle out of his reach. He knelt down and felt for a pulse at his neck. It was thready and fading.

Buchanan coughed, blood trickling out of the corner of his mouth. "All this because of a toothache!"

Murph just shook his head. "I told you that gloaters never prosper! But why??"

Buchanan smiled. His pupils dilated and he stared over Murph's shoulder at the bare bulb hanging from the ceiling. His head nodded forward, his chin resting on his chest. Frank Buchanan was gone.

Chapter 114

Carli picked herself up from the floor and came over to Murph as he reached down and closed Buchanan's eyes. She wrapped her arms around his shoulders and held him tight.

Murph put the pistol back into its holster and stood up, pulling her against his chest tightly. They stood quietly clinging to each other for a long moment. The adrenalin faded quickly, and the gravity of the situation descended on him.

"I've just shot the President," Murph sobbed.

Rick Neven grabbed his arm and shook him. "It's a damn good thing that you did! You saved my life. Thanks, Murph."

Sgt. Wolfe walked up, surveying the situation. "Excellent shooting, Doc. Three hits out of five shots fired." He bent down and examined the body, pointing at the logo on the windbreaker. "One shot right through the Great Seal of the President of the United States. Kind of symbolic. Rick Neven bent down and drew a knife from his boot. He used the tip to open the mouth of the body. "Missing a lower right molar. He's the fake one, all right."

Murph didn't need the verification. Frank Buchanan had been trying to shoot Neven. Murph had no choice to fire at him and, as Gabriel Levy had instructed, *don't shoot unless you intend to kill.* It was still a memory that would haunt Murph for the rest of his life.

Jean Buchanan was standing quietly outside the door of the bedroom, hands in her pockets. She seemed strangely unmoved by the carnage around her.

Murph stalked over to her and snarled, "Your husband is dead and you don't seem the least bit upset. What is it with you?"

Jean simply shrugged, dismissively. "He was merely a tool in the greater plan. His death is unfortunate but it does not change the course of events." She smoothed her hair. "From evil comes a greater good."

Murph resisted the urge to punch her. "You people keep saying that! What are you trying to do?" Murph swept his arm around the room, taking in the death and destruction, "From evil comes death! There is no good here!"

"You will see." She folded her arms across her chest, symbolically ending discussion.

"Your grandfather is dead." Murph played his trump card with as much force as possible. "Can any good come of that?"

It had the effect of slapping her in the face. Jean Buchanan staggered but caught herself, clenching her teeth, trying not to cry.

Murph pressed on the raw wound. "Yes, I know that Simon Cohen is your grandfather. He was shot by a Secret Service agent in the Treaty Room. His death has been covered up for now, until we can figure out your plan."

"But I spoke to him last night."

"It was by text. He told you that he couldn't talk because there were people in the White House who would overhear the conversation, yes?"

Her head dropped in resignation.

Murph continued. "When you called to have Capitano Liriano gloat about capturing Carli, I took his phone. I saw him enter his password, so we have been using the phone to text you. Margaret came into the White House to help mimic his style of conversation. While I was racing here, we tricked you into thinking I was still in DC."

A tear trickled down her cheek, but the fire of defiance returned to her eyes. "He was a great man, but his loss was inevitable. His vision will lead to the return of my people."

Murph looked deeply into her eyes, searching for something to work with. "He told me about the population of Jews in Europe and of the concept of *Rentrer*. His goal was to have the Jews return to Europe, but you have lost control of the US Presidency, and Simon Cohen is dead. How can your plans succeed now?"

"There is much that you know, but you still don't see. And you fail to understand!" She laughed—a cold, grating sound. "You can't stop it. When it happens, your President Buchanan will be forced to support it, just as *he* would have done." She pointed at Frank's body, crumpled on the floor.

"Your life is over. You will be taken into custody and you will disappear forever."

"You don't get it. It's not about me. This is about our people!" Jean smiled sweetly, "From evil will come a greater good!"

"Fine!" Murph realized that he had come to the end of what he was going to get from her. "We'll see what you have to say to other people more persuasive than me."

Murph took out his phone and dialed. "Are you in Susa?"

Rocco answered immediately. "Yes, we're here."

Murph gave the directions to the cave. "I have one guest for you for a while. Keep her on ice and see if she has any more to say."

It took only minutes, but to Murph it seemed like hours as his mind whirled. Rocco arrived and took Jean Buchanan into his care. Murph and Rocco secretly agreed that she would not be interrogated. Murph let her believe that Rocco was an agent outside of government control, who was not restricted in his interrogation techniques. When he left, Rocco also took the body of Frank Buchanan, wrapped tight so that no one could see who it was.

Rick Neven was surprised to release the First Lady, but he was secretly glad not to have that responsibility. "You're the boss!" he quickly admitted.

The choppers returned to pick up the Rangers and the remaining prisoners. The lead Blackhawk held Murph and Carli, with Valerie, Louisa, and Bernie Foa. Rick Neven and Sam Wells joined the group, so Neven could fill in his commander about the rest of the raid. It was a success, in that the Americans had been rescued safely and the immediate threat neutralized. There were only four wounded Rangers, none of which were seriously hurt.

The helicopters returned to Aviano Air Base quickly, and the local residents of Susa were left to wonder about the noise and commotion. Rocco helped foster the rumor that the Americans had conducted a drug raid. The convent was purported to have been used as a site to manufacture methamphetamine. The Vatican offered to take direct control of the property, and a new, brighter day for the eleventh century structure was planned.

Murph held Carli tight during the flight, while they compared notes on happened while they were apart. They landed sore and tired, but with a renewed sense of purpose. It was afternoon on Monday, and something terrible was about to happen. Rosh Hashanah was Wednesday. Israel was the key—of that Murph was sure. *But the key to what?*

Chapter 115

Upon landing at Aviano Air Base, medical treatment was provided for Lieutenant Schuster and the Rangers wounded in the raid. Private quarters were arranged for Louisa Perrin and Valerie David. Father Foa continued to provide support for the old women as they began to plan their future, making up for the seventy years they had lost.

Murph and Carli were in the briefing room, facing the withering stare of the base commander, General Travis Metcalf. They had been taken directly to the conference room with Captain Wells and Lieutenant Neven for the debriefing of the mission. Murph still had the green camouflage face paint smudged around his nose and chin, where he had not been able to completely clean it off without a mirror. Carli's hair was full of the white powder from the ruptured flour sack, now smeared with sweat on her face and ears.

The General was a career Air Force officer, having graduated from the Air Force Academy thirty-four years ago. At five-foot six, he was a bulldog of a man, built like a fireplug, but woefully short for the recruiting poster image of a fighter pilot. His hair was cut in a flattop, with gray flecks creeping into the brown of his sideburns. His ears were large, sticking out from the side of his head like an elephant. His ears were fiery, which was not a good look with the purple hue of his neck and the veins popping out of his forehead.

"Now let me get this straight," he barked. "You're a dentist, and you're a—well—a student, and you were on a raid with a Delta Force team that uncovered a plot to destabilize the world, but you don't know why! Have I got that right?"

Lt. Neven started to intervene, "General, I can explain…" Murph held up his hand to stop his friend, but then Metcalf cut them both off.

"That's enough out of you, Lieutenant. I'll deal with you and Wells in a minute." He turned to face Murph directly. "What do you have to say for yourself?"

Murph spread his hands wide, palms up, answering quietly, without emotion. "I am a dentist and my practice is in Washington, DC. It all began with the extraction of a suspicious tooth from a man calling himself Franklin Buchanan. That has led me to here. We have been shot at, bullied, nearly drowned, and chased all over the world. I have been forced to use deadly force and *I have had enough*. I just want this to be over. Rosh Hashanah is on Wednesday, and something terrible is supposed to happen." Murph placed his palms on the table, pushing himself up to his full height. He stared down at the General. "If it is in my power to stop the catastrophe, I will. General Metcalf, I would really appreciate your help, but I will go on without it if necessary."

Sam Wells muttered under his breath, "Jesus!"

Carli cringed, waiting for the blast. Neven leaned over, subconsciously getting out of the line of fire.

The General glared up at Murph but the dentist calmly looked back at him, regarding the commander patiently. Suddenly, the General's ruddy face split with a giant smile, and he burst out laughing. Shaking Murph's hand with gusto, he expressed his support. "Son, that took balls! I admire that kind of strength."

A voice came from the computer on the desk in front of the General. "See, Travis. I told you so! He's the real deal." General Metcalf turned the laptop around so they all could see the smiling face of Buck Buchanan. He was sitting behind the *Resolute* desk in the Oval Office. Margaret Farouk was behind him waving.

"Yeah, you were right. Just remember that I'm older than you. Even though you're President and everything, I taught you how to fly!" The General laughed, commenting to Murph. "I hate it when these bright young kids grow up and you have to salute them!"

Murph smiled, the tension receding from the room. "Hi, Buck. Hi, Margaret. How are things in Washington?"

"The usual. Confused and stressed." Buck leaned in toward the computer. "This is a secure line, so we can talk freely. Don't let anyone in the room there. Who are the Rangers with you?"

Murph pulled the officers into the view. "Captain Sam Wells and Lieutenant Rick Neven. They led the Delta Force team that rescued Carli and took the others."

"Congratulations, gentlemen. Job well done."

"Thank you, Sir."

Murph took out a pad and reviewed the notes he had been making since leaving Susa. "We don't have much time. Wednesday is only a little more than a day away."

Buck nodded. "So where do we stand?"

Murph tried to make his assessment as concise as possible. "Even though Cohen and the Pres...uh, Frank...are dead, Jean Buchanan still seems to think that their plans will proceed without change. Cyrille Bastien is unaccounted for. If we find him, we'll solve the mystery."

"What did she say?"

Murph scratched his nose, "She confirmed that this was all about 'her people.' We assume that this means Jews. Cohen was most insistent that he was a Jew but not Israeli. It would be safe to assume that his granddaughter would share that view. Their goal is to have Jews return to Europe—

383

rentrer. The question is how do they intend to make that happen, and why did it require taking over the presidency of the United States?"

Carli chimed in, "It seems that Israel is important. Cohen invested heavily in the complex at Atlit and had a major presence of mercenaries in the country. Just because we don't see any connection doesn't mean there isn't one?"

Murph reached out and rubbed the back of her neck. "I agree. In Israel, what facilities or organizations are under direct American control?"

General Metcalf piped up. "The only military asset in Israel is the US radar station at Mt. Keren, in the Negev Desert."

Buck agreed. "That's right. Travis, can you refresh my memory on Mt. Keren?"

"Sure thing. Mount Keren is a desert hilltop in southwestern Israel, five miles from the Egyptian border. About 100 US servicemen man a radar station there. They are the only foreign troops stationed in Israel. The portable X band radar is so advanced that it can spot a softball tossed in the air from 2,900 miles, and Tehran is only 1,000 miles away. The installation is capable of giving an advanced warning of a missile launch six or seven minutes before the Israeli's own radar, called Green Pine, would detect it. The earlier warning would give the Israelis 60% more time to sound the alarm and get people to shelters. It also allows a greater chance of launching interceptors to knock down the incoming missile before it reaches Israel. Then the wreckage of the missile would fall in the wasteland of the Jordanian desert instead of the heavily populated coastal plain. In the event of a miss, you might even get off another shot at the incoming missile."

"That's right." Buck tapped the table. "But it is up to the US officials to decide whether to share that information with the Israelis. The only people who see those radar screens are Americans. The information pipeline runs one way. No one could ever imagine a scenario where the Commander-in-Chief would choose to withhold an early warning that could save civilian lives of America's closest ally in the region—but he *could* give that order."

"Or he could have *already* given that order." Murph stood up, his chair falling backward to the floor with a crash. "If Cohen knew that the Iranians were planning a strike on Israel for Rosh Hashanah, he could have had his faux President issue the order to the commander at Mt. Keren not to inform the Israeli Defense Force of a missile launch. They could have even instructed them to deny a launch if contacted by the IDF, which would make the Israelis doubt their equipment, slowing their reactions further."

"Oh my God." Carli's hand was over her mouth in horror. "That kind of catastrophe would scare everyone in Israel, sending Jews fleeing the country—right back to Europe."

"From evil comes a greater good." Murph could see the plan with complete clarity. "They are willing to trade the lives of thousands of innocent Israelis to repopulate Europe with Jews."

Chapter 116

"General, " Murph consulted his pad, "Jean Buchanan seemed so sure that there was nothing I could do. Is there a way to have an order in place that could not be countermanded, no matter what happens?"

Metcalf considered this for a second. "It's possible to have an order that requires it to be rescinded in person, verbally, after proper authentication. Some of the nuclear launch orders are part of a series that, once the sequence is started, cannot be easily stopped."

"Who is in overall command of Mt. Keren?" Murph's pen scratched across his pad.

"CENTCOM. The Central Command includes the Med and Middle East. They're based at MacDill AFB in Tampa, FL. CENTCOM has command of us here, as well."

Buck said something to an aide off camera then turned back to Murph. "I'm going to make plans to go to MacDill on Wednesday for a surprise inspection. I can take direct control of the operations from there, if needed. Murph, I want you to go to Mt. Keren. Take General Metcalf with you. It's always nice to take a General along for muscle." Buck pointed into the camera for emphasis. "Personally size up the situation and make sure that the Israelis are notified if the Iranians, or anyone else for that matter, launches anything."

"Yes, Sir." Murph considered his options. "If it's OK with you, I would like to take Wells and Neven along too.

"Hell, yeah!" Neven blurted out. Wells whacked him in the arm. "Sorry, General."

"I like that enthusiasm, son!" General Metcalf began writing orders. "Go get your desert camo on and gear up. We're leaving as soon as we get an aircraft ready."

"Mr. President?" Carli's sweet voice cut through the commotion.

"Yes, Carli."

"I'd like your permission to go along to Tel Aviv. I know the Israeli Ambassador to the US and his wife, Shimon and Sarah Perski. We met at the State Dinner at the White House when Murph proposed. I could help them see what's going on without giving anything away."

Being a politician, Buck considered the possibilities. "Depending on what happens, it could be very valuable to have someone there to smooth things over diplomatically. Yes, I would like you to go. Make the arrangements to meet with Mr. Perski."

Murph whirled around. "But if there is a missile launch, you'll be right in the target area. You're staying right here, where you're safe!"

"It's a risk I need to take. You're going over there to stop it, I have to do my part."

"I lost you once and just got you back. I don't want to risk losing you again."

She hugged him. "Then be sure that no missiles get through." She leaned up on her tiptoes and kissed his cheek. "We're in this together. Nobody pushes us around!"

He relented, irritated at her stubborn nature but secretly admiring her courage. "Then let's get moving. We have a lot of planning to do."

* * * * * * *

Night was falling when they walked across the tarmac to the Air Force C-130 transport. They had not slept, but at least a shower brightened their mood considerably. Murph and Carli had hurried through the base exchange to purchase a change of clothing. Carli kept her black ballet flats and slacks, but added a new gray striped blouse, navy scarf and jean jacket. Murph was back in civilian black slacks and white sport shirt. In the evening chill, he proudly wore a black zip-front pullover given to him by the Rangers of the Delta Force team. He would always treasure it and the tan beret with the shield logo of the 75th Ranger Regiment. He had the beret safely stashed in his pack—a memento of his short time with the elite Army Rangers.

Carli wrinkled her nose at the sight of the plane. "Propellers?"

Murph could only shrug. "It's not a Gulfstream, but executive jets are hard to come by in the military. Hopefully, we will be able to sleep a bit on the flight."

Carli was not convinced, especially when she buckled in to the 'seat', which was little more than a canvas sling. Murph saw her frowning and leaned over.

"Remember, you wanted to come!" He kissed her on the cheek.

"Don't remind me!"

The flight was typical for a C-130, loud and bumpy. Carli and Murph were so tired that they hardly noticed, sleeping the entire way. It was not a restful sleep, but they were recharged when they landed in the pre-dawn darkness of Tel Aviv.

Murph had been in contact with Gabriel Levy prior to leaving Aviano. When the Americans had cleared Israeli customs, Murph met Gabriel. He was masquerading as a limo driver and was prepared to take Carli into the city for her meeting with Ambassador and Mrs. Perski.

Carli was quick to notice her familiar driver. "Gabriel?"

"At your service, ma'am."

She looked at Murph, her eyes narrowing. "I can handle myself!"

"I know. But it can't hurt to have a little extra help." Murph patted her on the back. "Besides, everyone likes a friendly face when they are in a foreign country."

Murph kissed her lightly and she was off into traffic.

General Metcalf was met by an Army Sergeant, who had been tasked with driving them out to Mt. Keren. They boarded the van and headed out of Ben Gurion Airport. The drive was less than two hours, the last hour in the vast tan wasteland that was the Negev Desert.

They arrived at the American installation, a series of concrete blast walls with the large rectangular radar peeking around the corners to see northeast into Iran. The guards manning the gate appeared casual enough, but Murph had been briefed by General Metcalf that they were really hand-picked members of the Israeli Defense Force in plain clothes. The sun was rising in the eastern sky, beating down on the desert. The temperature was rapidly rising through the eighties, right on the average for the middle of September.

Their access to the installation was swift. Having a two-star General and orders signed by the President opened any door quickly. Murph jumped out of the van and adjusted his sunglasses. The heat waves rippled over the yellow-brown desert surface. Wells and Neven piled out, as well, taking stock of the tight security at the installation.

Most of the staff there were guards for the facility. The information was fed directly to CENTCOM at MacDill.

Murph thought to himself that everything looks completely normal—too normal. It was Wednesday morning, but nothing appeared to be happening. Murph quickened his pace and caught up with General Metcalf.

"It's too quiet."

"Everything does seem routine here." Metcalf admitted. "Let's get inside and see what we find out."

They were ushered into office of the commander of the installation. Major Stockwell raced in, surprised to have a General making an unannounced visit.

He snapped to attention, his round, heavy rimmed glasses slipping down his nose. "General Metcalf. I'm pleased to see you." He really looked anything but pleased, but he was trying to recover. "But I have to admit that I'm confused. Why are you here?"

"Good. I'm glad you want to cut to the chase." Metcalf sat down heavily at Stockwell's desk. "Have you received any orders from the White House recently?"

The Army Major looked shocked. Murph thought to himself, *Whatever Stockwell was afraid the General had come to investigate, this wasn't it.*

"Not really. There was an NSA communiqué that asked us to track possible Arab terrorists crossing the border into Israel. That was a couple of weeks ago now." He stammered through his answer.

"Nothing about with-holding information from the Israelis?"

"No, Sir." Stockwell shook his head vigorously. "We couldn't do that here. Any communication between the Israelis and us goes through CENTCOM. That information is processed at MacDill AFB. It's not my call."

Metcalf looked impassive. Murph frowned behind Stockwell's back. "Major, did you see anything crossing the border."

Stockwell turned to face Murph, thinking he must be CIA. "Yes, Sir. There were several collections of Arabs that were suspicious. We turned that info over to the NSA through regular channels. I can get you the tape if you like."

Murph waved him off. "No, that's fine. I'll take your word for it."

A soldier ran down the hall and stuck his head in the office, spotted the General and snapped to attention. "Major?"

"Yes, Private."

"Is there an Agent Murphy here?"

Murph's eyes widened. "That would be me."

"CENTCOM's on the line for you. It's the President!"

Stockwell threw up his hands, "Then put him through, for God's sake."

"Yes, Sir." The private raced back down the hall then the phone on the desk rang.

Murph picked up the receiver. "Murphy."

"Yes, Sir. Please hold for the President."

The line clicked, and Buck was there. "Murph?"

"Yes, Sir."

"Any news at Mt. Keren?"

"No orders here, other than to report Arab incursions across the Israeli border."

"That may be it. I was watching TV coverage from Israel here for any signs and then saw her."

"Her?" Murph was confused.

"The woman who came and questioned me when I was held at Atlit. Her name is Ariella Joffe. She's an Israeli TV reporter. Kind of like the Israeli Katie Couric. We did some checking on her. She was a beauty queen when she was a teen, competing for her native Slovenia. She's a former Mossad agent who became a news anchor when she retired."

"That fits the profile of a European Jew."

"She's part of the group. Her current stories are about Arab/Muslim groups carrying weapons across the border into Israel to destabilize the Palestinian Israeli peace."

"I'll see what we can do from here."

"Thanks, Murph. I'll stay in close contact here at CENTCOM."

Murph hung up the phone and looked at the General. "We're looking in the wrong place!"

Chapter 117

Murph shoved Major Stockwell out of his own office and shut the door. Facing General Metcalf and the two Rangers, he passed along the news from the President.

"General, I need you to stay here, in case something happens that we need to address, plus you have access to the best communications in the region."

"Agreed."

"I need to get back across the Negev as fast as possible. Their plan is to create as much public havoc as possible, and here in the Negev is far too remote. They don't need an Iranian missile attack. They just need it to look like an Arab attack! Then the US issues a press release confirming that Arabs were tracked crossing the border to cause trouble in Israel. Once that video is released to the press, the US can't retract it. The blame will be spread on the Arabs, and the US will be complicit in that, even though we now control all the official channels. Cohen's billion dollar media empire is tough to stop once it's programmed and moving."

Sam Wells considered Murph's assessment. "I think you're right. But where will they attack? Israel isn't a big country, but we have to start looking somewhere."

"Someone once told me that Jerusalem is like a toy that kids fight over. It is one of the most revered holy sites for Jews, Muslims, and Christians. They all want it and will fight to the end to control it. If I were a Jew—but didn't care about the land in Israel, destroying Jerusalem would have a huge impact in the region—utter mayhem. And, blaming the Muslims would create sympathy for the poor Jews."

"That's really whacked out!" Neven's eyes crossed as he tried to comprehend it all.

"No, think of it from Cohen's perspective." Murph slowed down and put himself in the old man's shoes. "The last time something truly terrible happened to the Jews, the Holocaust killed over seven million of them and drove the rest out of their homes in Europe. The world felt sorry for them and created the nation of Israel to give them some place to go."

"From evil comes a greater good." Metcalf rubbed his jaw in amazement.

"So if I explode a small dirty nuclear device in Jerusalem and blame the Arabs, a wave of Jews will leave Israel and I—Cohen, that is, with my media empire—will be at the ready to welcome then 'back home' in Europe." Murph pulled out his phone as he was finishing his thought. "Cohen bought so many apartment buildings across western Europe so they would have someplace to go."

"Brilliant, terrible, and certifiably crazy—all at the same time." Wells shook his head in disbelief.

"We've got to get going." Murph tapped Rick on the shoulder. "Get us our driver back, and make sure the van has plenty of gas."

He dialed his iPhone. Gabriel Levy answered on the first ring.

"Gabriel, do you know Ariella Joffe?"

"Yes, she's a TV reporter—but she was also Mossad."

"Exactly. I have a positive ID that she was the woman who interrogated the prisoner at Atlit. She's part of the plot. We need to find her—NOW!"

"Carli just finished her breakfast with the Ambassador and his wife. We'll get on it right away and find Joffe."

"Good, I'm leaving Mt. Keren now." Murph considered whether he should talk over the phone, but speed trumped security at this point. "If you wanted to place a bomb in Jerusalem, where would you put it to do the most damage?"

Chapter 118

The drive from Mt. Keren to Jerusalem took just under two tedious hours, through the desert, up the coastal plain, then into the mountains. Murph phoned Carli and explained his theory. As much as she was horrified, she had to admit that it made sense.

Carli had found Ambassador Perski receptive to her concerns and story. She felt that he would offer any help they requested. Murph was becoming convinced that the Israelis deserved to know what he feared.

Gabriel informed Murph that his contacts had located Ariella Joffre at her TV studio. He and Carli were going to pay her a visit.

Murph then called Buck. It seemed odd to have the direct cell phone number to the President of the United States. With no time for pleasantries, as soon as Buck answered, Murph got right to the point.

"Buck, we have to tell them. They deserve to know."

"I've never met the man before. What a way to start? I have a rogue billionaire who is out to destroy the second largest city in your country. Have a nice day."

"That's one way to do it. However, it is a credible threat. The better way is to leave out any references to the faux President and concentrate on the billionaire. Start with: *I have been made aware of a credible threat of an attack on Jerusalem. It may be a nuclear attack. I have agents in Israel working on the problem. We can assist each other if you would like the help.* Then see what he says."

"That's a great approach. Have you ever considered a career in politics?"

"Not a chance!" Murph laughed. "Dentistry is much simpler – and safer. Don't get distracted. Just call Netenyahu!" Murph hung up the phone for emphasis.

* * * * * * *

Gabriel Levy parked in back of the local production office of Israeli Channel 2, deep in the heart of Tel Aviv. The building was a six-story concrete high rise, like the thousands of others that populated the capital city. Gabriel and Carli entered the lobby and paused at the desk, asking to see Ariella Joffe.

The receptionist called up, but Ariella responded that she was busy editing a story and they should make an appointment. Carli told the receptionist to tell Ariella that she had come from America to speak with her about her story on the *Rentrer*.

The receptionist promptly came back with the message that Ariella would be right down. Gabriel excused himself to go out to the car and make a call. Three minutes later, the phone at the reception desk rang. With obvious surprise, the perky receptionist said that Ariella wanted Carli to come right up to her office. She gave Carli the number and buzzed her in through the security door.

Carli reached the third floor office, knocked and let herself in. She found Ariella Joffre, her eyes wild with anger, sitting at her desk. Gabriel Levy sat calmly in a chair behind her, cradling a pistol menacingly in his hand.

"Our TV star decided she had to run a quick errand," he remarked casually. "She was heading for her car, but I convinced her to come back up and talk to you."

Carli smiled. "Excellent."

She entered the room and sat on the edge of the desk, carefully out of Gabriel's line of fire. In case anyone walked by in the hall, it looked like two girlfriends chatting about life at the office.

Carli's eyes turned hard and the corners of her smile leveled. "We don't have much time, so here it is. Simon Cohen is dead. So is Frank Buchanan. Jean Buchanan is in custody. The chance of your plan succeeding is nonexistent. There will be no *rentrer*—no coming home for your people. How would you like to help us, and save yourself in the process?"

Ariella sneered. "You know nothing, and I will not help you."

"That's about what I expected." Carli crossed her arms, waiting. "I think we should take her to Jerusalem so that she can film the end of the story herself." She started to get up.

"Wait!" Ariella's dark eyes widened into saucers. "I can't do anything. Cyrille will kill me."

"Bastien is our problem, and we'll have him soon. Tell me what your part of the plot is, for a start, then we'll see what use you can be." Carli leaned down close to her and whispered, "you may have been a beauty queen, but fear is not becoming. The sickly green color in your face doesn't do you any favors."

Ariella nervously pulled at her hair with her perfectly manicured nails. "I will show you the video we have prepared. That will explain everything."

Chapter 119

Murph's phone rang as they approached the outskirts of Jerusalem.

"Hi, Carli. I'm almost to Jerusalem."

"Then be careful. That's where they intend to explode the bomb."

"So we were right."

"Gabriel and I had a chat with Ariella. She's not nearly as committed to the cause as the others." Carli sighed. "She has a video package all ready to run as soon as the disaster occurs. It contains the images from Mt. Keren of the Arabs crossing the border with the nuclear device. It shows surveillance video of the team of Muslims bringing the device into Jerusalem. All they need is the carnage to complete the story. They have cameras already in place to record the blast and its effects. Oh, Murph, you were right. You have to get out of there."

"No. I have to try to stop it." Murph looked at Wells and Neven, who had heard every word. They nodded in agreement. "Rick and Sam are with me."

"But I'm afraid we're too late."

"Rosh Hashanah is the Jewish Day of Judgment. On this day, Jews seek forgiveness and clean the slate to start a new year. All I have to do is find the bomb and keep it from going off, or we all will be asking forgiveness directly!"

Carli was crying. "Don't make jokes!"

"Do you remember when we were in the Vatican? I know… it seems like years ago. We were with the little man in the white robes."

"Yes, of course."

"Then what did he say?"

"I…uh, I'm not sure."

"He said, 'Remember, The Lord is my shepherd, I shall not want. Though I walk through the valley of the shadow of death, I will fear no evil for You *are* with me.' I don't fear evil now, for I know that He is with me, guiding my hands."

"You expect God to tell you where the bomb is?"

"No. I don't see God's involvement in my life that way. In the Bible, the clouds would part and a booming voice would tell me where to search." Murph laughed, his heart suddenly very light. "I know that as long as I stay on the right path, I will feel at peace. If it is His will, the Lord will guide me. However, this is the Holy Land after all, so a bit of direct assistance would be nice."

"Oh, Murph!"

"Caroline Chamoun, I love you, and I'm going to spend the rest of my life with you. Wait for me there, and say a prayer for us. It's time for me to find Cyrille. I have a score to settle with him."

"I love you, too." Tears moistened her phone. "Just hurry back." But he was already gone.

Chapter 120

Jerusalem, located on a plateau in the Judean Mountains, remains one of the oldest cities in the world. During its long history, Jerusalem has been destroyed twice, besieged 23 times, attacked 52 times, and captured and recaptured 44 times. As they descended out of the mountains with Jerusalem spread out on the plain before them, Murph felt that he was entering the valley of death—for, indeed, death lurked somewhere in the walled city.

Searching Jerusalem, the sacred center of Judaism for roughly 3,000 years—of Christianity for around 2,000 years—and of Islam for approximately 1,400 years—with a population of 800,000 people was going to be like hunting for a needle in a haystack.

Their driver pulled the van over at the entrance of the city. Sam Wells was considering the map of Jerusalem on his phone. "Where would you like to start?"

Murph had been thinking about this. "If I were Bastien, the only place I would get the most emotional impact would be in the Old City. Now would be a good time for divine intervention, but let's start there."

Murph reached for the latch on the door, but it opened for him from the outside. A young man in rumpled khaki slacks, an olive t-shirt and tousled black bushy hair reached for his hand. "Dr. Murphy?"

"Yes." Murph pulled his hand back sharply.

"Do not be concerned. The Prime Minister sent us. My name is Avi." He shook Murph's hand. "We must hurry."

Sam and Rick moved to get out, but Avi asked them to wait.

"Your friends look too much like American soldiers. They would attract attention and slow us down. They must remain here."

Murph didn't like this, but it made sense. He needed confirmation, texting Buck quickly as he explained to the Rangers to wait with the van. If he failed, there was no use running. They were all too close to the bomb now.

Murph moved off with Avi as his phone chirped. "Netenyahu sending help to meet you in Jerusalem. Good hunting!"

Murph turned his phone on silent and checked the magazine on his SIG pistol. It contained a full 10 shots. He verified the safety and secured it in his waistband at the small of his back.

"Alright, Avi, where are we going?"

Avi ran to a waiting car, putting Murph in the passenger seat while he drove. "We begin at the most likely site. The Wailing Wall."

Avi drove like a man possessed, through the narrow alleys and streets of the ancient city. The residents of Jerusalem were blissfully unaware of the potential tragedy that awaited them. However, the city had an ever-present feeling of unease. Everyone seemed to be watching everyone else. The volatile mix of Jews, Christians, and Muslims created a tinderbox that was always smoldering just short of a full-blown fire. Tension was the rule.

The heat and humidity today added fuel to the fire. It was still late in the summer season, with a high well into the eighties. Rosh Hashanah was a high holiday, with the Jews wearing light, bright, happy colors to synagogue. Murph's challenge was to find Cyrille Bastien, the troll among the revelers, in the crowded city.

"My men are in position in the Old City. What does this Bastien look like?"

Murph described the bald-headed, bug-eyed troll in as clear terms as he could. Avi alerted his men and parked his car as close to the Wailing Wall as possible.

Avi led Murph into the plaza in the Jewish quarter, and Murph stopped. Standing 62 feet high, the sand color of the huge limestone blocks took his breath away. The sages said that praying at the base of the wall was valuable for "it is as if a man has prayed before the throne of glory because the gate of heaven is situated there and it is open to hear prayer."

Amid the bustling commotion of thousands of visitors, Murph closed his eyes and opened his mind. *Lord, help me!* He opened his eyes again, seeing the ancient wall. The golden dome of the basilica, the Dome of the Rock, appeared over the edge of the Wailing Wall. The al-Aqsa Mosque was also in view, and Murph could feel the presence of Jesus. This was the center point of the confluence of the religions. The corner stone of the Dome of the Rock, the Foundation Stone, was the most contested piece of real estate on earth, revered by Christians, Muslims, and Jews. He knew that it was here they would place the bomb.

Murph turned slowly around, scanning the crowd, his eyes squinting into thin slits.

Avi peered in all directions as well. "The bombers try to infiltrate a group to inflict the maximum casualties." He touched his earpiece. "My men do not see him. It seems to be a normal crowd for the holiday. There are no Muslims here."

"That's it!" It hit Murph like a bolt of lightning. "We've been looking for suicide bombers. But Bastien is not Muslim, and he is not here to commit suicide. They are Jewish and intend to live!"

Avi stared at Murph, not yet comprehending.

Murph grabbed him by the shoulders. "Tell you men the bomb is here, but the man who placed it is gone. We aren't seeking a person. We are looking for something big enough to hold the bomb that is just sitting here."

Murph scanned the plaza with new eyes. "Probably near the side where the Dome of the Rock or the mosque could be destroyed as well."

The base of the wall was covered with Jews praying. Some were placing scraps of paper with written prayers into cracks in the limestone. The floor of the plaza had wooden desks and chairs, where people were writing out prayers. The spaces under the desks and tables were deeply shadowed. A bomb would hide perfectly well here. It was probably only the size of a suitcase.

But residents of Jerusalem were highly sensitized to packages left unattended. If the bomb were under a desk, there was a high probability that it would be discovered quickly, foiling Bastien's plans to get away far enough.

Rejecting the floor of the plaza as too crowded, Murph looked up, along the line made by the top of the wall. He began tracing the parapet with his finger. He passed over the top of the Israeli flag, flying in the plaza. He could see the golden dome to his left and the al-Aqsa mosque to his right.

No one seemed to have access to the top of the wall, and yet there was a movie camera on a tripod. A lone cameraman slowly panned the video camera across the square. The logo of Israeli Channel 2 was visible in the distance.

Camera!

"Avi. When did they place TV cameras to film the Wailing Wall?"

"Dr. Murphy. There are no cameras here. Even for security. It is a holy place."

"Exactly." Murph began to run, pulling Avi with him, pointing. "There is a video camera on a tripod on top of the wall. It is up high, with a clear path to destroy the Dome of the Rock and the al-Aqsa Mosque, as well as the Wailing Wall and the entire Old City."

Avi recognized the danger immediately and called for support. Murph and Avi ran, climbing the ancient steps out of the plaza to the top of the wall.

Murph pulled out his phone as they ran. "Carli, tell Ariella that I've found a camera crew on the Wailing Wall. Is it theirs?"

Carli could hear their feet stepping quickly and Murph's labored breathing. She got the answer as quickly as she could.

"Murph, she says they never planned to have a crew film in Jerusalem. They have several remote cameras in the mountains to catch the mushroom cloud for maximum effect."

"That settles it, then." He put away the iPhone and lengthened his stride, climbing the stairs three at a time, with Avi close behind.

They burst suddenly onto the limestone surface that was the top of the wall of the old temple. The cameraman was stunned, turning quickly toward them. He reached for a silver suitcase lying on the ground beside the camera. Avi raised his pistol and expertly shot the cameraman with one shot to the forehead. The body fell backward and rolled off the top of the wall, falling to the plaza below. The screams of the faithful started a general panic, with people racing from the square.

Murph continued running to the camera and bent down. His suspicions were confirmed by a red light blinking ominously on the silver case, where a lock should have been.

"Do not touch it!" Avi shouted.

Murph sat back on his haunches, powerless to do anything, staring death in the face. Avi arrived to stand with him, guarding the bomb.

Minutes later, the bomb squad of the Israeli Defense Force ran up beside them. The lead technician turned to Murph. "Good work. You found the bomb. Now get out of here, and let me do my job. There's nothing more you can do."

Murph reached out and held his shoulder. "I can't possibly run fast enough or far enough to get to safety. If it's OK with you, I think I'll just stay here and pray."

The tech smiled. "That will make two of us!" He lowered his blast visor and moved ahead, joined by the remaining member of the squad.

With nothing else to do, Murph walked over to the Western Wall and sat down, his feet dangling over the edge. He closed his eyes and thought of Carli, seeing her face—sparkling green eyes and sly smile.

He opened his mind to form a prayer, but nothing would come. *Go back to the beginning.* He made the sign of the cross and recited slowly, savoring the words:

Lord, teach me to be generous.
Teach me to serve *you* as *you* deserve;
To give and not to count the cost,
To fight and not to heed the wounds,
To toil and not to seek for rest,
To labor and not to ask for reward,
Save that of knowing that I do *your* will.

Murph sat on the wall, his eyes closed, tears streaming down his cheeks, hands clasped tightly in his lap. The world spun around him. He felt at peace, for he was not alone.

Chapter 121

Murph nearly fell off the wall, turning to face Avi as the Israeli was shaking him by the shoulder. He helped Murph to his feet then embraced him, squeezing the air out of him.

"The technicians disarmed the bomb! We are safe!"

Murph looked up to Heaven. "Thank you!"

The team on top of the Wailing Wall was leaping for joy. Murph found the bomb technician and hugged him. They embraced quietly for a moment, and then Murph congratulated him on his bravery. The technician thanked Murph for the prayers. Both agreed in giving thanks to God.

Avi was pleased to drive Murph back to the outskirts of Jerusalem. They met Sam and Rick, who were relieved and not a little bit surprised to see Murph again.

"Boy, am I glad to see you!" Rick slapped Murph on the back.

"It was dicey, but we found the bomb before sundown and they disarmed it. It wasn't a powerful nuclear device, but it would have made a mess of Jerusalem."

Murph had Sam call the general and have the driver set a course for Tel Aviv. He had a few personal calls to make.

The call to Carli was quick. She was relieved. Tears were flowing, so he promised to see her soon. Murph then called Buck to report that the crisis had passed. They were planning to return to Aviano as soon as possible, then Murph and Carli would return to Washington.

Buck had already heard the good news from the Israelis. Murph was a hero in the country, but no one would ever know his name or how close Jerusalem had come to disaster.

Murph confided in Buck that his only concern was that Cyrille Bastien was loose. Murph believed that he would have been safely away from Jerusalem when the bomb detonated, which meant he could be anywhere. Buck promised the full power of the US to hunt him down and bring him to justice.

General Metcalf called Murph to say that he was ordered to stay on for a few days to monitor the situation. He would find Murph the next time he was in DC and buy him a drink— and a big steak.

Murph agreed with Gabriel Levy to meet at Ben Gurion Airport. Given the events of the past day, Murph, Carli, Sam and Rick were given a free pass through customs and allowed out to the waiting C-130.

Murph embraced Gabriel, thanking him for looking after Carli.

"I will see you soon in DC, my friend. I have loose ends to tie here in Israel."

"Agreed. We'll take a long bike ride and enjoy the peace and quiet."

The sun was setting, turning the matte gray paint of the C-130 transport black in the shrinking light. The windows of the airport glistened in gold, along with the concrete sides of the buildings in Tel Aviv. It was a beautiful night as Murph and Carli walked out to the plane, arm in arm.

Murph helped Carli buckle in as before. Wells and Neven settled in as well, facing forward. The four propellers began to spin, and the flight crew began raising the loading ramp at the tail of the aircraft.

Out of the corner of his eye, Murph spotted a hunched figure turn and run away from the tail. He quickly released his buckle and ran toward the rear door. "Bastien!"

"Wait!" The flight engineer shouted, but Murph continued running.

Murph turned over his shoulder, "Stop the plane! Everybody off!"

The ramp was closing, but Murph jumped on the gate and rolled off the side, landing on his feet. He reached behind his back and drew the SIG pistol.

Murph came around the end of the fuselage, under the tail of the plane. A man lunged out of the shadow, his fist striking Murph on the side of his head, spinning him around. The pistol tumbled out of his hand. As he looked for the gun,

403

Murph ducked and missed a second blow, but he felt a rope encircle his neck. Bastien had impersonated part of the ground crew, pulling the rubber wheel chocks to allow the plane to move. The rope connecting the two rubber triangles that prevented the wheels from rolling was now being used as a garrote to strangle Murph.

Bastien's pulled the dentist back against his chest, putting his lips against Murph's ear.

"Amateur! Did you really think you could beat a professional like me?" He tightened his grip. "Your luck ends now!"

Murph's vision began to blur, the edges turning red as the blood pressure increased in his head. He could see a glimmer of light growing behind him. *They're opening the rear door!*

Murph set his feet on the ground and lunged backward, slamming Cyrille's head against the metal ramp as it came down. Murph jumped again and there was another satisfying clang as Bastien struck the airplane. Murph was rewarded as the pressure on the rope released. He stamped down on Bastien's instep and swung back with his elbow to the assassin's ribs. Murph broke free, rolling to the ground, pulling the rope off of his neck.

Murph leaped up, swinging the rubber chocks at Bastien. They missed, but it bought Murph time to spot his pistol on the ground, where he had dropped it. Murph swung again. Bastien parried the blow with his long arm, the rope wrapping around Bastien's wrist. Cyrille pulled the rope out of Murph's hands. Rather than fight to hold the rope, Murph threw the end at Bastien.

The sudden lack of resistance left Bastien off balance. He stepped back and slipped on a patch of oil on the tarmac. Murph dove for the pistol, grabbed it and rolled over, coming up kneeling with his arms extended. Bastien reached into his pocket, backing into the deep shadow of the wing as he pulled his gun.

Murph fired three shots in rapid succession. The muzzle flashed from Bastien's gun as well—once down at the ground, then once at Murph. Murph could feel the searing pain in his side, where the bullet had hit him just above the left hip. He fired again at the retreating shadow, which staggered. Bastien lurched to the right, directly into the spinning propeller blade, spattering Murph with blood.

So much for being a professional! I'll take good luck. Murph thought. *And I'm always thankful for divine providence!*

The ramp was nearly down. Wells and Neven jumped over the side, guns drawn. Murph fell over, clutching his left side but still holding the SIG with his right hand. His left hand was covered in blood when Neven reached him.

"Where are you hit?

Murph reached up and grabbed Neven by the collar. "Get everyone off the plane!" It came out as a croak. "He planted a bomb!"

"What?"

"I saw him place something under the fuselage. It's got to be a bomb." Murph struggled to his feet, leaning on Neven. Murph put his arm over Rick's shoulder but his left leg was dragging.

Neven shouted over the engine noise. "There's a bomb on the plane! Get everyone away!"

Carli came down the ramp and looked at Murph. His face was spattered with blood, but the color was white. He smiled through gritted teeth, "Hi, Honey!"

"Just hold on, we're going to get you help."

"We've got to get away from the plane." He grabbed Carli with his free hand and led them all toward the lights of the terminal.

The engines began to stop, so the pilot had gotten word. Murph felt better as he saw the crew exiting the plane. The red lights and sirens heralded the arrival of medical assistance. Neven lowered Murph to the ground as Carli supported his head in her lap.

"Hang on, Murph. They're almost here" She kissed him on the forehead.

"Don't worry," he smiled weakly, "I've got plans for a wedding."

Murph saw her smile, her green eyes twinkling before the world faded to black.

Chapter 122

Beep...beep...beep. Murph heard the incessant, mechanical beep, forcing itself into the fog, piercing the silence as he wandered through the pine forest. He was looking for something. A cave? He pried his eyes open and turned. His vision was blurry but began to clear as he could make out the source of the irritation. The heart monitor registered 66 beats per minute. He followed the cords down, over the bed rail, and under the covers.

He started to roll over and felt the searing pain in his left side. *Bastien! Now I remember.* He fought to sit up but fell back as his heart rate spiked up suddenly. *Beep...beep... beep.* He felt the touch of a warm, smooth hand squeezing his fingers.

"Hey, sleepy! Welcome back!"

Murph raised his heavy eyelids and stared into emerald green eyes, slightly too large for her face, but the most beautiful sight he could remember. He was mesmerized.

"For as long as you have been sleeping, you could at least say something?"

Murph just smiled, content. "I'm just happy looking at you!" He tightened his grip on her hand.

"It's good to have you back. You had me worried there for a while."

"What day is it?"

"It's only Thursday afternoon. You were in surgery last night, and they kept you pretty well drugged today." Carli went to the window and drew up the blinds, revealing the ice blue sky and the golden mountains. "If you had to get shot,

Tel Aviv has some of the best medical care in the world. The docs seem to be impressed with what a tough guy you are!"

"I'm not tough—just persistent—or stubborn, depending on how you want to look at it." Murph pushed himself up on his elbows to get a better look at Carli. She stood there in profile against the window.

Carli winked at him. "You're plenty tough enough for me!"

"Bastien?" He hated to bring it up, but he had to know.

"You shot him at least twice. Then he stumbled into the propeller blade. He's gone." Carli shuddered at the memory of the bald assassin.

"Good. No more loose ends!"

"Well, there are a few things you'll need to deal with when you get up and around."

"How's that?"

"When they examined the plane, they did find the bomb Bastien had planted in the wheel well. Sadly, the pilot also found two bullet holes in his C-130. When you get back to Aviano, there's a Colonel Sheehy that plans to buy you a drink for saving everyone's life, but the Air Force may send you a bill for damaging government property."

Murph started to laugh, stopping short when the pain hit. "I think we know a couple people who could make that bill go away."

Carli sat on the edge of the bed. "Sam Wells and Rick Neven had to go back to Aviano this morning, but they told me to tell you one thing."

"What's that?"

"If you insist on continuing to use that pistol, they need to teach you how to shoot like a Ranger." She grinned. "They're going to take you out on the firing range and improve your accuracy. Beginners luck only goes so far!"

"And I thought I was doing so well!"

"I think you're doing great!" She kissed him, holding him for a long time.

"When do I get out of here?"

407

"Murph, I…well," Carli struggled with the words.

"Just tell me."

"Murph, you nearly lost your left kidney. The bullet tore things up quite a bit. You lost a lot of blood."

Murph sat quietly, holding Carli tight. "That's OK. You have two kidneys for a reason. If that one doesn't make it, at least I have a spare."

He forced himself upright, lifted her chin with his hand and looked into her eyes. "I just want to be with you. Let's go home as soon as I can. It's only one more scar, and…

"What?" She could see the smirk on his face.

"Chicks dig scars, right!?"

Carli threw her head back, laughing. "You're impossible!"

"But you love me anyway!" He pulled her down into his arms.

"Yes…YES, I do."

Chapter 123

All it took was a couple of days for Murph to begin to drive the staff at the Tel Aviv Sourasky Medical Center crazy. He was up and around, pacing the halls. They were amazed at the American's quick recovery and just as happy to see him go. They had no idea the cause of his wound, simply believing him to be another victim of gun violence. He probably deserved to get shot anyway, they thought.

Murph had arranged for Derek Whitman to pick them up in the G-550, whisking them quickly home to Washington. As soon as they were in DC, their presence was requested at the White House.

Murph returned to his condo, showered and shaved to be presentable. He selected dress jeans, a pale gray open-collared shirt, and black blazer. Carli arrived, casual yet elegant, in a little black dress with a coral sweater and kitten heels.

She studied Murph, noticing the loose fit of his jeans. "You've lost weight!"

"I was hoping my blazer would hide that."

"It will from everyone but me." Her tone was scolding, but she understood his pride. "You'll be back to normal in no time."

"It's been a rough couple of weeks." He forced himself to stand tall. "Exciting, though!"

"You could call it that."

He grabbed his keys off the desk. "Let's go see the President!"

* * * * * * *

It was a short drive, and they breezed through security. Agent Collins met them at the entrance, giving both of them a warm hug. The other agents and staff were awestruck, but the reunion was sweet, and Murph didn't care what anyone thought.

They were led directly to the Treaty Room, where Buck had dinner set for them. Buck embraced Carli, and she kissed him on the cheek. He grabbed Murph in a bear hug and it was all Murph could do not to cry out with the pain in his side. Buck could see his face tighten and apologized for forgetting the injuries in his excitement.

Murph and Carli were introduced to Buck's little girls, Laura and Blakely, who were a delight. Clearly, they were enjoying getting to know their father better, and Buck was determined to make up for the lost time. After dinner, the girls went off to bed.

Buck poured a glass of Jameson for Murph and then one for himself. Murph contemplated the amber liquid, savoring the whiskey. Carli continued to sip her white wine from dinner. Murph led Carli to the couch, sitting next to her. Buck chose the leather armchair and sat down.

"Thank you, Sir. The dinner was excellent!" Murph patted his stomach. "Much better than hospital food."

"Nothing but the best for you two. If not for you, I'd still be rotting in that condo in Haifa, waiting for Ariella Joffre to come question me."

Murph sipped his Jameson. "How is Ariella doing?"

Carli smiled. "She has been most cooperative. She's doing feature pieces, highlighting the low Jewish population in Europe, especially in France, Italy and Germany. Ariella is trying to entice Jews to consider immigration to countries in the European Union."

Buck nodded. "A foundation has been created to assist Jews and others who want to immigrate to Europe. The Vatican is using its considerable resources to help administer the funds and the property. The Simon Cohen Foundation has been created to spread his wealth to help those in Europe who need homes."

"It's designed to be self sustaining." This had been Carli's project while Murph was recuperating. He could sense her excitement and passion. "The apartments are not given away. The rent is subsidized, so that it's affordable, but the immigrants have to be committed. They have a stake in the game, so they will take care of the property. The rent they pay allows the money in the foundation to go farther and help more people."

"The work has only just begun, but I think it has real promise." Buck smiled. "Between Carli and Father Foa at the Vatican, it had been well planned and administered from the start."

Carli blushed. "I'm pleased to be able to help give people a fresh start in life. Cohen's plot was evil, but the spirit of *rentrer* has merit. Cohen's billions have a chance to make a difference."

Murph reached over and held her hand. "This honors the dreams of Father Gaspard. I know he would have approved."

Carli nodded, her eyes filled with tears. "I think so, too."

Murph turned to Buck and indicated through the window to the flag at half-mast. "I understand you are in mourning again."

Buck sighed. "Yes, while visiting Italy, Jean Buchanan was involved in a tragic car accident. Her vehicle was hit and tumbled off a cliff in the Cottian Mountains. She was killed instantly. It's been easy to look sad. It's wonderful being reunited with the girls, but I miss Gayle, my wife, even more now "

"But Jean is really...?" Murph asked for Carli, as she was shocked by the news.

"Jean is alive. She was transferred to Israel. They tried her quickly in a secret court. It didn't take long, since she was unrepentant. From what I was told, she remains defiant." Buck shook his head. "She was sentenced to life in prison and is somewhere in Israel, hidden from view..."

"Good. I'm glad she is no longer our problem. That's one less loose end." Murph ticked off his first finger. "I saw that Simon Cohen's death was reported as a heart attack. With the foundation started, his legacy is ensured." A second finger counted.

Buck agreed. "We know how twisted he was, but there's no need to step on a man's grave."

Murph sipped the whiskey, the liquid burning as he swallowed. "When you know his whole story, I understand his point of view. I don't agree with what he did, but I can see it from his place. In this case, from his evil we have been able to create a greater good."

"I'm glad of that." Carli was pleased.

She always likes happy endings! Murph thought.

Murph ticked another finger. "Bastien is dead. Frank Buchanan is dead."

Buck held up his hand. "Let me stop you there. We did a DNA analysis and the imposter was really a Jew from Ukraine named Grigory Abramov. He looked a lot like me in the first place. With some plastic surgery, he became a suitable imposter. They even changed his fingerprints."

Murph laughed. "But they forgot to look in his mouth. Too bad for them he had rotten teeth."

411

"No, that's really good for us." Buck stood up and poured more Jameson for himself and Murph.

"Thanks." Murph accepted the refill. "That's it for loose ends!"

Buck sat down heavily, resting his forearms on his knees, rolling the tumbler of whiskey between his hands. "There's one more."

Murph could tell the President was troubled. "What's that, Buck?"

"Should I resign from the Presidency? I have the chance to go now. In the eyes of the public, I've just lost my second wife. That's two tragedies in three years. No one would criticize me for wanting to leave Washington to be with my daughters."

Murph moved to the edge of the couch, staring intently into Buck's eyes. "Can you do the job of the President?"

"Yes."

"Do you want to leave?"

"No, there's so much work to be done."

Murph stood up. "Then it's settled!"

Buck rose as well, "How so?"

Murph smiled. "You're the right man for the job. You didn't want the job and didn't campaign for it. You are now the most powerful man in the world, but you didn't seek that power. You are a man of character who is beholden to no one." Murph reached out and shook his hand. "You're just the man I want in the job!"

Carli came over and hugged Buck. "Just be yourself! That's all we need."

"Yep, be the best President you can be. Your service to the American people will honor them."

Buck sighed with relief. "Thank you. I needed to hear that."

"Because you were willing to give up the power, I know you have the humility to be a great President." Of that, Murph was sure.

"I'm glad that you will be here to help me!"

"That's what friends are for!"

"Excellent! I'm glad to hear you say that." Buck sprung the trap. "I'm going to make you my special projects director. The two of you can investigate problems that I want quietly taken care of."

"Whoa, now!" Murph took a step back. "I have a dental practice that needs my attention!"

Carli chimed in, "And, we have a wedding to plan."

Buck wouldn't be denied. "Good. You can have the wedding here at the White House."

"Thanks, but no." Murph put his arm around Carli. "We talked about this on the flight home."

She nodded. "Father Albers is going to marry us at Saint Mary of the Assumption Chapel on the campus of Saint Ignatius High School. It will be a small ceremony for family and close friends."

"Then have a reception here in DC." Buck pointed out the window. "I have a really nice rose garden here, and the caterer is first rate!"

"OK—OK, you win!" Murph was laughing. "We'll have a reception here, then we're going on a honeymoon!"

Buck put his arms around them both. "Will you be going abroad?"

Murph shook his head. "No. I think we've had enough travel for a while."

"I just want something quiet—a place to get away." Carli had a wistful look in her eye.

Murph had been planning something, but he hadn't mentioned it before. "I was thinking about buying an old house on the water, maybe Sullivan's Island in Charleston. We could renovate it and make it a quiet getaway from the busy life here."

"It was beautiful there—what I could see before they dropped us out of the helicopter and we had to swim ashore. I'd like to explore the area."

"Then, it's settled." Murph was decisive, as always. "We'll honeymoon in Charleston."

The Jameson had provided warmth that was spreading slowly. Murph began to relax, for the first time in weeks. Carli snuggled under his arm, and he held her tight.

There was a knock on the door, and Darnell Collins entered.

"Mr. President, the Prime Minister of Japan, Mr. Nokamura, is on the phone. The North Koreans are threatening another missile launch."

Buck looked at them and shrugged. "Duty calls." He walked out of the room, down the hall toward the elevator, heading for the Oval Office.

Carli whispered. "He's going to make a great President."

"Yes." Murph tightened his hold on her. "But for now, all I care about is you."

Murph turned Carli toward him and kissed her, holding her tight. Looking out the window over her shoulder, the sun was setting on the south lawn of the White House. In the distance, past the Washington Monument, the statue of Thomas Jefferson stood silently facing them from the center of his memorial, regarding them across the still waters of the Tidal Basin. Murph closed his eyes and was at peace, with Carli in his arms. For a moment, at least, time stood still and all was right with the world.

Author's Note

I have always been fascinated by the hidden stories around significant historical events. We think we know everything about a moment in history, yet there are often narratives that go largely unnoticed. When discovered, I find that truth is often stranger than any fiction. It 's my desire to shed light on some of these tales, providing a historical backdrop for my fiction. In telling a good story, we can also expose these nearly forgotten memories and share them with the world.

I was intrigued with the story of Fort Hunt from the time I discovered that the camp at PO Box 1142 really did exist. The records are only recently being released and the oral history of the men and women who worked there are finally being collected and recorded. With the rapid rate at which the Greatest Generation is leaving us, this is a vital undertaking and I'm glad to see that these long forgotten veterans are finally getting the respect they deserve.

While Dr. Bloch is fictitious, a French physician, Marcel Petiot, was indeed convicted of serially killing over 150 Jews in Paris in 1944. Even within the brutal history of the Nazi rule of Europe, the abject evil of Dr. Petiot stands out.

There are even oddities present in the world today. Who would expect that there is a US radar installation at Mt. Keren in Israel? More than 100 US servicemen are currently stationed in the Negev Desert to provide early warning of attacks aimed at Israel. I collect these facts and wonder, "What if?" Curiosity leads me to want to weave these stories together.

My contact with the Jesuit educators at Saint Ignatius High School in Cleveland, Ohio fills me with the faith that good is possible in this troubled world, even if we have to periodically stand firm in the face of evil.

I am indebted to many people for the accuracy of the military and secret service components of the novel. The authenticity of what I write would not be possible without support. I want to specifically thank Fr. Lawrence Ober SJ,

Dave Tabar, Don Williams, Larry Shaw, Don Allen, Billy McGinty, and Bob Mooney. There are others that I must thank privately, since revealing their identities could compromise their positions in the military and other government agencies. You know who you are, so thank you from the bottom of my heart.

None of my efforts would be possible without the help and support of my loving family. Denise, Caitlin, Michael, Brian and Maggie have been with me through it all, keeping me grounded and giving me the time to complete my work.

My dedicated dental staff have listened to me tell parts of *The Black Swan Event* more times than they would care to remember. I would like to thank Sue, Robin, Juliann, Laurie, Sharri, and Kari for their patience and commitment as the story came to life.

My editor, Deb Bush, has been there through both books, hopefully with more to come. I appreciate all her caring and attention to detail. She always helps me speak with clarity, finding the power in my words.

I also am indebted to my loyal readers, for whom this book was created. The outpouring of love and concern for Murph and Carli made it impossible to allow their adventures to end with *The Curse of Sekhem Ka*. My plans for their future are clear, as Murph and Carli will return soon in *The Blue Star Conspiracy*.